Harriet Hudson was [illegible] degree in English Literature she became a [illegible] a London publishing company and is now a freelance editor and writer. She is married to an American, and they live in a Kentish village on the North Downs. This is her first novel under the name of Harriet Hudson, but she has also written, under the name of Amy Myers, three crime novels.

Also by this author, under the name Amy Myers

Murder in Pug's Parlour
Murder in the Limelight
Murder at Plum's

Look For Me By Moonlight

Harriet Hudson

HEADLINE

First published in 1989
by HEADLINE BOOK PUBLISHING PLC

First published in paperback in 1989
by HEADLINE BOOK PUBLISHING PLC

10 9 8 7 6 5 4 3

ISBN 0 7472 3182 6

Typeset in 10/12¼ pt English Times
by Colset Private Limited, Singapore

Printed and bound in Great Britain by
Collins, Glasgow

HEADLINE BOOK PUBLISHING PLC
Headline House
79 Great Titchfield Street
London W1P 7FN

For James
with love

ACKNOWLEDGEMENTS

The idea for this book was born on a summer's evening in the garden of a Kentish pub, but it would not have matured without the creative help and guidance of my friend and agent Dorothy Lumley and my editor Jane Morpeth, both of whom I thank most warmly.

My thanks are also due to Peggy Jones, T G Smith, Beryl Fisher and Marian Anderson, and to Messrs John Murray (Publishers) Ltd for permission to quote from 'The Highwayman' by Alfred Noyes published in *Forty Singing Seamen and Other Poems* and later *Collected Poems*.

Look for Me By Moonlight

'Yet, if they press me sharply, and harry me
through the day,
Then look for me by moonlight,
Watch for me by moonlight,
I'll come to thee by moonlight, though hell
should bar the way.'

Alfred Noyes, 'The Highwayman'

PROLOGUE

'There used to be hollyhocks . . .'

The woman spoke quietly, wonderingly to herself, though to the casual observer it might seem she merely passed a comment to her driver who stood slightly behind her, still holding the door of the old Alvis. But she was oblivious to the world of today, her dark eyes fixed on the old inn in front of her, devouring the length of its white and black-beamed frontage, its uneven peg-tiled roofs, its chimneys confidently seeking the sky as they had for four hundred years past.

Bathed in the golden sunlight of Kent's September, it was a restful, tranquil sight. Yet the woman's eyes seemed to search for something more. A slight sigh passed her lips, and the incurious driver caught the whisper: 'It's still there, Beth my girl. Still there. Still the same.'

Then with almost visible effort she brought herself back to the present, the reality of the post-war forties when Kent was picking herself up, healing the wounds inflicted on her people and her landscape, and proudly reasserting her independence, her survival once again against the threat of an invading enemy.

'Well, Barratt, what about a drink?' She spoke

briskly, and led the way without waiting for an answer through the low wooden doorway into the saloon bar. It was early, only just after six and the bar was deserted, save for a cat that stretched lazily and came towards them as if to offer its welcome in the place of the absent Mine Host. Now that she was inside, the woman felt an odd reluctance to look around, to face the memories she knew would come flooding back.

Barratt looked curiously round the old pub. Didn't think much of it, if the truth be told. Not a patch on the Elephant. No life. But there, the old lady took these fancies sometimes, and she paid a good wage so who was he to complain? Made a bit of change after all.

The woman seated herself, as if by habit, in a window seat, carved out of oak, threadbare chintz covering the wooden seat, and smoothed the kid gloves from off her hands.

'Evening, sir. Evening, ma'am.' Mine Host, young, eager to please because eager for custom in these days of post-war austerity. 'Nice evening.'

Not a man of Kent, the woman noted instantly to herself. Come down from London. After being demobbed, probably. One of the lucky ones.

'What can I get you?' he asked. Barratt was on his feet, but a firm hand stopped him.

'No, Barratt.' She rose, tall, strong, despite her seventy-two years.

She leaned almost lovingly on the oak bar, one hand spread possessively on the old wood. 'Two pints of your best mild and bitter, if you please. Teynham's.' Her voice was firm, loud.

The landlord cast her a disappointed look, for he had

glimpsed the expensive rings on her fingers. Beer? And ordering for herself? He opened his mouth as if to question the order, but something in those dark eyes made him hesitate. Beer it was. But: 'No Teynham's now, madam. All Sittingbourne Ales now. Tied house, you see.'

If he had not been concentrating on pulling the beer, he would have noticed the muscle twitching in the woman's cheek, the clenched hand gradually unfolding. Then she laughed. A deep belly laugh that made the landlord pause in astonishment and stare at her. The lines in her face crinkled as she threw back her head and her dark eyes glowed deep. Just for a moment, beneath the expensive fur hat, and the carefully groomed grey hair, the landlord saw the girl she must have been, and a light that would have made him wonder, had he been a fanciful man, what man had received the glory in those eyes, lain in those arms, and loved and laughed the nights away.

'No Teynham's Ale,' she repeated. 'I'm sorry, landlord, you must forgive me. But –' her voice trembled slightly, then recovered – 'I knew the Wheatsheaf years ago, and George Hamlin of Teynham's Breweries, all those battles, all that struggle –' there was a catch in her breath. 'Oh the pity of it.'

He smiled politely but uncomprehendingly, took the money and watched her carry with never a tremor the two full jugs back to the window seat. There was something in the confidence with which she had handled them that kept his attention. She'd done that a few times before, he decided. You could never mistake it. Barmaid, most likely, for all she looked more like a toff now.

The woman took her beer outside, as if something in the interior stifled her, and stood by the doorway, looking out across the small triangular green by the side of which the pub stood. Nothing had changed, not fundamentally, since before the old Queen died. Someone had built a garage at Parsley Cottage where old Mrs Tripp had kept her beloved goats, the small post office cum grocery on the corner had lost its Sharp's Toffee sign, roses grew where Bill the hedger had kept his vegetables. Where had they all gone – the Tripps, old Bill, Daniel Harbutt, the butcher?

Now sixty years later, over the green towards the pub there strolled a soldier in uniform and his girl, arm in arm, earnest, young and in love. Something caught in her throat as she watched them, something that might have been a tear blurred her eyes as she gazed into the mellowness of the setting sun; the figures were surrounded with a misty halo, the sound of the girl's laughter far away . . .

It was all there again, before her. She too had been that girl, laughing in the sun. She, Beth Ovenden, the black-haired, dark-eyed belle of the village, eighteen years old with her life before her, carefree and heartfree.

And then Richard had come.

PART ONE
The Landlord's Daughter

'He whistled a tune to the window, and
who should be waiting there
But the landlord's black-eyed daughter,
Bess, the landlord's daughter,
Plaiting a dark red love-knot
into her long black hair.'

Alfred Noyes

CHAPTER ONE

The sun was in her eyes. She couldn't see.

'It's coming, it's coming.'

Pippin's excited shout by her side made her turn quickly. Hitching up her skirts with one hand, she clambered on to the station fence, the morning sun warm on her back, to see the better along the track where, far away in the hazy blueness of the downs, a spiral of smoke in the air grew ever larger. The faint rumble increased to a hiss and a thunder, beating a rhythm to which her pounding heart seemed to be beating in unison.

Beth caught her breath in excitement. Every August it was the same. This moment she and Pippin waited for, pleaded with their respective parents for permission to attend, she winning it more easily than Pippin, the Squire's daughter. The arrival of the hop-pickers.

Outside Faversham station, the waggons from the local farms, decorated with garlands and ribbons, waited to greet the opening of the hop-picking season. Not that the hop-pickers were welcomed for themselves, but as a symbol of the harvest to come. Much as the youngsters of the village might enjoy the intrusion of this motley crowd into their midst for six weeks or more each year, their elders, with valuable crops to protect, viewed the event as a mixed blessing.

The steam engine thundered towards them, swirling black smoke belching forth from its innards. The waggoners leapt from their seats, ready to stand bastion against the tide of incoming humanity, the grooms to guard Miss Pippin. It was generally reckoned that Beth Ovenden could look after herself. No one would dare take liberties with that stalwart figure with the flashing eyes, as customers who ventured to try found to their cost at the Wheatsheaf. Eighteen she might be, but she had the independence of a woman twice her age.

With a final triumphant belch, the monster drew alongside the platform, and safe behind their barricade the two girls watched in awe as the flotsam of London's East End poured out onto the platform.

First appeared the luggage, bags, boxes, tin trunks, string-tied bundles, thrown from doors, passed out of windows by eager hands; then children tumbled out, ill clad, mostly unshod, some eager, adventurous, sharply appraising their new home, some shyer, holding back for the security of the known. After them clambered anxious mothers, shouting fathers, rotund grandmothers and ancient grandfathers, robust uncles, giggling girls, flashy youths, and a few solitary individuals with eyes already on the look out for the best ways of turning things to their own advantage in this new environment. For where the East End went, the criminal fraternity was not far behind. The railways had opened new vistas for them.

A Hop-pickers' Special had arrived, endless hours after it had left London Bridge the night before. The coaches were ancient, the journey was slow, but the fares were cheap. And after all, the hoppers reasoned, they were lucky. Their grandfathers had walked all the way from Whitechapel to get to this golden land. Yet cheap though the fares were, they were still too expensive for some, and it was not unknown for children to be secreted in trunks or sacks to emerge sleepy-eyed jack-in-the-boxes once safely on the station platform. There'd been little sleep for any on that long journey, packed like their beloved bloaters one against another in hot, steamy carriages. But the hoppers' spirits were undampened. It was late August, the sun was shining, and the adventure had begun. The air was full of noise, of movement, bags were hoisted, children gathered and the tide prepared to flow towards the exit and to look forward to their next battle – the fight for space on the waggons. Old hands were to the fore; those first timers who paused but briefly to get their bearings were lost in the flood.

Beth's eyes were everywhere, drinking in the excitement of the scene. In London it must be like this all the time. The bustle, the noise, the friendliness. Not like her quiet village. She would never want to leave Shepham of course, and *never* leave the Wheatsheaf, but all the same . . . She strained her eyes against the sun again the better to see the swarm as it swept along the platform, Pippin's hand clasped in her own.

She closed her eyes momentarily against the glare and, as she opened them again, in the dazzle a face appeared, just one, from the jostling throng in front; a pair of eyes, as blue as hers were dark, looked and laughed into hers. So strong was the gaze held that she looked away, then back hastily as the huddle came nearer, families clinging together determined not to be parted from boxes, trunks and children in that order. Caught up in their midst was a young man – no, two young men – their immaculate blazers and white trousers as out of place in the ragged, cheap-clothed mob surrounding them as two peas in a potato field.

The tall, dark-haired young man stared at Beth and Pippin appraisingly, impudently, as they clung to the fence, and in studied, if belated, politeness swept off his straw boater, then turned to his companion, overshadowed both physically and mentally by his friend's ebullience, saying: 'We're in luck, Rupert. Fair Kentish maids to greet us . . .'

'No, we ben't, you chuckhead,' retorted Beth fiercely, determined as usual to assert her dominant position, despite a moment's hesitation at the stranger's accent. No East Ender, this.

'Not maids? Better and better.'

A scandalised 'Oh' from Pippin as she took in the implication of his words made Beth turn on him more fiercely than she would have done herself. But for once her ready wit deserted her before those blue eyes:

'Not Kentish maids,' she said lamely. 'Maids of Kent we are – east of the Medway. That's what Father says.'

'Ah, you'll have to pardon an ignorant hopper.'

His companion, a quiet looking young man of about the same age, perhaps twenty-three, not older, had a worried eye on the still blushing Pippin. He began to utter words of apology, but was cut short by a hoot from Beth.

'A hopper? You're hoppers?' She threw back her

head and laughed, her confidence restored now. 'Why, you swells won't last a day in the gardens.' They were the oddest hoppers she'd ever seen. But she'd heard of this sort, all right. Smart Londoners who'd come down for the hopping, talking loudly of life in the open air and honest toil. They'd last a day and then go back, not talking so loudly this time, their hands smothered in green Zambuk ointment where the bines had rubbed them sore.

'What makes you so sure?' asked the tall one mockingly. 'I think we'll do all right, don't you, Rupert?'

Beth grinned, conscious of her inevitable victory now. 'Where be your luggage?' she asked scornfully.

'In the guard's van. Or was. The guard's getting it out for us,' said the one called Rupert, his face pink with embarrassment. He self-consciously pushed a strand of his straight fair hair back under his boater.

'Well, Mr Hoppers, you'll have to learn a bit about your trade. And that starts now. If you don't want to be carrying your trunks all the way to Shepham, you'd better look lively.' And with an air of triumph she casually pointed to where the waggoners, the exhausting task of sorting out each farm's ration of hoppers complete, were already pulling away. The waggons were packed to the gunnels with trunks and grandmothers, children perched on top of cases, string bags and sacks bulging ominously over the sides. The men were walking along beside. The two young men began to rush down the platform.

Beth jumped down off the gate, dusting off her hands. 'That's showed 'em, Pippin,' she remarked with satisfaction.

'Oh but, Beth, you were very hard on them – and they seemed quite nice.'

'Quite nice?' She eyed Pippin pityingly. 'You heard what they said to us. Come down from London, thinking we're like apples on trees, theirs for the taking. They'll learn different. You'll see.'

Outside in the yard the last waggons were already moving round the corner towards the Dover Road, the bells on the horses' harnesses jangling prettily amidst the raucous laughter and shouts and snatches of 'Two Lovely Black Eyes'.

Suddenly Beth caught hold of Pippin's arm. 'Why, Pippin, look –'

A vigorous argument was taking place between the two grooms by the Manor dogcart and the two young men, and a tussle over some luggage.

'It's a very large cart for just one person. And you *are* going to Medlars Home Farm. There's plenty of room for three. *And* the luggage,' she heard the dark-haired one expostulating.

'Squire's daughter don't travel with no hoppers.'

'I'm sure she wouldn't mind. *Noblesse oblige*, and so forth.'

'You'll have to ask Miss Pippin about that,' said the groom, spotting the girls coming with evident relief.

The young men spun round, and a slow smile crossed the lips of the dark one as Beth in the vanguard strode forward to do battle. 'Well if it isn't our – Maids of Kent. The Maids of Kent in all their grace – that's what the poet said. Now would you by your grace, Miss Pippin –' addressing his remarks to Beth, '– let us walk five miles or more when there's room in your conveyance?'

'You can walk ten for all I care,' said Beth sniffing.

'Beth,' said Pippin, plucking her sleeve, 'don't you think –?'

He glanced sharply from one to the other. 'Ah,' he said, instantly assessing the situation. '*You're* Miss Pippin.' Without giving another glance at Beth he made as if to appeal to the quiet fair-haired girl at her side. But Rupert was there first. 'We would be much obliged, Miss Pippin,' he said quietly. 'Little though we've deserved –'

Pippin glanced appealingly at Beth, then determinedly, as Beth was studiedly ignoring them all, nodded.

'It's all right, Harker,' she said to the groom, who with a clearly disapproving glare proceeded – without their help – to pack the offending trunks at the rear of the cart.

'Allow me, ma'am.' The tall young man was at the step of the cart, to hand Pippin up. Beth did not receive the same mannerly treatment. No sooner had she placed her foot on the step than a hefty heave under her bottom sent her stumbling into the cart with more haste than grace.

'Keep your hands to yourself, you –' she shrieked, whirling round to see a pair of blue eyes innocently gazing up at her – 'lazy London layabouts,' she muttered, disconcerted at then finding herself wedged in next to this annoying stranger. Why she could even feel the warmth of his thigh through her thin print dress and petticoat!

'Perhaps we should walk, Richard,' said Rupert uneasily. 'If the ladies would take the luggage . . .'

'Nonsense, I'm quite comfortable here,' said Richard, easing himself back in the seat. 'Except that - Miss Beth -'

She turned towards him unthinkingly, only to find his arm promptly encircling her waist.

'Ah that's much better. My arm was wedged, you see. Now I can lodge it much more restfully.'

Angrily she tried to wriggle away but to no avail. There was, he claimed, no room for his arm elsewhere.

'Look, Mr Hopper or whatever your name is -'

'Lyle. Richard Lyle, at your service, ma'am.'

And thus, so close she could feel his warm breath upon her cheek, they had come that first time to Shepham.

As they turned the bend in the road, and the cluster of red tiled roofs, with the church steeple their centrepoint, came into sight, she was filled as ever with a fierce possessive pride in her heritage, and stole a glance at her irritating neighbour to ensure he was sufficiently impressed. He was whistling something she could not identify and gazing at the village in front of them, but was aware enough of her glance to wink at her.

'That's Shepham,' she said ignoring this, but unable to restrain herself from the temptation of boasting of her village. Being in the lee of the highest fold of the downs it was not exposed to the bleak winds that swept the heights of the downs in winter and so had some woods and copses dotted around it. But hops dominated the village. Some farmers hedged their bets with supplementary fruit farming, but on the whole the flea, the fly and the mould, and the blight they could wreak on the hop farmers' fortunes were worse devils than the rains that could make or break the cherry and apple farmers.

The quiet village of Shepham had changed its livelihood over the years as often as the Vicar of Bray his religion. From sheep-farming and charcoal burning, to fruit farming; then, in the early sixteenth century always looking to the future, the already prosperous community put its money into the creation of the new hop gardens. Now Shepham was proud of its origins. Was not the very first English hop garden created nearby? There'd been problems to overcome. In the fifteenth century, some towns had tried to forbid hops, prejudiced against this foreign import from the Low Countries. But the hops had won. Now Shepham was a higgledy-piggledy mixture of houses: small cottages dating from medieval times; the larger Tudor houses; and, as the hop market expanded, many more recent houses hastily erected to accommodate the growing numbers of workers needed for the increasing hop gardens. Unusually for a village on the downs, although some of the village was strung out along the Faversham road, Shepham had a small triangular green, round which clustered a few shops and the Norman church. Facing it, almost at the apex of the triangle, was the Wheatsheaf.

The cart stopped. Beth gave Pippin a quick hug, carefully avoiding Richard Lyle's amused eyes, and jumped off the cart. She felt his gaze upon her, but determined not to give him the satisfaction of a backward glance, and ran up the path by the side of the green leading to the inn. It was a colourful sight, her hollyhocks giving a splash of colour to the white and black framed front, picking up the dull red in the peg-tiled roof. The frontage was the oldest part of the building, for the back was Tudor red brick.

As usual she felt a tug at the heart as she came up to it, solid and comforting. Her family had had this inn for over a hundred years; they proudly carried on the tradition they had inherited and always would. None but an Ovenden would own the Wheatsheaf now. She tried not to worry about what would happen when her father died. Her only brother had died at ten years old, a victim of diphtheria. She would think of something. The Wheatsheaf was her. She was the Wheatsheaf. To divide them was unthinkable. Her father had been licensee since his father died in 1866, twenty-eight years ago, and her grandfather for thirty-odd years before that and his father before that . . . though she knew little of her great-grandfather beyond the epitaph on his gravestone in Shepham churchyard, the meaning of which she had vainly pondered over as a child:

Stout of heart, his stout brought cheer,
But porter carried him to this bitter bier.
RIP William Ovenden, 1834.

Out Folkestone way, her father had told her, there were other Ovendens in the trade. Andrew had only sisters, who'd married and gone their separate ways with their husbands, but Beth's grandfather had had a brother,

Andrew's uncle, who had set up on his own. They'd lost touch. 'I never had much call to leave Shepham,' her father had said when she'd questioned him. 'The best village in all Kent or Christendom – no need to go arunning off to other parts.' But somehow it was comforting to know there were Ovendens elsewhere, besides at the Wheatsheaf. It made her feel, in some way, more secure in her heritage. The Wheatsheaf was a strange name for an inn in the middle of the best hop country in east Kent, but then the Wheatsheaf had been an inn before hops were firmly established in Kent; even when hops were still prohibited in the fifteenth century, thought of as a magic potion to delude the people. Down through the centuries the inn proudly carried its golden symbol on its signboard, the last painted by a gypsy who called one summer, and passed on his way, never to reappear. Every year when the casual pickers arrived, she wondered if he would return again, as so many rovers did to earn some easy money, but he never came.

It wasn't easy keeping a small inn going in a smallish village miles from anywhere dependent on the land for its livelihood, especially with the Temperance Movement so strong now. There'd been a spirit of live and let live at the beginning – then Joseph Higgins had come. An inoffensive man at first glance – until one saw the fanaticism behind the prominent pale blue eyes. He'd come out from Faversham where he worked as a solicitor's clerk for country air, he said. But it was no such thing. A lay preacher, he saw Shepham as a village of sin ripe for conversion. He'd been a year in Shepham now, and the village was beginning to divide, to be forced against its will to choose between the zealot and tradition. Or the life of evil, as Higgins put it. That life was symbolised for him by the Wheatsheaf. At first a joke to Andrew, Higgins was a joke no longer. Beer sales were down and the Wheatsheaf depended on its beer. There was little call for accommodation in a village off the main Dover Road. Folks that passed by were making for Ashford, maybe for Canterbury, where they'd find a meal and a bed more cheaply than the Ovendens could offer. For those that passed were not businessfolk, but itinerant charcoal burners, tree fellers, basket makers, pedlars or horse dealers. It was a hard struggle, but the Ovendens managed. They always had and they always would. Money was often short, but rarely lacking.

Andrew Ovenden's frown deepened when he saw his daughter.

'Late, aren't you? They'll be here soon. Expect me to manage them hoppers on me own, do you?'

His tone was not harsh. He was a slow, strong man, devoted to his daughter after the death of his wife ten years ago, the wife whom Beth so strongly resembled, and who had fallen victim to the same diphtheria outbreak that carried off his son. He'd sometimes thought of marrying again, but something had always kept him from it. There'd been one or two that would have been willing, but somehow it had never happened. Perhaps his wayward determined daughter had deterred them. 'A handful, that Beth Ovenden,' was the village's verdict on the little eight-year-old. Someone had even had the temerity to say it to his face. Perhaps it had been that which had decided him. I'll look after her in my own way, he'd thought, fired with a sudden possessive anger. And if his own way had resulted in her having a freedom disapproved of by the village, a freedom that developed into a sturdy-minded independence, it seemed a small price to pay for the loving, whole-hearted staunchness of his Beth, who flung herself into the running of the Wheatsheaf and into his welfare with such passionate caring. He was respected by the village, and it was as well, for that kept the customers faithful, even though they had reservations about some of his clientele. The Kentish villagers were clannish and would defend their own, even the eccentrics, against the world. They were a rough, good-humoured lot, mostly, that came to the pub; mainly farm labourers squeezing the pence for a beer out of the meagre wages that fluctuated with the seasonal work. The tradesmen and the postmaster came more rarely, the rector never. But even those who didn't patronise the Wheatsheaf, even before Higgins's advent, the Temperance lot, mostly had a good word for Andrew Ovenden. After all, the Ovendens had been Shepham folk for over a hundred years and the Wheatsheaf was part of Shepham.

'Get adoing now. Into the bar with you.'

Beth was puzzled. It wasn't like Andrew to be annoyed. Something must be awry.

'He's here again.' Andrew jerked his head towards one of the small private bars. Beth did not need to ask whom he meant. Unwillingly she went through the low lintel, taking care to keep the bar between herself and the portly man with the bowler hat who was leaning over it puffing contentedly at a small cigar.

'Evening, Beth.'

'Good evening, *Mr* Hamlin,' she replied shortly, 'and it's no use your expecting aught beyond your beer, for we're not selling.'

'Beer's what I'm here for, *this* time. Just to keep an eye on the place. Ensure you're not running it down that is.'

'No business of yours if we are. But we're not.'

'Small free house can't stand out in these days of competition. You've a bright head on your shoulders,' though it wasn't her shoulders he was staring at, she noticed. 'Teynham Breweries are the future.'

'We're staying a free house,' she said shortly.

'Till next Lady Day maybe,' he said, chuckling.

'What's Lady Day got to do with it?' she asked suspiciously.

'Didn't your father tell you? Well now, perhaps you don't know quite so much as you think, eh?' He reached out his hand to pinch her cheek, but she brushed him off as she would a bluebottle.

His face darkened. 'Don't try me too far, Miss Beth,' he said softly. 'I wouldn't do that if I were you. You might be needing me one day.' Without finishing his beer, or bothering to lift his hat, he heaved his large frame from the support of the bar and walked out.

'Can't we tell him not to come here, Father?' she asked angrily.

'Can't do that, my lass. Free house. All's welcome. You know the Wheatsheaf's motto: a free house and a friendly one.' But he avoided her eye.

'He must know we won't sell. What's he want here and –' suddenly remembering '– what's he mean about next Lady Day?'

Andrew blenched. Then he forced a laugh. 'Just an idle threat.'

'No, there's more, isn't there, Father?' She was suddenly quite certain of that, and when Andrew did not answer: 'Tell me,' she said fiercely.

'He just hopes I won't pay his bills, that's all,' said Andrew polishing a glass vigorously.

'He meant more than that,' said Beth slowly, remembering the look on Hamlin's face. 'He looked as pleased with himself as a dog at Fogge's feast.'

'He allus looks like that,' said Andrew uneasily.

'Tell me, Pa,' said Beth quietly.

He threw down the cloth and leant on the long oak bar hopelessly. 'You'll have to know, I suppose, sooner or later. Things are bad, Beth. We owe him money. He's given me till Lady Day to pay up the arrears.'

'Arrears? Arrears of what?' She stared at him aghast. 'The beer reckoning, you mean?'

'That – and worse,' muttered Andrew. He stared unseeingly at the silver tankard on the wooden dresser that he'd won in the village goal-running match years ago. 'Interest,' he went on with an effort. 'On the –' the word stuck in his throat, '– mortgage.'

There was a silence. Then as she said nothing, he burst out: 'I had to. No other way. We'd have gone for sure two years back when the harvest failed. It's hard times, Beth. All them foreign hops being imported. Folks leaving the land . . .' His voice trailed off hopelessly.

'How much?' said Beth heavily.

'Nearly a hundred,' he answered quietly. 'At five per cent. It's the usual rate,' he said eagerly, as if hoping to persuade her there was good in Hamlin still. Then his voice failed again. 'I can find the interest, Beth, but he's calling in the loan. That's what he says. If we can't repay by Lady Day we'll be out. The Wheatsheaf will be tied to Teynham Breweries, and since Hamlin owns Teynham's lock, stock and every grubby barrel of it, that will be that. Lucky if I can stay on as landlord, I reckon.' He stared at her in misery.

She steadied herself. Stay on under Hamlin's orders? Leave the Wheatsheaf? This could not happen. Not while she, Beth Ovenden, had a brain in her head.

'The Wheatsheaf belongs only to us Ovendens. It allus has. Allus will. Folks won't let Hamlin move in. You'll see. They'll help us –'

'Village folk don't have the money they did. That's what counts in the end,' he replied quietly.

'Money. So that's why you still let *them* come –' she jerked her head towards the other private bar. *Them.*

Sometimes they came by midday, sometimes by evening, sometimes by night. Not every day, perhaps twice in a week. There was an uneasy feeling in the Wheatsheaf then; the villagers did not avoid the inn, for there was no other in the village and no one wanted a three mile walk to the Plough at Westling, but they were hushed as though they, and not the others, were the outsiders. And those others – Beth always sensed their presence, even if she did not see them. She knew they were there. The travelling men.

When others spoke of travelling men they meant gypsies. The clannish, swarthy-skinned folk with the dark eyes who arrived silently in the woods and parked their gaudy caravans. They came at hop-picking time, and at other times too. But these were not *her* travelling men.

The name came out of her childhood, when old Bill the hedger would tell her stories when she was supposed to be asleep. He would talk, with a faraway look in his eye, of the days of old, way back in the thirties and forties when he was young. She couldn't ever imagine Bill being young, not with his old craggy face, gnarled hands, and bent limbs; she could never picture grown-ups as young as she. Bill would tell her tales of the smugglers of old, of exciting voyages across the sea from France in fishing boats, by night, laden with brandy, laces and rich perfumes. She was never sure whether they were heroes or villains, these mysterious travelling men, as he called them.

Then, as she'd grown older, she got it into her head that these travelling men were those that gathered in the old inn, stealthily and under cover of darkness. But now they were not covered with the aura of romance and adventure. For they were *here*. In her home. Alien, and somehow, evil intruders. Her father would laugh and say Old Bill had been filling her head with a lot of tales; yes, they were travelling men in the private bar, but they travelled the road for a living, Tom the higgler, who dealt in horses, Len the gypsy, two charcoal burners, Joe and Sam Rawlinson, who moved from forest to forest, George the pedlar. Yes, they were all travelling men. Tom the higgler seemed their leader, a rapscallion of a man with shifty eyes who could plead, persuade, bully or threaten according to his customer. Just business meetings they held, declared Andrew, exchanging information, meeting dealers from outside the county.

But his words failed to reassure Beth, and she always refused to serve in the private bar. Once she had, braving her fear, but they looked her up and down as though she were some prize mare herself, and muttered jokes and the coarse laughter she couldn't then understand. They wouldn't touch her, she knew that. Not because they were scared of her, or of the swift tongue she used as a weapon on the village lads, but because of Andrew's watchful eye.

'Is that why you have *them* here, the travelling men?' she demanded now again. 'We don't need them. Tell them they can't come here any more. We'll manage.'

'I can't do that, Beth.' He still avoided her look. 'We need the money.'

'But –'

Suddenly he lost his temper. 'It's seven months only to Lady Day. Now will you shut your mouth, girl, and get serving? The hoppers'll be here any moment. You've been out all afternoon with your fine friends. Think more about your home here, girl. Not Medlars.'

He was always wittery when he knew she had been out with Pippin. Why she did not know. It wasn't that he disliked Pippin. He'd been kind to the little fair-haired girl who had peeped shyly round the door one evening ten years ago hand in hand with her new friend, Beth. Until that is he'd seen who followed her. The Squire. Martin Scoones. His lips had set then, and his vigorous hands wiped the jug harder, paying careful attention to its rim, and ignoring the man who strode purposefully across the bar.

To eight-year-old Beth, looking on in wonder, it had been a strange scene that she remembered clearly.

'Your girl here, Ovenden,' the Squire had said gruffly. 'Beth.' A muscle twitched in Andrew's face, but he said nothing. 'Saved my daughter's life. Fell in the river. Your youngster jumped in and pulled her out. Brave little thing. Shouldn't have been there, of course. Trespassing as usual –' he glanced at Beth, who stared straight back at him, not a whit afraid of this alarming stranger. 'But there it is. Saved my Pippin's life. Anything I can do for her, you just tell me.'

Then Andrew spoke, full of an inexplicable anger Beth had never seen before. 'Nothing,' he said vehemently. 'There's nothing you can do for my Beth, Squire.'

Andrew had said little after that. He praised Beth for her courage, but explained she wasn't to see Miss Pippin again. They weren't her class. Miss Pippin had her own friends. Beth was surprised, but acquiesced. Beth had her own friends with whom she played in the fields, and hayricks, not like the gentle walks and croquet lawn of Medlars, Pippin's home.

But Pippin had shown herself a sterner stuff than her gentle exterior and shy manner suggested. She had a way of closing her mouth, pursing her lips and sticking out her small chin almost pugnaciously when crossed. She had persisted in treating Beth as her friend, turning up at the inn with no coachman in attendance, and staying with Beth like a faithful spaniel so Beth found herself forced to take her with her as an inseparable lieutenant on all her expeditions. Their fathers' prohibitions made no difference. Nothing would divide Pippin from Beth.

So gradually Andrew relented, though for some reason

son he never took to Pippin. 'Sly little thing,' he'd grunt, but when Beth protested did not argue with her. So Beth was invited to Medlars, shared Pippin's lessons, shared her nursery meals, and in return showed Pippin her world, the world of the badgers' sett, of tickling for trout, of blackberrying, hopping and riding the hay waggons. At first Pippin was an encumbrance, then Beth grew fond of her, and was her staunch friend and by the time they grew to womanhood their love was equal. And neither Andrew nor the Squire protested.

'Beth, where are you, girl?'

Andrew, clearly now regretting his confession of weakness, yelled irritably, startling Beth from her dreams. She had gone to the garden to gather some lovage for tomorrow's stew, but instead stood gazing at the back of the Wheatsheaf, trying to comprehend the full horror of what he had told her. She loved the Wheatsheaf best of all in the late afternoon light, covered with a pale wistaria at one end. The garden was aglow with flowers, and thriving vegetables and herbs. In the orchard next to it filberts grew between the apple trees, carefully cultivated by Andrew who did a fine trade with the Kentish cobs at Christmas time. But the garden was Beth's domain, the mulberry tree in the middle standing sentinel with its gnarled branches, and preparing now to yield its rich harvest.

'I'll never leave you, never,' she whispered softly to her kingdom. 'There has to be some way to raise the money.' She shut her eyes and prayed in case God might be listening despite her slack attendance at His temple. 'Please God, let me think of something. Help me, please.'

The sound of her father's renewed shout made her open

her eyes quickly. The hoppers must be here from the urgency in his voice. She ran quickly over the brick courtyard, her nostrils full of the heavy scents of the long evenings that would float up to her as she lay in her bed on a summer night, making her long for she knew not what. In through the back door past the huge old kitchen to the large room which William the barman and her father had already stripped of billiard tables to accommodate more profitable custom. The door to the cellar was open and from its depths she could hear William cussing as he pulled casks on to the barrow. A large sturdy young man of twenty-four, William Parslow had always been part of Beth's life. He reminded her of her father in many ways, hovering over her, slow moving yet, miraculously, always there to pick her up if she fell over as a child; a big brother; her staunch ally. He was the son of the village postmaster, and to his father's annoyance chose to work at the Wheatsheaf rather than with him. Beth did not bother to question why, for to her William was just there. He was easy-going, yet shrewd and perceptive. Every so often he was obstinate. And one thing he was obstinate about was hoppers. He disliked them, one and all.

Andrew's attitude towards the hoppers was mixed. He welcomed their trade but their physical presence was often a different matter. It was disrupting, threatening to their peaceful existence in Shepham. Trusting none of them, he insisted on a deposit for each glass which would then be retained for the evening.

The pickers were a mixed group – there were the East Enders who were down for a good time, as well as the money, and brawling and fighting were far from rare occurrences at the Wheatsheaf. Andrew would throw them out, lock his doors and let them fight it out in the street. Then there were the gypsies, an itinerant population during hop-picking time. Clannish, they kept themselves to themselves, no trouble to anyone, save when two rival tribes met. Then there were the solitary ones, nature's outcasts like Big Stan, six foot five and a deaf mute, but the quickest fingers in the field; old Michael with his scarred face – an ex-sailor they said, who lost a leg Shanghai way; and Auntie Nell, who appeared as regular as clockwork on the first day of the season with her sacking clothes and her round face and happy smile. Where did they hide the rest of the year, Beth wondered? She could not believe they really existed outside Shepham, and she never felt hop-picking had truly begun till their familiar faces appeared.

The room was already full, and Sylvie the barmaid cast her a reproachful glare. Sylvie was a plump twenty and had been working at the Wheatsheaf for two and a half years, six months less than William. Indeed, Beth often thought that's why she had come – to be with William. But if so, William showed scant signs of appreciating it. Conscience-stricken as Sylvie struggled with a tray of beer, Beth rushed to her rescue.

The hoppers were in a happy mood now that the all important question of accommodation had been hammered out. Even though the council had stepped in some years ago with regulations over housing things were slow to change and, apart from the lucky ones who could boast a partitioned corner of a barn or outhouse, most slept under canvas in the fields. Little wonder they filled up with beer, and often after the inn had closed at ten would prefer to sit outside carousing into the small hours, despite the fact that at dawn they would be in the fields.

'Wotcher, duck. Over here.' A raucous shout directed her tray of stout.

'What's the hurry, love?' An arm about her waist checked her.

Smiling, she disengaged herself. There was no harm in them – yet. Not this early in the season.

'Well, if it ain't Black Bess herself.' The slow whining drawl compelled her unwillingly to look towards him. She didn't know his name. Only his face. A weasly-faced man in his mid-twenties, always solitary, always a watchful eye and wandering hands. He hadn't liked it last year when she'd pushed him away from her, after he'd grabbed her outside the inn. Not that she cared. With relief she saw the familiar face of Big Stan, his painful grunts of pleasure at seeing her, a smile on his anxious face.

After two hours of pushing through the mêlée of hot steamy bodies, the smell of bloaters which they had cooked for their supper still pervading the air, she felt her stomach heave. She put down her tray and ran quickly into the garden, gulping down the sweet night air.

She recognised him immediately although his back was to her, leaning nonchalantly against the wall by a window. The window of the private room, where *they* were. The travelling men.

'Be doing a spot of eavesdropping, are de den, Mus Lyle?' she enquired sarcastically. He spun round at her voice.

'Ah. The landlord's daughter.' He came forward without a sign of embarrassment, and propelled her forward with him into the garden. 'Don't put on that village talk with me, Beth.'

'And who asked you to call me Beth, Mr Lyle?' she flashed.

He stopped by the mulberry tree and gave the question some consideration. Then grinned at her. The air was still warm around them, a hundred scents filling the dusk, trapped by the red brick walls.

'I've known you a long time, Beth.'

'I never met you till this afternoon,' she said indignantly.

'Long ago, before that. When Adam delved and Eve span, that's when we met. Don't you believe that?'

'No,' she said prosaically.

'Is there no romance in your soul, my Beth? Do you not wonder, ponder, on the glories of the East, want to ride like Sheba in all her magnificence, discover the Nile, fight with Zulus, ride a camel by the light of an Eastern moon? Does not the air around us make you feel that in such a night as this stood Dido with a willow in her hand and wafted her love to come again to Carthage?'

'That's Shakespeare, and no it doesn't,' she said obstinately, though it cost her something to say it, with his dancing eyes so near. 'It makes me think that these roses smell better than those bloaters back there, but it's bloaters I'll be cooking for the rest of my days.'

He walked over to the rose bush and snapped one off for her. 'Here, Beth, here's to your dark eyes. You don't want to spend your life with bloaters, do you? Don't you wish I would sweep you off on my white charger, off to the stars?'

'Then who's to look after the bar?' she said, provokingly, determined to puncture this heady talk. 'And Mr Lyle, it's precious little way you'll get if the travelling men catch you spying at the window again.'

'Who? Oh them. Spying? I was merely on my way back from the privy.'

'You had your ears pricked up like an old sow in beans,' she said firmly.

He laughed. 'Perhaps I paused just for a moment. But I reject the sow. Um – those travelling men – where do they travel? The path of Marco Polo? Do they follow with their caravans the road to Mandalay?'

'They're not gypsies,' she said, misunderstanding. 'Just business folk.'

'What sort of business,' he asked, frowning.

'They're horse dealers and the like,' she said. 'Father says.' And if they weren't, she thought to herself, it was Shepham business. None of his.

'Then why do they scare you?' he said lightly.

'Scare me?' she said, firing up immediately. How dare he see into her private thoughts. 'Nothing don't scare me, Mr Lyle. It's just that –' Something in his face suddenly encouraged her to go on – tell him what she'd never even told Pippin. 'It's the Seven Whistlers, see. The fishermen say when you hear the Seven Whistlers calling –' and seeing him look mystified – 'birds that is, curlews, there's bad times on the way. And it seems to me I hear them most when they're here. I heard them tonight – only when they've been here, the travelling men.'

'And what kind of bad times could they bring you,

Beth?' he asked gravely, passing an arm round her shoulder. So wrapped up was she that she did not even notice. 'They don't threaten you, do they? Hurt you? Molest you? You're a lovely girl, Beth.' He looked at her there in the dusk against the rising moon, her black hair tumbling to her shoulders, her bosom rising and falling quickly with her agitation, and thought that lovely was an understatement. She was beautiful.

'No, not me,' she said impatiently. 'Bad for the Wheatsheaf. I can look after myself.'

'Can you, Beth, can you?'

In the dusk he reached out for her quickly, suddenly, but Beth was the quicker, mood instantly changing, laughing and twisting out of his arms like a kitten, and running down the garden through the back gate into the orchard to slip round and back to the Wheatsheaf. But, guessing her intention, he was through the side gate to meet her as she ran round the corner tumbling smack into his arms and, keeping her pinned close to him, he planted a full bodied kiss on her lips as they parted in surprise. Just for an instant she relaxed against the warmth of his mouth, giving herself up to a sensation that was new to her. Then, recollecting, she speedily opened her eyes, shot an indignant glance at him and pulled herself away, facing him warily, coquettishly, waiting for his next move.

'Can you, Beth, can you?' he repeated, pulling her to him again and smiling at her in a way that she thought her heart would turn over within her. But that he should not know.

'If you be looking for a milkmaid,' she said sweetly, 'Mr Fine Gentleman down from the town, amongst us poor peasants, you'll not be lucky. I be an innkeeper's daughter, and you'll have to pick a lot of hops to catch me.' And pushing him away with all her might she broke free and ran back to the inn, not heeding his husky, whispered . . . 'Beth, wait . . .'

His words she might forget, but the memory of the touch of his lips on hers remained with her as she went to bed that night in the attic room with its sloping roof by the dormer window, and lingered as she drifted into sleep.

CHAPTER TWO

'I don't dare, Miss Beth.'

'Oh, William, don't be such a chuckhead. No one will know.'

It had been hard to persuade him, but then Beth was very persuasive. She could talk William into almost anything.

'You be up to summit, ben't you?' he asked suspiciously.

'Of course not,' she replied indignantly, looking as innocent as she could manage.

'What be you awanting Shurland's for, then? Never gone there on your own before, have you?'

'I have to start sometime,' she said offhandedly. 'Now, William, all I want is for you to take me in the dog cart. Not so difficult, is it?'

'Suppose not,' he said grudgingly. Little did she know how she made him feel when she looked at him like that. All shivery, confused and hot at the same time. It hadn't always been so. She'd been like one of Mrs Tripp's pet kid goats to be looked after, cosseted, protected from harm. Then one day she'd come into the post office – not quite a woman, not quite a girl. She'd looked at him and smiled. And he'd told his father he was going to work at the Wheatsheaf now. No two ways about it. At a village dance he'd once put his arm hesitantly round her waist, but it made no difference to his devotion when, without even thinking about it, she firmly removed it. He merely, as it were, stepped two paces back. All the same he was going to protect her, keep her out of trouble. And he had a feeling she was up to no good this morning.

'You tell me why you're going, Miss Beth, and I'll take you. Fair, ain't it?'

Beth bit her lip impatiently. But she knew William in these moods. 'If I promised you it was for the Wheatsheaf,' she said slowly, 'that it was really important – is that enough? Will you believe me?'

He looked at her carefully and surrendered. 'Reckon I will,' he said.

She was silent all the way to Canterbury, worrying about what she was going to say when she got there. She rehearsed it all again in her mind for the tenth time.

'A half hour I reckon, William.' She smoothed her gloves nervously as they arrived outside the Canterbury premises of Shurland's. She'd have to keep 'em on for her hands were rough, from the garden and the washing, for this important meeting. She arranged the skirts of her best purple Sunday dress carefully, smoothing back the fullness over her hips. She looked like a lady, with her best hat squashed firmly on top of her black curls, modestly arranged for the occasion. She felt ready for anything and anybody, even the awe-inspiring Mr Shurland.

'Sure you don't want me with you?' asked William, staring straight ahead.

'No, William,' she said kindly. 'I – I – it's, best this way. You do see?' Why did William always make her feel this way? With his transparent devotion, he was like a large sheep dog waiting to be patted.

He shrugged and looked away, and Beth hurried, conscience-stricken, into the red-brick house that served as offices for the Shurland's brewery. It needed all her powers of persuasion to gain an interview with the great man, and when she was actually in the dark ornate office, with its smell of leather armchairs and leather-topped desk, all her nervousness rushed back. She stared hard at the picture above Mr Shurland's desk, a print of 'The Pickwick Club' by Seymour. She gulped and stared at the waistcoat buttons of the foremost fat man, then forced herself to say: 'I – We need your help, Mr Shurland. A loan.' It was best to come straight out with it. It was her way.

Mr Shurland ceased to look like a benevolent Mr Pickwick himself and glanced at her severely over the top of his glasses.

'You told my clerk that you'd brought a message from your father, Miss Ovenden.'

'I didn't think you'd see me otherwise,' she said honestly.

'Your father does know you're here, however?'

'No.'

'My dear young lady' – he half rose to his feet.

'I may be a lady, Mr Shurland,' she said firmly, more firmly than she in fact felt, 'and I may be young, but I don't think you ought to call me dear. I've come to talk very important business, and I think you should just listen and I'll explain.'

Perhaps it was the intensity of her eyes, perhaps curiosity, perhaps shock, but Mr Shurland subsided speechless into his leather-covered armchair.

'You have five minutes, Miss Ovenden. Just five minutes.'

She breathed a sigh of relief. From now on, it would be easy. She could just tell the truth. And for Mr Shurland it would make sense. He had always been a reasonable man, not like Hamlin. She'd known him since she was small. True it was somewhat different being chucked under the chin as a seven-year-old from sitting here intending to discuss money, but it was the same man facing her, she must remember.

Quietly, firmly, she told him all about the mortgage, and therefore the need for the loan.

'I'll need it for nine months, Mr Shurland.'

'A loan, my dear –' he coughed hastily, 'Miss Ovenden? Is there any reason why Shurland Ales should be interested in saving a little house like the Wheatsheaf? A mere minnow,' he boomed.

'Yes, there is a reason. You can't afford to let us freehouses go, in case Teynham Breweries gets hold of us –'

He shot a quick glance at her, and paused for a moment to think. He was a little shaken.

He'd been going to try to bluff me, thought Beth instantly.

He eyed her keenly, saying slowly, 'My dear young lady, if we needed you we'd buy you out.'

'You can't,' she said triumphantly. 'Not while Hamlin holds the mortgage.'

'Ah,' he sat back and drummed his fingers on his

leather-topped desk. 'What terms do you offer?' he asked at last.

'Two and a half per cent for nine months,' she said. 'Six per cent if we can't then repay for a further year.'

Now he did laugh. 'Two and a half per cent,' he exploded. 'We're a brewery, Miss Ovenden. Not a lending institution.'

'I know, Mr Shurland.' Hold on, Beth, she told herself, here we go. 'But we want to go on stocking your beer - what with the hoppers here now - but it seems to me we might have to cut down again to meet Mr Hamlin's demands. We get better terms, see.' She looked modestly down at her lap, her fingers intertwined closely, tensely. She could feel him staring at her, calculatingly.

'Very well, Beth. I like your spirit,' he said suddenly. 'Keep the big businessmen out, eh? Very well. I'll do it.' He slammed his hand, hard on the table. 'Two conditions.'

She looked up hopefully.

'Three per cent.'

She breathed a sigh of relief. This is what she had calculated on. It was all going to plan - she would worry about how to tell her father later.

'And double your order with us.'

She gasped. Four barrels a month? Fine while the hoppers were here but how about the winter? They'd have to cut out Teynham's - suddenly a scheme leapt into her mind, complete, bold, just possible. She jumped to her feet and forgot all about being a business woman and behaved like an excited young eighteen-year-old. 'Mr Shurland. You're an angel. A real Kentish saint.'

'And I will need your father's approval,' he added sternly, emerging from her hug a trifle flustered.

'Father, we can do it. Really we can.' Beth was almost in tears. Did he not see it? It was all so clear in her own mind. Yet Andrew was angrier than she had ever seen him.

'It's a risk, Father,' she said pleadingly. 'But anything is better than Teynham's.'

'Shurland?' he shouted. 'Even if we repay Teynham's mortgage, how the devil do we know Shurland won't do the same to us in nine months' time? All tarred with the same brush, these brewers.'

'He won't because we'll repay him.'

Andrew laughed. 'Taken leave of your senses, girl? How can we?'

'We'll have the hopkin here for one thing.'

'The hopkin?' Andrew's eyes bulged.

Beth swept on in her excitement. 'You see, there's the tithe barn outside. We'll have it there. The villagers don't like them using the village hall anyway. We'll have their favourite foods for them – buy it in. Their bloaters, and Chelsea buns, and everything they like, and we'll cook it for them as well as the flead cakes and all the usual things. It'll be good for the Wheatsheaf. We'll get Sam Jelks in with his accordion. And we'll get Eddie up the oasthouse to cook the potatoes in the ashes all day long, and –'

He cut across her excited outburst. 'Fine words, Beth. But do you think we can make enough in one evening to pay off Hamlin? You're out of your mind – all passion and no sense. Just like your mother.' He was quiet suddenly, thinking of the fiery girl that Beth so closely resembled.

Beth swept on. 'And we'll cook for them *every* night maybe. Make them pay for the food. Then they'll come here, specially if it's raining, rather than cooking in the fields.'

'And who's to do the work, eh?' In spite of himself Andrew was listening.

'Me – and well, there's William and Sylvie –'

Sylvie despite her buxomness was as nimble with feet and hands as any barmaid they'd ever had.

'Sylvie's behind the bar with me.'

'Then William and I'll manage.'

He heaved a sigh, and looked at the books in front of him, 'It's worth a try, I suppose.'

'There's something else too, Father. We'll have to cut Teynham Breweries' order altogether. We'll brew our own, for those who don't like Shurland's. Like Grandfather did.'

'Brew our own?' He gaped at her again.

'We've still got the equipment. Needs a bit of cleaning maybe, it's been here a long time. Remember how you used to do it when I was small? Got a way with malt has Andrew Ovenden – they still say that in the village.'

'I haven't brewed up since your mother was alive,' said Andrew, thinking back to those early days of his ownership of the Wheatsheaf with Elizabeth, laughing, high-spirited like her daughter – Elizabeth with her laughing eyes and lovely ways . . .

And Beth was just like her with her dancing mind, and quick wits. He'd resented it sometimes when Elizabeth seemed to be running things, suggesting he did this and that to drum up trade. It was his job. She could never leave anything be. And now Beth was doing the same. He sighed. Well, perhaps she was right. Perhaps he was set in his ways. Perhaps the old inn needed a shake up. But there again Beth was young; she didn't always see the pitfalls.

'We'll never do it,' he said, despondent again, full of a sadness from the past.

'We'll have nine months, Father. *Anything* can happen in that time! Don't you want to save the Wheatsheaf?'

'Want? You out of your mind lass?' he roared. She had said the right thing. 'By God we'll have a go.' And by God he would – even if he had his own methods that he would never discuss with Beth.

Even ten years of acquaintance with it had not robbed Beth of that lift of the heart which the first sight of Medlars brought. As she walked round the curve in the drive that brought her within sight of the gracious old Queen Anne building, she felt the same rush of feeling, the same rush of awe as the awkward eight-year-old who had hung back as Pippin seized her hand and tugged her towards the house for the very first time. Cloistered as it was in the seclusion of its grounds, she had never seen Medlars before and it was to leave an indelible impression on her mind, a far-off vision of another world, a world from which she was far removed, yet welcome to enter. And enter it she had, on every occasion possible, and had come to love its mellow warmth as a friend, its beautiful furniture, paintings, books, with a kind of wonder, rather than envy, that these things existed.

Medlars was part of Shepham, part of village life, in a way that Chartboys, the part Tudor, part Stuart mansion at Westling Forstal was not, although it was almost as close to the village. Chartboys sat on the highest part of the downs, faced away from the village, down towards Doddington and Lenham, as if to proudly reassert its independence of Shepham. Built of stone, it lacked the warmth of Medlars for all its imposing castellated facade. Lady Charing, widow of the ninth baronet, was almost a recluse. Her only child had been killed at Rorke's Drift, and it was said she waited only for the day that she might join her soldier son and husband. Once a year she was seen at Shepham Church, at Christmas, black veiled and silent in the Charing private pew. How different to Chartboys was Medlars, with its warmth and life.

As Beth walked through onto the paved terrace at the rear of the house, she heard a laugh - Pippin's laugh. Pippin did not often laugh outright and Beth was intrigued. Whom could she have with her? She ran down the long path of the rose garden, pulling her pink cotton dress impatiently from the bushes that caught at it, towards the walled vegetable garden at its side, from where the sound had come.

She stopped short as she opened the gate. Pippin was indeed not alone. She was with Richard Lyle and his friend - what was his name? Rupert something? It was a strange tableau: Pippin with her hands over her face as though embarrassed at her hearty laugh; Rupert standing protectively by her side and Richard a way apart, with them but not of them. The sudden stillness was broken as Pippin ran up to her, throwing her arms round her neck.

'Beth, darling, I'm so glad you've come.'

Beth frowned as she looked over Pippin's shoulder and met Richard's eyes. She did not altogether trust the innocence she saw there.

'Good day, Miss Ovenden.' Richard bowed towards her.

Not bothering to acknowledge the courtesy, she said abruptly, 'What are you doing here?'

His eyebrows rose, but Pippin answered for him.

'I met Mr Lyle and Mr Bonner in the village,' she said shyly, glancing at Rupert, 'and as they were so interested to see Medlars I brought them to meet Father. They have been making me laugh so much, telling me about the hoppers: poor Mrs Glubb who got thrown in the bin and Big Stan – they kept emptying his basket when his back was turned –' She went into a peal of laughter, in which the two men joined, though Rupert cast an apologetic look at Beth's shocked face. How could they laugh at poor old Big Stan? Couldn't they see he wasn't quite like other people? And Pippin joining in, too!

'You see, Beth,' Pippin continued, 'Mr Lyle and Mr Bonner aren't really hoppers –'

'They're frogs in disguise,' cut in Beth rudely.

'Beth!' Pippin was herself shocked now. 'They're training to be lawyers. They are here for their holidays.'

'Just amusing themselves in the country with us poor peasants.'

'No indeed, Miss Ovenden,' said Rupert earnestly.

'We need the money for our next term. Indeed you misjudge us.'

Beth cast them a look which implied she much doubted this, at least as far as Richard Lyle was concerned. But she was also aware of Richard's eyes upon her and that she made a striking picture in her pink cotton dress and matching sunbonnet.

She opened her mouth to make a scathing comment. Then she remembered. The Wheatsheaf. Maybe he could help her in her plans. Her true feelings could wait a little. So she changed her mind, and managed to smile instead. 'Lawyers. Fancy,' she murmured, retying the bow of her sunbonnet.

Richard had clearly been expecting something of a different sort from her lips, but when he looked at her suspiciously all he saw was an expression of admiration remarkably like Pippin's. 'Let me show you the famous medlar trees, Mr Lyle. You really ought to see how the manor house gets its name.'

Beth took his arm firmly, an act which he regarded with some surprise, but accepted with alacrity. The trees, which generations of Scoones had carefully tended, were at the far end of the walled garden, their fruit now coming to its lush harvest.

'I've never tasted a medlar - one must indulge in all life's experiences, Miss Ovenden, don't you think?' And he plucked one from the tree, biting into it.

'Yes indeed, Mr Lyle,' she laughed as he spat it out in disgust.

'Most amusing, Miss Ovenden,' he said grimly.

'All life's experiences,' she mocked. 'Don't you know you never eat a medlar till it's fallen, and rotten?

Most folks don't like 'em at all. You taste 'em at the end of the season when they're on the ground and it'll be a different story.'

'If I last till the end of the season,' he said ruefully. 'It's hard work, hop-picking. Now if I lived in a place like this –' He glanced up at the mellow red brick building and the mature gardens in front of it '– I wouldn't need to.'

'Shall you be at the Wheatsheaf tonight – er, Richard,' she asked innocently.

'If you look at me like that, obviously.'

'And the other hoppers?'

'What about them?'

'Won't they come? It'll be more comfortable than the fields. After all, it looks like rain tonight. We could cook for them – anything they like, every night if they like. And then we could have the hopkin there –' she rushed on eagerly.

'The what?'

'The party on the last night of the hop-picking. Plenty of food. A dance. We've got a tithe barn, you see. Perfect. Go on, suggest it. They'll listen to you. You're to be a lawyer, talk 'em into it.'

He stopped, disengaged his arm and looked at her narrowly. 'And why, my beautiful Beth, do you want –' He broke off. 'Ah. Need the custom, do you? It's not for my blue eyes you want me tonight.'

'Course not,' she said angrily.

'You must need money badly to be courting the hoppers every night.'

'Will you do it?' she asked obstinately.

'I might,' he said casually. 'I might at that. But there's a price.'

'What?'

'Well –' He looked at her consideringly, seemed about to say something, then changed his mind and said lightly, 'I want one of those figs behind you. They look delicious. The green bursting figs that hang upon the red-brick wall.'

'Mr Wilde, is it not?' said Pippin coming up close behind with Rupert.

'Yes, indeed, Miss Pippin,' Richard said.

'Not, I trust, a favourite poet of yours, Miss Scoones,' said Rupert, clearly a little shocked for some reason.

Beth looked on the trio scornfully. Poetry! Who had time to waste on poetry when there were important things to be done. It was all right in its proper place, when you could laze about lying in the meadows with a book in your hand. Real life wasn't like that, however. It was about survival and fighting for your own. And what use was poetry for that? They might be students, might 'need the money' but she could tell that they came from families that would never let them starve. Just the same as Pippin. Though Pippin was different. Pippin was Pippin and who could feel resentment against her for being born to a life where money was never a worry? They none of them understood what life was about. People and places were important. The Wheatsheaf was important, because it was a home. And homes meant folks. *Her* folks.

It seemed the summer would never end. When she looked back, it seemed as if it had all been a golden glow of sunshine, the occasional September storm clearing again to blue skies and warmth. By now the last of the huge hay waggons had deposited their loads, the apples were ready for picking, smelling sweet and fresh in the orchards. The cherry crop had been disappointing this year, for all their spring glory of blossom, but round about Shepham apples were the main fruit crop and hundreds of boxes were already on their way to the London markets. Everywhere the smell of harvest was in the air. The hop season had been good, and Shepham was content.

As if finally to concede that Michaelmas was here, the last day of hop-picking produced a continuous fine drizzle. Beth was in despair. What of the food, the outside fires and the cooking she had planned for the hopkin? No one would come. There'd be no money – the money she so badly needed.

It hadn't been so easy as she'd hoped, getting the hoppers to come to the Wheatsheaf regularly and to eat. Richard had helped in the beginning but then his enthusiasm had seemed to wane. She had been so busy, and she saw him less and less; on the last occcasion, he had had his arm round that Hetty Didcot, the Jezebel. Taking this as a direct slur upon herself, she had resolved to do without his help. As the numbers of hoppers appearing at the Wheatsheaf fell, she sallied forth to the gardens herself to cajole them into coming. She was no stranger to the hop gardens. In a village like Shepham every child was involved in the hop-growing cycle. There were jobs children could do, twisting the skeins of string into balls, helping with the dressing of the hops, the endless hoeing. Everyone had to play their part.

'We need them hops, Beth,' Andrew explained gently when she had protested as a youngster over sore hands and tired legs. 'Everybody must help. It's village business.' When she was nine she had started to pick hops, squatting on an old box, bines across her lap, endlessly picking off the hops, dropping them into any receptacle at hand, then emptying them at intervals into the big five-bushel baskets at the last moment when the measurer came along, so the hops would weigh lighter and fill the basket quicker. Then there were the endless discussions with the tallyman. Mrs Tripp, with whom she picked her hops, was a redoubtable woman. Any tallyman daring to argue with her risked a sweep of her large black brolly. Now the Butcher system of stringing was accepted all over East Kent work was easier for them, for at least they could sit, unlike the folks in the Weald who had to stand over huge canvas bins all day while the poles were unhooked and laid across the bins. But it was a long day. They started at 7.30 and went on till 5.30 with only half an hour for lunch. Woe betide any that ignored the horn calling them back to work. And how she used to long for the shout that heralded the end of picking for the day: 'Pull no more bines . . .'

The only part of hop-picking she'd liked had been riding on the waggons with the pokes of hops to the oast house; to see their funny cone hats turning with the wind. They had seemed to her like little castles when she was young, the dryer within, the castle's keeper. She loved the smell of the brimstone that the dryer put on the fire to give the hops that extra special tang, the flickering of the sulphur flames on the fire, and the taste of the potatoes they let the villagers cook in the ashes.

The dryers lived in the oast twenty-four hours a day during the season, the most important men in the whole of the hop-picking. A good dryer could make or break a farmer, irrespective of the quality of the hops. They knew their importance, but rarely traded on it.

She still liked the oast houses, but the hop gardens with their mud and their noise were a different matter. Babies were born, there was love-making in secluded spots and cooking, sleeping, suckling – the whole of life was conducted there, for all to see. Yet on these people depended the future of the Wheatsheaf. And so she went there, encouraging them to come to the Wheatsheaf, with a laugh, a joke, a toss of the head, a promise of cooking their favourite foods. Gradually, but surely, she wooed them.

The battle won, today she had a different mission at the hop garden – to make last minute arrangements for that all-important event, the hopkin.

Despondently she picked her way once more through the mud to the fields. Her hair clung limply round her face, her cape was insufficient protection against the insidious rain. Her boots squelched through the mud. Bill Saddler and his family, regular pickers for fifty years, organised the hopkin so far as the hoppers themselves were concerned. And they would be in the field getting the last of the bines stripped. There was a relaxation tolerated today in the fields, the garden manager turning a blind eye to the frolicking. At 6am that morning the horn had blown and picking had commenced as hard as ever, with everyone anxious to gain as many notches as possible on the tally sticks before the great pay out on the morrow. Shouts of good-humoured laughter rang out despite the rain which was still falling at midday. Cries for lost children were interspersed with snatches of 'Champagne Charlie', and 'The Man Who Broke The Bank at Monte Carlo'.

Beth had to search hard for Bill avoiding the hands put out lackadaisically to grab her, not too persistently, for they were aware she might wreak revenge this evening. Over the weeks the Wheatsheaf had established itself as the community eating place and Beth was the acknowledged queen of the proceedings. She encouraged this for it might mean more money for the Wheatsheaf. She seemed to have grown up in the last weeks, Andrew had thought admiringly, acquired a sense of controlled responsibility now that she had a purpose, and lost the headstrong, will-o'-the-wisp passion of her adolescence. All her energies were directed now to the making of money to save the Wheatsheaf. Only one thing could distract her. Richard Lyle. She found herself watching to see if he were present, rejoicing if she saw his tall dark figure perched on a table in the corner regaling the crowd with stories. Sometimes he and Rupert would dodge the picking, and they'd all go on a picnic taking Pippin; sometimes Rupert alone would come, Richard's absence ignored, unexplained. His elusiveness and air of mystery both infuriated and intrigued her. The sooner he went back to London the better! He'd never kissed her again like that first night, only light pecks on the cheek that infuriated her. But he'd only to laugh, and smile at her, and turn away as she might she would find herself longing for his arms about her still. After the hopkin tonight she would never see him again. And good riddance, she told her burning heart.

In some places the villagers waited till the hoppers had

gone before holding the hopkin. In Shepham they played fair. Or reasonably fair. They had two hopkins, one for the outsiders, one for the home pickers after the foreigners had gone. Even Pippin went to the second one, once Squire himself had appeared. Only the hardiest of the villagers would attend tonight's hopkin. Not that that worried the East Enders. The gypsies would have one corner of the barn, the casuals one corner, and the East Enders another. Gradually as the evening wore on there would be modest fraternising, as the music got into its stride.

'You got the potatoes organised, Bill?' Beth asked wearily, pushing a lock of wet black hair from her face.

He nodded, not even taking the time off from stripping his bine. Of course he had the potatoes organised. 'Gladys'll make up a party to fetch 'em,' he assured her.

'The lollyman's called at the Wheatsheaf already. Now what about herrings, Bill?'

He jerked his head. 'Over there, girl.'

At the side of the field a small crowd was surrounding the fishman in from Whitstable. News of a hopkin travelled fast and the fishermen would venture even to strange inland territories for wider custom. But Beth was not fated to reach him. Her way was barred by a crowd of roistering hoppers.

'Footshoe, footshoe.'

'Get off, you clutter'ucks,' she shrieked, as hands grabbed at her feet. Woe betide any visitors who refused to allow their feet to be wiped or to donate money to the hopkin. Beth cried in vain – today nobody was sacrosanct. Any excuse and a non-hopper entering the field was a good chance to bring the old custom into play.

'I be organising the hopkin,' she shouted irritably. 'I'm not giving you money. You're paying us.'

''Ear that? She's not giving the likes of us any money. We know what to do with the likes of 'er, then eh?' In a trice she was lifted off her feet by two youths and borne off.

'Into the basket.' Half the garden took up the cry.

'In with her.'

She was unceremoniously upended and tipped into one of the five bushel baskets where she lay higgledy-piggledy in the strong-smelling hops, skirts tumbling round her waist, her feet over the side, exposing her drawers for all the world to see, and unable to move from her ignoble position. Tears of vexation came to her eyes as she struggled to gain a hold and scramble out. Then from her ignominious position she saw someone elbowing his way to the front of the laughing crowd, remove her chief tormentor, and peer down at her. Richard Lyle shook his head sadly.

'Oh Beth, Beth, must you always be so undignified?'

'Get me out!' she hissed, too angry even to be embarrassed.

He bent over and, with a strength surprising in his slim frame, lifted her up in his arms and out of the basket. The crowd, having had their amusement, melted away in search of a new victim.

'I suppose you want me to thank you?' she stormed, tidying her skirts.

'Tonight will do,' he said, eyeing her with laconic

amusement. 'You can dance with me. Be my hopper's mate.'

'Why me all of a sudden?' she cried. 'Hetty Didcot not coming?'

It still rankled. Not that she cared a fig for Richard Lyle, but to see him with that draggletail had been a shock. She'd gone up to the gardens one day on her usual mission, and seen him by accident. Not in the gardens. She'd gone by an unfrequented footpath and seen him kissing that besom just the same as he had her, Beth. She'd had to come closer in order to pass and seen him push her down into the long grass. Then he'd seen her, whispered to Hetty and they'd laughed. Laughed – at *her*, Beth Ovenden.

'Still jealous, then?' he enquired now as she recalled this humiliating episode.

'Jealous of you?' she retorted scornfully. 'Why, I wouldn't be jealous of any man that Hetty Didcot looked at.'

'You can't think I'd notice Hetty Didcot when you're around, my Beth? Your generous heart won't let me be alone tonight?'

'I'll be working,' she said defiantly, though the thought of spending the evening with him made her heart race.

'Then you'd best go back where you came from,' and, before she could protest, he had picked her up and was holding her threateningly over the basket.

'Dance with me?' he hissed in her ear.

'I'm coming, Beth,' Pippin's voice was determined.

'But it's not fitting you be there. Your father wouldn't like it.'

'Pooh. I'm coming.'

'Wouldn't it be better if you come to the villagers' hopkin? It's going to be rough tonight, you know what they're like.'

'You'll be there,' Pippin pointed out.

'I'm different, I can look after myself.'

'So can I, you know,' said Pippin quietly. 'And, after all, Rupert and Richard will be there.'

Beth glanced at her, and wondered. Perhaps she could look after herself. She was a self-willed little thing. Perhaps that was why she liked her so much. All the same she couldn't get out of her mind that she had to protect her.

'Now that's settled,' said Pippin, 'what shall I wear? This?' She held up a white satin dress.

Beth shook her head firmly. 'No, too gentrified for a hopkin.'

Just for an instant she imagined herself clad in white satin held close in Richard Lyle's arms, saw his admiring glance as she mentally pushed the neckline lower – then she laughed at herself. What had she to do with silks and satins? She was a working girl and always would be. No, let Pippin have her silks and satins, she was born to them.

'Let's see now,' she said enthusiastically, attacking Pippin's wardrobe. Pippin looked at her consideringly. Sometimes she thought she'd be quite lost without Beth. Life had been a puzzle, a nightmare to her after her mother had died, and then it seemed as if Beth had come to take her place. Beth would tell her what to do, make things easy for her. Only now ten years later was she beginning to feel the stirrings of confidence, of wondering what life would hold for her, whom she'd marry – for marry she would. Her father would arrange something, though she would insist on a say in it. Suddenly she was quite sure about that. Sure about the sort of man she wanted.

'This,' said Beth, holding out a pale blue full-skirted cotton dress.

Pippin made a moué of disgust. 'No.'

'Then this. Oh, this.' Beth pulled out in excitement a peach-coloured dress trimmed with lace at the bodice and the hem, with artificial roses sewn down the straight front of the skirt.

'Yes,' said Pippin slowly, fingering it. 'Yes,' but her mind seemed to be on something else. 'Beth,' she went on slowly, 'Richard likes you, doesn't he?'

Beth sniffed. 'And plenty of others too.' Even Pippin should not know the effect that Richard Lyle had on her.

'But you specially,' Pippin persisted.

'Maybe.' Her voice was careless, but a glow came to Beth's face. 'Yes, perhaps he does.' She hummed, twirling around holding the peach-coloured dress against her. 'No,' she said regretfully, 'it's your colour, not mine. Anyway,' she said quickly, changing the subject, 'how about you and Rupert? Rupert follows you around like – like a sunflower the sun. Do you like him?'

'Oh yes,' said Pippin. She blushed and would not meet Beth's eye.

Beth glanced at her. So she was right. Pippin was attracted to Rupert. And who better? Well-educated, his father a sir so Pippin would be a lady. As gentle as Pippin herself. But not a weak man, she guessed, for all he was often overshadowed by Richard.

'Pippin,' she answered warmly. 'Yes. Who could not?

And he likes you,' she added teasingly. 'Can't tear him away from your side. Has he kissed you yet?'

Pippin looked shocked. 'Of course not,' she said indignantly. 'He did –' she hesitated '– hold my hand once. That's all right, isn't it?' she asked anxiously.

Beth looked at her fondly. 'Yes, that's all right. Do you think he'll come a-courting?'

Pippin glanced at her, and then her eyes fell away. 'Do you think this shawl, perhaps?' she said lightly, changing the subject.

'The bloaters, the bloaters,' Beth cried in anguish. She'd forgotten to put them on, though the fires had been ready some time. Thank goodness fate had been kind – the rain had gone and the sun had smiled. She cast a critical look around the tables. There were the rows of huffkins laid out, and of course pride of place to the hoppers cake, a marvellous concoction with wine and lemons and fruit that had taken her much time to bake. Then there was the bread pudding, Twenty-one Pie, oast cakes and, since the lollyman's visit, for the children aniseed balls, Spanish shoelaces and brandy balls. One table – outside – smelled of the seafood brought in from Whitstable: whelks and mussels. Now the cooking was done Beth was looking forward to the evening. She had put on her best white dress, for all she'd stopped Pippin wearing white. But then Beth only had one decent dress. She had found some late red roses with which to decorate it. It was a bit low for a hoppers' dance but, there, she could look after herself. In fact she rather liked its effect. Only her hands let her down; hands roughened from garden, bar and cooking work.

Other than that she looked just like a lady. But one thing spoiled her pleasure. The travelling men were there, even this evening, in a private room. Whenever they were there that indefinable menace hung over the Wheatsheaf.

'Beth, hold the bar for me. I'll be off to the private bar to tell 'em they'd best be gone,' said Andrew, putting down his drying cloth.

'Why are they always so anxious not to be seen?' she demanded of her father. He merely stared at her expressionlessly, and repeated, 'It's time they were gone.'

No one would come into the bar this evening – not when it was known that the hopkin was in the Wheatsheaf's barn. With all her love and fierce possessiveness for the Wheatsheaf there was still this shadow over it. Why? Surely there must be some reason other than the one her father gave?

Andrew came back, avoiding her eye, and without a word she left to attend to the food again. She picked up a plate of oast cakes in the large rambling kitchen and took it across to the barn. The hoppers were already arriving, erupting into the newly cleared tithe barn like they had on their lives eight weeks ago. William was in charge of organising the hoppers – thank goodness. She would be looking after the food, and Sylvie the drinks. The hoppers were dressed in their best: bright scarves at neck, plumes in the women's hats, and gleaming cheap jewellery blossoming on their bosoms. They brought with them the scent of the hop fields, and other smells beside, for baths were unknown to the hoppers. Crossing to the barn, Beth was brought to a stop – the travelling men were hurrying from the private bar down to the side gate, already shadowy, black, in the shorter September evenings. As they left, another, familiar, figure came round the corner sauntering towards the barn. Richard.

She stared at him, aghast, suddenly feeling sick.

'My Beth. Lovelier than ever,' he said lightly though for a second she could swear he was as shaken as she.

She ignored his greeting. 'Were you with them?' she whispered.

'With whom?' he asked nonchalantly.

'Them. The travelling men. You *were* with them, weren't you?'

He took her hands and kissed each of them in turn. 'You've been reading too many girlish romances. As usual, I'm much duller. I've been to the privy. Why did you think I'd been with them?'

'Beth? Richard?' Pippin's voice interrupted them.

'Pippin, you look lovely,' he said turning to her. Pippin blushed but Beth immediately felt a pang of jealousy, which intensified when he bore Pippin off into the barn, his arm round her waist, leaving Beth standing staring after them. He threw over his shoulder: 'Don't forget. I want my reward later.'

The evening was hectic. Beth flew around serving food, her face flushed with the heat, her nostrils nauseated by the smell. Yet she kept a permanent smile on her face, determined that this evening should be good. They must remember it, for the future of the Wheatsheaf might depend on it. Each bloater she served, she told herself, was a penny for the Wheatsheaf. She caught fleeting glimpses of Pippin dancing with Rupert, sometimes with Richard, her face lit up radiantly. Richard was dancing, first with an old grandmother then with Hetty Didcot. How could he! That draggletail. Why, she'd even left her corsets off. But as time went by Beth began to wish she could follow her example – though not for the same reasons. After all, her figure didn't need any artificial holding up and what was the point of flattening your breasts when the Good Lord gave them to you in a different shape? She watched the way Richard was holding Hetty – close. On an impulse she rushed inside to her bedroom, and tore off her dress, then the corsets, reverting to the little one she'd worn as a girl. She looked at herself doubtfully in the mirror, but her chemise and the dress itself with its boned bodice seemed firm enough, and happily she went downstairs with renewed enthusiasm. The demand for the hot food had diminished now; they were on to huffkins and Kentish hop-picker's cake.

As the evening wore on, things got rowdier. She found herself dancing with William, then with various strange men – but no sign of Richard. She told herself she didn't care. That tomorrow he would be gone and she'd never see him again anyway, so what did it matter? Yet she did care. The air was full of the smell of unwashed human bodies. How could Pippin stand it? she wondered. She was suddenly dispirited. Fancy her, Beth Ovenden, belle of the village, ignored by a mere Londoner.

'Wassermatter, little lady?' An arm round her waist whirled her round. 'Hey, a nice little bundle here.' It was him. The hopper she'd had trouble with last year. But he had no chance to exploit his advantage, for with a mere 'What you got, Ben?' she was seized by yet another pair of hands, forced down on to a lap, hot breath searing her, while Ben went on to pastures new. A resounding slap made her assailant loosen his hold. But only momentarily. With a hiss of rage he said: 'Fire in your belly, eh girl? Elsewhere too I'll be bound. Let's find out,' and he pulled her back against him, planting his lips over hers, thrusting his tongue into her mouth, squeezing her to him till she could hardly breathe. All round the merry crowd surged, oblivious and uncaring. With a grin of triumph, he crowed, 'What's this then? Nice, oh, very nice,' as his hand fastened greedily over one breast.

'Let me go, you –'

'Yes, let the lady go. My property.' Richard Lyle was standing over them. To Beth's amazement, the man did let her go, a deprecating smile on his face. Then Richard had pulled her away from her tormentor, through the throng to the outside. She saw William's face watching them, black with a puzzling, unaccustomed anger. Richard led her into the garden and leaned her against a wall where the hollyhocks grew strong. His arms pinioned her there, as he looked at her flushed, indignant face and the honesty that shone out of it, an honesty he was irresistibly drawn to – and yet which scared him. But none of this did he let Beth see, as he asked mockingly: 'Couldn't you wait, Beth?'

She was still shaking with panic and anger combined. He took out his handkerchief and wiped her face. She turned her face from him and spat. 'I feel dirty –' she muttered.

He led her down the garden to the well, dipped his handkerchief in the bucket of water and wiped her face over. Then he gave her some to drink out of his cupped hands. 'How's that?'

'Better.' Then, 'Why me?' she burst out angrily. 'They wouldn't dare do that to Pippin.'

'Perhaps Pippin wears corsets,' he remarked casually.

She gasped and blushed. 'But – you can't tell –'

'There's a certain – um – swing when you walk that has its attractions. And a certain outline –' He put his hand on her left breast, lightly, fleetingly. Instinctively, her hand came up to push it away.

'What about Hetty Didcot, then?' she asked crossly. 'Won't she be missing you?'

'To the devil with Hetty Didcot,' he murmured, catching her hand and drawing her to him again. Then putting one hand behind her head, caressing her neck, with the other he released her carefully pinned black hair, already dishevelled by the exertions of the evening, and let it fall round her shoulders, and kissed her. This time she reached out for him, her lips open, warm, tender, meeting his – only to find they were withdrawn.

'There,' he said, lightly, 'that'll have to do you. Till next year.'

She opened her eyes. 'Next year?' she repeated wonderingly.

'I think I must have hopping in my blood. That or something else,' he said teasingly. 'You'll wait for me, won't you? Not go running off with any costermongers, up to London's bright lights?'

She shuddered anew at the recollection. 'It weren't just the corsets,' she muttered, scuffling the ground with the tip of her satin shoe. 'They wouldn't do that to

Pippin whether she was wearing 'em or not. Why me then?'

'Pippin's a lady.'

She reddened angrily, unable to believe her ears. How could he do it? Leading her on then saying something like that. 'And what about me?' she said, almost crying again. 'You want me to wait for you. Aren't I a lady then?'

'You?' His blue eyes looked into hers, the laughter momentarily absent. 'You are my Beth. That's all I know. Part of me. Now and forever, you are my Beth.'

And on the morrow he was gone.

CHAPTER THREE

'Cherries be blowing late this year,' grunted Andrew, glancing out at the white mass of petals fluttering on the breeze. 'Don't bode too well for the summer, do it, lass?'

'Nonsense,' Beth said stoutly, busy with her mushroom catsup. She was beginning early this year for the hopper invasion. ''Tis just that winter held them back, that's all. Most likely be the best summer for years.' She spoke more cheerfully than she felt. Even her spirits had been lowered by the winter that had only just passed into spring. The coldest spell for ninety years or more, so they said. Even old Mr Trimlett in the village, reputed to be over a hundred, couldn't remember a winter so severe. Weeks of nothing but white mounds of unbroken snow, great piles that offered a bleak landscape from waking to sleeping. The village was cut off with scarce enough food for man, let alone beast, and Beth's prowess at baking had been severely tested, for food was all that kept the revenue of the Wheatsheaf going. She had gone through her mother's recipe books time after time, and had been reduced to boiled batter pudding, so low was her store cupboard. Thank Heaven she had had enough potatoes to make yeast, or they would have been in a sorry state. No beer deliveries had got through, and their own supply of home brewed beer had been running out. They'd been forced to start on the March brewing supplies before it was really ready to drink, and complaints hadn't been long in coming in. That had meant buying in more barrels from outside – and yet more credit.

But the shortage had brought one good result – young Beth Ovenden's gooseberry and elderflower wine had suddenly acquired favour in the village and, encouraged, she had watched her supplies dwindle and the tills rattle. True, much was chalked up on the old slate they kept behind the bar clock, but it had been mostly redeemed after the thaw eventually came. Shepham was too small a village for it to remain unpaid. Andrew had traipsed through the fields braving drifts, leading Nelly and the cart during the worst of the weather to bring back a few essential deliveries for themselves and others, but even Faversham ran short of food.

'Under four weeks to Midsummer Day.' Andrew broke into her thoughts. 'What you going to say to Shurland?' His tone was sharp, but Beth knew there was no malice in his words. He was as sick with anxiety as she, and it showed in his gruffness. 'Ain't got enough, 'ave 'ee? Just like I said. You paid off Hamlin and now we're in worse debt to Shurland. Proper businesswoman you be.'

She swallowed hard. 'We'll have to carry it over, like I arranged,' she said more coolly than she felt.

He laughed sarcastically. 'Yes, at six per cent. And you reckoned Hamlin was hard on us!'

She fired up. 'Who would you rather deal with? Shurland or Hamlin?'

'When you're in debt, girl, they all be the same. All in it to make money. No one is here just to bail the Ovendens out of trouble. You'll see. If you have to over-carry that loan at six per cent - another year and old Shurland be boss here.'

Beth said nothing, but added the chillies to the mixture on the range and stirred vigorously. He had reason on his side and she knew it. But she had hope on hers.

''Tis not all black, Father,' she said encouragingly. No point in letting Andrew get into one of his moods. The whole pub would be affected then and that drove away custom. 'We can repay half,' she pointed out, 'on Midsummer Day. And the interest. We'll carry the rest over and - and work up trade.'

'We work our hind legs off as it is, Beth. What with brewing our own Ovenden Mild and you serving food, all that fuss for mighty little return. We can't do no more. Village don't have the trade.'

'We'll manage,' she said confidently. 'When the hoppers come, you'll see -'

'When the hoppers come,' he echoed scathingly, but fell silent.

When the hoppers come, she thought, caught unawares by a lurch of her heart, would he be with them, as he had promised? Or had it been a whim to pass a summer in the country, to take love lightly and pass on his way? Like the gypsy of that golden summer, who'd vanished into a world of his own far away and never came whistling up the village green again.

Not a word had she heard from Richard Lyle, since

he departed last October, though Pippin had heard from Rupert several times. She had even met him at Christmas at a ball in Sussex, but if news had passed between them about Richard Lyle it did not reach Beth and, dear though Pippin was to her, Beth was too proud to ask. Let him come if he would. Let her forget him if he would not. Yet when she danced at the village dances with Robert Chace, the rector's son, who was much smitten with her, she felt other arms around her. When with great daring he'd kissed her, she had responded for there swam before her not the earnest, round face of Robert, but a pair of blue eyes laughing from a devil-may-care face that would not be denied.

She looked at her hands ruefully, those hands he'd kissed so often, stained now with field mushrooms. Have to get some lemon to them. They were almost as bad as they'd been last autumn stirring in the malt for the brewing and measuring out the hops.

It had been her idea they should start brewing again but, enthusiastic as she was about it, she dreaded brewing days: her washing copper out of action for the brewing, every one of her large kitchen pans, preserving pans, tubs, even the milk pans purloined to cool the nearly boiling worts. Not just for the day itself, but well beforehand so that they could be scrubbed out with lime chloride, scalded and washed, ready for the day. In theory brewing was Andrew's job but, somehow, Beth found not only her own time but much of William's and even Sylvie's had to be devoted to it, Andrew seeing himself more in the role of master craftsman. On the day itself the kitchen boiler and other pans were filled with water and boiled for an hour and the resulting liquor, when exactly the right temperature - and what anxious moments went into determining that - was run into the mash tun which Beth had rescued from its rotting death in the barn. Then the malt was added and the stirring began. Oh, that stirring. Beth's arms ached and even William's muscles felt the strain by the time it was over. Finally the tap in the bottom of the tun was opened and the wort ran through to fill Beth's pans and tubs from where it would be poured into the huge copper. Now came the part Beth enjoyed - adding the hops to the boiling liquid, enjoying their heady smell, feeling that at last the unprepossessing mess was on the way to becoming beer. But William and Andrew did not enjoy it. They watched it anxiously as a farmer might a new-born foal.

Then, once again, the wort had to be cooled to exactly the right temperature before the yeast was added in the fermenting bin. At this stage sleep was dispensed with as it was watched constantly for a day and a half, Andrew and William taking it in turns, to ensure that the temperature did not rise too high for Ovenden Ale. At last, when tempers were frayed and nerves at breaking point, there would be a conspiratorial sigh between the two and the bungs would be driven home in the casks.

Beth's wines were rather scorned by William and Andrew besides the brewing of the beer, and Beth was left to get on with it very much alone. Beer always had the first priority, it seemed, on her pans. All the same, she'd bottled six dozen bottles of elderberry wine last autumn to add to the elderflower wine she'd made in the summer, and pickled three dozen jars of walnuts ready for next year. Still, it had been worth it. She was beginning to work up a nice little trade with her catsup and preserves in Mrs Parslow's store. The wines were selling nicely, and now rack upon rack of rhubarb wine awaited maturity. Up till now there hadn't been much call for it in the pub, but it opened up a train of thought in Beth's mind. It was a popular drink with ladies. 'Fifty per cent of this village is women,' she had said excitedly to her father. 'Why shouldn't they come to the Wheatsheaf too?'

'It ain't their place,' Andrew had said, glaring at her. He was a traditionalist.

'Why not?' argued Beth fiercely. 'Why ever not?'

Andrew had been furious when she converted one of the private rooms into a parlour where women might come. Not only for elderflower wine, for Beth's active mind had gone racing ahead. *Teas*, and her scones for example. The room had remained empty for many weeks until William loyally persuaded his mother to accompany his father one Saturday night. Mrs Parslow sailed in, face pink but determined as she crossed the threshold of sin. 'A glass of elderflower wine, if you please, Miss Ovenden.' No tea for Mrs Parslow. A second glass had in due course followed the first, and also in due course a second female customer followed her example. The parlour gained a small precarious toehold at the Wheatsheaf.

'Another of these new-fangled ideas of Beth Ovenden's' was the male verdict, to be tolerated, provided it did not intrude on the serious business of the Wheatsheaf. Joseph Higgins, the temperance lay preacher, with his pale long face and fanatical eyes, had remonstrated with the ladies but, when in an attempt to cultivate extra trade Beth introduced afternoon tea and cakes, he lost the battle.

He had arrived, he and his pale shadow of a wife, one afternoon, flanked by three henchmen, as Mrs Parslow departed, and barred her path.

'Surprised I am to see you, Mrs Parslow, partaking of refreshment in the Devil's house.' His voice low, grating, as unctuous as a snake's carried, as it was meant to, to Beth standing in the doorway. He may have felt that one woman on her own was no match for five, or it may have been that he had underestimated Mrs Parslow.

She was a large woman – William took after her, not his quiet, thin father – and resented being stopped in her path on her way to cook her Herbert's tea. She put out a restraining arm as Beth ran to join her. She could cope alone with Higgins.

'The Devil's more to do than to argify with me over tea and huffkins, Mr Higgins.' She answered pleasantly enough but, to those who knew William's mother, the underlying tone of her voice would have made them beware.

'Pray to the Lord, Mrs Parslow, to lead you not into temptation. He will deliver you,' Mrs Higgins put in helpfully.

'The Lord has His work cut out in this village keeping His eye on His so-called disciples, I'm thinking,' replied Mrs Parslow firmly.

At this Higgins had been unwise enough to lay a hand on Mrs Parslow's arm, thus bringing Mrs Parslow's large red umbrella into the action. This, combined with a steady stream of Kentish abuse, defeated Higgins without Beth uttering a word. Yet she knew that his enmity was not for Mrs Parslow but for the Ovendens and for her in particular. Each time his pale blue eyes flickered over her she felt defiled as if his mere look could touch her.

'The Lord will not be mocked,' he shouted as, red and in retreat, he went back down the green. 'The time of the Lord will come.'

Since that day he had left the Wheatsheaf in peace, and the afternoon trade had grown. This afternoon, however, no one had come and Beth had a rare hour or two of freedom.

Beth gave up the unequal task of trying to make her hands as white as Pippins's, tied on her straw bonnet and set off to pay a long overdue visit to Medlars. She had not seen Pippin for three weeks. Pippin was nineteen now, six months older than Beth, and she had been swept into a world of balls and visits under the aegis of her Aunt Phyllis who had intervened in the motherless household to superintend her niece's social life. Beth swung between envy and practicality. After all, her common sense reasoned, did she really want to go to dances with red-faced rich landowners' sons, who'd never pulled a pint in their lives and who danced as if they were oxen? She'd as soon gallop around with the village lads. Pippin was welcome. Schooling had finished now, save for Pippin's drawing and music lessons in which Beth did not share. What did Pippin *do* all day now, she wondered, with no garden to tend, no washing to do, no baking?

She turned into the lane that led to Medlars, which

lay half a mile from the village. The banks on either side were studded with pink ragged robin and buttercups, the woods beyond thick with bluebells. She passed Farmer Judd's orchard, in full bloom now, and plucked a sprig of apple blossom for her bonnet, making a mental note to give his beer a long pull in compensation when next he came to the Wheatsheaf.

Something in her was leaping excitedly. The indefinable quality in the air that was spring had come at last, the slight sharpness in the warmth that spelled of excitements to come, of summer heralded. Her step lightened and she was almost skipping along. They'd find a way through their problems, she was convinced. If you worked hard enough, if you were determined, you would find the way. That's what Father had always taught her, and he must believe it himself now.

The gardens at Medlars were springing to life again after the long harsh winter, the lilacs in bloom and the drive bordered with huge purple and red rhododendrons. The warmth of new-cut grass from the lawns filled her nostrils as she walked up the drive, meeting the Squire who had come through the arched gateway at the side of the house. She saw little of him now that lessons were over, and for one moment he seemed to hesitate as he saw her and she thought he would wait to speak to her. But he changed his mind and, with an abrupt 'Afternoon, Beth,' he continued on his way to the stables. Pippin, sitting in the drawing room, noticed her pass the window and flew to meet her, beating Jervis the butler to the door, much to his disapproval.

'Beth, I was longing and longing to see you . . .'

'Then why didn't you come down to Wheatsheaf?' asked Beth practically.

Pippin pulled a face. 'Father said –' She lowered her voice. 'He says I should not, now that I'm – well – a young lady, he says. I must not go to public houses.'

Beth had her own opinion of what being 'out' involved. Staying in, more like. But then Pippin always was rather a cuckoo. She looked at her affectionately. How pretty she looked today, with her fair hair swept up behind in loose curls, a pale green figured silk skirt that picked up the lights in her greenish-hazel eyes, and a soft white lawn blouse. These styles flattered one so slim as Pippin, but Beth's own more generous curves simply refused to budge to current fashion. She looked all behind, like Farmer Judd's rent, as the village saying went. Not that there was much call for current fashion behind a bar.

'What do you do every day now?' asked Beth curiously as they sat down in the drawing room.

'Oh lots of things,' Pippin said vaguely. 'I visit, and then there's letters, clothes – you know.'

Beth did not know. 'No more hop-picking for you?' she said sadly.

'No,' said Pippin without regret. 'It gives me too many freckles, and I have to think of my complexion now.' She caught Beth's look and laughed a little shamefacedly. 'Silly, isn't it? But I won't miss the Hop-pickers' Special. Nor our picnics. Oh Beth, I shall see just as much of you, shan't I? You must come here, we'll have tea, just as we always did. Go shopping. All sorts of things. You can come with me to some of the balls. Why not?' Her eyes gleamed with pleasure at the thought.

'No more hopkins for you, though?' Beth teased, but was surprised by Pippin's reaction.

'I – I shall if I want,' she said obstinately. 'After all, that's a village thing. I ought to go. Anyway, that's a long way off. There'll be lots of things before then. When Rupert comes –' she added offhandedly.

'Rupert?' asked Beth quickly. 'Have you heard from him, Pippin?'

Pippin reddened slightly. 'I met him last week,' she said casually. 'In London at an exhibition. We took tea together. He says they will be coming for the hop-picking again, after their final year at university is over. Then they come here before going to Inner Temple in the autumn to begin their legal training.'

'They?' Beth said sharply.

'He – and Richard. Richard Lyle,' added Pippin unnecessarily, fiddling with her skirt and glancing at Beth from under her eyelids.

Beth was still, emotions churning through her heart. So he had not forgotten. He was coming again. Her heart danced, but she disciplined herself to think rationally. Not a word had he sent. 'You'll wait for me, Beth.' It had been a light-hearted comment, that was all. What a fool she was to waste a thought for him.

But all the same it was a long time until August and the arrival of the hop-pickers.

The robed figure strode ahead. The Reverend Chace, a twinkle in his usual impassive grave expression, took the ceremony in as good part as his parishioners. Once a solemn necessity, it now was half-frolic, this Rogationtide beating of the bounds. No farmers asked for a blessing on their fields and so that part of the ceremony had been abandoned. For the young folk it was an exciting event. Children were dragged along by older brothers and sisters, as part of the ritual, to see where the marker stones were so that they in their turn might pass the knowledge on to their children. And thus would Shepham live.

Old folk came too, not of their own free will, but chivvied by the rector that their long memory of the ancient boundaries might be shared with all. Even old Trimlett was there, carried in his chair by four stalwart youths, eyes watering with excitement as his utterances were suddenly of such importance.

Miss Monk, the wild-eyed lady of indeterminate age who lived outside the village with three cats, large garden and orchard, and whom some claimed was a witch, was striding out in her old-fashioned, wide-skirted black gown and red petticoats, poking with a stick in the stream to clear a marker of weeds. William, approaching her to help her across the nailbourne stream, now in flood, received short shrift: 'Take your hands off me, young Parslow. Not in my grave yet.'

William grinned and returned to Beth's side. ' 'Tis the Midsummer Dance in three weeks, Miss Beth. The Saturday before Midsummer Day this year,' he pointed out casually.

'So it is,' Beth said equally offhandedly. Dances, she thought indignantly, when Midsummer was the all-important time of repayment to Mr Shurland! She had now just over £50, the minimum Mr Shurland had said he would accept as first payment on the loan, plus the interest.

'I'd be mortal pleased if you was to be my partner,' said William awkwardly, ''Course,' he added hastily, 'I know I'm not much of a dancer, but –'

'Get along with you, you great sprollucks,' Beth said affectionately. 'What would Sylvie say if you and I was to go together?'

William flushed and muttered, 'I can ask who I likes, can't I?'

Beth thought quickly. She did not want to hurt William but she did not want to announce to the village so clearly that she was William's girl. After all, there was Robert Chace and – no, it would not do.

''Tis all right, Miss Beth, I understand,' said William hurriedly, swiping at the cow parsley in the hedgerow with a stick, and affecting nonchalance. 'You got other things on your mind. Can't repay Shurland – that it?' he asked abruptly with a perspicacity that took her by surprise.

'Not exactly,' she said slowly, half reluctant to get drawn into a discussion about the Wheatsheaf and its finances and half welcoming it since it diverted her attention from other matters that William would never know about.

'You might as well tell me, Miss Beth,' he said quietly. 'Reckon if the Wheatsheaf's going to survive, you'll *have* to tell me.'

'Have to?' she echoed indignantly. 'I don't see –'

'No, you never do,' he said, just as quietly, but when she turned to him she saw a rare anger reflected in his pale face. 'You just believes everything everyone tells you. You don't think there's evil in no one. And sometimes that ain't a good thing. Even when it's your own father.'

He looked at her dispassionately as she took this in, her cheeks flushing red, and she turned to him in fury. It wasn't going to be easy for her. But she had to know. After all, it hadn't been easy for him. Andrew Ovenden had been a second father to him all his life, and was a good employer, though perhaps employer was the wrong word for what he felt about working at the Wheatsheaf. He loved it, not with Beth's emotional, instinctive passion but with a reasoning, devoted detachment that the Wheatsheaf meant something important, that it was necessary for it to survive just as it was necessary for England to survive. And so he had to tell her.

'Before you start shouting at me, Beth, just listen. I wasn't born blind and I've been around Wheatsheaf a long time. I know when something's wrong and something's been wrong for a long time. Now I've found out what it is. And it ain't Hamlin.'

'What?' she said, intrigued and alarmed, and noting the 'Beth'.

'Such as what's underneath that old thatched barn at back of orchard,' replied William grimly.

'That's only used for storing old barrels and fodder,' said Beth puzzled.

'Ever seen the trapdoor in the floor under the big vat? Gives way to a cellar underneath. Very useful for storing things you don't want prying eyes to see. And those travelling men as you call 'em,' he went on rapidly, the colour rising in his broad face. 'It's not right. They still come here, you know. And you should hear why. Reckon most of the village knows or guesses. 'Tis smugglers they are, Beth.'

'Smugglers!' she said, stopping abruptly on the path. Then she laughed, relieved. 'Oh, William, you're joking. There aren't any nowadays.' Whatever she had been expecting, it wasn't this.

'In the old days, see, Wheatsheaf was a safe centre for dividing the spoils. It were on the old smugglers' route to London. Brought ashore on the flats at Seasalter to Blue Anchor Corner, over to the Wheatsheaf through Herne Hill, then on down to Blue House Farm Lenham way. Then up the old road to London. No London trade now of course. Not for fifty years or more, since the Customs got smarter. Now that the tariffs are lower there's no call from London for the stuff. But it still goes on. 'Tis a tradition, see, in some families. They never known no other way of life and ain't got the wit to think of one. And the Wheatsheaf generally been part of it.'

'True enough,' said Andrew angrily as Beth hurtled through the cellar door where he was adding finings to the beer. 'Though what cause William had to go atelling you for, I don't know.' Beth had half hoped against hope that he would deny it, laugh and ruffle her hair as he had so reassuringly when she was a child.

She tried to take it in. The travelling men had been part of her nightmares for so long, it was hard to grapple with the fact that it was now a real nightmare. And a threat. For, if contraband was kept here, the Wheatsheaf and Father were in danger. She tried to calm herself, to think clearly. It needed but one enemy – an enemy like Higgins – to tell on them and then what? A fine for the smugglers, but for father the loss of the licence for sure.

'It's dangerous, Father.'

'I've done it for ten years or more and nowt's gone wrong yet. This ain't women's business, Beth. Men's work.'

'Of course it's my business. If you lose your licence – go to prison –'

'We've got to make a living, girl,' he said roughly. 'Saints alive, d'yer think the village trade is enough to keep us going? Tom the Higgler's all right – honest enough in his way. They ain't let me down yet. They pay me well. And they don't come here so much recently. Got somewhere else maybe. I don't enquire.'

'You said the extra money came from the Farmers' Benevolent Society meetings, Darts Club and the like –'

'So it does – about five per cent of it. Rest comes from brandy and tobacco. It's what brought you up without help from others –' He broke off, and his lips closed firmly.

'But suppose it goes wrong?' she cried.

'Suppose nothing, girl. While I'm here you don't know nothing. You're the landlord's daughter, that's all. Just because you fancy yourself up as a business lady don't mean you has to know everything.'

'I can do more for the Wheatsheaf at the kitchen stove, I suppose,' said Beth bitterly.

'You could do worse, at that,' retorted Andrew angrily. 'There's Joe Higgins just waiting his chance to close us down. Him and Goodfellow, that meddling new policeman. We've got enough enemies in this village without you stirring up more.'

She shivered as she watched Andrew stomp upstairs. Higgins with his cold, fishlike grey eyes and sweaty hands. She'd sooner face that East End costermonger than Higgins with his lisping voice and fanatical blank-eyed stare.

She dropped the blue dress over her head carefully for she did not wish to undo her half hour's work in pinning up her hair. She had swept it back above her ears, with curls hanging down at the back, a style that displayed her long white neck to perfection. The hair was arranged in as careful an imitation of Pippin's as she could achieve with her mother's old iron hair tongs. For all she affected not to care about the Midsummer Dance she had taken great pains to look her best. She pulled the huge bell sleeves down and admired the slimness they appeared to give her waist. She was going to look as different from the village girls as possible. Hetty Didcot was married now (and was suspiciously large with child though that was not unusual in Shepham), but there were many others, young and fresh sixteen- and seventeen-year-olds inclined to regard her, Beth Ovenden, at not quite nineteen as an old maid. She would show them.

Nearly the whole village seemed to be crammed into the village hall, spilling over outside in the orchard at the back, and onto the green at the front. Old folks were ensconsed proprietorially around the walls, young folks intermingled in ever-changing permutations of partners, all masked to add to the excitement.

'Miss Beth, may I have the pleasure?' William, clearly recognisable despite the obligatory mask, his hair gleaming with pomatum, his cheeks flushed, stood before her square and stocky, and she danced away in his arms to the vigorous accompaniment of the village band, none too sure of their tempo. She noticed Sylvie standing by the wall watching, in an unbecoming dress of red satin, a glittering, malevolent expression in her eyes. Mostly Sylvie avoided encounters with Beth apart from those strictly necessary in the course of business, but recently her animosity had been overt. Unusually busy in the bar, one day Beth had called out: 'Fetch some more of the rhubarb wine, Sylvie.' When nothing had happened Beth impatiently went in search of her, to find her helping William in the other bar, and demanded to know why the wine had not come. Sylvie had turned on her with: 'I don't allus dance to your tune. I bain't like William.' William had flushed a deep red, and said nothing, and after a quick look at him Beth had replied quietly, 'Would you get it now please, Sylvie.' Without another word, Sylvie did. Yet Beth, glancing at her now, at the dance, sensed her continuing jealousy.

By the time Beth had danced three times with William and once with Robert Chace, also recognisable since he announced his identity, she was hot but exhilarated, though Robert had held her far too close for her liking or for his peace of mind apparently.

His hand had slid up and down her back far too enthusiastically for a rector's son, and she had had to decline an invitation for a breath of air. As the evening wore on, couples appeared and disappeared, looking guilty or complacent according to their characters. Beth stayed resolutely inside, a fact which did her no service when it came to the impromptu beer-drinking competition. Despite all her protestations she found herself bodily lifted and placed on the platform. 'Beth Ovenden's the prize', yelled the wit. 'A kiss and a dance with the landlord's daughter.'

'Put me down, you strommocks –' yelled Beth. 'I'll be no part of –'

But her voice was drowned in the yells as the twenty or more contestants surged forward.

'Half an hour's allowed,' called the youth who had ordained himself master of ceremonies for the event.

At the end of twenty minutes only three of the drinkers were left in, William stolidly avoiding Beth's eye as he drank, and two others.

By five pints and twenty-five minutes one had fallen out and, half a pint later, William with a grunt of disgust put down his glass and lurched outside.

With a crow of triumph the winner leapt onto the stage to claim her and swept her down, tearing off her inadequate mask with one hand.

'Get off, I don't agree to this,' she hissed. He grinned at her and ignoring shouts to claim the kiss, swept her into the throng. He held her far too tightly in strong arms and she had to keep her head back to avoid the smell of the beer oozing from him. Why ever had she come? She hated this beery lecherous crowd! She tried to pull herself away, but he grasped her the more firmly, then pulled her head towards him and placed his mouth on hers, his lips surprisingly gentle. She shut her eyes to escape the horror until the lips should be withdrawn again and the smell recede.

'Wearing your corsets tonight, I see,' he whispered.

Her lids flew wide open, to see the blue eyes gleaming at her through the mask. The eyes of Richard Lyle.

She stumbled from the shock and would have fallen but for his arm.

'Outside,' he said. And led her protestingly to the back door, with ribald comments following them.

'I've no dishonourable intentions. All that beer –' he said, pushing her before him outside, taking her into the orchard still unable to find words.

'Are you going to watch?' he enquired.

Blushing, she turned away. 'Manners of a farm hand,' she remarked scornfully when he'd finished, 'as well as looking like one,' staring critically at his country style drill trousers and square-toed boots. 'What game you playing at now, Mr Lyle?'

'I thought you'd be glad to see me back,' he said, hurt, tossing his mask away.

'Glad!' she echoed indignantly. Her legs felt weak, but something inside her seemed to be hammering up and down.

'My university examinations are finished, so I flew to your side, Beth. Naturally. I thought I'd spend a few weekends down here cherry picking perhaps till the hops start, or do some hop-dressing, hoeing. I've heard there's a good inn nearby –' His eyes danced at her.

'We're full,' said Beth quickly. The thought of Richard Lyle under the same roof was scaring, yet life suddenly seemed to have taken on a new excitement, and the blood rose in her cheeks.

'Not room even in your bed?' he murmured.

'That there is not,' she said scandalised. 'My bed's my own, Mr Lyle.'

'With that black hair and that figure? You're cruel, Beth.' He pulled her towards him and kissed her again, a long slow kiss that made her head swim with pleasure. But he should not know that.

'Tell me you're glad to see me back,' he murmured into her cheek.

'If you're to lodge at Wheatsheaf,' she said breathlessly, 'we'd best be moving,' and she turned away.

'Beth –' he caught her arm. 'Tell me.' His voice was almost pleading. He had hardly known himself what brought him back, but now, face to face with Beth once more, her dark eyes shining into his, he knew at last.

Beth swallowed and turned away, she could not look at him as she said simply, 'I'm glad you have come, Richard.'

The Thursday of Midsummer Day dawned bright and clear as larksong. Beth hummed as she dressed. Her best white blouse with the yellow and white tucks was really too ornate for a business meeting but she decided to wear it anyway. They had something to celebrate. Fifty-three pounds in her handbag to give to Mr Shurland. She ran downstairs to get the hot water ready for Richard's washing bowl. For once she had other things to think about than Richard Lyle. He was off to Dover today with some companions, he'd said, and would be back this evening.

'Companions?' she'd asked, when he had left on Monday, saying he would return on Wednesday with two young ladies.

'They're friends of mine going to France and I said I'd see them to Dover. You can put them up, can't you?' he had asked carelessly.

'I suppose so,' she said, puzzled. 'But why here? It's out of the way for Dover.'

'It's a good excuse for me to stay here, isn't it?'

And so he'd arrived in a hired carriage from Faversham last night. Beth didn't know much about London, but she knew about women. She'd seen that type before. She'd tried to talk to them, but Richard had discouraged it, laughing and talking with her till she didn't know what she was doing. They were Hetty Didcots, both of 'em, and no better than they should be. Hetty had just given birth to a son, 'come early' she claimed. Beth had sniffed to herself when she heard that.

Now she filled the three water bowls and jugs and placed two of them outside the girls' rooms, and the third outside Richard's. She was glad they'd be gone when she got back from Canterbury. Then she would have Richard to herself to talk about the day. She ran downstairs again to join Andrew in the cart. He'd insisted on driving her himself. 'No slip of a girl is going to run my business.'

William, left to mind the Wheatsheaf, looked after them wistfully as the cart departed down the side of the village green, their old horse George pulling slowly as if resentful at this early morning task. A blackbird, startled from its worm, flew indignantly across their path.

'You seem happy enough, lass,' said Andrew, noticing Beth's sparkling eyes.

'Who wouldn't be happy? The roses are out, the sun is shining. 'Tis Midsummer Day and - oh, Father, we've half the money to pay Mr Shurland.'

'And suppose he won't give you credit for another year?'

'But he will. He said he would.'

Canterbury was already full of shoppers, bustling and hustling under the shadow of the majestic cathedral. Beth gave a quick look at the awe-inspiring façade and passed a quick prayer of thanks to the Almighty for this glorious day.

Gathering the folds of the yellow shantung skirt in her hands she jumped down from the cart when they reached the brewery, earning a reproving look from Andrew. Time Beth got over her hoydenish ways if she fancied herself a businesswoman.

The clerk in the reception office looked embarrassed, wary. 'Mr Shurland,' he repeated. 'Mr Shurland –'

'Yes, man, yes, we've an appointment these three months.'

He looked down at his desk as though something deeply fascinated him there. 'Mr Shurland's ill –'

'Ill?' said Beth. A small cloud of unease swept over her. 'When will he be back?'

The man looked evasive. 'It's his heart, so they say. After - what happened.'

'Who's standing in for him?' asked Andrew abruptly.

'No one is exactly standing in for –' began the man nervously.

'Perhaps I can be of assistance.' The door to Mr Shurland's office opened. A familiar portly figure stood on the threshold, smiling in an imitation of benevolence.

'Hamlin,' breathed Andrew, his cheeks going pink. 'What be you doing here?'

'Mr Hamlin please, Mr Ovenden, now we're doing business together again.' Hamlin's voice purred.

'Our business is with Mr Shurland, not you,' said Beth more bravely than she felt.

'Alas, dear young lady, our mutual friend Mr Shurland is not available.'

'Then we'll be back when he is,' said Andrew, preparing to depart.

'I do not make myself clear perhaps,' added Hamlin smoothly. 'There is no Shurland's any more. Mr Shurland wisely decided to sell his brewery to me. Teynham and Shurland Breweries, and soon we'll drop the Shurland's. There'll always be a place for Mr Shurland on the board if he should recover but *I* do the business. Now what was it you wished to discuss? The matter of the repayment of your loan perhaps.'

'Sold out? To you? He'd never do that willingly,' said Beth fiercely. 'What happened?'

'The money, Miss Ovenden,' said Hamlin smoothly, ignoring her question.

Beth put the money on the desk.

'My dear young lady, I had understood the loan was one hundred pounds plus interest at three per cent.

'It was understood that we'd have another year to pay,' said Beth fiercely, 'at six per cent if we paid half now. And we'll do it.'

'Understood was it? Not by me, Miss Ovenden. And

I see nothing to that effect in Mr Shurland's files. Not that I'm doubting your word, but I'm a businessman, Miss Ovenden. If I do not have that money by the end of trading today I shall reluctantly - very reluctantly - be forced to call in the loan. You understand my position?'

'By God, I understand you, Hamlin,' Andrew roared. 'You double-dealing shuck.'

Hamlin smiled coldly, but his eyes narrowed. 'Interested to hear your opinion of me, I'm sure, Mr Ovenden. You won't be wanting to stay on as manager after I take over the Wheatsheaf, then. You wouldn't want to work for a scoundrel. I'll keep the girl on though. Handsome piece. She'll have to be more pleasant to the customers, though.'

Andrew started towards him with a roar, but Beth held him back. 'I'll thank you to remember you're not landlord of the Wheatsheaf yet. We've until the end of the day. Till then we'll have some respect. Come, Father.'

Hamlin's jeering laugh rang in their ears as they walked down the stairs.

'And where do you think we can lay hands on fifty pounds by the end of the day?' asked Andrew, already defeated.

'Your travelling men. How about them?' asked Beth desperately.

'Them? They ain't seen that kind of money in a month of Sundays.'

'Squire?'

'I'll not ask Squire for a penny,' said Andrew obstinately.

'But he's been kind to me, Father, I'm sure he'd help for the Wheatsheaf.'

'No,' said Andrew, in tones that brooked no further discussion.

'Then it's Mr Shurland, ill or not.'

Everyone knew Shurland's house. Ancient black-beamed walls overhanging the street and leaded windows, gables and dormers. Fourteenth century they said. One of the sights of the town, and once renowned for its open door of hospitality. It had seen none for a long time. The chintz covers looked dull and the furniture in need of polish. Shurland, wrapped in a shawl, sat in a tall armchair, his face grey – 'dried like an old hop', thought Beth looking at him compassionately. Her heart sank, but she steeled herself at least to try.

'Miss Ovenden,' he muttered, barely focusing on her as she knelt by his side. 'Young Beth. It's got to come, you know. Progress. No room for people like us, eh, Ovenden?'

'There has to be,' said Beth fiercely. 'Or the whole trade will be at the mercy of folks like Hamlin.'

'I thought that once,' he grunted. 'My father, my grandfather, built up Shurland's. I thought it would go on for ever. But business – I never did understand it. Not Hamlin's sort.'

'Then you mustn't let the same thing happen to the Wheatsheaf.'

'What's one small pub with things as they are today?'

Beth hesitated, choosing her words with care. 'It's like Kent,' she said at last. 'She's always kept her independence. She's stood and fought. Even William the Conqueror. He never properly conquered Kent.'

Shurland smiled at her, his face shrunken. No resemblance to Mr Pickwick now. 'I'm too old to take on Goliath.'

'We can defeat him as easy as David did,' said Beth eagerly, 'if you'll only help. Lend us the money to pay off Hamlin.'

The longcase clock with the moon face ticked slowly in the corner as Shurland relapsed into gloom. 'I never wrote it down, you see,' he said. 'No need. It was a matter between gentlemen – begging your pardon, Miss Ovenden.' Her face fell. Then he went on, 'I'm not a rich man. But if it comes to getting back at Hamlin, I'll loan you the money.'

She caught her breath. 'We'll repay you by the month,' said Beth recklessly, jubilantly. 'We need fifty pounds. We'll pay you four pounds a month. Plus interest at six per cent. We'll pay, oh yes, we'll pay.'

'We'll require a receipt, Mr Hamlin,' flinging down the banknotes on his desk.

'That old fool Shurland, I suppose,' said Hamlin softly. 'But it isn't over yet, Miss Ovenden. Be sure of that.'

The evening of Midsummer Day and her eyes were like stars. She had had but one glass of her own gooseberry wine and it tasted like champagne. She had won a round against Hamlin. She had never understood the malevolence in his eyes whenever he talked to Andrew or herself, or quite why he should want the Wheatsheaf so much. But, being Beth, she never pursued the thought. It was enough that the Wheatsheaf was safe for the moment.

It was nine o'clock and the sun was setting on this glorious day. Suddenly she could stay in the crowded smoky bar no longer and ran out into the garden to gloat alone, to glory in her triumph. She unpinned her hair, letting it fall around her shoulders, luxuriating in the freedom. *Her* garden. *Her* heritage. Hamlin should not set foot here. She closed her eyes in happiness and gave herself up to joy as she swung herself slowly round the trunk of the mulberry tree, the folds of her blue chiffon dress swirling around her.

Then strong arms caught her from behind and Richard Lyle was kissing the nape of her neck, her shoulders, slipping the dress from them and caressing them with his hands. 'Beth,' he whispered.

Laughing, she twisted away and turned to him, eyes sparkling. His face was mysterious in the dusky evening light with the scents of the roses trapped by the warm walls around them.

'Beth, tell me why your heart is like a singing bird tonight. Why you're so – so –'

'I don't know what you're on about. There's no birds hereabouts. Just us two,' she murmured, smiling at him from under her lashes, lowering her voice.

'Don't look at me that way, Beth.'

'What way is that?'

'Like all the mystery of Sheba was in your smile, and the beauty of Helen in your body,' he said, drawing her close to him. 'Beth, you're magic tonight, intoxicating.'

'No, that be my gooseberry wine intoxicating you.'

She twisted away again from his arms. She was in a mood not to be caught yet awhile, sure of herself. Sure of him. 'Got rid of your other young ladies, have 'ee?'

she asked carelessly, smelling one of her red roses as though every nerve in her body was not awake for him.

He put his arms around her and turned her around. 'Yes, they're gone. Now tell me what makes you so –'

'So what?'

He swallowed and said nothing.

She smiled at him, knowing the magnitude of her victory. 'Let's walk,' she said. 'Father will be looking for me.'

A flame leapt in his eyes. He took her hand. 'We'll go a roving then, you and I, into the gentle night.'

Her heart beat faster, an excitement taking over that had little now to do with wine. He led her, hand clasped in hand, into the orchard, and through into the meadow that led to the nailbourne.

'Now tell me,' he commanded, passing an arm round her waist.

'We've saved the Wheatsheaf.'

He frowned. 'Saved it? What from?'

'From old Hamlin. He wants it, you know. He's threatened us. Like he did last year. He thought he'd got it this time but, provided we work and work for another year, we can fight him off. What do you think of that?'

'The Wheatsheaf means a lot to you, doesn't it? Why? Because it's home?'

'Oh no, more than that,' she said, shaking her head. 'It's a symbol. It's something that has always stood, you see. For centuries it's been here, seen bad times, seen good times, been a haven, a warmth for people to meet in, everything that's parish business goes on here.'

'It would still go on even if Hamlin took over, wouldn't it?'

'No,' she said. 'It wouldn't be the same. It wouldn't be . . .' she hesitated, 'a harbour, like England really – standing solid, keeping foes out. Unshakeable. If the Wheatsheaf were sold it would be like old Boney invading England.'

'You frighten me sometimes, Beth,' said Richard soberly. 'You're so – you expect so much. People change, places change. You realise that, Beth? Neither England nor the Wheatsheaf can go on for ever as they are. Things have to renew themselves or they die. England can't just cut herself off and nor can the Wheatsheaf. She's part of the world and sooner or later she'll get drawn into its problems.'

'But not while I'm here to protect it,' said Beth fiercely. 'The Wheatsheaf I mean, not England.' She laughed and hiccuped. 'But who cares tonight? It's safe.'

She threw herself into his arms, and did not stop to think in her joy how strange it was that this seemed perfectly natural. He lifted her off her feet high into the air and held her there for a moment, then put her down and held her close. 'Beth,' he said huskily. 'I'll be here too. We'll protect it. Nothing will happen to the Wheatsheaf – not while I can do anything. Oh, Beth.' There was a strange note in his voice, then silence as his mouth found hers and she was tight against him. All sorts of sensations happened to her mouth, then to the rest of her body and she found herself murmuring into his ear, her hands running through his unruly black hair, touching his cheeks, his lips, his hair. Then he gathered her in his arms and laid her down on the cool grass with the warm scents of the evening. Her body arched into his and she heard him catch his breath, felt his hands at her breast, trying to slip the dress over her shoulders, then an impatient sigh before his lips met hers again, and his hands pulling at her skirts. The leap inside her as his hands touched her body brought her to her senses. With a faint cry, she rolled aside, pushing his hands away, sat up and with an unsteady breath said, 'What are you at, Richard?'

'Beth?' he said, puzzled. 'Beth,' and reached out a hand.

'No,' she said sharply. 'I'll not be a Hetty Didcot.'

He drew in his breath sharply. 'It's not like that, Beth. You know that. You *must* know that. It's all right. You love me.'

She stared at him in the dusk. Too honest to deny it, but taken aback by his arrogance in assuming it.

Victorious in her silence, he came close again and took her by the shoulders, 'I love you too, Beth –' And he knew it was true.

'If you love me,' she cried out in anguish, 'you'd give me time –'

'Time?' he asked. 'But why? If it's not today, it will be tomorrow or the day after, so why not now, when the wild roses are blooming around us and you have me in your toils as ever woman did man – and we're happy –'

As his lips sought hers again her senses swam. How easy to let him take her on a wave of sensuousness, how easy to be his, to be his lover for ever. But the niggle of honesty that was Beth Ovenden overcame the woman in her.

She pushed him away, but gently this time: 'No,' she

said quietly. 'Not yet. I don't know you, Richard. Not enough. Not what you're really like.'

The air was suddenly chill between them. He kissed her forehead, got up and walked quickly away. And the woman swept over her, and her whole body ached for his arms.

'We've got to get rid of those smugglers, Father. They're creeping back. Been here three times this month. We've got to get a decent custom here and we'll never do it while the travelling men are here. One whisper and Hamlin will oppose the licence being renewed, even if you're not arrested.'

Andrew looked at her sharply. 'Perhaps you're right, girl,' he said grudgingly. 'That cellar's vulnerable. They're putting too much stuff in there and the Customs are a might hotter than they were a year or two back. Three times the numbers of seizures last year, I heard, than they were getting a few years back. *And* convicted over five thousand men. I'll not be one of them. I'll tell them to go and go for good.' He paused. 'Pity in a way. End of a tradition.'

'Better that than the end of the Wheatsheaf.'

'I remember your grandfather telling me about the old days,' he said, not listening. 'That's what put it in my head after your mother died. I heard tell of haystacks growing twice the size in a single night. About the signalling systems all the way along the coast.' He chuckled. 'Folks'd stand at their doors, rub their noses or some such signal, and the runners'd start. Carry the news to the next step. And about old Reverend Patten of the Seasalter Company. Sounds almost respectable, don't it? Running smuggling from a parsonage.'

'I remember Bill the hedger telling me about them,' said Beth with a shiver. 'That and the Seven Whistlers.' Her face clouded. 'But it's nearly the twentieth century now. Those days are past. We've got to go for a richer trade.'

'You'll not make out of the Wheatsheaf anything but a village pub,' said Andrew decisively.

Beth did not reply, but in her mind's eye she saw a line of noble carriages, depositing men of rank and title at the Wheatsheaf's door, perhaps even a coroneted carriage. Women, too, in furs and silks, with ostrich fans and jewelled head-dresses. They said that now there were horseless carriages over in France, they might soon come here, going twice the speed of horses. If they caught on . . . But her vision faded, faced with the immediate problem of how to make their supper out of half a cold rabbit and a bunch of carrots.

'Are you going to greet the hoppers, Pippin? After all, Rupert will be there,' Beth teased.

'And Richard –' Pippin cast a sidelong look at Beth, who turned away. Beth, for no reason she could explain, had never told Pippin about Richard's half a dozen visits to the Wheatsheaf. It was a secret between her and Richard. Something special. Though the visits were clouded because of her puzzlement over the girls. Two each time. A dozen in all so far.

'Who are they all, these girls?' she had asked again of Richard one evening, when for the third time he brought down two lady friends.

'My sisters?' he ventured hopefully. She cast him a

scathing look and he laughed. 'They're young ladies who are going to be governesses or dancers in Paris,' he told her finally.

'But why with you? You aren't a dancing master, are you?'

'I act between the agent in London who signs them up and the employers in Paris. That's all. Most of the girls haven't been out of England before and they need an escort to the boat. I need every penny I can make now, you know. It costs about ninety pounds just to get into one of the Inns of Court. You're expected to have private means and, though I've some, Pater doesn't allow me enough to, well, enjoy myself at all.'

He could hardly blame his father. On coming into his mother's estate only a year ago he had managed to lose half of it, and his father, a country vicar of abstemious habits and horrified at his son's waywardness, had sequestered the remainder, keeping a strict eye upon its use. Richard took after his mother, a tempestuous and dark-eyed beauty whose only means of rebellion against her noble and illustrious family had been to marry an all but penniless vicar. That the marriage had succeeded owed much to them both, and her early death had driven her husband into a retirement from the pain of the world that left him no inner resources for coping with his son, whose fatal attraction to money was only rivalled by that to women.

'But why not go straight to Dover? And why won't you let me talk to them? There's nothing wrong about it, is there?' she asked, suddenly suspicious.

'Sometimes just a little,' he said, smiling at her. 'They're under age, some of them, you see, and they have very unhappy lives at home.'

Her frown deepened. 'Then it's illegal –'

'They're going of their own free will. They're your age and you wouldn't let anyone stop you doing what you wanted, now would you? Where's your adventurous spirit? Wouldn't you like to be going to foreign parts with them? Like Isabella Bird?'

'Yes,' she said, 'but I can't. I've got the Wheatsheaf.'

'The Wheatsheaf. Always the Wheatsheaf.'

'Yes,' she said quietly, 'always the Wheatsheaf.'

That conversation had been at the beginning of the month, and she had not seen him since. But now the hoppers were coming . . .

She turned her attention back to Pippin.

'What will Mr Barnham say when Rupert arrives? He's a much better catch than Rupert, isn't he?' Mr Barnham, a young Sussex landowner, had shown more than a passing interest in Pippin.

'Do you ever think of marrying?' she asked Pippin boldly.

'You're being silly, Beth. I shan't get married for ages, and especially not to Martin.' Pippin threw a rose at Beth from the vase on the table, hitting her on the cheek.

'But you'll have to marry sooner or later, won't you?'

'So will you.'

'I've got the Wheatsheaf to think of, before I think of marriage,' said Beth grandly.

'A husband could help in the pub. William now, or Robert Chace, though I hate to think what his father would say.' Pippin giggled.

Beth kept her own counsel. How could Pippin even

think of Robert Chace when she above all had seen the spell that drew Richard and herself together. They had never spoken of it, for it was understood.

'No,' she said, 'the Wheatsheaf is something I've got to do on my own. Don't you see?'

Pippin did not. She stared uncomprehendingly, then said brightly, 'Let's have tea.' It was one more tiny thing that made Beth feel she and Pippin were being driven apart, not because they wanted it but by the ways of the world. Pippin was born to be married, that was her role and what would suit her. She'd be protected by men all her life - and why not? But she, Beth was different. Pippin, as if sensing her sudden irrational despondence, slipped an arm through Beth's. 'I'll be coming to meet the hoppers, just as I used to. I'm still Pippin, you know,' she said, glancing at Beth anxiously. 'Not Philippa.'

'I'd almost forgotten you had a real name,' said Beth. 'You'll always be Pippin to me. Always.'

There they were, striding along the platform at Faversham station, as happy as the swarming hoppers surrounding them. Exactly as a year ago. Now she was here, she was suddenly reluctant about Richard Lyle finding her waiting for him, and Pippin's being here somehow made it worse. She saw his hair first, black as the rook's wings, no hat upon that mop of unruly curls. Then as a plump grandmother moved she saw his face, a fleeting glance at her, the blue eyes, and they were swept along the platform towards the exit.

'Well, there they are, Pippin,' she said unnecessarily.

'Shall we give them a lift?' asked Pippin laughing and jumping off the gate.

A rhetorical question, as Richard Lyle was already strolling over to the Medlars' governess cart when the girls arrived in the yard, Rupert hesitating behind.

It seemed as though the long winter had never been, the fights, the back-breaking work to make the Wheatsheaf pay. All that was important now was the hoppers were here - and with them Richard. Beth's heart was as light as the hoppers', seeing six weeks of holiday ahead. No matter it rained some days, no matter the barns leaked, that privacy was minimal, that payment was low and the work was hard. They would remember that soon enough, when the binman set his horn to his lips to summon them for the reading of the Rules that first morning, but for now it was summer, it was meeting old friends, exchanging stories, singing songs, marching to the Wheatsheaf.

It was a day of expectation, of hope, and summer was in Beth's eyes. For Richard was here, here for six whole weeks of golden harvest.

'Beth.'

Beth started up from her work in the herb garden and brushed the hair out of her eyes. To her amazement it was Rupert. He seemed ill at ease for all he seemed older and better looking than a year before.

'I've come -'

'About Pippin?'

He reddened. 'No,' he said quietly. 'About Richard.' Beth was still. 'He's been staying here, hasn't he? He brings girls, young women, down here, doesn't he?'

Beth was silent at first, defensive, then she said with a burst of relief that her worries could be shared, 'Yes.

Governesses, dancers. It's against the law, I know, but he says –'

'Is that what he told you?' Rupert interrupted. 'They're *not* governesses. It's much worse,' he said grimly. 'I can't stop him. *You* must. You know how headstrong he is. He may choose to believe they're dancers – at least I hope he does – I hope I don't shock you, Beth –'

'Shock me?' An icy cold swept over her.

'The girls may think they're going to be dancers or governesses but they're not. They're – well – to become unfortunate women.'

Beth stared at him and, seeing she did not understand, he blurted out: 'Whores, Beth, abroad. He doesn't take them to Dover, but the way they used to take French POWs when they smuggled them back to France after the Napoleonic wars. From Whitstable way.'

'The white slavers,' Beth whispered, unable to take it in, hardly able to frame the words. She'd read about it several years ago. 'You're wrong, oh, you must be wrong, Rupert. They stopped that traffic.'

'No, it still goes on. The girls have to be got out of the country secretly now because they watch the ports both sides. Richard got involved with the smuggling group down here – oh yes, I know about that – did a little brandy and tobacco smuggling last year, but that wasn't enough for him so he set up a two-way trade sending the girls back by the same boats that brought the smuggled goods.'

'I won't believe it,' said Beth faintly. Richard? But then she heard her own voice as if to mock her saying that June night: *I don't really know you Richard. Not enough.*

'He can't know,' she burst out beseechingly.

'Perhaps he doesn't. Perhaps he's just the escort, not the man behind it. But he's involved all right. You must stop him. Or he'll wreck his career at the bar.' He looked at her gently. 'I'm sorry, Beth. You don't deserve this. He just wants to stir life up in search of excitement, and then gets into scrapes like this.'

Don't you ever want adventure? Beth heard Richard's voice cry again, and she wept for her highwayman.

CHAPTER FOUR

There he was. Picking hops. But not as most of the hoppers were hop-picking. Richard had his arm round a buxom girl in a gaudy yellow dress, with his other hand slowly picking the hops from the bine laid across her lap. Beth watched him for a few moments dispassionately.

She was tired and listless, for she had slept little the previous night. The hot sun and the noisy jesting hoppers all around her merely added to her depression. Children were screaming, whether with laughter or tears was all one. Nimble practised fingers stripped hops from bines into any old receptacle, up-ended umbrellas, picnic baskets, shopping bags, periodically emptied into the large five-bushel baskets. Snatches of music-hall songs floated from neighbouring drifts. Behind her the sound of a bell denoted the lollyman's arrival, and the children promptly swarmed out of the alleys to greet him. The smell of fish borne on the breeze was making her feel sick; the hoppers ate lunch early in the gardens.

Her mood changed to a bitter anger. She stood behind Richard, arms akimbo, until her shadow falling across the couple made Richard look round. An immediate grin crossed his face. He was not in the least abashed. He merely gave the lady a tight squeeze, released her and stood up.

'Beth, what delight,' he murmured, looking her up and down, lazily appraising, a look that yesterday would have enchanted and today alienated her still further. It was as though he were a stranger.

'It won't be delight you're feeling when I've finished with you,' she replied shortly.

His mobile face twisted into a mock grimace. 'Ah, this sounds as though it is likely to be painful. Perhaps I'll continue hop-picking. The measurer will be round soon.'

She caught his arm, as he turned away. 'Not so fast, Mr Lyle.'

He shrugged and, eyes twinkling, said, 'Then, as what you are going to say is clearly not going to be pleasant, I suggest we walk apace.' A squeeze of the buxom - and, Beth noted, toothy - lady's shoulder, and taking Beth's arm, he walked her firmly from the hop-garden.

The meadow was quiet after the noise of the garden as the hoppers' voices receded into the background. To their right in the distance was the grey outline of Chartboys. The oast houses in the fold of the downs below were the only other sign of human habitation in the wide vista over the green downs far away to the distant blue haze where lay the Weald. Richard put an arm round her waist and she let it rest there, momentarily forgetting what she had come about. Then, as she remembered, she indignantly threw the arm off, ignoring the reproach in the innocent-looking blue eyes.

'It's those women,' she began uncertainly, by no means as sure of her position as she had been earlier. Then she pulled herself together. Right was right.

'Not serious, my petal. But as you do not favour me,

what can I do but seek elsewhere? Euphelia serves to grace my measure. Chloe is my real flame.'

'Who's this Chloe?' she asked suspiciously, diverted from her purpose.

'The poet Matthew Prior,' he replied, laughing at her.

'Oh. Anyway,' she went on firmly, 'it's these dancers and governesses you've been taking to Dover.'

'What about them?' he asked idly. 'Not jealous of them, are you?'

'I'm not jealous of *any* of your women,' she replied instantly.

He grinned at her lie, and whistled carelessly to himself.

'They're not dancers, are they?' she plunged on desperately. 'They're going to be – be – whores, aren't they?'

There was a brief silence, while she dared not look at him. Then he burst out laughing. 'I see my friend Rupert has been to see you. He has this foolish idea that I'm some kind of pimp –' and seeing she did not understand – 'master-criminal, white slaver, leading these girls to doom and destruction. It all comes of Rupert leading such a dull life; he has to make up these melodramatic stories.'

'I believe him, Richard.'

He laughed again, but to her mind it was somewhat forced. 'Oh, Beth, what can you know of vice and corruption, living here in Shepham. Do you *really* think I'm a white slaver? Look at me.' He took her by the shoulders, gazing into her eyes as though by the very intensity of his gaze he could make her believe him.

'I don't know, Richard,' she said slowly, moving from his touch. 'But there's something in you I don't understand. Something wild –'

'Like you, my Beth –'

'No, not like me. You and me mean different things by adventure. I want to be free, to do what I choose, yes, travel and do things. But you want excitement, danger. You think of yourself as some story-book highwayman, robbing people at pistol point and then handing their money back with a gracious bow. Like Robin Hood. But life's not like that. A highwayman really is only a low-down criminal.'

His lips tightened, and he grabbed her roughly by the shoulders: 'Goddamn you, Beth. Don't try to "understand" me. No woman's going to smother me, hold me – you're all the same, trying to make me something I'm not. You're right. You don't know me at all.' His face was pale, and anger blazed momentarily from his blue eyes. Then with an effort he laughed, released her and kissed her lightly on the cheek: 'Now be good and say you love me, Beth.'

She backed away. 'Don't you talk down to me, Richard Lyle. Coming here with your London ways, and trying to be lord of manor with *me*. I'm Beth Ovenden, the Wheatsheaf landlord's daughter, and I don't need no London criminal to tell me –' her voice broke.

'The landlord's daughter,' he echoed softly. 'Beth, don't let's quarrel. If it'll make you happier I'll stop this – um – dancing trade. Though you're wrong, you know,' he said hastily. 'They really *are* dancers –'

'If you believe that, Richard,' she said slowly, 'you're believing what you want to believe, shutting your eyes.

Ask questions up in London about it. Tell Customs at Dover when you board –'

'I'll give it all up, if only you'll be nice to me again,' he said cajolingly. He took her hand and pressed it to his lips then, seeing she made no demur, took her into his arms and kissed her, not the desperate hungry kiss of that Midsummer evening, but sweetly, tenderly, a kiss that spelled summer, as light as the butterflies that danced around them.

Yet as they walked back to the garden hand in hand, he said casually, 'Just one more run. I'm pledged for that. And these really are going to be dancers. They've an engagement at the Folies Bergères in Paris.'

She started to protest, but he said quickly, 'And after that no more. My word on it. The word of Gentlemen Dick, the fearsome highwayman.'

'Let me buy you a dress, Beth,' pleaded Pippin, fingering the gauzy charmeuse at her Canterbury dressmakers. 'Please. Look at this cherry colour. Wouldn't you like that?'

Beth reddened. 'No.' She lied, for it was the most lovely colour she had seen.

'You know, Beth,' said Pippin slowly, shooting a swift glance at her, 'pride will be your undoing one day.'

'There's nothing wrong with pride,' said Beth stubbornly.

Pippin went on pretending to examine lace, then said quietly. 'I think there is. Don't you think you should think about other people's feelings sometimes? I'd really like to buy you a dress. You could wear it to the hopkin,' she added cunningly. 'It could be ready by then.'

Beth was silent.

'Not everybody's as strong as you, Beth.' Pippin sensed her advantage. 'Give in to us just once in a while.'

Beth looked at the cherry charmeuse again, then smiled ruefully and gave Pippin a quick hug. 'I'm just jouttering,' she said. 'Take no notice. I'd love a dress, and you're my dear sweet Pippin to think of it.'

'Now, which do you think –' And it was half an hour before the all important question of trimming and tucks was settled, and a further two hours before Pippin had arranged to her satisfaction two evening mantles, three day dresses and four white blouses, and measurements had been taken. It was after six o'clock therefore when the landau drew up in front of Medlars' portico.

'I've brought you here so you will stay to supper with me,' said Pippin smugly.

It took ten minutes for her to override Beth's protestations that, although in theory it was her free day, she would be needed at the Wheatsheaf. And when at nine o'clock after supper Beth rose to go: 'Do stay a little – Father won't be back tonight at all, and it's so quiet without anyone except Moumou to talk to.' Beth exchanged looks with the large white Persian cat; Beth had always disliked this particular cat, much as she adored most animals, and Moumou returned the compliment.

'Away all night? Does that often happen?'

'No, it's special. He's a magistrate as you know, and the policemen from London came to see him this morning.' Pippin was clearly longing to impart the whole story to her. 'They're planning a joint ambush on some *smugglers!*'

'Smugglers?' said Beth faintly. 'Where?' The word was a whiplash.

'Out Seasalter way.' Pippin noticed nothing odd. 'They're landing contraband apparently – isn't it exciting? – and as smuggling's been increasing in the last year or two the customs want to make an example of them. But they've got to time it very carefully, because they can't pick up the smugglers until after the boats have left again, because the boats are going on somewhere else for – oh Beth,' her voice dropped, 'for what do you think? White slave traffic! Smuggling girls to the Continent. That's where Father and these London police come in –'

'Where, Pippin, where are they going?' Beth's voice cut in with deadly calm. 'You must tell me.'

'Well –' Pippin stopped, clearly bewildered at Beth's reaction.

'Pippin, I've got to stop it. I must. Richard! Oh, I can't tell you now, but –'

'Richard?' echoed Pippin. 'Richard Lyle? What is he to do with it? You can't mean he's a smuggler?'

'Perhaps worse,' admitted Beth wretchedly. 'He says he's not a white slaver. They're dancers. He was going to stop it. This is his last time –'

Pippin stared at Beth, her face impassive with shock. Then words tumbled from her lips: 'They're landing the brandy and tobacco on the Seasalter beach and the Seasalter customs men will be waiting to catch them in the next stage on the journey inland, well away from the beach. An ambush in Cut Throat Lane. But then the boats are going to Whitstable Harbour to pick up the – the women – they're coming down on the Canterbury to Whitstable railway line to the harbour station this evening and will wait till after dark for the boats to arrive.

Beth –' her voice rose again, 'do you really think Richard's involved?'

'He doesn't deny it,' said Beth miserably, 'but he says it's harmless.' Her voice broke and Pippin leaned across.

'I'll do anything,' she said, 'anything I can to help. I'll come with you to warn him –'

'Don't be a goose, Pippin,' said Beth laughing and crying at the same time. 'You'd be no help.'

'I could bring the carriage,' said Pippin. 'The coachman's with Father. You can't go by railway. It's too late, and you'd never get back. And you'd be noticed in your old cart. I'll take the carriage. I can say we were looking for Father. No one would suspect me of being mixed up with smugglers after all –'

'But who's to drive?'

'Fetch Rupert,' said Pippin eagerly. 'He'll be at the Wheatsheaf, won't he? He can drive us.'

Beth rushed into the barn, still dazed at this new resolute Pippin. The hoppers were in good form tonight, the cacophony of noise rasped at her pent-up nerves. There was no sign of Rupert. She fought her way through the crowd and caught at the sleeve of Bill Saddler who was involved in a heated discussion on the rival merits of Yarmouth bloaters and Whitstable oysters.

'Mr Rupert? Not 'ere, darling. Both gone to London till Monday.'

'*Both*? Together?' asked Beth, with a sudden hope.

'Mr Lyle went orf yesterday. Mr Rupert today. See 'is family, 'e says.'

Hope died. What could she do now? She could hardly drive herself. William? No, she looked up at the clock, he was needed at the pub till 10.30 and it was only 10 now. But dark enough for the landings already to be taking place. She must hurry. Besides she could not drag William into danger. He had no love for Richard Lyle, she knew that. She could not trust a hopper. There was only the one way out. *She* must drive. And she must wrap herself up to look like a coachman. Wear men's clothes. The possibilities raced through her mind. Her father's clothes would not fit her, but Richard still had some clothes at the pub. Perhaps she could squeeze into them. With a jacket, cloak, she might pass.

She opened the door of Richard's room – she still thought of it as that though the only sign of his previous occupancy was the large suitcase in one corner. She pulled out a pair of drill trousers, and a shirt. Too long of course, but otherwise it worked with a belt and, her hair stuffed into a cap of father's, and her own boots, she would pass for a callow youth. Enough to drive along the coast road without comment.

She slipped down the back staircase where there was no risk of Andrew seeing her, out of the kitchen door and round into the alley between the bar and barn where the hoppers were still carousing. She hurried past the open door. So intent was she that she walked straight into someone coming the other way – William.

Something about her averted face alerted him. 'Miss Beth!' in tones of outrage. 'What you adoing, for lorsake?'

'Be quiet, William. Oh, do be quiet. And let me go,' she said angrily, for he was gripping her wrist none too gently.

'What be you up to? No good, that's for sure, dressed like that –'

'Let me go,' and she snapped up her wrist, and freed it.

But he stood barring her way. 'You don't get by me, Miss Beth, till you tell me what you be at.'

'Very well,' she said viciously, 'but not here. Please not here.'

She led him swiftly up the back lane towards Medlars, for she had no wish to walk along the village high street. What should she do? She had to trust him.

'Richard Lyle,' William commented gruffly when she'd finished. 'He's no good, Miss Beth. I could have told you. No good, and you running after him –'

'I'm not running after him,' she said fiercely. 'But I've got to save him. If only for the Wheatsheaf,' she added cunningly, 'otherwise we'll be dragged in when the police start investigating and find out they've been staying here.'

He stood thinking, until she could have screamed, still holding her firmly by one wrist: 'You're right, Miss Beth,' he said finally. 'There's the Wheatsheaf to consider. Very well, I'll go. Warn 'em. Bring 'em back.'

'I don't want you to come, William. I can drive.'

'I'm not asking your permission, Beth. I'm telling you. And you ain't coming with me.'

'I'm coming –'

'That you're not. You'll do him no good – nor the Wheatsheaf – running around the countryside dressed indecent. I'll take the old cart. Not Squire's carriage.'

'I want –'

'What you want's of no interest. If it's the Wheatsheaf you want to save – or Mus' Lyle – you'll stay here. Or I'll be in and tell your father.'

Beth bit her lip. 'All right,' she said. 'I'll go to tell Miss

Pippin. But hurry, please, please hurry.'

'*I'll* go to Medlars,' said William.

'There won't be time,' said Beth in an agony.

A slight look of compassion softened his face. 'You can trust me, Beth,' he said more gently. 'Now for lorsake, get back in your skirts so's your father don't catch you.'

She sat by her open window, staring unseeing into the dark garden. Groups of hoppers still caroused in the barn, the sound of Andrew's raised voice came to her from time to time. But her thoughts were not on the Wheatsheaf; they were centred on William and his journey through the lanes – 10.45, according to her little French clock on the mantelshelf. Surely now he'd be past Faversham, into the winding inland road to Whitstable. Or would he take the coast road past the Sportsman Inn? No, too dangerous with customs men ready to pounce; any traffic at that time of night might arouse suspicion. No, he'd be going through Goodnestone, Down Forstal, then that stretch of open country. She was remembering from her last visit to Whitstable for the blessing of the sea ceremony. He might be at Borstal Hill now, even the High Street, the harbour would be crowded with fishing boats and fishermen waiting for the night tide – no doubt why they chose this time to make the pick-up.

And there amongst them would be Richard. She tried not to think about him. It hurt too much. Suppose he were caught. His career would be ruined. He might even be imprisoned. She would not see him again.

It was midnight before they returned to the Wheatsheaf. Even with her vigil at the window Beth could not be certain she heard anything. She strained her ears. Yes, the faint unmistakable sound of George's whinny. She ran down the back stairs thankful that she and her father slept on opposite sides of the house, and slipped out through the kitchen door. She saw William, a dark figure outlined against the dark sky, walking towards the barn. Taking a candle she ran, her heart in her mouth. Was he alone, or –

Richard was there. Without stopping to think she flung herself into his arms, so great was her relief, and was unaware of William quietly departing.

'There's no need to worry, Beth. The girls are in your haybarn till the morning. Then William and I'll drive them to Ashford early, before your father's about. They can go back to London.' His voice was completely calm, so matter of fact that she raised her head to look at him.

'Why?' she asked, flatly.

He shrugged. 'Money,' he answered casually. 'The thrill.'

'You knew,' she said wearily. 'You knew they were going to be unfort – whores. And you talk of thrills?'

'Beth, they had positions in the Folies Bergères, that's all I knew –'

'Suppose they talk when they're back in London?'

'They won't. They'll disappear. I know these girls, Beth – you don't.'

'But it's you – what it's doing to you – it's not right when you don't know what's to become of them –'

'Yet you still wanted to save me, Beth, didn't you?'

She was silent. Then she said stiffly, 'You'd best have your old room back till morning. We'll go up the wistaria way though, case Father hears us. No sense waking him now. Best he don't know nothing about it.'

She marched without a backward look from the barn round to the back of the house, and pointed: 'Up that way, there, that branch there –'

'You go first.'

'That I will not,' she whispered indignantly. 'Up with you. I'll light your way. In at my window there.'

'Is this the way all your lovers come?' he whispered.

'No lovers for me,' she said forthrightly. 'Men are more trouble than they're worth.' She was beginning to recover her composure.

He held out his hand to help her over the sill, and caught her as she dropped into the room, then held her in his arms.

'I haven't thanked you yet. William –'

'You can best thank me by getting to your room –'

But he held her the tighter, drawing her towards the white-counterpaned bed. 'It's a long time to morning, Beth.' Then his lips were on hers, first sweet, then urgent. Yet still she found the strength to push him away.

'Your room's out there, Richard,' she said, gently enough.

He looked at her for a moment, and shook his head ruefully. 'Will you have the whole summer gone, Beth? And autumn fall?'

And she was left alone.

The next morning it seemed a dream. Richard's room again stood empty. She drew in deep breaths of the day, fresh air. This was real, this was important, not those adventures of night, that nightmare she never wanted to repeat, with the illusions that the dark brings in its wake.

She leant back against the kitchen door thankfully. It was over.

But she was wrong.

'Beth, in here with you.' Andrew ushered her into the private bar. Cross from being drawn from her baking, her irritation changed to wariness when she entered the bar and saw Andrew's visitors. Two bowler-hatted men rose to their feet as she came in. George Goodfellow, the village policeman, did not. There was no love lost between Beth and PC Goodfellow ever since the time she'd stopped him from interfering with Miss Monk's giving her herb potions to the villagers. Besides he was Temperance, one of Higgins's lot. Now he was glowing pink with his own importance.

'These gentlemen,' Andrew said with indignation, 'seem to think we have something to do with a smuggling racket here. Seems there was supposed to be a landing last night, though no one was caught. I told 'em it were nonsense, that they're welcome to look around. They're interested in summat else, too, seem to think you can help. I told 'em you was busy but –'

'Sergeant Perkins, Metropolitan Police, Detective Division, miss,' said one of the two bowler-hatted men, a bland fatherly looking man in his forties, introducing himself. 'And this is Mr Sampson of the Whitstable customs house.' Mr Sampson did not look bland. He was weasly-faced and shifty-eyed, Beth instantly decided.

'You know a Mr Lyle, miss?' the sergeant asked.

'One of the hoppers – yes.' She tried to inject a note of surprise into her voice.

'They want to know if he's been staying here. I told 'em yes,' broke in Andrew.

'He's been once or twice,' she said guardedly.

'What was his business, miss?'

'He – he came to see me,' she said firmly, avoiding Andrew's eye. 'And now he's hop-picking. Staying on the farm. Not here.'

'We think he may be mixed up with something rather unpleasant.'

Her heart sank. 'I think you must be mistaken,' she said, puzzled. 'He's going to be a barrister. Going to Inner Temple in the autumn. He's hardly likely to be mixed up with anything against the law.'

'There's some say Jack the Ripper was a barrister,' said the sergeant jovially.

'Jack the –'

'Mind, I'm not saying Mr Lyle's a murderer, miss. But we're just interested to know when he stayed here this summer. When did you last see him?'

She hesitated. 'A few evenings ago – when he came to the Wheatsheaf.'

'And you didn't see him yesterday at all?'

'I imagine he must have been at the farm.'

'No, miss. He left on Friday for London. And he was seen getting on a train in London bound for Canterbury on Saturday. With two young ladies.'

'Well?' Her voice remained slightly puzzled.

'We know he left the train at Canterbury, but he never turned up where we was expecting to see him. Nor the young ladies.'

'Where was that, Sergeant?' asked Beth, her mind crystal clear now.

'Whitstable, miss. There's folks ready to say they think they saw him there, but he wasn't there when we arrived.'

'Then they were mistaken,' Beth said coolly. 'I didn't want to tell you naturally. But if it's that important – Mr Lyle was not at Whitstable last evening. He was with me.' She stared straight at the sergeant.

'And what time did he leave you, miss?'

'He – he didn't.' She paused. A hundred thoughts raced through her mind and left but one. She must save Richard. 'He was with me all night.'

There was a sharp intake of breath. Beth stared at her lap. She did not dare look at her father.

'Thank you, miss,' said the sergeant evenly. 'He did tell us he was with a lady, but we had to confirm it, see?'

'My daughter,' Andrew shouted when they'd gone, eyes blazing. 'By Heaven, how could you, Beth? A whore.' Her face whitened.

'You don't understand, Father.'

'I understands all right –'

'It was partly to save the Wheatsheaf.'

'Save the Wheatsheaf!' he snorted. 'Everything's to save the Wheatsheaf. You even have to go awhoring to save the Wheatsheaf now.'

'No,' she shouted back. 'But if they'd caught him, the trail would have led back here. Even William saw that –'

'William?' roared her father. 'You dragged him into this?'

'He insisted. He went to Whitstable to bring them back. Richard was there, you see,' she said miserably.

'It seems I'm no longer master in my own pub. You even send my barman to pimp for you –'

'No,' she cried, choking on her own words. 'When he

got here, Richard slept in the room he's always had. But I couldn't tell the police that. That's no alibi.'

'I don't believe you, girl. You go to all that trouble to save him, and you try and tell me he didn't have his way with you –'

'There's plenty do it, even if I did, which I didn't –'

'But not Ovendens,' he roared. 'Haven't you any respect? Who'd you think would marry you if this gets out? Do you think young Master Lyle is going to marry the likes of you?'

She flushed. 'There's no cause for him to marry me. No cause.'

'No, because he's gentry and you're not. You're a fool, Beth.' He looked at her bitterly. 'Like mother, like daughter. Headstrong. Self-willed. I don't believe that he slept in another room. I've seen him looking at you, and you at him. Not the first time I'll be bound. Under *my* roof. I tell you, Beth, I'll not forget this. You've had too free a hand. Sooner you're married the better. Not that any self-respecting man will wed you now. Ruined. George Goodfellow will make sure the news gets round quicker than if you put a postcard in the post office window.'

Sylvie was the first, oozing false sympathy, her solid frame quivering with delight. 'Sorry to hear about your trouble, Miss Beth. Men are rascals, aren't they? And that Mr Lyle. He's a real devil. I don't wonder you fancy his bed.'

'Do you want to keep your job here?' Beth retorted, at first startled then angry that she and Richard should become the sniggering point for the village.

'You can't give me the order of the sack,' said Sylvie triumphantly. 'Only Mr Ovenden.'

'Then I'll –'

'I be thinking Mr Ovenden'll need all the help he can get,' replied Sylvie cryptically, with a smug smile.

The next move was unexpected. 'Beth,' roared Andrew's irate voice. 'In parlour. Hurry yourself.'

Startled, she entered to find the Squire sitting awkwardly in one of the armchairs, his large frame looking out of place amid the shabby chintz-covered chairs.

He rose as she came in, and she saw in some astonishment his face was red with embarrassment.

'Good of you to see me, Miss Ovenden.' He paused as though he did not know what to say next, then plunged on abruptly. 'I hear the police have been to see you. About this smuggling problem. Why did they come to you, eh?'

She flushed. Why should she answer? Was it a trap to see if she would reveal more to him than to the police? She must be careful.

'They just wanted to know about one of our lodgers. His movements and suchlike. Mr Lyle they was interested in.'

There was a silence, and her heart beat the faster. Had the news reached him yet? She hoped not; she wanted to keep his good opinion, but guessed it would inevitably reach him – and Pippin! The thought struck her sickeningly. She could explain to Pippin. She'd understand of course. But the Squire was a different matter.

'Yes, my daughter told me he was staying here. She's worried about you, Miss Ovenden. Asked me to smooth things over with the police. Make sure there's no trouble still brewing for you or this Lyle fellow. I gather he's a friend of young Rupert Bonner. Well, I've done it. Seems to be no further problem. I'm fond of you, you know,' he went on devastatingly. She gazed at him open-mouthed. Fond of her? The aloof, gruff Squire? She had thought him hardly aware of her existence. 'Wouldn't like to see you mixed up in anything that could cause trouble. Dangerous times, Beth. You might not realise . . . enemies, you can make them when you don't mean to. This pub's not good for you. Pubs and women don't mix. Not decent ones, that is.'

Beth stiffened. 'The Wheatsheaf's my home, Squire. And no one, not even you, is going to say anything against it.'

'I've nothing against the Wheatsheaf, Miss Ovenden,' he said hastily. 'But talk gathers round a pub. Rumours. I'm just saying be careful.'

'Yes, Squire,' said Beth, completely bewildered.

'You take after your mother,' he said after a pause. 'Hot-headed. Impulsive. Lovely woman.' He took up his hat. 'I'll help if I can.'

She stared after him, astonished.

They came that evening. After chapel. She heard them where she was serving in the saloon bar. Led by Higgins, the Temperance Band of Hopers marched down the village street chanting, banners held high proclaiming 'Out with the Whore of Babylon', naked flares illuminating pale fanatical faces. The words of the chanting were indistinguishable, but their menace was clear. The marchers filled the yard in front of the Wheatsheaf spilling over onto the green, singing hymns to their god of hate, for Christianity never entered into it. Chanting, raucously shouting. There must have been two hundred of them, men and women, not all from Shepham, but strangers they had never seen before. As the rumpus continued the villagers straggled from their homes to see what was going on and were drawn in like moths caught in the flame of Higgins's eloquence. From the barn spilled the hoppers, alerted by William and drawn by the prospect of a fight, in which they were not for once concerned. Clasping glasses in hand, they stood taking in the scene, not prepared to get involved.

'Someone's planned this,' said Andrew peering through the window with Beth at his side. The few drinkers that evening stood nervously behind them. 'They mean business. Look at them flares – '

The first egg hit the window, followed by rotten fruit splashing dripping down the panes. Then came the first stone thrown by an unseen hand amid the sea of menacing shapes grey in the fast fading light. A window pane shattered.

'Fetch out the whore in her shame. Let her answer before the Lord.'

Andrew went to the door, and shut it behind him, an imposing sturdy figure facing the manic Higgins.

'Get away from me and mine, Higgins. These are my premises.'

'Shame on you for siring the whore that lives under your roof –'

'No one calls my daughter a whore,' roared Andrew and plunged forward to grab Higgins.

A banner thrust at him caught him on the temple and

he fell like a stone. Maddened by blood lust, the crowd surged past him and over him, towards the door, women in the fore. One of the crowd enraged by the sight of a glass in a hopper's hand swept it in a fit of temperance fervour from his hand. Where they would not fight for Beth Ovenden the hoppers fought for their own. One hundred East Enders were more than a match for two hundred villagers. The fight was fierce, vicious and swiftly over outside; the arrival of a reluctant Goodfellow, urged on by the Squire, dispelled the last of the rioters.

Dimly Beth heard the Squire's voice raised above the mob: 'What's got into you? This is *Shepham*.' Inside though the battle continued. Frozen with fear Beth stayed behind the bar, as the maniacal women, led by Higgins, burst through the door and dragged her out, tearing at her hair, at her clothes, pulling them off her. She was on the floor by the time Richard came, closely followed by William. Shouldering their way through the mob, they wrenched her assailants off her, and threw themselves across her body till the rabble retreated, chivvied out by the hoppers, their mania subsiding. Only Joseph Higgins remained, picking himself up from the floor, eyes blazing, shaking with fury, a demented beast, staring at her torn clothes.

'I'll have you yet, Beth Ovenden,' he shouted, as William came forward, and grasped him by the collar. 'You'll rue the day that you gave yourself to that Devil's spawn there. The Lord will wreak His vengeance upon you. And I, His servant –' he broke off, choking as William swung him off his feet and over the threshold into the dark of the night.

* * *

Richard helped Beth to her feet.

'There, my honey, there,' he said, pulling her clothes back over her, exclaiming when he saw the bruises already coming out and the deep scratches on her white skin. He pressed his lips to her shoulder, as William came back into the pub, lips tightening as he watched. His arm was round Andrew, half helping, half dragging him. The Squire, ashen-faced, walked behind.

'Mr Ovenden's hurt,' he said briefly. 'I'll take him to the doctor in my carriage. No need of the runner.'

Freeing herself from Richard's supporting arm, Beth ran to her father, examining the deep gash on his forehead.

''Tis nothing,' said Andrew, his voice weak, but still irritated. 'Just bind it up. No need of doctors. And no need of you, Squire, thanking you. Obliged for your help, but we'll manage alone.'

Beth's fingers gently explored the wound. 'I'll make a comfrey compress, Father. Will bind it up easy.'

'I'll sleep in the bar tonight,' said Richard. 'They may be back. We'll not risk it.'

'Reckon I will too,' William said quietly. He had no intention of giving Richard Lyle another opportunity to sneak into Beth's bedroom. The news had spread further than Beth's enemies.

'I'll have no one attack my daughter,' said Andrew gruffly to Beth, when they were alone in the kitchen, as she applied the compress to his temple. 'Whatever you've done, you're an Ovenden. Beth, whatever I said, you can forget. You're worth more than that scum all together. Just keep out of sight a while –'

'No, Father,' said Beth quietly. 'Would make the village think I've done something to be ashamed of, when I haven't. And even if I had bedded with Mr Lyle, how many of them have done the same before they married? The hypocrites. No, they're after the Wheatsheaf - and they won't succeed. Ever.'

But her desire to fight was quickly quenched, her defiant resolve broken. She visited Medlars. She had to find out what Pippin had heard - *if* she had heard.

Pippin ran to greet her as she had always done, but there was a nervousness in her eye, an awkwardness in her manner.

'What's wrong, Pippin?' Beth asked quietly.

'Father's so angry, Beth,' she said all with a rush. 'I don't know why. He doesn't seem to want you to come here any more. I said it was ridiculous even if -'

'Even if what?' Beth asked bleakly.

'Even if you were a - even if you had - oh Beth, did you?'

'No, Pippin,' she replied as evenly as she could. 'I had to, to save him, you see. You believe me, don't you?'

'Yes, Beth. I always believe what you tell me. You're my friend. But why, tell me, why you did it? Are you in love with him?'

'Yes,' said Beth bluntly.

Pippin stepped back almost as though Beth had struck her, and her face blanched. In a tone almost devoid of expression she said after a moment, 'It will mean trouble, Beth. No good can come of it.'

Beth flushed. 'Because he's gentry? And I'm not?'

'No,' said Pippin offhandedly, 'but Father -'

'If he doesn't want me to come here,' said Beth proudly, 'I won't, but you could come to the Wheatsheaf?' she asked desperately. If Pippin were to desert her, too – but this thought was too dreadful to contemplate. Pippin was *always* there. Yet the doubt was written clearly on Pippin's face and it seemed the very foundation of Beth's life was suddenly threatened. What was the good of fighting if there were nothing left to fight for? She willed Pippin to answer, to give her hope for the future.

'Father doesn't –' Pippin hesitated, then a slow smile crossed her lips. 'But I'll get round him, Beth. He'll do anything I want. Anything.'

'Beth.' Richard came up behind her, the sharp strong smell of hops clinging to him. 'You did all that for me? Told the police I'd been with you – oh Beth, I only just heard – I didn't understand.'

'You told 'em yourself,' she said indignantly, her fingers continuing to weed vigorously round the herbs. 'Some gentleman you are.'

'No, Beth. You can't think I would do that? I told them a lady's honour was at stake, because –' he hesitated. 'I'd arranged with Hetty Didcot to give me an alibi if the worst came to the worst, her husband being away at sea. She's a good sort, you know, Beth,' he added awkwardly. 'Do you really think I'd have risked your reputation suffering?'

'I don't know what to think.' The tears were pouring down her face. 'Even Father doesn't believe me that I didn't –'

'Then I'll tell him –'

'He won't believe you. And does it matter now, after this? It'll be a nine days' wonder, and then they'll forget about it.'

She had been trying to convince herself of this for the past two days. The hoppers had helped, spoiling her with a sympathetic rough humour, and she had managed to overlook the odd snigger and leer. But seared on her mind for ever was her memory of that night. The malice of the mob, how quickly her village had divided itself against her, with civilisation left behind, people she'd known and liked all her life, fighting like animals.

'Then why haven't you been out? Your father tells me you've stayed at home. Are you afraid of what people will say?'

'They've said it all as far as I can see.'

'Come out with me now, openly, Beth. Show them you're not ashamed to be with me –'

'I can't, Richard,' she said in a low voice. 'I'm scared.'

'My Beth scared?'

'Yes,' she said simply. 'I've lived here all my life. I can't face them –'

'You've faced policemen, smugglers and worse for my sake. Will you not come with me now and face your fellow villagers?'

'But old Higgins –'

'Can only have power to hurt if you hide away. Come.' And as she still hesitated, he said gently, 'You must, Beth. Otherwise people will say I've tired of you. That I've had you and left you.'

The red rushed into her cheeks.

'Put your bonnet on, and walk down the village street with me. Now!' he commanded.

He tied the ribbons of her bonnet under her chin and took her hand. They walked in silence over the green to the village street. She imagined she saw Mrs Parslow behind her window and her heart jumped in panic. Miss Wilson, the village schoolmistress, stern and uncompromising, was walking towards them on her way to the post office. Again Beth flinched and would have turned back but for the strength of Richard's hand. Twenty yards, ten yards, five yards and still Miss Wilson studied the ground. Then with a faint colour in her cheeks, the teacher raised her head.

'Good afternoon, Beth. Mr Lyle –' somewhat more grimly.

The pressure of his hand relaxed a little and she was aware of the sweat in her palms. Bill the hedger was in his front garden, tending his beans. He straightened up, hoe in hand. 'Afternoon Beth. 'Tis a fine one again.'

She began to breathe more easily and felt a tear prick behind her eyes. The knot in her stomach began to relax. Until she saw, chatting outside Harbutt the butchers, two of the women who had attacked her. But a quick glance at each other and a muttered, 'Afternoon, Miss Ovenden', followed.

'How can they?' cried Beth wonderingly to Richard, when they were past.

'It's the mob instinct – one strong leader and they play the tune. Just as they followed Higgins so they'll follow Miss Wilson. Though I doubt if they're feeling too proud of themselves for what they did to you. You'll see, people will start drifting back to the Wheatsheaf now, and this will all be forgotten.'

'I won't forget,' she said quietly. 'And you, Richard. Will you forget?'

He smiled at her but said nothing. They passed through the hop garden and out through the rickety wooden gate. Not until ten minutes later when they were lying in the long meadow, bathed in golden afternoon sunlight, a bright blue dragonfly circling nearby, did he speak.

'You asked me if I would forget, Beth. No. You are my soul, the best part of me, Beth. How could I forget?'

'And what will you do at the end of the season? Leave?' she said scornfully, hesitant to take the troth his words seemed to offer. 'You won't think much of Shepham now. And now you've given up the smuggling?' If there was a faint interrogation he did not acknowledge it. This question hung over her like a shadow.

'Go back to Inner Temple, eat my dinners diligently, read for the bar examinations for three years. Then do like all young barristers. Take chambers and wait for clients.'

A shadow passed over her sun.

'You'll not come hop-picking again?'

'Why not? I'm still a student in between the law terms. But I don't think you're interested in whether I come hop-picking again or not. I think you want to know what plans I have for Beth Ovenden.'

'I do not so,' she said indignantly, her pride ruffled.

He picked a daisy, and began to pluck it in the traditional manner. 'I love you, I love you not.' She sniffed, with something of an attempt to return to her old manner. Yet she took quite an interest in his progress and her black glossy head was close to his as the petals diminished in number. 'I love you.' One more petal gone, three left. 'I love you not.' Two disappeared together. They both stared at the one remaining.

'You cheated,' said Beth slowly.

'That I did not. 'Twas the impassioned nature of my soul impatient to reach an end. I do love you, Beth. Do you believe me?'

'What place in a highwayman's life for love?' she murmured, suddenly and gloriously sure that he did love her.

'We can rove and adventure together throughout the whole wide world.'

'But it's so nice *here*.' She lay back on the grass, smiling at him.

He bent over her, leaning on his elbow, the other hand playing with a lock of her hair. Then he said softly, hoarsely, 'Beth, now the village has given us this bad reputation, and accepted it, thinking we're lovers – even your father –'

'Yes?'

'There's no harm in making it –'

She looked at him for a second. The only man she'd ever love. She reached up her arms and drew him down to her.

And his lips were in her hair, calling her sweet names, around her eyes, lost in her sweetness. And then found hers with an urgency and sweetness both together that made her gasp with pleasure, and as she sought for breath she felt his hands under her skirts, then removing her clothing, then stroking her bare skin, making her gasp aloud with pleasure. The world swam a thousand miles away as he was on her and with her and around her;

for a few moments there was pain, and he stopped to soothe her, then with muttered passionate words he was part of her and she was lost forever in his love.

'Beth?' His voice was strong, jubilant, excited. 'Let's get married. We'll go off round the world, chase butterflies in Turkey, dig for gold in Peru, hunt zebras in Africa –'

'Me in Africa,' she laughed. 'Do they need barmaids there –' She struggled up, straightening her clothes. He pulled her up and whirled her round. 'You see this haystack? You can see the top of the world from there. Have a look. Up with you.'

'I don't see the world,' she said laughing, as he pushed her up and she lay spreadeagled, her skirts awry, on the top of the stack.

'What do you see then?'

'I see Judd's farm, the old oast house, the Stour down there, and in the distance the Weald. That's all.'

'You're wrong, heart of mine. That stream's a canal with gondolas on it. Venice. You have but to stretch a hand and we'll be there. That oast house is the Taj Mahal and all the wonders of the Orient. The Weald, oh, the Arabian desert –'

'It sounds hot –'

'Then we'll go to Venice first and I'll love you as we drift along in a gondola –'

'And what do we do for money?' she asked practically though her heart sang like a bird.

'It will be there,' he said. 'Just come. Forget about the Wheatsheaf – forget about the Temple. Oh Beth, just marry me and come.'

* * *

The hopkin that year was mingled sweetness and sadness. The end of a month that had whistled into the wind in ecstasy and enchantment, through which Beth floated in a cloud of happiness. Now dancing in Richard's arms in the red charmeuse dress, she was aware that deep down something was wrong. She wanted to marry Richard with all her heart, to go with him up to London. Yet something held her back. Not the Wheatsheaf. Not fear of the future. But something deeper. Something that when she was not with him worried her, something that finally she had had the courage to face and to define. And now she had to tell Richard, somehow to explain it to him, when she could not yet properly explain it to herself.

'All this talk of gondolas, it's not real,' she said when they were alone in the garden. 'You've got to go back and make yourself a barrister. Finish what you've set out to do. Otherwise how will you ever respect yourself?'

'That's not for you to worry about,' he said, kissing the nape of her neck. 'And I'll look after dull old things like money. And we'll have lots of it.'

'By smuggling? Or by honest ways?' she asked sharply.

'As true and honest as you yourself, Beth. But I need you with me –'

'Yes, I think you do,' she said slowly. 'But we wouldn't be happy – not till I know for sure you've put all that behind you. That you'd never get in with that lot again.' She shuddered.

'With you I could –'

'You've got to do it by yourself, Richard. Not just because I'm there. You've got to go to the Inner Temple and work. Then come down at the end of the term early next summer –' She faltered. It was eternity. 'And then, we'll get married. When the roses are out. When Shurland's paid off.'

'Shurland?'

'The Wheatsheaf,' she explained. 'I couldn't go away leaving it not yet saved. When we've paid off Shurland, and you've started to work for your examinations, then I'll come to you. London, the Orient, Venice –' It was the hardest decision she'd ever made.

'Beth –' She stopped his protests with a kiss and folded her arms around him. The night was still before them.

CHAPTER FIVE

Christmas drew near and no word from Richard. It had been her decision that they should part until the next summer, yet as November fog gave way to bleak December, Beth longed for him to break that promise. The strength she had found to send him away until the next year faltered as she found herself on her own trying to cope with the everyday round of life at the Wheatsheaf, juggling bills and payments, sorting out the hundred and one minor problems that occurred daily. Once her father would have coped, but since the Higgins-inspired riot he had become withdrawn, leaving more and more of the daily decisions to her. The wound on his head had healed but the mental scar remained. To Beth, however, he was more gentle, rarely shouting at her now, content to leave much of the running of the pub to her. He had even lost interest in the brewing. Where his spirit had been dented hers strove to increase, but it was a battle, at least at first, to treat the villagers who had supported Higgins and attacked her, with her former friendliness. A period of readjustment was necessary, a period that as Christmas approached seemed to be over.

But as that problem receded, the other for Beth took its place. Ceaselessly she questioned herself in the damp loneliness of those November days as to whether she had done the right thing in sending Richard away. Had she lost him for good? Useless to tell herself he was no loss if so, for everything in her cried out for him. Several times she was on the point of writing to him then held herself back, too proud, too honest to go back on what had been her own decision. Instead she fell back on dreams. Dreamed that she was in his arms again. Dreamed that he would appear magically riding out of the sunset to sweep her off as he had promised. Then, after such thoughts, she would laugh at herself for her weak will, and set to with renewed devotion to the stirring of the plum puddings. Plum puddings were so much a part of her life that when, not Richard himself, but a letter arrived she greeted it – as one would dismiss a dream – with a frown. Wiping her sticky fingers on her apron she carefully prised open the envelope . . .

. . . The train drew in with a triumphant belch to Charing Cross railway station. Beth was torn between her desire to hang out of the window and her reluctance to appear other than completely ladylike before Pippin and her formidable Aunt Phyllis as disapproving chaperone. She compromised by standing fidgeting in front of the window toying with the leather strap as the train approached the platform and was rewarded by a large smut of soot in one eye. Pippin dealt with the emergency to the ruin of her best lace handkerchief, whilst Aunt Phyllis watched with pursed lips. It was difficult enough to chaperone Philippa but Beth Ovenden was, well, impossible.

Impatience won. As the train drew alongside the platform, Beth had opened the door regardless of decorum and, before even the porters could enter the carriage, she was out impatiently tugging the train of her new emerald green two-piece costume and was in Richard's arms. His lusty kiss drew a scandalised gasp from Aunt Phyllis, who averted her eyes to the relatively more acceptable sight of Rupert kissing Pippin's hand. Yet, once freed, Beth was overcome by a sudden shyness, both men seeming alien in their town clothes and in this strange environment.

'You be all dressed up like a Christmas goose,' was all she could manage in the way of loving greeting, though the feelings at the back of her throat threatened to choke her, overwhelm her. Fortunately Richard did not seem to take this amiss, but turned to where Pippin was waiting to greet him, her face upturned for his kiss. Then he came back to Beth and tucking her arm into his, marched her off down the platform, leaving Aunt Phyllis clucking disapprovingly to walk behind. She was even more disapproving when, obligingly helped into a hansom by Richard, along with the luggage, she found the carriage moving off at a smart pace and her charges waving goodbye to her from the railway station, four large smiles in evidence.

Emerging from the railway station, Beth found the Strand bewildering, a world that passed before her eyes like a magic lantern show, and seemingly as real. Carriages, horses, pedestrians milled everywhere, a cacophony of cries from flower sellers, roast chestnut vendors and bootboys filled the air. With the early falling dusk the gas lights twinkled the Strand to a galaxy of stars. In a daze and clutching Richard's hand, Beth passed the Gaiety, the Savoy, Gatti's, Romano's – once mere names, now before her in all their elegant reality.

The Hotel Cecil, their destination, seemed a haven of quiet after the hubbub of the thoroughfare, but the wonders of the room she was to share with Pippin brought her to new heights of ecstasy as she flew from one delight to another, to Pippin's slightly superior amusement. It was so good of Pippin to have thought of suggesting Beth and Richard join them for New Year. Especially when Pippin was still a little shocked at what had happened last summer. Beth could tell Pippin still had not really approved by her avoidance of any mention of Richard's name, and the comparative rarity of her visits.

'Oh, Pippin, aren't you happy? Both of us here, with Rupert and Richard, and – oh – *everything*? And the New Year the day after tomorrow. 1896. What will it bring, Pippin? Oh what will it bring?'

'Happy, Beth?'

'Happy?' she echoed. Afterwards, she could feel happy at the memory perhaps, but now she could not. The last twenty-four hours had been such a whirl, a kaleidoscope of impressions that had not yet dimmed. The visit to the Gaiety to see *The Shop Girl* the previous evening had entranced, captivated, and swept her into a world she had not known existed. Clutching her ostrich fan with fingers trembling with excitement, she had sat enraptured as Seymour Hicks as the young medical student and Ellaline Terriss as the shop girl bewitched their audience.

She went to bed that Monday night singing, tunelessly (for song was not her strong point) 'with a naughty little twinkle in her eye', and with Richard's face alternating with Seymour Hicks's before her. She glanced at Pippin sitting before the mirror brushing her long fair hair: 'Her golden hair was hanging down her back,' Beth teased. 'You'll have Rupert singing that to you for evermore now.'

'You're talking nonsense, Beth,' said Pippin, continuing the long even strokes.

'I know. But isn't nonsense wonderful? On a night like this?'

That brought her back to the present, and Richard's 'Happy, Beth?' as he almost dragged her up the long flight of steps. For all her country upbringing Beth was exhausted. Walking in London was tiring, and they had seen the new Tower Bridge, walked round the Tower of London, the National Gallery, the Monument – and now St Paul's. Yet Richard seemed indefatigable, and even Pippin was gamely keeping up. Pippin . . . Beth had been amazed at Pippin's so readily conniving to shake loose from the restrictive shackles of Aunt Phyllis today, and now she was walking sedately, Rupert's hand firmly clasping hers, a slight flush on her cheeks.

'Tonight's New Year's Eve, Beth,' Richard whispered, 'and tomorrow the first day of the New Year. Our year, Beth. Remember? Are you still going to marry me?' He held her close in a gallery below the windows of the cupola.

'Yes, Richard. Oh yes.'

'I didn't hear you say it. Louder.'

And she said it louder and the waves of sound carried it round and round the echoing gallery. She clasped her hand over her mouth and blushed and laughed.

'The Whispering Gallery,' he explained. 'See.' And turning to the wall he murmured confidentially, 'I love Beth Ovenden.'

The glorious words echoed from every wall, time and time again, as Pippin and Rupert stared at them unsmilingly from across the gallery. Oblivious to everything but Richard, it seemed to Beth she was the happiest woman in London.

The euphoria lasted till the dinner that evening at the Savoy to greet the New Year. Quite suddenly and inexplicably Beth came down to earth. One moment she was admiring the breathtaking beauty of the scene, the next she saw only puppets dancing before her, a world of marionettes, pulled by strings from an unseen hand, that had nothing to do with her. She looked to Richard for reassurance. Perhaps it was the champagne, perhaps merely a trick of over-tiredness, but she saw her three companions, Richard, Rupert and Pippin, as in a tableau, motionless in time, just as she had seen them in the Medlars' garden that day so long ago sharing – sharing what? She did not know, but it was something from which she was excluded.

Forcing herself back into the party mood, she laughed and joked, and failed to notice the passing time.

'Oh,' said Pippin, 'Listen! The New Year. It's beginning to strike.' They all four jumped up in a hurry to reach the dance floor. Beth, tripping over someone's feet, found herself clutching Rupert for support. And so Richard's arm was flung casually round Pippin as the New Year dawned and the band struck up to welcome 1896.

'Rupert, I'm so sorry,' said Beth apologetically, as

they sat down at the table to await their return. 'You should have been dancing with Pippin to welcome in the New Year.'

'And you with Richard, Beth,' he retorted quietly, his eyes fixed on the slim fair-haired girl. He hesitated. 'I think she did it on purpose, Beth.'

'Pippin?' Beth was astonished. Rupert must be in love to feel so rejected. 'Oh no, it was my fault. I tripped. She wouldn't do that. Pippin's the sweetest girl in the world.'

'Is she, Beth? Is she?' he said slowly. 'I hope so, Beth, for your sake. You need her friendship.'

'I have it, Rupert,' she said simply. 'Pippin would not be cruel to you in that way. Martin Barnham isn't important to her. I think she really loves you.'

He smiled sadly, and said no more.

She pushed the hair out of her eyes where it had fallen as she cooked. She felt as if she were carrying the whole burden of the Wheatsheaf herself, her father going about the inn quietly and without superfluous words. It was March, but still cold and summer a million years away. Even William was withdrawn. He had never referred to what had happened that summer with Richard - nor its sequel. But she knew it had hurt him, that he was contemptuous of her for loving Richard Lyle. She had expected him to marry Sylvie, but he did not. Sylvie threatened to leave, changed her mind, and went the more sullenly about the place, having seemingly given up the struggle to win William's affection. Pippin Beth rarely saw, though she knew she had visited London once or twice. But if she met Rupert, if there was word of Richard, Beth had not heard.

If he's forgotten me, good riddance, decided Beth. She could never fit in that artificial world, the world of make-believe in which Pippin, Rupert, and Richard belonged. She knew she never could belong, would never want to. But sometimes her own world, her future, looked very bleak. She told herself that she would not see Richard Lyle again. She told herself she did not care. Yet she lied.

'You'll not cross my threshold, Hamlin.' Andrew barred the way.

Hamlin turned expressively to his companion, a large thickset man in his fifties. 'My dear James, I told you Mr Ovenden has his own quaint ways of doing business. It's business I'm after, Ovenden. Money in your pocket. I warrant you can do with it. Matter of an outstanding bill to my partner, Mr Shurland. Personal of course, so I daresay you won't be in too much of a hurry to pay if off. Couldn't keep up with the monthly payments, I hear. Haven't got much time left now, eh?'

Andrew's face purpled, but Beth stepped in. 'We'll hear him out, Father,' she said coolly. 'Words never hurt no one. Then he can be on his way.'

'If it isn't young Beth,' said Hamlin. 'Quite the businesswoman eh?'

Two dark eyes glared unflinchingly back at him.

'This is Thomas James,' he said. 'Brewery contact in the city.' Beth gave a fleeting glance at their carriage, grander even than the Chartboys' carriage. 'Now what we're here for is to rent one of your private rooms. We'll pay you a good rent.'

'What for?' asked Beth abruptly.

'I've no objection to explaining,' James took over. 'It's a reasonable question. I own a brewery in London and I'm interested in local connections with the smaller breweries and in Kent businessmen. We need a meeting of local brewers here and the Wheatsheaf is central –'

'Why not Faversham? More convenient than this.'

'If you understood business matters, my dear, you would understand that it is best conducted sometimes away from rivals' eyes, best to come into the country where inquisitive rivals can't be watching your every move.'

'I don't like it,' said Beth.

'Your father, my dear, is the licensee. What do you say, Ovenden? I'll offer you six pounds a month.'

Beth gasped. 'Father –'

But Andrew's eyes had lit up. 'I don't like it, Hamlin, and I don't like you. But that don't stand in the way of business. The first sign of anything illegal and you're out.'

James looked shocked. 'I don't intend to set up a gaming shop, Mr Ovenden. You may rest assured of that. I suggest we take the room for a month and see if you are satisfied that we're not master criminals.'

Beth turned angrily on her father. 'They're paying too much. There's something fishy – can't you see that?'

But Andrew was already accepting the money.

The painfully accumulated hoard of money in Beth's closet slowly mounted. They would repay Mr Shurland, just in time perhaps, for he had never regained his health. He should have the balance of the loan and interest in full. It was June now and the end of the law term. Would he come? Or would he wait for the hopping? Still no word from him. One postcard - of Ellaline Terriss - in March, and that was all.

That postcard was under her pillow now. She reached for it, as she sank into the feather bed thankfully. It had been a busy night in the bar, the warm June nights bringing customers out a-plenty and giving them an unaccustomed thirst. No message on the postcard, just the card itself, but she knew the writing. Bold, black, confident writing that resurrected her longing for him and brought it to painful life. Where was he? If he was still true to her, why did he not come or send a word? She remembered Bill the hedger saying to her last autumn: 'He's the light of the devil in his eyes, Miss Beth. Easy now.' She blew her candle out, and settled down to sleep firmly dispelling the all intrusive thoughts of Richard.

Deep in her first sleep, somewhere in her troubled dream of fighting hoppers and apple-pickers, an apple hit the ground with insistent force. Then another. And another. And a hopper whispering Beth, Beth, over and over, and she could not reach him. She awoke with a start. Half in the real world, half in a dream, she heard a knock at the window, and as she sat fearfully up in bed there was a hand grasping the half-open window.

And a voice. *The* voice. Richard's voice.

'Open the damned window, Beth. It's stuck.'

Automatically, still drugged with sleep, she got out of bed, coming to her senses as the night breeze played onto her face through the open window.

He was there, clinging to the wistaria. He grinned as he saw her.

'Hurry up, Beth. I'm damned stiff. I've been sitting up

in the mulberry tree all evening, waiting for you to go to bed.'

'Serve you right if I left you there,' she hissed indignantly. 'Who gave you permission to climb up my wistaria?'

'It was you showed me the way,' he pointed out. 'Are you going to leave me here all night? Because I'd like to mention that I'm about to fall off.'

She jerked the window free and, in a trice, he was standing by her side.

'You can't stay –'

But the moonlight streamed in through the window and the months of winter were swept away in the reality of his arms.

'Tell me now you don't want me and I'll go,' he whispered, holding her to him so hard she could feel the warmth of his body through the thin lawn of her nightgown. His lips found her mouth and his hands her breast.

'You know I do,' she said. 'Oh Richard, you know that. But why do you have to keep popping up like a jack-in-a-box. Why didn't you write? Why leave me so long –'

'Did you doubt me, Beth?' His eyes were serious as he looked at her. 'Ah Beth, you couldn't have. Not you.'

All the miseries and hesitations of the last months fell away in one glorious moment of certainty and faith. She looked into his eyes, rejoiced at what she saw there, and put her arms around him.

'I've waited long enough, Beth. I've done all you told me, and now I've come to claim you. Eight months is a long time to sleep alone –'

* * *

She counted it out again, it was no mistake. There was ten pounds missing. She counted it once again even more slowly. There was no doubt. It had gone. A wave of desolation spread over her. How could she find ten pounds before the end of another week? She would have to let Shurland down. Ask him to wait another three months. Already she'd had to go back on the arrangement she'd recklessly offered to pay back each month. It had been possible up till Christmas but after that, with receipts falling, she'd had to visit him to ask him to wait till June for the balance. He'd agreed, almost seeming to take no interest in the matter, his eyes apathetic, and she had not been in touch with him since save a letter to announce she was coming. She bit her lip. She hated to go back on her word for a second time. Then she grappled with another thought. Where *was* the money? No one knew where she kept it but her, unless someone had come across it by chance. And there was only one person to whom that could apply. Sylvie – who hated her. She did not hesitate. She found Sylvie glossing the oak wainscot with boiled beer and beeswax.

'Where is it?' she demanded.

'Where's what, Miss Beth?' enquired Sylvie, busily continuing her task.

'The ten pounds you took.'

Sylvie laid down her brush slowly and turned round to face her. The look of mean triumph on her face was all the proof Beth needed.

'What ten pounds?' she asked scornfully.

'Oh Sylvie,' said Beth wearily, 'there's no need to bluff it out. We're alone here. Just tell me why, that's all.

You knew that money was to save the Wheatsheaf. Don't you want that to happen? Do you want it to be always in debt?'

'Oh no, miss, I don't want that.' There was now a definite smirk on her full face.

'Tell me why,' shouted Beth, taking her by the shoulders in her anger.

'I should leave me alone, miss, if I were you. If Mr Hamlin were to know you was bullying me, 'e wouldn't like it.'

'Hamlin!' exploded Beth. 'We own the Wheatsheaf, not Hamlin. We employ you.'

'Not after Midsummer you won't, miss.' Sylvie was openly triumphant.

'Oh yes, we will. Mr Shurland will extend the loan in view of what you've done.'

''E don't hold the loan no more. Mr Hamlin does –'

Beth stared at her, unable to take it in, hoping she was lying, but premonition sweeping over her.

'Mr Hamlin,'e took over the loan from Mr Shurland. 'E got into trouble, see. Poor man. Dying, they say.' There was little sorrow in her voice, however.

'And even if this is true, where do you come into it?' asked Beth slowly.

'He'll want someone to run Wheatsheaf. No more Ovendens for him, see.'

'He's hardly likely to choose you,' said Beth scornfully.

'No, he'll ask William. And William and me have an understanding now –'

'Does William know about this?' asked Beth in horror.

'Of course, Miss Beth,' Sylvie replied smugly. ' 'E's allus wanted to run Wheatsheaf, ain't 'e?'

It was two miles to Westling. Richard had rented a cottage there for the summer to share with Rupert when he came down. He was tired of the rough accommodation given to the hoppers. But Beth did not mind the walk this afternoon. It gave her time to think. The cottage was outside the village itself, small with an overgrown garden, remains of last year's bolted cabbages at one end, rambling roses and cornflowers fighting among the weeds near the cottage itself, but inside all was sparkling, primitive though it was. She found it without difficulty, and found Richard in the garden, taking a scythe to the nettles that threatened to engulf the path.

His face brightened when he saw her. He tossed the scythe carelessly aside, and went to greet her.

'You're just in time. You can make my tea,' he jested, then frowned as he saw her face. 'There's something troubling you, Beth?'

'I need some money,' she said bluntly.

He exploded with laughter. 'Every woman's cry,' he said. 'A very loverlike greeting. And why, my beloved, do you want money?'

''Tis the Wheatsheaf,' she said.

He heaved a mock sigh. ' "'Tis the Wheatsheaf." Of course.' But he listened in silence while she told him.

'I'll be a pauper coming to you. And Hamlin! Oh, I tell you, Richard, there's trouble brewing. I feel it –'

'Sweetheart,' he said laughing. 'All that worries you is ten pounds – you shall have it. Right now.'

'But can you spare as much?' she said, alarmed.

He shrugged. 'I have some by me in the cottage, and I can easily replace it when next I go to London.'

''Tis a lot of money,' she said frowning. 'I've no wish to be beholden to you for long. We can repay it by hopkin time.'

'Very well. If it makes you happier to repay it, hopkin time it is. Now come inside and start paying me the interest.'

But she clung to his hand suddenly shy, and hesitated before entering.

'Do you still want me, Richard? As your wife, I mean?'

'You can repay me the money as a wedding present,' he said, stroking her hair. 'At hopkin time. Harvest time. Yes, this time, oh, my Beth, oh, this time,' as his arms went round her, 'I'll not leave you behind.'

The summer passed in a golden haze of lovers' meetings. The Wheatsheaf was safe, Hamlin was paid off, the suspicions and worries of that time forgotten as Richard filled Beth's every thought. Now that the travelling men had disappeared, not a cloud was left in the summer sky. Even the private room still rented by Hamlin was no longer occupied.

'Where do you think they've gone, the travelling men, William?' she asked. Not that she cared. They'd left the Wheatsheaf and Richard had no longer any contact.

'Gone to another pub, Faversham way,' said William shortly. 'Good thing too. 'Specially at the moment.'

'What do you mean?' said Beth curiously. 'Especially at the moment.'

'Now the hoppers are here,' said William quickly, avoiding her eye.

'There's more than that, William. Now tell me.'

'Well, I did hear that they was planning something big next Saturday. Faversham Creek at nightfall. Out by the pub there.' Beth shuddered. Even the mention of the travelling men still made her feel ill – and she was thankful that the Wheatsheaf was no longer involved.

Folkestone washerwomen they called them, those large black clouds that appeared without warning in a summer sky. And they came that week.

Beth walked round the corner with a tray of beers for the hoppers, right into a familiar figure. The twisted leering figure of Tom the Higgler.

'I'll open the door for you, my pretty,' he said. 'Then you can thank me like you're pleased to see me.'

She took the tray to the barn, then returned and opened the door of the private room.

They stopped their talk instantly, wary looks changing to lecherous ones as they looked her up and down. One of them put out a hand to touch her, but another of them pulled it back with a soft muttered word in his ear. There was a snigger and they watched her warily.

'What are you doing here?' she demanded.

Tom shrugged. 'Business, lady, just business.' He grinned showing blackened teeth. 'Want to help?'

'I want nothing to do with you. This is Hamlin's –'

'We're part of Mr Hamlin's business, ain't we?'

There was a chorus of murmurs.

'I know your sort of business,' she said scornfully, aware of the trembling in her legs.

'Not now, miss. We've seen the error of our ways. After you so kindly helped us last summer. Mr Lyle told us. Didn't realise you liked us so much. Makes you like one of us, don't it?'

'Vermin,' she said with scorn.

'Easy now, miss. Police might like to know who it was spoiled their fun last summer.'

'There's nothing you can prove,' she said scornfully.

'How about young Mr Parslow then?'

William. She could fight against them for herself, but could not endanger him. She bit her lip. 'All right, you can stay. I know – ' she faltered and went on bravely, '– you're planning something big. But nothing in the Wheatsheaf. Nothing,' she repeated vehemently.

The men looked at each other. A slow smile crossed Joe Rawlinson's face. 'That's all right, miss. We understand each other I see. Nothing in the Wheatsheaf. Hear that, lads?'

'Beth, 'tis the police, they want a word with you.' William put his head into the crowded bar.

'The police!' she exclaimed. 'What do Goodfellow want here?' Wiping her hands on her apron, she left William in charge of the bar and went to the private room. Her father had gone to Canterbury for the evening, and it was hard enough to manage without him without the aggravation of Goodfellow and his sanctimonious prying ways.

But it was not Goodfellow. She was greeted again by the bland avuncular face of Sergeant Perkins of the Metropolitan Police. And the Squire. So it was bad then. She avoided the Squire's worried, slightly accusing look.

'I hear PC Goodfellow saw a few of them smugglers – or I should say Tom the Higgler's men – in here the other evening, Miss Ovenden,' he began without preamble. 'I'd like to have a word with your father.'

'He's not here,' said Beth warily. She might have known Goodfellow would cause trouble. 'Mr Hamlin of Teynham Breweries lent them the room.'

'Is that so, miss? We can ask him about that of course. It just seemed a coincidence like – us having heard there's a landing on – and them being seen at the Wheatsheaf. You being friendly with them, we thought –'

'I am not friendly with them,' Beth retorted angrily. 'They came to the pub, that's all. I didn't know they were coming – and – and I hate them,' she burst out.

'That's as may be,' he said, eyeing her thoughtfully. 'But there's no denying it's a coincidence.'

'Search anywhere you like,' said Beth defiantly. 'You won't find anything, now *or* tomorrow.'

'We searched last year, miss, you see. And we *did* find a few interesting things. We never did anything about it, 'cos that occasion – for some reason –' he held her eye, 'we never did catch 'em at it. But we let your father know how things stood and give him a warning. So if you knows anything about tonight, I think you might be wise to tell us. Otherwise it would look very ill for your father. Very bad indeed. We'd have to take him in. I've a warrant here somewhere,' he added casually, fumbling in a pocket. 'We could just wait till he gets back.'

Why did Father have to be out this time of all times, thought Beth desperately. It looked so bad for him. If she did not tell them now about the landings the implication was plain, he would be arrested – and the Wheatsheaf – what would happen then? Panic began to take over from reason and the thought of the threat of the travelling men being removed forever from the Wheatsheaf decided her. She owed nothing to Tom the Higgler, and she had to save her father.

'Faversham Creek,' she began wretchedly . . .

'I've nothing to say to the likes of you. Come pushing in here –'

'Beth, you've got to –'

'Who gave you the right to call me Beth, *Mrs* Grayston?' asked Beth in a voice heavy with sarcasm. Hetty Didcot, the brazen hussy, bursting into the bar with all the men looking at her and that indecent dress –

'Please.' Her long painted face was pushed close to Beth's.

'All right, come to private bar,' said Beth wearily. Would the evening never end? Hetty Didcot followed her into the private room, clutching her toddler by one grimy hand.

'I don't know why you hold against me so much, I'm sure,' sniffed Hetty. 'Or perhaps I do?' she said grinning and glancing at the toddler and then back at Beth.

The implication was unmistakable, and Beth went cold with shock. Richard and Hetty Didcot in the long grass. Why had it not occurred to her before that Hetty had been carrying Richard's child when she married? The realisation, as she nerved herself to look at the blue-eyed youngster, made her faint for the moment, then she recovered. Whatever had happened in the past was gone. Theirs was the future, hers and Richard's. But it made her none the warmer towards Hetty Didcot.

'I've not come here to trade insults, Beth Ovenden.

I've nothing against you, and it seems to me we've a lot in common.'

'In common?' Beth tried to conceal her outrage.

'George Goodfellow tells me they was going to ask you about the landings tonight. That right?'

'What if they did? You've no love for Tom the Higgler, have you?' said Beth belligerently. 'He did you no good turn once, I recall.'

The look on Hetty's face did not bode well for Beth. 'No, but I have for Richard Lyle.'

'Richard?' echoed Beth stupidly. 'But –'

'And your father too. You must have realised. No,' she said, her voice filled with scorn, 'the mighty Beth Ovenden don't see nothing she don't want to. Don't think neither.'

'But Richard's changed – you're wrong – he –'

'Of course he ain't changed. Richard won't never change.'

Beth stared at her dumbly. The woman was right. Of course he hadn't changed. That's what he'd come down for. Not to see her. Always the highwayman. There'd always be the one last adventure. And she had betrayed him.

'Did you tell 'em the place?' And interpreting her silence aright, 'Then it's too late. Cursed be you, Beth Ovenden, for your headstrong blind ways.'

Please, oh please let Rupert be in the barn with the rest of the hoppers and not gone to his parents. Her prayer was answered. He listened to her story in silence, then put his arms around her. His lips were tight and a battle seemed to be going on in his normally placid self.

'No, Beth, I won't do it,' he said at last. 'I've bailed him out of trouble too often.'

'But Rupert –' Beth was suddenly scared. Why was he so hostile? Richard was his *friend*. 'It's his whole career, his life –'

He looked at her gently. 'Beth, you go through the world blinded by your own honesty. Don't you see? Oh, don't you see how it is?'

'I don't see anything except I love him. And there's Father and the Wheatsheaf,' she went on desperately.

He did not say anything for a moment, then said reluctantly, 'Very well, Beth. But I do it for you. Not for him.'

The cart rattled and jogged along West Street. Across the creek on their right was the Faversham Customs House and Beth glanced at the large square white building fearfully. Would Richard soon be there? Was he already there, handcuffed, hurt, dead? She curtailed her imagination. In harbour, at the top of the creek, the paddle-tug *Pioneer* was moored for the night, and a dozen or so other vessels, for Faversham was a busy port. Ideal for smuggling where boats coming up the Swale at all times of day and night would cause no comment – and those that stopped on the strand before entering Faversham Creek would if the times were chosen right escape all notice.

'Don't turn here,' she ordered. ''Tis so quiet, they'll wonder at it in the Customs House. Take next turning through Davington, past the Priory, and round by the pond to the powder-works road.' The grim gaunt buildings of the Marsh powder-works dominated the horizon to their left as in the pitch dark, only the lanterns to guide him, George picked and stumbled his way along the uneven lane. The noise of the cart clattering over stones seemed deafening in an ocean of flat stillness.

'We can't take him no further,' said Beth, bumped and jolted in the cart. 'Leave him here. Take him out of sight of the Ham Farm road and you wait with him. We'll be heard otherwise. I'll do rest on foot. 'Tis too dangerous for you to come. I can make an excuse for being there, you can't.' She spoke more bravely than she felt, for the dark silence of the night disorientated her, and the thought that every shadow might be an ambush made her want to cling to Rupert for safety.

'I'm coming,' said Rupert simply. 'I won't let you go alone. We'll just take one lantern. You hold my hand. Is there a path?' He stared out across the dark, dimly illuminated by the clouded moon.

'There's one to the left by Oare Creek,' said Beth, heart beating loudly. 'Or we cut over to the one by Faversham Creek in Powder Monkey Bay. But 'tis too dangerous and too long that way. We'd best perhaps go straight over the field to the Hollow Shore. There's a light in the Shipwright's Inn still. That will guide us. It's safe enough for sheep, so it's safe enough for us.'

Stumbling over the tussocks and clumps of marshy weeds in the dark, they made their way across the last half mile, the occasional indignant baa of a sheep sending their hearts to their mouths. Soon the Shipwright's Inn at Hollow Shore was in sight, a dark shape against the sky now it had closed for the evening with just one light in an upstairs window.

'That's where the police will be waiting?' asked Rupert.

'No,' said Beth. 'Too obvious. They're probably in the barge building yard over there.' She pointed to the other side of Oare Creek. 'That's the best vantage point for the strand to catch the boats making the landing.' She tugged at Rupert's arm – 'Look!'

Silhouetted against the moonlight, on top of the high creek bank was a slim figure, unmistakable, defiant, staring out towards the sea along the creek.

'The idiot,' muttered Rupert savagely. 'Has he no sense?'

'All he wants is his highwayman's hat,' choked Beth, torn between anxiety, relief and a ridiculous desire to laugh at the unreality of the scene. She squeezed Rupert's arm. 'I'll go.'

'Take care, Beth, take care –'

She ran as best she could over the last twenty yards of the field, no need of the lantern now, through the courtyard of the pub. She ran up the bank, oblivious now to the dangers of being seen from the shipyard, and caught at his arm. He turned with panther-like reflexes, eyes distant, fierce, those of a stranger. Then, as quickly he recognised her, realised the reason.

'Where?' he whispered, his eyes glinting hard in the night light.

'In boat-yard, I reckon. Oh Richard, I –'

'Then it's along to Powder Monkey Bay for us. Darling, come.' He picked up his lantern to wave a warning signal to the dim shapes of half a dozen boats already approaching the strand. Dark shapes squirmed from behind rocks, the whole beach seemed alive but silent. Then it exploded into chaos as the crack of a pistol came from the boat-yard and the huddle of shapes on the beach dissolved into twenty different entities, leaving but one. One who wavered then fell. With horror in her heart Beth recognised him. It was her father.

'Come,' said Richard urgently to Beth, tugging at her arm. 'Quickly. Run.'

'Father,' she said desperately. 'My father's here. He's fallen. That's *him*.' The grip on her arm tightened, as he stopped, looked at her, looked towards safety and back to the nightmare on the beach.

Everything in him was urging him to run. The instinct of the hunted, the fox. Live to fight another day. He tore his eyes from the dark horizon and looked at the girl by his side. In those brief seconds of decision, her dark pleading eyes full of confidence changed his life for ever.

'For you, Beth,' he laughed, kissed her quickly and jumped down the bank, racing into the middle of the mêlée where customs men and police were battling with the gang and moving into the water to prevent the boats from leaving. A helpless spectator, she watched as he picked up Andrew, half dragging him back to the bank.

They were almost there. There were two, then suddenly five or six. He made no attempt to resist them. Her last sight of Richard and her father was of them being led away by two policemen. He threw her but one mocking, rueful glance over his shoulder, and his fine features were etched forever on her memory.

Why was Jervis taking so long to answer? 'Hurry, hurry, oh please, hurry,' Beth murmured to the unresponsive door knocker. As he opened the door at last Rupert came up behind her, breathing heavily from running up the drive, and put one hand on her shoulder preventing her from entering.

His face was pale. 'I thought you'd be here, Beth. I told you to wait until I came to the Wheatsheaf.' His tone was peremptory, quite unlike the Rupert she knew.

Beth turned impatiently to go into the house for they were wasting time, but he caught at her wrist. 'Don't go, Beth!' he said sharply. 'Don't involve Pippin in this – *please*.'

He spoke to deaf ears. She pulled her wrist away, and ran into the house where Pippin was still breakfasting – alone. There was no sign of the Squire. Beth ran to her as she looked up in amazement.

'Pippin, you've got to help,' she burst out. 'Richard's been arrested and Father, too, and he's hurt – oh, Pippin, can you do anything? Talk to your father. *Please*. For me.'

Pippin looked past Beth to where Rupert stood in the doorway.

'Richard?' she said dazedly.

'Rupert, tell her, explain she must help,' said Beth desperately, whirling round. But Rupert's eyes were fixed on Pippin and he said nothing. It was as if Beth did not exist.

'I'll go straightaway,' said Pippin. 'Of course.' Her face took on a determined look.

Then, only then, did Rupert speak in a flat, emotionless voice: 'I'll come with you.'

'I'll go alone, Rupert. It's better that way.'

'It's more than smuggling, miss. Much more. Matter of

bank notes.' Sergeant Perkins was waiting for her, studying the lists for the weekly darts' match, when she returned.

'But my father. How is he?'

'All in good time, miss. You see, a record is kept of all stolen notes and, funny thing, a banknote stolen in London turned up here in Canterbury and Mr Hamlin tells us he had it from you. Now how would that be, miss? Your father get it, did he? Seems a bit out of his line.'

Her mind was crystal clear. The ten pounds Richard had given her. Stolen money. Of course. Her heart sank. He would have had to have found something big. Just to smuggle brandy wouldn't be exciting enough. And he'd told her he had reformed.

'I really can't say. We get a lot of notes passing through our hands,' she forced herself to say offhandedly.

'Not ten pound notes in a pub this size, miss?'

'Sometimes', she said, obstinately. 'You don't think I'm a bank robber, do you?'

'No, miss, but we think you've been involved. Perhaps you knew about it. Perhaps you didn't. There's quite a trade in stolen banknotes in London. Don't pass them in this country – too risky, because the numbers are recorded by the Bank of England. So they're taken over to the Continent, passed around there and when a foreign customer presents it to the Bank of England they have to honour it. See? Clever. Seems someone's had the bright idea of following in Ikey Solomon's footsteps. Takes brains to think of that. Brains like Mr Lyle's got. Seen him recently?' he shot at her.

'I seen him, but I don't have no ten-pound notes from

him,' said Beth defiantly. 'Hop-pickers don't have that kind of money.'

'We'll have to see about what he can remember, miss. He might have a better memory than you, if it comes to a question of whether your father's involved.' He smiled at her pleasantly, raised his hat and walked out, leaving Beth alone marooned in a sea of uncertainty and fears.

'Any news, Beth?'

'No. He wouldn't say anything about Father.'

'Anything I can do?'

'I don't want no help from traitors.'

'Traitors. What's this then?' said William, puzzled.

'It was all a trick, weren't it, William? she said bitterly. 'One of Hamlin's. He planned this whole thing. And he got hold of you and you turned against us.'

'I don't know what you're on about, Beth.'

'I'm on about Sylvie,' she threw at him.

'What's Sylvie got –' His face was black with anger.

'Hamlin wants you both to run the Wheatsheaf when he's got rid of us, don't he?'

His face flushed red. 'I don't know who's been telling 'ee stories, Beth, but you're a fool to believe them.'

'How do I know what's true any more?' she asked wearily.

'How do you know, Beth?' he retorted angrily. 'Because I worked here for years, that's why. Because you known me since we was babes in arms. Because you know full well Sylvie don't mean a thing to me, nor Hamlin neither. Only thing keeps me here is you and Mr Ovenden and I tell you, Beth, there's been times in the last year when I precious near walked out you act so daft the pair of you.'

All that day she waited, going about the essential business steadily, hardly aware of what she was doing. William ran the bar, and they had nothing to say to each other, each consumed with worry.

In the late afternoon Andrew returned, his arm in a sling, grey, unshaven, tired, avoiding her eye. Relief flooded over her, and she ran to him. 'Come and sit down. Is it over? Your arm – Richard's free too?' She hardly dared to ask.

'Thank the Squire,' he said slowly. 'Yes, Lyle goes free.'

She burst into tears with relief, while Andrew regarded her detachedly.

'Squire argued they hadn't anything on me. No proof they hadn't dragged me down there as a hostage – after all, you come after me – and you told 'em where landing was,' he pointed out, 'and Mr Lyle come too to save me. That's what Squire said. Anyways, none of them notes was found on us, thanks be. Nothing to do with that, I had.'

'Why did you do it?' she burst out, though she had tried to keep from saying it.

'Why?' he said dully. 'Do you think your pickled walnuts is enough to keep us going? I didn't want to worry you – kept the men away so you wouldn't know – I didn't know Hamlin was in with 'em. Double-crossed Tom the Higgler and all, he did. Reckon 'twas he dropped hint to police. Lyle came down with his fancy ideas –'

'But he tried to save you,' she cried.

'Aye,' he said grudgingly. 'Aye, he did. Not all bad. Anyways, he's free with a caution to watch his step.'

The joyous relief flooded her heart. 'I'll go to see him, Father. You can see to bar tonight, can't you. I must go to him – or did he say he'd come here?'

'No,' said Andrew quickly, and something about the way he said it made her look at him. His eyes fell and she saw in his face something that she feared to ask.

'What is it, Father?' she said at last, licking dry lips. 'Tell me.'

'There was a price to pay, lass,' he said awkwardly. Then, looking at her, he burst out, 'God alive, I don't want to be the one to tell you, Beth. I don't like him. Never have, for all he tried to save me. He ought to tell you himself, like a man.'

'What should he tell me, Father? *Tell me*!' she said, panic welling up inside her.

'He's got to marry Miss Pippin.'

The words made no sense. Richard – marry Pippin?

'Why,' she cried disbelieving, 'that's ridiculous. You've got it wrong. *Rupert* is to marry Pippin.'

'No, Beth,' he said quietly. 'Miss Pippin asked her father to get Richard off provided he agreed to marry her.'

She was very cold, very quiet. Then she laughed in relief. 'No, you must have misunderstood, Father. Pippin's my best friend. She's doing it for *me*. It was her way of getting Richard free; now he is, she'll say she's changed her mind. She knows he's going to marry me –'

'For God's sake, Beth,' Andrew roared in anguish, 'you don't see further than your own nose. You think too well of people. She ain't doing it for your sake; she's doing it for hers. She allus does, self-willed little bitch. She's twisted you round her finger, and her father too, since she was eight years old, and you with your loving headstrong heart thinking her so good. She allus wanted 'im. I sees more than you think.'

She stared at him dully. 'But Rupert –'

'Rupert nothing. It was Richard Lyle she lusted after, but he had eyes only for you. Didn't you see she were allus around, come to the hopkin, taking you to Lunnon so as to have an excuse to see 'im –'

'I must see her –'

'She won't see you, Beth.' His words were final.

Through cracked and painful lips she managed to cry – 'Richard.'

She did not sleep that night. She did not weep. She sat at the window looking out at the darkened garden, filled with roses that Richard would never see. She would never hear his laugh again, never lie within his arms.

Heavy of heart and limb she dressed in the morning and walked slowly towards Medlars. As she turned into the lane she stopped and, fearing to face the truth, haltingly retraced her steps.

'I'm going back to London, Beth.' Rupert came into the garden, awkwardly twiddling his hat between nervous fingers. 'I came to say goodbye.'

She swallowed. 'Did you know?' she asked simply.

'I wondered,' he replied. 'I – tried to warn you. But you seemed so confident – so sure – I couldn't make you see the danger. Besides, I wasn't sure myself. Richard was so much in love with you. How could I know? It was just that Pippin was –' he reddened, 'never quite there when I kissed her. I thought it was shyness, until I saw the way she looked at you in St Paul's and then at the dance –'

'He's been forced into marriage,' she burst out vehemently. 'But he's free now, and Richard's not too fussy about keeping his word. Squire can't go back and have him arrested now, so maybe he'll not marry Pippin. Yes, that's it,' she said eagerly.

'You don't know Richard very well, do you, Beth?' said Rupert gently.

She was about to deny it, then she reheard her own words: 'I don't really know you, Richard,' and was silent.

'Beth, I have to tell you, forgive me – I've talked to Richard. He – he's not that unwilling to marry Pippin. He wants to –'

'Wants to?' She turned a face of such misery to him that he blenched but forced himself to go on.

'He loves you, I know he does, but – well – he's ambitious, Beth.'

'And I won't make a barrister's wife, is that it? I'm not a lady?' She forced herself to say it, remembering again Richard's laughing hurtful words, 'Pippin's a lady . . .'

'If the world reckoned things right,' Rupert said bitterly, 'it would count you the gentlewoman and Pippin the – the whore!' he burst out.

Beth touched his flushed cheek gently, torn from her own anguish by the sight of his.

'Buying love with money,' he went on. 'Her money.'

She shook her head. 'Richard said money would just come when you loved somebody. He wouldn't sell himself for money –'

'He is fond of Pippin, Beth.' Rupert quietened down. 'And it's easy money. No risk. He's weak-willed. Yet he needs *you*. He should be marrying you.'

She stared at the roses so lovingly tended, she thought of the lonely nights, she thought of the baby inside her, Richard's baby, that for the last few days she had known for sure was coming, and part of her died. The laughing careless girl that had been Beth Ovenden had gone for ever.

He came that night, climbing the wistaria and knocking for her to open the window. Like an automaton she rose and went to the window, but would not let him enter. Astride the sill, he put a hand on her arm. 'Beth.' Her breast rose and fell under the high-necked cotton nightgown with harsh panting breaths, and she thought her heart would burst with love as he looked at her with pleading tenderness.

'Beth, you know me now, through and through. You know I love you.'

She turned her head aside, and heard her own voice say coldly: 'Go and say such things to Pippin.'

'Don't be harsh on Pippin – she feels badly about it.'

She gave a short laugh.

'I promised her – would you have me in jail, Beth? Shut away for years? Twenty maybe. Disgraced, my life gone. Not to feel the sun on my face, adventure ahead? I promised Pippin –'

'You made a promise to *me* too, that you'd give up this wild life –'

'Can I give up life itself? I told you I needed you, Beth, but you wouldn't come –'

'You're weak.'

'You're too strong, Beth. Don't blame us weaker wills. I'll be good to Pippin.' She closed her eyes in pain and, try as she would, a tear escaped from the lids.

'Go away, Richard, go away,' she said hoarsely.

'We could still see each other –'

'No,' she flung at him in horror. 'You made your decision. You must live with it. As I shall.'

He leaned in towards her again and touched her cheek, then gripped her arm. 'Don't be so hard, Beth,' he pleaded in a low voice. 'Help me, give me the strength and I'll tell the squire to go to hell, tell Pippin to go to hell, and we'll to heaven together.'

She felt as though life itself were being torn from her body. She had only to speak, to tell him of the baby in her womb, and he would stay. Only to plead her love and he would not leave. But she could not speak the words, would not hold him to her by her own pleading. If he did not love her enough to make the decision his own, then she would not, could not, make it for him. Her pride, the curse of the Ovendens, stood between her and everything she wanted.

'Go away, Richard,' she said steadily, pushing him away. As he clung to the wistaria she closed the window behind him.

She heard his last despairing cry: 'Beth!', but she made no answer.

CHAPTER SIX

She retched miserably into the bowl. As she lifted her head, the very roses of the wallpaper seemed to mock her, vibrant and colourful with a life that was closed to her. She, Beth Ovenden, whom she thought so superior to the girls in the village, was no better than Hetty Didcot – if as good, for Hetty Didcot had never given herself airs.

A dull ache spread over her body that had nothing to do with the child that was growing in her womb. Pain seemed to hit every nerve of her body as the force of her loss swept over her. Richard had gone, leaving her to the life she'd always said she'd have to face – bloaters, baking and hard work. The haystack where she and Richard had travelled the world together had vanished. The thought was too immense for her even to think of that other betrayal, that perhaps grosser betrayal, for it was of friendship and trust.

'Work, girl,' Andrew said, gruff with compassion, as she desultorily polished the glasses. 'Work. There's nothing like it. Go and pound some dough. Let your feelings out. I reckon I know how you're feeling,' he added awkwardly. 'I tell 'ee, Beth, there's nothing certain in this world, not where love's concerned.' His mouth took on a bitter twist. 'And, after all, there's still the Wheatsheaf. It's still ours. I may have acted wrong, but we're through that now. You be sure you keep it, girl. No matter what happens, you hang on to the old place.'

But what use was a building when its love and life were gone, when the spirits within were crushed, and hope extinguished? Year after year serving behind the bar, cooking food, baking and with a child to bring up – the prospect stretched before her like a life sentence.

By the middle of the afternoon the walls all about seemed to stifle her. Trade was non-existent this afternoon and, grabbing her sunbonnet, she ran outside into the garden to attack the earth. She picked one or two ripe tomatoes, and noticed that the apples were ripening nicely. The Kentish Pippin. Everything reminded her of the dull ache of disbelief inside her. The apple blossom had just fallen when Richard had come and now they were almost ready for the picking – the bitter fruit. Her mind could think of nothing but her own misery: the laughing Beth Ovenden who had teased and flirted with Richard Lyle in a garden full of scents and the soft night air had died and left in her place what?

'Betrayal, Beth, is never easy,' her father had said. 'Makes you fair doubt the senses of your own eyes, sometimes.'

She had believed that Pippin was her true friend – yet all the time she had wanted to take Richard from her – and had done so without thought for her. 'I love Beth Ovenden,' Richard had cried triumphantly to the world. But had he? He could not or he would not have done this thing. He had been amusing himself with a village girl, and all the while Pippin had waited for her chance. She forced herself to think of Pippin and Richard together and the bitterness grew. Then she pulled herself together.

This wasn't like Beth Ovenden. Where was her pride? She must go to see Pippin, hear it from her own lips. Perhaps even now Pippin was preparing to come down to see her, to tell her it was all a mistake. Yes, that was it – a mistake. She would tell her that she hadn't realised how much Beth loved him. Full of a sudden irrational hope she put down her trowel.

'Miss Philippa is not at home.' A wave of revulsion suffused her, part physical, part emotional. Beth lifted her head high and said proudly to the blankfaced Jervis: 'I am sorry to have missed her. Tell Miss Philippa I called, but that it was not of the least importance. She need not bother to return the call.'

The doors of Medlars closed in front of her. As she had walked up to the house she had seen a slim figure at one of the windows, a figure quickly withdrawn. She had thought Pippin had been coming down to meet her, as she had for the last twelve years, beating Jervis in her eagerness to greet her friend. Beth's heart had leapt, willing still to hope, to believe that Pippin was not guilty of such betrayal.

Now she leaned against the pillar of the portico to steady herself, and she gazed out over Medlars' gardens to the blue of the distant Weald. Just below, Shepham lay serene in the fold of the hill, the grey Norman tower protruding above the warm red roofs as it had done for centuries past, a symbol of peace and endurance. But today it brought no peace to Beth. Her girlhood was past and she had become a woman.

She could not face returning to the Wheatsheaf right away, she needed time to reflect now she knew it was true. She would not go through the hopfields; she could not bear to walk there with its throng of bustling humanity, carrying on cheerfully with the business of loving, birth and death. She wandered out through the home farm, hardly conscious of where she went.

Had Pippin always been a deceiver? Had her love for Beth always been false, because she was a leech that drained without giving? No, said Beth, honesty unwillingly dragged from her. Yes, contradicted her evil voice; she gave only when it was at no cost to her. She gave of her life at Medlars freely – because it suited her to share it with someone. Gave generously when it did not deprive her. Yet what of Rupert? She had been so attracted to him. Though had she actually said so? Or had Beth just assumed it, because Rupert was so much the sort of person she thought Pippin should marry – whereas Richard, with his recklessness, his wildness, she had assumed would frighten Pippin. She had been wrong. It had been that quality attracted her. And she was face to face with the realisation that she had never really known Pippin if that were the case. Would Richard now that he was to marry cease to be an adventurer? Or would he sweep Pippin off to Venice – to Araby?

She cried aloud in pain to the trees, throwing her head back and closing her eyes against the sun, and when she opened them again and looked back along the lane they were full of sun-mist, clouded. And it seemed as if in a dream the laughing shouts and cries coming towards her were part of a monstrous charade from hell sent to taunt her.

The waggon was decked with flags and flowers, garlands around the horses' necks; the waggon piled high with corn moved at a snail's pace towards her, perhaps thirty, maybe forty men and girls running along beside. On top of the hay sat a girl, clad in white and crowned with flowers and clasping a stook of corn sheaves.

Beth stood aside to let them pass; oblivious in their joy they swept by for the world had no time for grievers. They were bringing home the corn, crying the neck in the old tradition of taking the last stook to a neighbouring farmer who had not yet finished harvesting. Up aloft was the Ivy Queen, and gazing up at her into the sun it seemed to Beth it was Pippin sat there, shining and golden, bringing home the corn, triumphant in her harvest.

And black-haired Beth Ovenden who had fought for her own, was forced to the ditch to let them pass. Then as she was pressed up against the bank, there was a clasp on her shoulder. Tom the Higgler. 'Leave me be,' she said wearily. 'Oh, leave me be.'

He grinned, his evil breath floating over her from between blackened teeth.

'Miss Ovenden of the Wheatsheaf, the whore of Shepham, who'd have thought it, now. All alone, eh? No Mus Lyle? Gone off and left you, 'as 'e? Like 'e left us?'

The last word came out as a hiss. 'Squire got your father and Lyle off. No such luck for us though. And who we got to thank for that, eh? There's ten lads in prison and the rest of us fined. All thanks to you, my fine lady.' He was pinioning her against the high bank and, with a sudden resurgence of her old vigour, she knocked his hands away and stood free, facing him.

'You've haunted the Wheatsheaf like an evil demon all my life, Tom, you and your kind. No more. The Wheatsheaf can stand alone. It doesn't need your money. You live on people, prey on them –'

His face darkened. 'That so, me lady? Seems to me you ain't quite realised 'ow we feel. We know as was you told on us, laughed on the other side of your face when you found out your father was involved, didn't you? And your precious Mus Lyle.'

'I had to tell,' cried Beth. 'Don't you understand? It was Hamlin arranged it all. He set you up in the room, then made sure you were betrayed. He just wants the Wheatsheaf.'

But from his black face, she knew he didn't believe her. ''Twas you told 'em, my pretty. Mus Lyle told us to keep off you, but now 'e's gone, ain't 'e?' He put out his hand and clawed at her breast before she could knock the hand away. She pushed past him and ran quickly down the lane, his jeering laughter ringing in her ears.

A cloud blotted out the sun as she passed through the churchyard and the church loomed grey and forbidding above her. Would Pippin be married in this church? Would she have to endure the very sight of Richard marrying another woman? She shivered as, high above, she heard a bird singing. A wood-lark. No, a longer and sadder note. She was still. She must be mistaken. But no, it called again. The plaintive cry of the curlew. The Seven Whistlers. Misfortune, or death, sadness. But it had come already. There could be no more. She tried to regain her composure. But even the Wheatsheaf seemed forbidding as she walked over the green. As she entered the door the curlew called again.

'Taken your time, girl, ain't you? Hoppers be here already waiting to be served, and a rare turn-out in the bar. News has got round. Want to see I'm back, see what a fool I made of meself. Can't handle everything myself, you know.' Andrew's tones were gruff but it was concern, not anger, that shone out of his eyes. 'Afore ye go in bar, Beth, Squire was here this afternoon.'

She stiffened. 'He told me,' Andrew paused awkwardly. 'He told me 'tis all been arranged. Mr Lyle has gone back to London today – get him out of the way Squire said. So you needn't bother your head about seeing that good-for-nothing.' He didn't mention the furious row he'd had with the Squire, the result of bitterness that had been stored up for years. 'God knows why Squire wants him in the family,' he continued. 'Miss Pippin allus did know how to get her own way. If you ask me he's trying to make it up to her acos –'

'Because of what?' asked Beth, curious despite the pain that seemed to be choking her.

'Acos her mother died young,' Andrew finished lamely.

Beth did not notice, she had lost interest. Richard had gone. Sadness, relief, joy, anger all struck her at once. It was settled; she could not go to him, tell him she'd changed her mind. It was over.

'And Miss Pippin's to follow next week, stay with her aunt up in town, and get married up there.' Andrew paused, looking at her anxiously. 'They thought it best. Not have it here, that is.'

Her lips compressed. 'Do they think I'd forbid the banns, then, Father?'

'None of that, Beth,' he said gruffly. 'Seemed best, that's what he said. And I agree. We got our lives to be getting on with here without that sort of upset. They'll live up London of course. So you can forget him. Best be looking for a husband here, Beth. Vicar's son's out of course.' She winced at his unconscious cruelty. 'What about that Mr Rupert? He was very fond of Miss Pippin, he said. And you, too, I reckon –'

In spite of herself, Beth smiled. Poor, gentle Rupert. To be foisted with her, Beth, with all her problems. Two lonely hearts together. 'I'll think about it, Father,' she said gravely.

Would this day ever end? As if in deliberate contrast to Beth the hoppers seemed extra boisterous that evening. Their demands were almost impossible to meet. The smell of the bloaters made her feel sick and she was forced to hand over to Sylvie, who glanced at her curiously. Ever since the summer they had simmered in armed but passive hostility, not speaking more than was necessary for the running of the Wheatsheaf. Sylvie was too valuable to lose and William had clearly had words with her, for her hatred of Beth had seemed to intensify.

As the evening wore on, Beth's depression grew. By nine o'clock she could bear the noise no more, and slipped out of the pub, through the orchard and wandered down towards the river. The fields were lush and green with evening dew as she walked through, her dress brushing against the long grass. The river was running fast, mysterious and compelling in the fading light. She closed her eyes. How peaceful it looked, just running on to eternity. A cold, peaceful eternity. So easy. So different from this world of hers. What did the future hold for her? A bastard baby, the whole village rejoicing at her downfall. If marriage lay ahead with one of the village lads, then housework, field work, dull, dull toil. An endless succession of children. Or she could stay on working with her father, an old maid but no maid, the butt of every cheap male jibe in the village. Move away? How, with no money and a child? What future could there be for Richard's baby, without his father. A child born of him would be clever, restless, and what would he do? Was this the life she would want for him? Go and see Miss Monk and plead for one of her special potions? She shuddered. No, she could not kill Richard's baby. It would be part of him, something longed for and feared at the same time. A constant reminder of her wasted life. Better perhaps to end it now, slip into the cool water and just lie down to sleep. It would be very easy . . .

There was a rustle in the bushes. She froze, then relaxed. A rabbit, fox even. But it was no animal. A hand grabbed her round her neck from behind, forcing her head back, choking her, strangling her.

A voice in her ear. "'Tis the Lord led me to you this day to do His work. To force the devil out of you, Beth Ovenden.'

Higgins. She knew instantly that he was mad: it was lust, not religious fanaticism she'd seen all these years in his eyes.

Now she was being dragged to the ground, still that gripping hand round her throat rendering her incapable of action, incapable of speech, incapable of anything save terror and but one thought - she wanted to live.

Not die. And die she surely would, for he'd not leave her alive to bear witness against him, after he'd forced her body. She was on the ground, his mad pale fanatic face leering down at her, thick lips besmearing her face with spittle. His large soft pudgy hand pinioned hers above her head while the other fumbled desperately with her clothes. She wriggled her legs frantically and he sank the weight of his body on her to stop them. Her brain became icy clear as he tore at her skirts, pulling them to her waist and feverishly ripped open her drawers. She painfully pushed up her hands with all her strength, the ground cutting deep into her back and when he began to lose balance, with her last ounce of strength, she brought her knee up hard into his groin. With his cry of pain, she rolled him off her to the side where he doubled up in agony.

Sobbing, she scrambled to her feet and ran. Ran over tree roots and over stubble. Over fence and boulder. Anything for life, sweet life. By the time she reached the orchard she realised she was alone, that he was not following her. She stumbled into the pantry, covered in mud, retching, to be caught in William's arms.

'My sweet life, Beth. What's wrong?'

'Higgins,' she croaked. 'Higgins.'

'He did this to you?' William's face darkened. Answering William's shout, Andrew came rushing in, and freeing herself from William she ran to him. He cradled her in his arms, no woman now, but his little girl running to him for help. 'Did he – ?'

'No, I fought him. He –' She ran to the sink and was sick into it. William looked at her, then at Andrew and turned for the door.

'Where be you going?'

'After Higgins,' said William grimly.

'No.' Andrew's voice was sharp. 'They'd have us all, him and Goodfellow, if you lay a finger on him. This time we do it right. We go to police at Canterbury tomorrow. Chapel or not, we'll have him thrown out for this.'

'But if they don't believe me –' Beth croaked.

'They'll believe you. Stand right out. Show them you're not ashamed of anything. We got to make a stand against Higgins. He'll cause trouble, believe me, girl. There's trouble coming, and we'll need all we can to overcome it. I've no doubt Hamlin's behind it all, but we got to win our own village first.'

Beth took some time to get to sleep that night, and when at last sleep came it was fitful, a half-sleep half-waking, where nothing seemed real, all life a monstrous nightmare.

She did not dream of Richard, or of Pippin. Instead horrific images of giant hoppers and bloaters filled her mind, of hopfields scorching hot under the sun with merciless binmen and the endless toil, of the raucous uncaring shouts of the hoppers around, while she lay, powerless to move away: then of the camp fires over which the bloaters were cooked, fires building up from little more than faggots of wood to enormous piles of logs and sticks, dry crackling wood so that the flames roared high and she, Beth Ovenden, was the sacrifice.

The hoppers' shouts went on, and the smoke was in her throat, her eyes, yet drawing her irresistibly towards the fire, whose red hot centre beckoned her on, on, till it seemed she must succumb to its embrace. The smoke was clouding her mind, dimming her vision . . .

. . . 'Beth, Beth, wake up, girl.'

Now Andrew was adding his voice to the hoppers'.

'Fire! Beth, wake up! Wake up, Wheatsheaf's on fire!'

New sounds dimly penetrated her sleep, her eyes dragged open to a world of smoke, in her nostrils, in her throat, in her eyes. So much simpler to close them, close them . . .

'Beth!' Andrew's strangled voice was nearer, hammering, hammering at her dreams.

She was very near the fire, now so very hot . . .

'Beth, wake up.' He was shaking her. 'Come back, come back. Get up, fire. We're on fire.' She stared up at him into a gloom that had nothing to do with the bedroom she'd always known, in which red shapes danced eerily on the sky outside, sending flickering shadows into the room.

Andrew had a scarf round his nose and mouth and was pulling her out of bed wrestling with her reluctant limbs. Then with a roar half of the ceiling fell in, a splintering crash and sparks as the heavy beam across the window top fell sideways . . . and the sky was above them, flames leaping towards the heavens.

Tears were running down Andrew's face as she focussed at last upon it. 'Get going, girl. We've got to get out. Here, tie this round you.' He seized the kerchief from his own mouth and nose and put it round hers, for a few seconds she sensed the blessed relief of water on her face. They stumbled to the door and opened it to find only a wall of flame.

'The window,' Andrew said hoarsely. But it was

blocked by the beam that had fallen across.

Below the window they could make out a sea of faces standing in their back garden, white upturned faces. Men were throwing buckets of water vainly at the flames, forming themselves into a chain from the well. A cheer went up as Andrew's face appeared at the blocked window.

'Steamer's on its way from Faversham,' came one shout. 'The manual won't reach. 'Tis round the front. No ladder high enough afore steamer come. You'll have to jump'. Half bemused, Beth could only think that this was part of her nightmare. Then a burning spark landed on her face, and fear began.

'Steady, lass,' said Andrew. 'Panic won't help. Can you get through space?' He hoisted her up, but it was hopeless. The space was too small, the beam immovable and licks of flame were creeping under the door. Andrew left her side to throw the contents of her washing bowl at the door and they receded. While she watched helplessly, he leapt on a chair, tearing away the broken tiles of the roof with his hands to enlarge the window space.

'There, lass,' he said tensely, his hands bleeding, ''tis big enough for you.'

'For me,' she cried. 'But –'

'Up with you. You first. I'll follow. Happen they'll be here with tools by then.' He unceremoniously pushed her up on the chair. Through the noise of the crowd below they could hear a new sound as the Merryweather steamer arrived, and its pump set going, belches of steam adding to the smoke-filled atmosphere. As Beth managed to squeeze herself out through the hole, the ladder was erected and the fly was being pulled up. Then a uniformed fireman was swarming up, seizing her, pulling her through the hole. Pinioning her skirts to her, he tipped her over his shoulder and descended carefully. Then she was on the ground, and Bill was putting his coat round her bare shoulders.

'My father!'

She looked up at the window, to which the fireman was already climbing once more to see her father's face, pale and set, flames dancing behind him in the room. And she saw it happen. With a crash the remaining roof gave way; what had been the window disappeared in a cloud of debris, the face had disappeared and the flames triumphantly leapt towards the sky. A voice that did not seem to be her own was screaming from a long way off, distanced further and further as she sank oblivious into Mrs Parslow's arms.

She came to in the barn where they had carried her. Instantly she was awake. 'Where's Father?' she demanded of Mrs Parslow.

'Hush now, Beth. They're doing all they can, my pretty.'

She started to struggle to her feet. 'I must go –'

'No!'

But, pushing aside the restraining arm, she was up and out into the garden. In the front the manual engine was valiantly pumping away, four men on the pump, a bucket chain attacking less serious outbreaks. This side the flames were dying down, the fire was almost contained.

She pushed her way to the back of the Wheatsheaf where the steam engine was still in full action, shooting powerful jets of water at the flames.

'Father,' she said, clutching the nearest shoulder, 'where is he?'

An arm round her shoulder. 'William got him out, lass, but –' She saw William then, outlined against the leaping flames, kneeling over something lying on the ground. They tried to keep her back, but she would have none of it. Blackened skin, no hair, this thing could not be Andrew. It seemed impossible that he could be alive, and he was barely so.

'Father.'

He heard her, for he moved, but could not see her. 'Beth,' he said so low she had to bend very close to hear. 'Beth, I did my best for you. 'Tis yours now. The Wheatsheaf. Keep it going, lass. There's allus been Ovendens –' and then no more.

Beth Ovenden stood up slowly. She looked at her father's body, she looked at the ruins of the Wheatsheaf, she looked at the circle of silent villagers.

A small cluster of people gathered round her, anxious, sympathetic, and unable to help. As she slowly, dispassionately looked round the villagers, she saw two hostile, triumphant faces, Tom the Higgler's and Higgins's. And she knew, if she needed telling, that the fire at the Wheatsheaf had been no accident.

They wanted to take him to the undertaker, Mr Burgess; they said it was not fitting he remain in the Wheatsheaf, just her and the body. They wanted her to go to Mrs Parslow's, said it was not fitting she remain there.

But she would not let them. 'The Wheatsheaf is his home,' she explained carefully. 'He stays here.'

''Tis not safe here. Leave it be till tomorrow.'

'No.' Her voice rose sharply. 'He stays here.'

'Let the girl be,' said William, roughly pushing the concerned crowd aside. 'He'll stay here.' He looked round. The steamer had departed, the manual been driven back to the Tudor Barn where it was kept, and beer money distributed to the pumpers. They were left outside the Wheatsheaf, one third destroyed, its innards exposed to the elements.

'Who'll give a hand here?' William's voice was steady.

'I will, William.' The rector came to help, followed by his son. At that, there was no shortage of volunteers, and Andrew Ovenden entered the Wheatsheaf for the last time.

Some of the posts of the stairs were blackened but they got Andrew's body up to the dining room on the first floor, where they laid it to rest on the long oak table, covered with a cloth.

'We'll need a guard against looting,' said William to the rector.

'Is Goodfellow here?' asked the rector.

'I'll not have him, Rector.'

The rector met his eye. 'Very well. Jim Backus. You'll stand a turn?'

Jim nodded: 'I'll stand sentry till dawn, William. Reckon you can do with some sleep.'

Beth stood by silently, power gone from her hands. Helpless. She stood by, as in a dumbshow, as though this were nothing of concern to her.

'And you come with me, dear,' said Mrs Parslow.

'No,' said Beth quietly. 'I live here, the Wheatsheaf is my home.'

'But you can't, m'dear. It isn't proper that you, a maid alone – '

'I'll stay here,' said Beth. 'I'll not leave Father and I'll not leave the Wheatsheaf.' And, unbidden , the tears held back so long began to roll down her face.

'I'll stay with her, Mother,' said William.

'But 'tis not fitting –'

'There's a powerful lot of things not fitting about tonight,' said William grimly. 'And this is the least of them. Get you back to bed, Mother. And never fret.'

They were alone with the ruin of their lives. Beth, usually so strong, now helpless: William in command. 'There's a bed made up this side –'

'Not Father's room –'

'No, not that. You'll take another. We'll see how things look in the morning. But to bed with you now, Beth, after all you've been through, in your condition . . .' and seeing her look at him, he blushed. 'Sylvie told me – guessed – you know what women are.'

Her pride crumpled, and she swayed towards him. William picked her up as if she were a child, and slipping the coat and the rags of her nightdress from her, put her into the lavender-scented sheets and stayed with her holding her hand till exhausted she fell asleep. Then he took himself a chair and sat by the window gazing out over the darkened village green until the dawn rose.

CHAPTER SEVEN

Only Bill the hedger was real, sitting in his shabby parlour, gnarled and old, smoking his briar pipe and smelling of the earth he had tended all his life.

The last five days had been a dream that she had had to endure, of which only the odd scene would come back to her conscious memory from time to time: standing behind the Wheatsheaf, in the cool garden, looking up at blackened ruins, William's supporting arm round her; William talking, endlessly talking, to Joe the undertaker, to the rector, to uniformed police from Faversham, while she stood dumbly by; of people coming to her, uttering words, of her replying, though not with her conscious mind; of William continually stocktaking, shifting bottles; talking to her gently, but her not comprehending. Then of dressing that morning, in her funeral black, knowing that it was Father's funeral but feeling nothing. It seemed long, long ago, yet it had been that morning.

A 'men only' funeral, William had suggested, but she had looked at him bewildered. Of course she would be there. She was an Ovenden. His only child.

The black-plumed horses, the villagers, unfamiliar in their funeral black, had seemed to distance the reality from her. The road to the church was lined with villagers and hoppers for once united. No funeral black among the hoppers, and she was glad of it, for dressed in their Sunday best and self-conscious as they were, they seemed a handle to everyday life to which she could cling.

The group round the graveside had bewildered, almost frightened her. Relations she had met but rarely, some not at all, turning up to claim their share of a man Beth had thought was hers alone.

'You'll be coming to live with us, my dear.' Andrew's sister was nearly sixty with button-black eyes, and a determined though kindly enough face, nothing of Andrew in her. Her husband had stayed in the background fidgeting awkwardly. Their elder son, flanked by his own family, passed from her memory as soon as his muttered condolences were over – the youngsters stared at Beth with ill-concealed curiosity. Three Ovenden cousins, born of Andrew's uncle, stood stiffly by the graveside, identity-less faces in the silhouetted tableau of the day.

'I live at the Wheatsheaf,' Beth had replied to her aunt, puzzled at her statement. She could not understand everyone's anxiety over her. Eventually her aunt gave up trying and confined herself to platitudes as her only means of communication with this wayward niece.

The Wheatsheaf . . . Beth clung to this one anchor. Medlars was gone. No word from the Squire, no sign of him at the funeral, she realised, dully and without pain. 'I'd like to help,' Squire had said. But what could he do – now? There was no comfort now at Medlars.

Over the whole day, Hamlin had hovered like a black

cloud. 'I'll be along to see you. Hardly fitting now. Have to observe the proprieties. I'll be along to see you when everything's sorted out. I've had a word with your solicitor already, I'll give you a good price. You'll not find me unreasonable.'

Beth stared at Hamlin. He was actually smiling. 'Price?' she echoed. 'Price for what?'

'Why, the Wheatsheaf, my dear.'

'But it's not for sale,' she said, puzzled.

Hamlin laughed, reverting to his old manner. Then, remembering the occasion, he said soothingly, 'You're confused, my dear. I'll be along.'

It all meant nothing to her. She passed through the rest of the day dry-eyed and calm.

The Wheatsheaf. Andrew's words: 'Keep it going, lass. There's allus be Ovendens at the Wheatsheaf.' This was where she belonged. Not in dear Mrs Parslow's parlour where the party had gathered, nor in her aunt's Folkestone pub. And Hamlin had no part in it. She walked, then ran, down the path from Mrs Parslow's to the Wheatsheaf, and ran round the ruined side of the house into the garden. It was the first time she had been alone there since the fire. The sun had not yet reached the back of the house, and she shivered. In the shade the house looked alien, forbidding, gaunt. They were hers, these blackened ruins, one side of the Wheatsheaf gone. Now that even her father's body had left its home, she was aware of her solitude. Even the charred remains of her former bedroom did not bring her back to a world of pain. But she forced herself to look, to remember, to mourn. Slowly she approached the house, over the bricked yard. The wistaria was gone, a solitary black stem lying on the ground. She picked it up, charred and burned by the fire. The wistaria she had grown from a cutting taken at Medlars when she was ten; all that was left was a blackened stump. The blackened stump of her life, Medlars, Pippin, Father, the Wheatsheaf. And Richard, who in love had come to her, climbed this wistaria, was gone. And for this blackened stump of a tree the pain of living began to make itself felt for the first time since her father's death.

Then she was running; hardly knowing what she was doing, she stumbled to the far end of the orchard, once a gateway into the meadows of love, now an exit into an unknown dark world. There were her father's two bee-hives, only a few worker bees crawling over them at that moment. As she stared at them, the half-forgotten superstitions of her childhood came to the fore and her lips began to move. Everything around her was quiet, save for the hum from the hives, where once her father's voice would have been calling for her from the inn – 'Beth, Beth, where are you?' She strained her ears to hear, and the cry went on coming, nearer.

And then William was beside her, kneeling down, putting his arm around her. 'Beth, what are you doing here?' he asked, his voice gruff with anxiety.

She looked at him bleakly, then turned her head to the hives. 'I'm whispering his death,' she said simply. 'Telling the bees, so they don't leave.'

'Hearts alive,' he said gently. 'You don't believe that old superstition, do you, Beth?'

'I don't know,' said Beth, wearily. 'I don't know. But no one told them. I thought it might help.' She stood up unsteadily, while William, powerless to reach her in this mood, muttered words of concern.

'Why don't you come back now?' he asked awkwardly. ''Tis best for you to be with folks today.'

She gave him her full attention. 'No,' she said earnestly. 'No, I couldn't. You go back, William. There's someone I must see before I come back.'

She ran, as so often in her childhood, to Bill the hedger. There was no need to explain to Bill. He knew it already. She could not tell him about Richard, about the baby, but her grief, her desolation, there was no need to put into words.

'You be in trouble, Miss Beth,' he said slowly.

'Father –'

''Tis more than your father, more than the Wheatsheaf, bain't it, my rose?'

'How do you know?' she said listlessly.

'Gracious heart alive, I've known you since you was a baby. Can't remember the times I rocked you asleep talking. Dere ain't nothing you can keep from me, Miss Beth.'

But there was one thing.

'Ah,' he continued, looking at her withdrawn face, 'love's a terrible thing. 'Course, with my Sarah, God rest her, we were powerful happy, but didn't seem like that when she passed over. Why, everything seemed like end of the world. But it all passes, my dear. Life can twist us like a twig of hazel in a hedge, and we'll go its way just like it wants. 'Tis when we try to bend de other way it hurts.'

'I thought life wanted me always to run the Wheatsheaf,' she said wryly. 'But it's over. It's gone.'

And Richard, had she been trying to bend life the other way? No, no, that she could never accept.

'Harkee m'dear, life's never over, not even though the sap's stopped a while. Sap rises, and in the winter it falls, but that don't mean 'twon't come to life agin, if you just let it be a while. Terrible worrier at life, you be. Like a rose, you want to be out ablooming all de time. Got to wait a bit. An emmet, that you be. Trying to be movin', no matter what. Won't work.'

'But if I don't fight, everything will be lost,' she said hopelessly. 'You've got to fight.'

'There's seasons for fighting, and seasons for sleeping,' Bill said firmly. 'When it's time to start fighting again, then you'll know. But it's no use flying against nature. It may be tomorrow nature'll want you to fight, maybe not for another year or more. But one day you'll hear her say, Beth Ovenden, now you come along.'

That evening Beth sat on a tree trunk in the meadow, trying to put her thoughts in order. Bill was right; she should take things calmly. But how? In the fold of the hill beyond she could see the cowls of the oast houses; cows were grazing in Seven Acre field, under its sentinels of ageless, green elms. To her left in the orchard was an old spade, leaning against a damson tree – where Andrew had never finished digging out the stump of the diseased apple-tree. The basket she used for fruit picking lay on its side in the tall grass, a spider's web across its width, silvered by the September dew. The damsons would be ready soon, and the Kentish Pippins. Despite the faint lurch of her heart, she forced her thoughts to continue uninterrupted, to smell the freshness of the apples on the trees, so different to the devastation behind her. To her right one of the smaller hopgardens, silent now that the pickers had stopped work for the evening. These things would go on. Long after her problems were laid to rest, and her with them, the sap of Kent would go on rising, its fruitfulness and mellow warmth succouring generations to come, giving strength to its yeomen. And the Wheatsheaf would go on standing – or her Father would have died in vain. That somehow this would be achieved, she knew, without at this moment seeking to question how. She got slowly to her feet, took a sharp stone, and carved a single letter – O – on the cherry tree sapling in front of her. The Ovendens were here, and here they would remain.

Yet what of the child she was carrying? The awareness that this must soon take precedence over everything else swept over her. Then she let that thought be. One problem at a time. Time enough for that, when she had made the Wheatsheaf her own again.

'Most of beer's gone, Beth.' William was practical, calm, efficient.

'High in stock, were we, William?'

'Just had monthly order.'

They were partners now. They had to be. Somehow it had never occurred to her that William might leave, as had Sylvie, now that Andrew was dead. He fixed up a room for himself at the Wheatsheaf, and the murmur of dissenting voices from the village quickly died down. Beth accepted the situation as completely normal. It was only after some days that it occurred to her that he was afraid for her. Afraid, that in the absence of any action by the police, for lack of evidence, Higgins might come again. But nothing happened. It was as if she and William went about their work in a void, while Shepham held its breath, waiting.

Only one beer room was left – the saloon. The taproom and public bar had gone. The private rooms remained, and so did the parlour. The fire had demolished the left hand side of the building entirely, save for the attic, although the roof had fallen in over the dormer and the floor was unsafe. The fire had licked the cellar to an inferno, ruining the beer that remained through heat.

'We've our own left,' she said obstinately.

'Only three barrels, now,' William pointed out. 'And no bitter. And –' he hesitated, 'we've lost our brewer.'

'*We* can do it,' said Beth, more resolutely than she felt. 'And there's the wine that I made last winter – and the elderflower I made in the summer will be fit for drinking soon.'

'Won't be drinkable yet awhile,' William pointed out practically. 'It's beer we need, Beth. And where's money to buy hops to brew our own? If we're to woo back the hoppers from taking waggon to Westling, we'll need beer. Now.'

'We'll have to buy more.'

'Do you have money?' he asked forthrightly.

She shook her head.

'And there's something else, Beth, you haven't thought of,' he went on gently. 'There's no licensee now. Can't reopen without one.'

How could she have overlooked that? Father had been licensee all her life, and now he was gone.

'And even if you get over that problem, Beth, where's money coming from to rebuild? Won't get a licence like this, half falling down. Higgins and Hamlin will be up, opposing it, sure as there's a dog in Dover.'

Hamlin. She had almost forgotten him.

He did not long leave her in peace. He arrived the next morning with Mr Makepeace, the manager of their Canterbury bank, whom Beth had only ever seen once before. She had been a child then and this stiff and starchy man had completely overawed her – the years had done little to change him, but much to change her.

'He's offering a good price, Miss Ovenden.'

Hamlin stood pompously by.

'I'll not sell,' she said emphatically.

'You don't have much alternative, Miss Ovenden. Your father left no money, you know.'

She flushed. 'I think that's between you and me, Mr Makepeace, not to discuss before others,' tossing her head towards Hamlin.

The bank manager shot her an inimical glance. He was not used to being taught etiquette by twenty-year-old girls.

'It's common enough knowledge,' said Hamlin jeeringly. 'Now look here, Beth, you've got to sell to me; there's nothing else you can do. You've no licensee. You can't pay for a manager, nor stock, nor rebuilding. Sell to me, and you can stay on as barmaid. Even live here, how's that?'

The thought made her tremble with disgust. 'I'll not work for your sort, Hamlin. Any more than I'd work for Tom the Higgler.' She stopped, her tormented mind racing on. 'Tom the Higgler,' she repeated staring at him.

'He'd do anything you say, wouldn't he? Like – like burning down the Wheatsheaf,' she flung at him.

His face went purple. 'By God, girl, you'll go too far one day. I offer you a good price, job thrown in, and you spit in my face. Why would I want to burn down the pub I want to own? You'll apologise for that, my girl.'

She hid her face in her hands, then looked up at him. 'Perhaps not,' she said at last. 'Perhaps even you wouldn't go that far. Wouldn't have the courage. But you're here to scavenge what you can, aren't you?'

'I made you a reasonable proposition,' he said softly. 'What can you do with this ruin otherwise?'

'I'll live here,' said Beth obstinately. Suddenly she knew that was exactly what she would do. 'I'll live here, take in washing, work on a farm, anything. But I'll not sell to you, Mr Hamlin, now or ever.'

'You'll come crawling to me one day, girl,' said Hamlin viciously. 'And you'll pay for it then.' He came up close to her and seized her by one arm, hissing in her ear. 'You've spoiled one too many of my plans, woman. This,' he jerked his head towards the ruined pub, 'is just the beginning. Remember that, girl.' Not bothering to raise his hat, he stalked off to his carriage, leaving the bank manager to move nervously from foot to foot.

'Very foolish of you, Miss Ovenden. Very foolish. I can do no more for you, if you won't accept my professional opinion. Young women should take note of the advice given them.'

Young women, thought Beth wearily, as he followed Hamlin into the carriage. What difference did sex make to feelings? Yet because she was a woman she could inherit the pub, but not the licenseeship, despite years of training.

She went back into the parlour and sat down in the oak window seat to think. There must be an Ovenden at the Wheatsheaf. Her uncle – but he already had a pub. His sons – they were Ovendens.

She discarded the thought. 'Once let your Aunt Rose in and you'll never get her out,' her father had said. Her sons looked as though they might follow in her footsteps. No, that was no answer, save in desperation. There would be Ovendens at the Wheatsheaf but it would be hers, somehow. Gone were her thoughts of taking in washing, of living by any means other than that she knew. The Wheatsheaf was an inn; it had always been so and so should remain. Then she smiled to herself. The answer was so simple.

The hardest part had been to walk up the lane towards Medlars, steeling herself to face the dearly loved driveway, and to see the red brick house that had been a second home, to know that that life was past, to see the gardens where she and Pippin had played as children, and to know that she was now forced to come cap in hand to Pippin's father.

She wore her green two-piece, the skirt barely closing now. But she had to look what she did not feel, a competent woman of affairs.

It steadied her to see the Squire equally ill at ease, pacing his study with uneven steps, his big busy eyebrows drawn deep in a frown, voicing awkward embarrassed condolences. She knew from the tone of his voice that it had not been dislike of Andrew Ovenden that had kept him from the funeral. It was Pippin.

'But the next licensing session is not for several months –'

'I thought perhaps you might be able to get me a temporary licence, Squire, you being one of the magistrates.'

'In whose name?' he demanded.

'Mine.'

'You.' His eyes goggled. 'But you're a woman.'

'I'm the owner,' she pointed out. 'I've a staff.'

'But women can't be licensees – good heavens, whatever next.'

'There's no reason why not.'

'People wouldn't respect a woman. How are you going to cope with drunks?'

'They respect *me*,' she said. 'And there's Mr Parslow. Just till next session, that's all I ask.'

'Out of the question,' he said abruptly. 'I've told you my feelings about women in pubs at all – let alone running them.'

'Very well, then – William Parslow. Just temporary, mind, till we get something sorted out.'

'Possible,' he grunted, 'but I'd have to put up a good case. And what is it, eh?' He fidgeted with his snuff box, avoiding her eye.

Beth was taken aback. What a silly question. But she blurted out, 'Because the Wheatsheaf's always been there. The village *needs* a pub.'

'Been a lot quieter there, so I'm told, now the hoppers go over to Westling.'

'But the hoppers go home. And then the pub is the centre of the village. It always has been. That and the church. It only lives if there's a pub in the village. 'Tis more than a drinking place. It's there all the village business goes on. The Christmas Club, the Funeral Club monies are there, all the social clubs meet there, farmers, darts' players. It's always been so. Where else is there for them to go? Messages for the doctor come there –'

'And smugglers meet there –' put in the Squire grimly.

'No,' said Beth firmly. 'Oh no. Not again.'

There was a silence, and he was looking at her almost humanly. 'They've made one attempt to close you down, Miss Ovenden. Do you think they'll rest at that? There'll be more trouble as long as you're there. We want no more trouble in Shepham. I'm sorry to remind you, but Andrew Ovenden went to his grave with a stain on his honour, and it'll need time to clear the air as far as the police are concerned.' He hesitated. 'I can take no more risks for the Ovendens.'

'Then it's for me to clear the stains,' said Beth quietly. 'Give me a chance, Squire, and I'll – we'll – turn the Wheatsheaf into the kind of pub that the village can be proud of.'

'Very well,' he said at last. 'I'll put your case to the board. But it's temporary – and conditional. The first sign of trouble of whoever's making and it's rescinded.'

'Me licensee,' said William, wonderingly. 'But –'

'No buts, William. We've got three months to impress the board, if Squire gets you a temporary licence. But we need to reopen immediately even before we start to build.'

'*Build*? But how, Beth? We've not a penny. Unless we accept Hamlin's money.'

'Rupert'll lend me £50, he says. For the building materials.'

'Will he now?' said William, looking at her strangely.

'All very well, but where's the money for the beer coming from?'

'Credit. We'll have to get credit.'

'Fine words, Beth, but who round here would give us credit? They may be sorry but they reckon the day of the Ovendens at the Wheatsheaf is over. They're believing what Higgins's lot are saying.'

'There must be someone, somewhere, if only we look.'

It took over a week to find a brewery willing to take credit. They found it in an unlikely place, the middle of Maidstone, a small brewery with but two tied houses.

'I like it,' Jim MacBride said approvingly when Beth had finished. 'You don't know whether you'll be licensed, whether you'll have a pub to serve beer in, whether you can afford to pay me. Well, I've always liked a challenge. Women too.' His eyes flicked over her admiringly. 'I went up to London last week and happened to see that Mrs Despard, female suffragism they call it. You remind me of her. Dark eyes. Determined. And after all, if a woman can rule the country, one can rule a pub. That's what I say. But I'll want interest.'

'Look alive, Sylvie,' said William impatiently.

Sylvie cast a reproachful glance at William. The only reason she'd come back was that it had occurred to her that William was seeing a dangerous amount of Beth. Sylvie would work for practically nothing to be near William. And nothing was what they had. But she could keep an eye on William, and William would need a wife now if he were going to be a licensee. It wasn't going to be Beth Ovenden if she had a say in the matter.

William cast a look around the bar. All seemed ready for the evening of the reopening, and it was big enough for the meeting. The hoppers were already drifting into the barn and the familiar, by now welcome smell of bloaters was beginning to permeate the air. Beth had never thought the day would come that bloaters would smell so sweet. Today it meant the Wheatsheaf was in business again. That encouraged her, for while William was to dispense drinks she, Beth, had to make the most difficult speech she had ever made in her life.

'I'm nervous, William. It's seven and no one here yet. Save for them.' In the barn the hoppers were beginning their usual rumpus. 'Let someone come, oh, please let someone arrive *soon*.'

And someone did. Mr Tong the baker came through the door, pink with embarrassment at being first, twisting his hat in his hands, followed hesitantly, then with more courage, by several others. Soon there were twenty or more villagers sitting stiffly in their chairs, drinks in front of them, awkward under the new regime. Beth Ovenden the landlord's daughter was one thing, owner was another. And alongside William Parslow, too, as new licensee.

'You all knew my father,' Beth began steadily. 'Some of you remember his father beyond that.' She chose Mr Harbutt in the front row and held his eye firmly. 'The Wheatsheaf is a village pub, and we want to keep it so. But it's going to be difficult –'

'Teynham Breweries would buy you, miss,' pointed out the baker rashly. 'Still be a village pub and Mr Hamlin, he'd build it up again, restore it, like it was new.'

'No,' she said quietly. 'I won't sell to Teynham's. I've got two choices. Either I close the Wheatsheaf down and live in it as a house, which means you'll have no village pub, or –'

There were rumbles of disquiet.

'Or the village have to help me get it going again. Help us rebuild it so as we'll get a proper licence.' There was another stir of unease as men looked into their beer. 'I've got the money for the materials, but I want some volunteers to build her up,' she went on. 'And we've only three months to do it in.'

'You're asking a lot, missus,' pointed out one braver than the rest. 'We've our own work to do. Why help you for nothing?'

'For my father's sake – he was a good friend to you all. Didn't he lend you money when your first-born came, Bill Simmons, and you out of work? Didn't he give you a job, Tom Hardwick, when factory closed down?'

'It's true enough,' Tom conceded. 'But it don't seem right to work for a woman.'

William came out from behind the bar. 'You're not working just for a woman,' he said steadily. 'I'm here as licensee. You all know me.'

'What needs doing, miss?' asked one guardedly, though it was obvious enough.

'I need bricklayers, carpenters, roofers, fitters –'

'No roofer in village, miss. No tiler that is, only Sam, and he's a thatcher – and what are we to get out of it?'

A few hoppers were beginning to gather at the doorway, interested spectators.

'Free beer while you're working.'

A laugh went up at this. 'You'll never afford it, miss. You don't know how much we do drink.'

'Do I have any volunteers?' Beth swept on.

Each looked furtively at the other, then to their drinks.

Beth's heart sank. It had to work. 'Aren't there any men left in Shepham?' she asked fiercely.

'Not to work for a whore!' Unnoticed, Higgins had pushed his way through the hoppers, henchmen gathered behind him. 'Why listen to this strumpet, who urges you on with lust in her heart to do her evil work, takes you from your wives to do the devil's work. Heed her not and cast out sin –'

With a roar William launched himself at Higgins, bringing him to the floor, and grappling with him. The villagers shrank back, and Higgins's henchmen dragged William outside.

The villagers were already shrinking out of the doors as Higgins faced her in triumph: 'The Lord avenges His own –'

'The Good Lord will take his revenge on *you* Higgins,' she shouted hysterically. 'You dare take His name in vain you, you – animal. You burned down this place, you with lust in your heart and evil in your mind.'

His face leered. 'What's that in your belly, Beth Ovenden? And you trying to talk these innocents into rebuilding for you. What will their wives, their sweethearts, say if they work for a whore carrying Richard Lyle's bastard?'

She flew at him, the unexpectedness of her attack making him stagger. 'I'll have the police to you, Higgins, this time, disrupting a peaceful public house.'

'Police. And lose your licence?' She went for him, but he seized her by the arms. The villagers had melted away but the hoppers had not. Seeing the strength of an army coming towards them enlivened by the thought of a fight, Higgins's army was soon routed. But it seemed the victory was Higgins's for her meeting was ended, the men upon whom she had relied for the rebuilding of the Wheatsheaf disbanded.

'Recognise me, me old china?' Despondently she glanced at the hopper who had come to her aid. She did recognise him. It was her tormentor from previous years. Ben Perkins. 'I'm a new man, now. Got meself married. Always did think you was a nice little piece. Don't like to see any tub-thumper with his hands on you.' The other hoppers began to gather round. 'Now listen, me darling. Me an' me mates were listening to your problem, an' we gotta suggestion. We're all for individual enterprise as you might say, an' we like it down 'ere. Now the hopping's at an end in a week or two, what say we 'ang on a bit after that? Build the place up again.'

She stared at him blankly, unable to take it in.

Mistaking her expression, he hastily said, 'Just for our grub an' booze, see. Do a bit of fruit picking maybe in between whiles. I reckon as 'ow I can find twenty or so willing to 'ave a go. What'd yer say?'

'No,' she said wearily. 'It's good of you, but it's no use fighting Higgins. If we build it up, he'll knock it down. He'll never let the village come here in peace. Not till Hamlin owns it.'

'I thought you was a fighter. You fought me orl right. Regular bulldog bitch you was. Thought you 'ad a bit of life in yer.'

A fighter? Beth lifted her head. A fighter? Old Bill's words came into her head. 'When the sap begins to rise, you'll fight. When you're ready, you will fight.'

Andrew's death, Pippin's betrayal, the loss of Richard, all came together. She'd fight. By God, she'd fight. And win.

She grinned at the man. 'Grub and booze, eh? No bloaters though?'

'Saturdays only, missus.'

The work went rapidly after the hopping season. With the adept ways of the East Enders, things just appeared, mysteriously acquired. Carts were borrowed, bricks carried in, some looking suspiciously old, clapboards, and ragstone arrived, barrowload after barrowload. A pile of peg tiles grew overnight. Day by day she watched the Wheatsheaf come alive again. The villagers watched sullenly, unwilling to turn aside, but unwilling to risk Higgins's wrath. Then came the day that Percy Twist sauntered carelessly by, watched a minute, then with decision strode towards the working men, threw off his coat, and was up the ladder.

'Here,' he said gruffly, 'you ain't never fastened a clapboard in your life. Give it 'ere.'

The glazier came next, just to show them how it should be done, and stayed to fix the new dormer. In the event, the rebuilding of the Wheatsheaf united hoppers and villagers as nothing had before. 'Not going to have our village pub built by a load of foreigners' was the general verdict.

By the end of October all was done. Beth by now was arranging loose capes over her dress, and had taken to unfashionably full skirts. With the Wheatsheaf rebuilt, another worry presented itself. How could she go before the licensing magistrates as owner – and prospective licensee – with an illegitimate baby clearly showing?

'When's it due, Beth?' asked William, awkwardly.

'Lady Day,' said Beth wryly. 'Like all reckonings.'

'What will you do? If magistrates ask you about it?'

'I'll – I'll say 'tis none of their business,' she tried to say bravely.

'You could marry me,' he said gruffly.

She laid a hand on his shoulder. William was a brother to her, a partner, part of herself and part of the Wheatsheaf. She could not think beyond that. Marriage was no part of her life now. Marriage had meant Richard, and was closed to her now forever.

'Yes, they're married, Beth.' She had taken the news impassively. It had happened, and her life was ahead of her to be lived somehow. 'I just came down to see how you were,' added Rupert. He looked thinner, and older, a shadow over his face, where once there had been just innocent hope for life ahead.

Beth sat down carefully. He should not see how her hands trembled beneath the all-enveloping cape. 'You're a kind man, Rupert,' she said slowly. 'I'm doing well enough, thanks to you. What of you? You're back at Inner Temple?'

'Yes.' He paused. 'You wonder how I can when it means I'll be seeing Richard –'

'Yes.' Her pain swept over her again.

'Beth.' He took her hands. 'Beth, does it hurt very much?' She merely smiled. 'For me also.' He hesitated.

'I thought she loved me, Beth. I really did. She was so sweet, so confiding, she was so –' he reddened '– warm in my arms. We'd even talked of how life could be for us. I could offer her a life she'd want, not the wife of a struggling barrister, but in the country. A home like Medlars. Or we could have lived here if she'd preferred, but –' his face grew white and pinched. 'I'll never understand it. I'd blame it on Richard, but I know she planned it. He'd never have changed, Beth. He had one chance, and only one. You. But he didn't take it. He's always taken the quickest path to money, however dangerous, and then when he gets into trouble, takes the easiest way out and leaves other people to suffer.'

'Stop,' said Beth in anguish.

'I'm sorry, Beth. How do you think I feel though, knowing he'll not change his ways and knowing he's married to Pippin?'

Beth had not thought of this, and considered it. 'You think they'll not be happy?' she said slowly. She had not thought past the unbearable fact of their marriage; how they would fare after that she had not contemplated. It was too cruel.

'I cannot see it is possible. But it's of little matter.' He gave a twisted smile. 'It's all past. I have to look ahead, and so do you. I shall have to marry, I think quite soon.'

He sat beside her on the mossy seat and took her hand. 'My father wants me to marry. He's ill and wants to see an heir before he dies. He has someone picked out for me – I like her well enough. But –' he paused. 'I – would *you* marry me, Beth?'

'Me?' Beth turned startled eyes upon him. 'Me, Rupert?' A smile came unbidden to her lips at the thought of Beth Ovenden as the mistress of Draycott Manor, the future Lady Bonner.

'You find the idea amusing?' he asked quietly.

'No, oh no, Rupert. I was smiling because it was wonderful of you. To trust me. Want me. But it wouldn't do.'

'It could,' he said. 'I mean it, Beth. I've thought a lot about it. I know you love Richard and I love Pippin. But that's past and we must get on with life. I'm not like Richard, I could try to make you happy. You'd have plenty to occupy you at the Manor – '

'I was born to the Wheatsheaf, Rupert.'

'I knew you'd say that,' he said, 'so I have another suggestion. I could stay here with you. Take the licence. There'd be no problem with the magistrates. No problem with money.'

'You?' She turned amazed eyes on him. 'You run the Wheatsheaf?'

'Why not?' he said quietly. 'I'm not like your father of course. I'd have to change it. But we could build it up with my money, make it a fashionable inn, a hotel. I like the country life, and I love Shepham.'

Her vision of a prosperous, successful Wheatsheaf rose tantalisingly before Beth's eyes, before she regretfully let it fall.

'No, Rupert, it can't be.' She hesitated. 'In five months I shall be bearing Richard's child.'

In the startled pause that followed, she could hear her own heartbeat. 'Now do you ask me to marry you?' she said wryly.

'No,' he said, putting his arm round her. 'Now I'm telling you you *must* marry me.'

Tears pricked at her eyes, and she smiled at him mistily. 'Oh Rupert,' she said. 'You're such a – *gentleman*. But you haven't thought. Your father wanting to see the succession assured – another man's child?'

'It would be *our* child,' said Rupert stoutly.

'No, every so often you'd remember. Every time you see Richard you'd remember. No, but thank you, oh, thank you.'

'Beth,' he said wistfully, 'your pride again. Take care, take care. Will you never learn?'

'I told you, Miss Ovenden, any trouble and I'd not defend your case to my fellow magistrates. And what do we have? A disorderly brawl.'

'That's Higgins,' she said, white to the lips. 'But he's lost now, and the villagers know it. There'll be no more trouble, now the pub's rebuilt.'

'Rightly or wrongly, there'll always be trouble while you try to keep that pub independent,' said the Squire shrewdly. 'If you sell out to Hamlin you stand a chance. Otherwise no.'

She laughed. 'I haven't come all this way to sell out to Hamlin now. We've got the Wheatsheaf rebuilt, we've got a supplier on good credit terms. We've just to get through the winter season and then next year –'

'You need a licensee,' said the Squire. 'Don't want to be brutal, but that's the truth of it.'

'William –'

'Tch. There's you an unmarried girl, and a boy not much older, running the pub, sleeping on the premises. Not a very good advertisement for an orderly house, is it?'

'Then let me be the licensee,' she said quietly. 'Where's the harm save that I'm a woman. I own the place and the villagers are on my side now.'

'We'll have no woman licensee,' shouted the Squire. 'I'll not have it. And certainly not *you*.'

'Why not me?' she demanded. 'What's wrong with me? Do you not think I'm businesswoman enough?'

'Yes,' he said, 'you're clever enough. You've a good head on your shoulders.'

'Then why not try it? You could persuade your colleagues –'

'No,' he said peremptorily, 'and that's my last word.'

'What have you got against me?' asked Beth, pleading now. 'Save that I'm a woman? What's to become of me if I don't get the licence. Surely you care for me just a little? You've been so kind to me over the years, and not just because of one small thing I did as a child to save your daughter's life. You must have liked me to educate me, to see me –'

'Stop,' he said abruptly. 'Damn it, stop.'

'You can't just cast me off now, when I need your help.' She held her head proudly.

'Beth –'

She stiffened in surprise. The word had come out naturally, as though he had long thought of her so.

'You don't make this easy for me.'

'You don't make things easy for me, sir.'

He sat down at the table opposite her, then rose again as though he could not rest. 'You're my daughter, Beth.' That was all. Just a plain statement. When she said she did not understand, he tried again: 'Andrew Ovenden was not your father.'

'I –' She started to speak, but stopped, for she did not know what she had intended to say.

'Elizabeth Ovenden was your mother, of course,' he went on gruffly. 'She was very lovely, Beth. It was only once. Mary – my wife – was very ill while she was carrying Pippin, and – well –'

The world had gone mad. Father not her father. This stiff, unbending man who passed like a shadow in the background all her life was her real father. All those years and he had been simply Pippin's father to her. The Squire. No love demonstrated, no special tie emerged of which she, at any rate, had been conscious. And Pippin – if Squire was her father then Pippin was her half-sister. A wave of pain swept over her. She steadied herself. She must not think about that. Not now. Perhaps not ever.

'Did Father know?' she said through stiff lips. Then she remembered. Of course he had known. She remembered his dislike of the Squire; his opposition to her seeing Pippin.

'We agreed you were to be brought up as his daughter. Absolutely. He wanted no money, would take none, then or later. He said you were to be his daughter completely. An Ovenden.'

An Ovenden. Beth was very still. She was not an Ovenden. All these years of the Wheatsheaf and the Ovendens, and now she found she was not one. Yet *Father* had said she was an Ovenden. He meant it. He'd brought her up to be one, and so she would remain.

'My mother,' she said painfully, 'she was unfaithful then?'

'You're very young,' the Squire said slowly. 'You'll

find it difficult to understand. She loved your father, but she was younger, your age, alive, vivacious. I was – well, persistent – it was just a summer afternoon.'

'I was the result,' she said bitterly.

'I wanted to be closer to you, Beth. Giving you the freedom of Medlars – educating you, was all Ovenden would allow. Always fond of you. Did you realise that?'

'I –' She broke off. Had she realised it? She thought of the years she'd been accustomed to seeing this big, grey-haired man silently sitting reading his newspaper, while she and Pippin laughed and played around him. Working in the library while they played draughts at his side. Walking in the gardens while they bowled hoops and played hide and seek. Anxiously demanding of the governess *both* the girls' progress. Always there, in the background, unheeded, unacknowledged. Her father.

She buried her face in her hands. 'Too much,' she whispered. 'It's too much.'

He was instantly apologetic, patting her shoulder gruffly. 'Shouldn't have told you yet. Bad time, Beth. You've had a bad time.' She raised her head gratefully.

'The Wheatsheaf,' she began. In the topsy-turviness of her spinning emotions, she tried to cling to the one thing which made sense: 'For all those missing years, you must give me my inheritance.' She had to spell it out. 'Give me the Wheatsheaf.'

'No.' His face reddened. 'I'll have no daughter of mine running a pub. You can stay there, if you insist, with a man running it, but you sell to Teynham's. I hold no brief for Hamlin, nor he for me, but it'll give time to sort out something for your future. Something more suitable. You can come here, live with me if you like. Run the house. I'll acknowledge you now Ovenden's gone.' He was almost pleading. 'But no more of pubs.'

She smiled bitterly. 'It's too late, Squire. The Wheatsheaf is my life. I was locked out of Medlars the day that Pippin decided to marry Richard Lyle.'

He was uncomprehending.

'Did you not know that Richard and I were in love?'

His face darkened. 'I heard the story. But that's all over. He's married to my daughter now. I want no more –'

'But I'm your daughter too and your first grandchild will be born in March. To *me*,' she said, laughing and crying all together. She took off her coat and smoothed her dress over her stomach. 'I'm having Richard's baby,' she said starkly.

His face was grey with shock. 'He took advantage of you, did he, Beth?' His face was torn with hope that this was so. 'By God, I knew he was a wrong 'un. I should never have let Pippin talk me into it. He seduced you? You're not loose, are you? My daughter?'

'No,' she said proudly. 'This is a child of love, Squire. And everyone will know who's the father unless you let me be licensee of the Wheatsheaf. Your son-in-law.' It was her last hope. Bluff. Everyone would know anyway, but he was not to know that.

The Squire stared at her, defeated.

'You may think it's blackmail, but by what you've told me today, Squire, I think I have to fight for what I want. You've let me suffer alone – although you say I'm your daughter. You did not help when the Wheatsheaf burned.

Your daughter took the man I love and betrayed me. But by Heaven, I'll have something. The only thing left to me: the Wheatsheaf.'

'Very well,' said the Squire slowly. 'On one condition, Beth. I'll not support you as licensee. But be married within the fortnight and I'll see your husband gets it – whoever he may be.'

PART TWO
Before the Morning Light

'One kiss, my bonny sweetheart, I'm after a prize tonight,
But I shall be back with the yellow gold before the morning light.'

Alfred Noyes

CHAPTER EIGHT

The logs sputtered in the inglenook, casting sparks onto the tiled floor. The smell of applewood, so familiar, so timeless, caught her for a brief moment off guard and Beth was held in the grip of an age that was gone. How often as a little girl she had stood watching her father raking out the ashes, piling the logs by the fire's side; now she had a sudden image of her mother pushing the peel with its load of uncooked bread into the brick oven glowing with a heat whose waves reached as far as the little girl who watched so wonderingly.

Five years ago the fire had come, and one era of the Wheatsheaf's long history had abruptly ended. So carefully had the chimney been repaired that there was little sign of the scarring it had received. The arched vault of the old bread oven had collapsed and though it, too, had been repaired it never seemed the same. Beth used the oven in the kitchen, though the long-handled peel and the iron ember rake remained hanging in the inglenook as memorials to a way of life now past. The good companions which had belonged to William's grandmother stood sentinel in the hearth hiding the new brick that betrayed the tragedy of 1896, scars carefully camouflaged over to hide the hurt that was buried deep.

The life of the Wheatsheaf had continued after its pause as if uninterrupted, as solid as the Pax Britannica in this new century. The old queen had passed away and with the coming of Edward VII to the throne there was an excitement that befitted the dawn of a new age. Yet no one doubted that the old order would still prevail. The empires that had opened up under Victoria's rule would expand, for they were rooted in an ageless tradition of benevolent despotism that could never be eroded.

After the death of Andrew Ovenden the pub had quietly, slowly, reverted to its usual business. After the initial shock a combination of laziness, shame and loyalty had sent the villagers back to the Wheatsheaf where, to their surprise, everything seemed as it had been before – save for the face behind the bar. No mention was made of the tragedy. The darts, the goal-running, the bat and ball clubs had resumed their meetings, the regulars reclaimed their accustomed chairs. If a glance was given at the photograph of Andrew Ovenden hanging in the parlour no comment was made, whether through shame or because the past was past.

'Mama, Elizabeth stuck.'

Beth turned to see her cherubic fair-haired son toddling stolidly into the room. 'Oh, Owen, where this time?' she asked resignedly.

'In the tree.'

Of course it would be in a tree. And of course it would be Elizabeth in trouble. 'I told you both not to go climbing trees without Papa or me,' she said firmly. Seizing her two-year-old by the hand, she marched through the quarry tiled hallway out into the spring sunshine. The mulberry tree was coming into leaf and, from the terrace, she could see the mischievous face of her four-year-old daughter amid its branches, glaring defiance at her.

Tight-lipped, she helped her down, trying to keep back a sudden surge of laughter as Elizabeth's brown eyes twinkled at her, her tangle of dark hair falling over her face. As soon as she was safe upon the ground, she deemed it time to relax her charm. The thin arms unwound themselves from Beth's neck and she sped away.

'Not so fast, Elizabeth.' The tone in Beth's voice stopped the little girl, who slowly turned to face her doom. 'I told you not to climb trees, didn't I?'

'But, Mama, I like it.'

A smack produced rebellious eyes, and a stormy countenance, as she faced Beth defiantly.

'You shouldn't smack me. Papa doesn't like it,' Elizabeth ventured hopefully.

'Papa likes what I like for you,' said Beth firmly.

Salvation, however, was at hand. Elizabeth spotted her father, brought to the door of the Wheatsheaf by his daughter's yell. Immediately the blue eyes turned from defiance to self-pity, filling with tears, and she ran towards him to be scooped up in William's strong arms.

'Mama smacked me.'

William's eyes met Beth's across the heaving shoulders. 'Then I expect you deserved it, young miss.' He planted a kiss on her head and set her down, whereupon she was immediately diverted by her next pursuit – chasing a hen who had ill-advisedly chosen this moment to appear for lunch.

Beth sighed. 'I try, William, but she takes no notice of me. It's you, you, you –' Her voice dropped in despair.

William looked at her evenly. 'Perhaps you care for her too much, Beth.'

Shocked, and taken by surprise, she stared at him. *Care* for her too much? Did he mean? No – she dismissed the thought. Elizabeth had always clung to William rather than to her. Yet she was conscious of no difference in her attitude to the children. But did she – the thought passed irrepressibly through her head – did she turn away from Elizabeth in case she might love her too much, in case she might see in Elizabeth's eyes another's face? She pushed the thought away impatiently. That could have nothing to do with the present. The children were different, that was all, as all children were. The surprise was only that William could think that she still cared for what had happened all that time ago. They had been married nearly five years now. At first there had been a refuge and a haven, finding in William's comforting arms oblivion from torment, and then content. William was of the land, as she was herself, sturdy as the Kentish oaks. Season after season would pass in their marriage. Each year the mulberry tree would come into flower, would fruit and be harvested, then rest again; a cycle of eternity like their marriage.

These things she loved, the red roofs of Kent, the gently sloping green meadows, the smell of woodsmoke curling out of the Wheatsheaf chimney, the daffodils poking their green sprouts up in the spring, the apple blossom and cherry blossom, the cowls of the oast houses, everything that was Kent. Somehow William was part of all this and, as she came to rely on these things more and more as her heritage, it seemed to her that he had given them to her as his gift and she loved him for it; he had given her back her homeland.

But not all was peace in Shepham, not all tranquil with the Wheatsheaf. At first it seemed as though it might have been. Joseph Higgins's power as a preacher began to fail. Little by little, his flock deserted him and returned to the old grey stone church that had guarded Shepham for seven hundred years. Defeated by the turning of opinion against him, Higgins had left the village and, with his departure, the divisions at last began to heal in earnest. A sense of justice brought even Higgins's supporters round to Beth's side after the fire and her marriage met general approval. Gossiping tongues were stilled. She had chosen Shepham. Those who still nursed resentment nursed it in silence – until a new rallying point appeared a year or two later.

For two years ago, as if to take up Higgins's mantle, George Hamlin had come to live nearby.

A late eighteenth-century house built in the newly fashionable grey stone and made gloomier by its unusual north-facing aspect had been for sale between Shepham and Charing. This dull, classically styled mansion, as unwelcoming as Hamlin himself, was now the property of Hamlin and his sharp-faced wife.

Hardly had the news reached the Wheatsheaf than Hamlin himself condescended to visit them. William paused fractionally in his trimming of the lamps and then continued his task. It was left to Beth to say in an even voice: 'Good evening, Mr Hamlin. I heard you were living round these parts.'

He appeared somewhat disconcerted by the new Beth. Perhaps he did not recognise in the calm, dignified Beth Parslow, her hair drawn smoothly up behind her head, the tempestuous Beth Ovenden with whom he had sparred so long.

'Always been fond of Shepham, you know that, Beth - Mrs Parslow.' He ordered a beer, one of their own brewing, as if in sign of conciliation. 'Business good, is it then?'

'Well enough, Mr Hamlin. And with you?'

'Thriving, Mrs Parslow. Thriving.'

Civil words, an armistice, a no man's land. Whether there was more war to follow was unclear. It was not like Hamlin to give up what he had set his mind to; he was still extending his brewery's empire. The Star and Garter at Charing had been the latest acquisition and the Plough at Westling had long been in his domain.

'If you ever want to sell –'

'We won't be selling.' William's calm voice now intervened.

Surprisingly, Hamlin had said no more, nor had he troubled them in two years. Occasionally he would call in for a drink, sometimes even eat the simple luncheon that Beth prepared for the local workers. If his ambitions still included possession of the Wheatsheaf he gave no sign of it, and the uneasy peace reigned.

Other difficult situations had been resolved too. Sylvie no longer worked at the Wheatsheaf. Two weeks after Beth had married William, she had married a farm labourer at the Medlars Home Farm. Her husband did not drink in the Wheatsheaf, and Beth rarely saw Sylvie except a figure in the distance wheeling a perambulator. If she harboured rancour, Beth was too busy to be concerned about it. It fell to her to look after the books and accounts for the Wheatsheaf. And somehow the ordering had fallen to her lot as well. William was busy enough with running the bar and cellar, and had taken all the responsibilities for the brewing onto his shoulders. On brewing days he would call in a couple of local farm-hands to help and somehow seemingly half the village fell into the habit of calling in to give advice, the process being a never-ending source of interest.

The books, and looking after the house and kitchen, serving at the bar, exhausted her, but left her vaguely unsatisfied.

'I'm going to start my preserves again, William,' she had declared. 'Your mother is always saying she could do with a larger, more regular supply in the shop. And the village store wants some. We could sell them outside the village, too. Faversham maybe?' Her eyes gleamed on distant horizons.

'Now, Beth,' William had said patiently. 'You ain't got the time. Nor, I reckon, the energy. Be still once in a while, won't you?'

'I'm going to try, William,' was all she had said. It had been difficult, and selling to Faversham was still an unfulfilled dream. But Beth Parslow's clover vinegar, Indian soy and walnut catsup were in steady demand for Mrs Parslow Senior's post office shop. Then, greatly daring, she branched out into glycerine jelly for the skin, and polishing pastes. But it was hard work.

However, one chapter of Beth's life had not closed.

Beth clearly remembered the day that it reopened and reflected on how strange life was that it could bring such whirligigs of fortune. After Sylvie left they had managed alone for two months. Then one day Beth, heavy with child, had looked up from polishing the floor, conscious of someone watching her.

'You ought not to be doing that, Mrs Parslow.' Hetty Didcot stood before her, an old-fashioned black-quilted mantle clutched round her for warmth, a bright orange feather stuck jauntily in her wide-brimmed hat.

'Thank you, Mrs Grayston. I'll manage,' Beth had snapped back automatically.

'You allus were stiff-necked,' remarked Hetty without animosity. 'Come now, give us the cloth. That the polish?' She seized the jar and rag from Beth's astonished hand and set to work. Within ten minutes the floor shone, the task complete.

'Thank you,' said Beth awkwardly, wary but too weak to protest.

'I heard you was looking for a barmaid,' said Hetty slowly.

Beth was suddenly fully alert. 'No!'

Hetty flushed at her tone. 'I'd make a good barmaid.'

'I don't want your sort in here.' Hetty had left rebuffed without another word. Was it hurt that Beth had seen on her face? If so, she refused to recognise it.

'You were hard on her, Beth,' said William quietly afterwards. 'She's a good worker, so I've heard. You're prejudiced, that's all. You think about it. Past's over and we need a barmaid.'

'She's loose,' said Beth defensively.

'I'm thinking she's had a hard life, Beth. Maybe she were flighty when she was younger, but she had a bad time with that husband of hers. And now he's gone. It's difficult to live down an old reputation, Beth.'

She turned away.

'Beth – you hear a lot of things behind a bar, and it did seem to me you might have been what you might call jealous of her at times. Perhaps you didn't get to think about her side of things.'

'William,' said Beth violently, 'why, oh why, do you have to be so *reasonable*?'

Somehow, however, later that morning she had found herself walking along the narrow pathway to Hetty's cottage. The cottage was small, one up, one down, half lathe, half clapboard, badly in need of paint and repair. Several peg tiles were missing from the roof. Inside, though, it was spotless, as Beth noted when Hetty opened the door. Hetty's face darkened when she saw her visitor. Beth kept her eyes resolutely from the toddler who plucked at her skirts.

'Mam, who's that?'

'I've come to apologise, Mrs Grayston,' said Beth stiffly. 'I spoke hastily. I hope you'll forgive me.' Pure surprise crossed Hetty's face, though not scorn. Emboldened, Beth went on: 'And I've come to say if you want to be barmaid, we'd like to have you. 'Twon't be big money at first, 10s a week and your food while you're there, but we'll increase during the hopping.'

Hetty's undoubtedly painted mouth had fallen open. 'Reckon I'll come then,' she said slowly. 'Mrs Parslow, I need the job, see.' She hesitated. 'But I don't need it that much. Seeing as 'ow you'll be employing me, I'd best say my piece afore I take on the job. We have had some hard words between us over the years, but we ought to leave that behind us. We've both had a hard time – my Jim's gone, you know that – gone off Shanghai way and won't be back he says. And there's always that old business between us. We'll have to forget all that. I'll work well for you, Mrs Parslow, but nothing personal, nothing personal at all. We'll leave that out of it, if you please.'

Hetty had worked well and hard at the bar, leaving Beth more time to work on building up her trade in preserves and wine. Hetty was popular with the customers, her dresses not overlow nor her ways overloud. Whatever society she might keep at the cottage did not accompany her to the pub. What Beth did not see, she could ignore. There had been but one difficult moment. The arrival of the new barman a year ago. Now used to organising everything behind the bar, with the help of William as cellarman and Beth as stocktaker, Hetty saw no need for a new barman. But William had been adamant. Perhaps he saw the fatigue in Beth's eyes when, exhausted by the birth of Owen, she had to struggle back to work in the pub. Perhaps he needed another man around the place. Hetty had been even less amenable when she saw who it was . . .

The hop-pickers had left early that season. Picking had been swift and the harvest good, and the 'foreigners' had departed a few days earlier than usual, back to the East End, some still with proceeds from the hop-picking, some penniless again but happy. They had left in boisterous fashion, the sound of their song left floating on the wind as the Hop-pickers' Special drew out – leaving but one behind.

'What be you doing here, Ben?' said William amazed,

interrupted in the midst of the delicate task of adding the yeast to the fermenting tun for the batch of Ovenden Mild. 'Miss the train, did 'ee?'

'Nah,' said Ben, fingering his neck-scarf. 'Thought maybe I'd hang me 'at up a while 'ere. That wort's still too 'ot to take the yeast, Mr Parslow.'

'We're not open till ten,' William pointed out, annoyed at this slur on his expertise. 'And how come you're such an expert on Ovenden Mild?'

'Other side o' the bar,' said Ben succinctly. 'And used to work in a brewery, see?'

William frowned. 'You want to work *here*, Ben?'

'That's right, gov.'

'We need a cellarman,' William said doubtfully. 'I'll have to talk it over with Beth. Meanwhile, as you're so knowledgeable, take hold of this pail and pour it in the tun.'

Yet, somehow, by the time Beth arrived it had all been arranged. Love of country air was Ben's professed reason for staying, now that his wife Gladys was expecting. Whether there was more to fear in Whitechapel than the difficulties he might find in Shepham they did not enquire. Apart from some initial animosity from Hetty, jealous of sharing her limelight, he fitted in astonishingly well.

At first the villagers found it difficult to accept the transition of alien hopper to Shepham resident, but they gradually came to accept him simply because he ignored the fact that he was being treated warily. His wife took in washing at which she proved so adept that the Shepham women ceased to scorn the idea of a dirty London hopper doing anything and began to look to their laurels. Their five-year-old son, Daniel, was beginning to talk in a strange mixture of Kentish and cockney, and the eighteen-month-old baby was regarded as a Shephamite by right.

New faces had thus slipped into old ways, and to Beth standing under the mulberry tree that spring day in 1901, with her children around her, it seemed that things must ever be so and a wave of thankfulness swept over her.

'Run along in now, Elizabeth,' said William firmly. 'I've to speak to your mother.' Elizabeth looked interested. 'About the accounts.' Her face fell, and she ran off.

'I've a letter for 'ee, Beth,' he went on with no inflection in his tone as he extricated a square white envelope from his apron pocket. 'London postmark.' She frowned. 'With a crest,' he continued.

'A crest?' she repeated. A tremor of unease stole over her. William felt it too, she was sure, for he did not look at her as he handed her the letter. 'Don't go, William,' she said sharply, as he turned to go inside again. 'There's no secrets between us.'

Yet her fingers trembled slightly as she opened the envelope and took out the stiff sheet of white paper. Her eyes went straight to the signature. Rupert. *Sir* Rupert Bonner. His father must have died and he had inherited the baronetcy then. Her stomach muscles relaxed a little. What had she been hoping – or fearing?

'It's from Rupert,' she said to William flatly. 'Rupert Bonner. You remember. He wants to come to stay a night or two. Tuesday next.'

William regarded her steadily. 'And you, what do you think Beth? Wise, is it?'

'It's a long time now, William,' said Beth. 'We've two

children. We've something we've built ourselves here at the Wheatsheaf. Not just what we inherited. 'Tis nothing to me whether Rupert Bonner comes.' Yet her fingers clutched tightly at the stiff paper.

'But he were a part of it all. And he wanted to wed you.' His voice had relaxed and his face softened nevertheless.

'He didn't care for me,' said Beth. ''Twas a business arrangement, for convenience at a bad time. You've nothing to worry about on that score.'

'That I know,' said William. 'We've done well, Beth, haven't we? Well enough?'

Beth looked at the wistaria coming into leaf and beginning to establish itself once more on the walls of the old inn, and heard the two shouting children. 'Yes, William, we have. And Rupert shall be welcome here.'

Yet for all her calm words she found herself making extra careful preparations for his room, filling bowls with pot-pourri, turning down the sheets herself with special care, placing lavender beneath the pillows, as many jobs as she could think of to drive from her mind the image of the Rupert of the past and to fill it with thoughts of his present visit.

Whenever that stilled nerve deep inside her stirred she quelled it fiercely, fearfully, but finally the thought would not be denied. *He would have news of Richard.* 'Tis curiosity, that's all, she told herself firmly. I'd just like to know what happened, how he fared. But when Elizabeth upset the pomatum mixture she was preparing for William, the child was surprised not to be scolded as rigorously as she expected by her mother.

She would not think of him. She would not. He had

chosen his life and she hers. The pain of those first months agonisingly imagining him in Pippin's arms, longing for him still, had passed into a numbness that she had welcomed as a friend. She had trained herself, if her thoughts were treacherous and turned to Richard Lyle, to think of him objectively. He was no doubt a father by now, a successful barrister, a model husband, with never a thought to spare for the wild days of youth. If he and Pippin came to visit Medlars, she never saw them, nor heard word of it, and she presumed that it was more likely that the Squire - she still could not think of him as Father - visited them in London. She and Hetty spoke only of the Wheatsheaf and its business - never a word of Richard Lyle. And so it would, and must, remain.

Rupert had changed in five years. Beth wondered if she had changed as much, if time had marked her face in the same way. The lines of his thin face gave it a character that had been absent in the young student. But he'd been a qualified lawyer for at least two years now, as well, presumably, as running the estate.

'Beth.'

The moment he spoke her sudden reticence fled. He was still Rupert, however severe his city clothes made him look.

'I thought you'd have had one of these new-fangled motor cars now, and here you are arriving by Mr Mann's cab,' she joked, to hide her shyness at seeing him again.

He smiled. 'I do have one but I thought the London, Dover and South-Eastern would get me here more reliably. I didn't fancy being stuck on Charing Hill dressed like this.' He had flung his ulster over the back of a chair and she looked admiringly at the well-cut morning coat and striped trousers and severe Whitehall collar.

'Well, you look different from a hop-picker, that's for sure.'

'I came straight down from a meeting in London,' he said, as if in apology for his un-Shephamlike clothing.

'Business? Lawyers' meeting?'

'No. Something else.' He did not seem disposed to continue. All the time he was looking at her, as though his mind was elsewhere. 'I'm sorry to stare so, Beth, it's just that, I didn't expect it to be such a shock seeing you again.'

'I've changed that much?'

'No – yes,' he paused, searching for the right words. 'You're handsomer now than you were five years ago, your beauty's settled down, more serene, but you've lost –'

'I know what I've lost,' she interrupted quickly. 'But perhaps that's a good thing.' She had not reckoned that, whatever she felt about resurrecting the past, Rupert might not feel the same. Might even *want* to talk about it.

'I'm sorry –'

'Don't apologise, Rupert. No need for that. But I – ' she hesitated – 'those times are dead. I've a new life now. I'm happy –'

Owen bounded through the door, followed by William in hot pursuit. 'Now I told you,' he was shouting, 'your mother's got a friend in there. She don't want you –' But the two-year-old, not unnaturally, took no notice.

'Good to see you again, Mr Rupert - Sir Rupert, I should say,' said William gruffly, his face flushed.

Rupert crossed to him and shook his hand. 'It's good of you to have me, William - and no sirs in Shepham. I hoped I was amongst friends here.' William looked more cordial, as Rupert continued: 'The Wheatsheaf looks prosperous. You've done a wonderful job.'

'We manage,' said William shortly.

'No, more than that,' Rupert persisted. 'I'm sure you still have difficulties here, but the place looks loved, cared for – a home.' His eyes wandered round the bar wistfully.

'Aye,' said William simply. 'You're right. It's a home.'

Rupert stretched his legs out in front of the fire which, for all it was May, still flamed in the hearth, lit, he suspected, for his benefit. He had changed into a velvet smoking jacket, and the lines of tension were already fading from his face. Surrounded by the old oak panelling and beams, the smell of beeswax mingling with the applewood log smoke, he was immediately transported back to a world he'd thought had past. When he had come he had vowed that what lay ahead was to be a new beginning for him; only the future would be important. He had known that to include Beth in his plans would be difficult, but had determined to surmount the problem. Now he realised it might be more difficult than he had thought. He had not reckoned with his own nature, that simply being back in Shepham might strip the years off him relentlessly, and expose the young student, raw, inexperienced, passive, the victim of others' actions. It was not going to be easy to remember he was the thirty-year-old man who was here to direct others, not to suffer.

The door opened, and a little four-year-old girl catapulted in, tumbled over, stood up, and stared. A grin crossed her face, lighting up the tempestuous brows to instant sunshine.

'Hello,' she said carefully. 'Mama said I wasn't to disturb you, so I'll just look. That's if you don't mind,' she added as a polite afterthought.

'Not at all,' Rupert replied equally politely. 'Would you not be more comfortable seated?'

This excess of politeness flummoxed his visitor.

'I'm Elizabeth,' she volunteered. There was a pause. 'Why are you staring at me? I said I was going to look at you.'

'I'm sorry,' said Rupert humbly. 'I – was admiring your eyes.'

'Why? Mama mostly looks at my hands, or my stockings because they're dirty.'

Why? Because the irrepressible twinkle in those dark eyes made him uneasy. The kind of uneasy spell that Richard Lyle had always cast over him, with the hypnotic charm that his daughter – for she could be no other's – already possessed. He told himself that Elizabeth was William's daughter by rights now. And so she must remain. Yet the thought of Richard Lyle rose unbidden into his mind. The death of his father had meant a welcome release from the obligation of being in close contact with Richard Lyle and his wife, an opportunity to break the ties easily and without rancour. He suspected Richard was as glad as he. Not for Richard had been the difficult struggle through penniless early days in chambers. With his usual luck, and some influence, he was already doing well in criminal law within two years of being called to the bar, and was already known for his flamboyant impassioned pleading that could hypnotise a jury. An up-and-coming man. He had seen them for the last time two years before, when he attended a party at their country home in Hampstead. He had stayed for a short while and then left, unable to bear the brittle charm of the new Pippin: fashionable, elegant, an admirable hostess – but where was the real woman? Had there ever been one? His last sight of Richard Lyle had been a reproachful gaze, part triumphant, part pleading and part the look of someone trapped. He had seen Richard's name in *The Times* since then, defending such and such, defending – never the prosecution, Rupert noted. His future was assured. The past left behind, he had settled down with Pippin to a brilliant career, with their three-year-old son – and, as he had read in the press, a new daughter born three months ago.

As he gazed solemnly at the little girl in front of him, Beth appeared, forbidding in her best evening blouse and blue chine silk skirt. Elizabeth cast one look, clearly debating whether to stay to argue the matter with her mother or to disappear, and chose the latter course.

Without saying a word, Beth set down Rupert's dinner on the small mahogany table, busying herself with the arrangement of plates and knives and forks, perhaps staving off the inevitable moment when the purpose of his visit should be revealed, lest it bode some change to the ordered existence on which she depended.

'Beth, sit a while.'

'I can't – I –'

'Please.' Beth reluctantly sat down. 'You've two very lovely children, you and William,' said Rupert naturally.

She looked at him gratefully. 'Yes,' she said, simply.

He looked at the plate of hot dressed crayfish in front of him. 'You've lost none of your touch as a hostess, Beth. Do you still cook bloaters for the hoppers?'

'No, they cooks their own,' she smiled. 'I've grown wiser now.'

'Beth, I want you to come for a walk with me after I've finished. There's something I have to ask you.'

She grew rigid. 'Not to do with Elizabeth, is it then?' suddenly fearful. She had seen the way Rupert looked at her.

'No, nothing to do with her or – with the old days.'

She relaxed. 'If William doesn't mind, then.'

She did not have as much time now to tend the garden, but the lilac was in bloom and the trees proud in their spring growth. They walked out in the dusk through the orchard, the apple blossom scattering around them, its strong scent filling the air. 'No bees now?' he asked, glancing at the empty hives huddled together in one corner.

'No, that was Father's pleasure,' she said sadly. 'Rupert, tell me why you've come now.'

He took her hand. 'Come, Beth. I want to show you

something. He led her through the orchard gate, up the gentle slope of the meadow till they stood on the height of the downs overlooking the valley below, and the hills around.

'You see that?' Rupert pointed to the east. 'That building?'

'Chartboys, you mean?' she said puzzled, straining her eyes in the dusk to where the huge old house stood outlined against the evening sky. 'Where old Lady Charing used to live?'

'Yes. It's mine.'

'*Yours*?' She gaped at him. 'You mean, you inherited it when she died. I didn't know.'

'No, I bought it.'

She said nothing, and he looked at her anxiously. 'You don't mind, do you, Beth. You don't resent my living so near? I always liked Shepham and –'

'But I don't understand,' she said bewildered. 'What about your home in Buckinghamshire? I thought you'd inherited the house and estate there? Have you sold it? Why Shepham? Not because of Pippin?' She could have bitten her tongue out.

'No,' he replied stiltedly. '*Not* because of Pippin. Oddly enough, nothing whatsoever to do with that time, except that I came to know and love Shepham then. It's something quite different.'

He smiled crookedly at her. 'It's a long story, Beth, but I want you to understand it. Because I want you to be a part of it.'

'*Me*?' she asked weakly, her old fears sweeping over her. She wanted to fight him, tell him to leave her; not to awaken her with memories of her past or talk of the future. Her future was clear. She had set it out.

'Yes. You. You see, Chartboys is mine, but my main home must remain in Buckinghamshire because of the entail on the estate. I intend to use Chartboys for something quite different – a sanatorium for tuberculosis – for consumptive patients.'

Whatever she had expected, it was not this. The idea was too alien to absorb at once.

'But why, why? You're not a doctor.'

'When I asked you to marry me, Beth, you thought I was being chivalrous; an idle offer made in a difficult period for both of us. You were right, we probably wouldn't have been happy, I couldn't have run an inn. But you were wrong too. I knew I had deep roots here in Shepham that had nothing to do with Pippin. That something here, in the very air, answered a need in me. It provided a peace I had never known. The air is wonderful on the downs, and it's air that consumptives need, not warmth. It's so healthy here – look at the way the hoppers return, year after year, pale, sick after their year in London. They come here for six weeks and go back different people. The rich pay the earth to go to sanatoriums in Switzerland – or to the big hotels along the south coast, but they can get just the same here, with all the peace and quiet that Kent can give them. What better place than Chartboys with its view into the infinite blue beyond.' He swept on, almost oblivious of her.

'Do you know that last year alone fifty-three thousand people died in this country of tuberculosis? And do you know that although doctors *know* what causes it, and have known for fifteen years, there is no hope whatsoever of a cure in sight? That they even know how eventually it will be cured – but goodness knows when that will be? That the only medicine ever to be effective is just cod liver oil, and rest and quiet, with gradual exercises. That the only cure is to lead a different kind of life and people have to be taught how to live that different kind of life, if they are to fight the disease successfully?'

'But why? Rupert, why you?'

His face was overcast with emotion.

'Is there consumption in your family, Rupert?' she asked gently. 'Your father?'

'No, Beth. But my son –'

'Your *son*?' she interrupted.

He smiled wanly. 'I did not mean to be so dramatic, Beth. Yes, I have a son.'

'And your wife, Rupert?'

'No, I have no wife now,' he said quietly.

His eyes were fixed on the grey crenellated outline of Chartboys. She said nothing. He would speak if he would. They were silent for perhaps five minutes before he spoke, first slowly, with difficulty, then more easily as if the words no longer pained him.

'Her name was Marie, Beth. She did not have your strength. She was loving and lovely, good of heart and pure of soul, with the kind of honesty that you would recognise. She had all the qualities that I thought Pippin had, till I discovered differently. She gave me herself, trusted me in everything, gave me her love, and gave me my son. And I couldn't love her in return.' The last words were wrung out in an anguish of pain. 'God forgive me, I still love Pippin. The guilt, Beth, the guilt – can you understand?'

She shivered, 'Oh yes, I understand, Rupert,' and

closed her mind to the thought, closed her mind to all save William.

'She died, Beth. She cheated me of the chance to make things right for her.'

'She died of consumption?'

'Yes.' The monosyllable was abrupt, ending the conversation, so Beth thought. But he continued. 'When she came out of the sanatorium they told her not to have a baby. She knew how much I wanted one, so she didn't tell me. When she found she was pregnant, she came to me overjoyed, but the doctor told me that she should have an abortion. If she had the baby, the disease would in all probability flare up again and kill her. I tried everything to persuade her, Beth. Believe me. But she was adamant. She would have the baby, the doctors might be wrong. I was cruel and told her the chances were the child would develop the disease. It hurt her, but she still went on; said the doctors didn't know everything. But they did. It killed her, less than a year after our son was born.'

The ravages of grief were evident now on his face.

'And now you're punishing yourself because you think you didn't try hard enough to persuade her to have the abortion,' said Beth quietly.

'You always did see things clearly, Beth.'

'Not always,' she said bitterly.

The dew was damp, rising through her clothes, but she was so wrapped up in his story that she did not notice. 'But how did she get consumption, Rupert? Is it in her family?'

'No, in her background,' he said simply. 'The conditions she grew up in. She was a hopper, you see.'

'A hopper.' Beth stared at Rupert, scarcely seeing in him now the pale shadow of Richard Lyle that he had been those years ago. How youth can be blind. She had been so oblivious, wrapped up in her own troubles, that she did not even take time to notice Rupert whom she had casually called her friend.

'But - *you* - married a hopper? What did your father say?'

'He was livid, but he was won over by Marie. Everyone was. She was so kind, Beth. All that time when Pippin was - I thought I'd go out of my mind. That night when Richard came back free and I found out for sure that I'd been right - that Pippin was to marry him - I wanted to kill myself. I went down to the river - and she found me there. I'd often seen her looking at me, I'd helped her a few times - she wasn't strong - and she developed I suppose a sort of gratitude, devotion, quite undeserved. Somehow she was always there. And when she found me that night - well, she was so loving. I didn't seduce her, Beth. She *wanted* me to love her.'

'And then came your son?'

'Oh no,' he said. 'After that first time, I was careful. When we went back to London I missed her - and I went on to find her. Selfish. Just selfishness. She said it would be bad for me as time went on, that I would need a different kind of woman. I told her I didn't need any woman, but that she could -' he swallowed '- come and live near me in London if she liked, go on seeing me, but that no one could mean anything to me because of Pippin. She understood that, but she loved me so much she thought she could only bring harm to me by continuing to see me. So she went away. I realised then how much I missed her – selfish again – I found it harder and harder, not easier, to keep on seeing Pippin and I thought marriage would help. *Any* marriage. If it's fashionable to marry a Gaiety Girl, I thought, why not a hopper? I think I just wanted to break every convention there is. I married her and was happier than I deserved ever to be and didn't realise it. She died two years ago.'

'And you're opening the hospital for her sake?'

'Partly,' he said. 'And for my son's.'

'Your son has inherited the disease?' she asked in horror.

'No, they think now the disease can't be inherited. But children of an infected parent are more likely to develop the disease. He shows no sign yet, but at his age he wouldn't. He was born early and has never been strong though, and I want him to be able to fight it. That's why I want him to be brought up here on the downs, with their fresh clean winds sweeping across. Buckinghamshire is lovely, but it's not Kent. I can't have him at Chartboys though – it wouldn't be right to surround him with sickness.' He took her hand and held on to it. 'Beth, would you let him live at the Wheatsheaf with you? Till he's old enough to go to boarding school?'

Seeing her flabbergasted face, he added, 'I'd pay for him, of course, and he's a nice child, delicate, but –'

'Rupert,' she said, laughing and crying all together. 'Steady. You're as impetuous as –'

'No,' he said, forestalling her lest the name slip out and chill the air. 'No, I'm not impetuous. I've thought this all out very carefully.'

'You're a romantic then.' She shook her head. 'You

haven't thought carefully enough. I could bring him up if William agrees. He'd be company for Owen. But we can't bring him up as a gentleman – fit to be your heir. It isn't fair on the child. If he goes to boarding school after being with us, he won't know the ways of the gentry. You're not thinking clear.'

'He'd be alive though,' said Rupert.

'Maybe. But he could live in a lot of places other than a country pub for that,' said Beth bluntly. 'You've some other reason as well as good country air and cooking, haven't you?'

'Perhaps,' said Rupert. The shades of the dark were gathering around them. Beth shivered in the cold air, but he did not notice. 'I want you to help me, be involved in Chartboys, Beth. I want you to be part of my life here. I can't be here all the time. I know you won't leave the Wheatsheaf of course, but I want you to be an overall manageress – to oversee the place when I'm not there. There'll be a board of patrons of course – I couldn't manage all the costs myself – and a head matron, but it needs another eye, a caring all-seeing eye to make sure it's being run as I want it run.'

Beth was very still. Something strong leapt within her. An unaccustomed thrill of excitement. Something new. Something that would be different every day, a gate into a new world. But that gate was bolted.

She shook her head sadly. 'You're kind to think of me, Rupert, but you know it's impossible. There's William and the pub – not to mention the children. Besides, I've dreams of my own,' she added rather wistfully. Dreams she saw no prospect of ever fulfilling.

'You've staff –'

'I threw my lot in with William and the Wheatsheaf five years ago. I can't go back on that decision now.'

'Before you say no finally, come and look round the place with me tomorrow. Please. Please, Beth.'

'Very well.' No harm there surely? No, no harm. But maybe there was. There might be more to this than just his son. Perhaps Pippin's shadow still hovered over them. Did Rupert want to cling on to Beth – as a reminder of her? But this brought with it too hurtful thoughts, dreams that she had ignored for the past five years and suppressed again as she blew out her candle later that night and climbed in beside William, slumbering peacefully beside her.

CHAPTER NINE

'I feel proper daffy dressed up like this,' grumbled William, as the brougham turned into the Chartboys' drive. Elizabeth was hanging out of the window with excitement and Owen was crying loudly because he could not see. William ran a hand gingerly round the collar of his evening bow tie.

'Rupert told you there's no need,' Beth pointed out shortly. William had made such a ridiculous fuss already about leaving the pub for once in the fully capable hands of Hetty and Ben.

'If we're going to have supper at the big house, then I'm going to be dressed proper,' William had said firmly, wriggling awkwardly in his corner. The dinner jacket was undoubtedly a shade too small. Hardly surprising, since it must have been one of the first ones ever made twenty years before and had been handed down as a souvenir from William's grandfather, who had served twice as a councillor. Beth fingered the folds of her own old blue charmeuse dress, ill-adapted to the new shape of corset. It was ridiculous. They were merely going to dinner with Rupert, coping with a makeshift staff commandeered from his town house – no doubt with some grumbling on their part. Beth stepped down from the brougham with care, determined not to give the slightest inch to the somewhat supercilious driver who clearly thought Kent a great social come-down after Buckinghamshire.

Rupert was standing on the front steps to welcome them; Beth noticed with relief that he too was dressed formally. She did not want William's great effort to pass in vain. The children seemed for once overawed by the vastness of the Chartboys' façade. Even Elizabeth clung to her mother's hand as they climbed the steps. Owen took one look at the stone lions and cried. William picked him up, pacified him and set him on his shoulder. It had been Rupert's idea the children should come. They should meet his son as well as Beth. It could do no harm, he had pointed out, no matter what Beth's final decision. Rupert took them into the one furnished room in the house, a small withdrawing room in which a temporary dining table had been imported.

'You've told William about my plans?' enquired Rupert.

'Everything, no secrets between us,' Beth replied, a trifle guardedly.

'Beth is to make up her own mind,' William said stiffly. 'We can manage at Wheatsheaf without her if she's a mind –'

'But, William –'

'And you told him about Arthur – my son?'

William turned a puzzled look on Beth who looked embarrassed. She had hoped this particular plan of Rupert's could wait until after tonight. 'What's this then?'

'No,' said Beth awkwardly. 'I told you, Rupert, 'tis

not fair on the child. There's nothing to discuss.'

'What is it then?' asked William implacably.

Rupert explained, while William listened, his face revealing nothing. 'So you see, William, why I said no,' said Beth firmly.

'Just for a year or two until he's seven, and goes to school,' said Rupert. 'What do you think, William?'

'Beth has the last word on this one,' said William loyally. 'I'm not against it, but 'tis her decision. I like plenty of children about the place.'

Beth flushed. She knew William wanted more children, but after Owen's birth she had failed to conceive again.

'But William,' said Beth in reproach, 'I –'

'Perhaps you should meet him straight away,' said Rupert quickly, pulling the bell rope by the marble fireplace.

The child entered reluctantly, peeping from behind his stoutly built nanny. He was fair, fairer even than Owen, and thin, with blue eyes too large for his small frightened face – or rather what could be seen of it as he remained hidden sucking his thumb behind the nurse. Seeing his father, his anxious face relaxed a little and he ran to him, burying his head in his father's embrace. Muffled sobs were his only response to Rupert's exhortations to greet the visitors.

'What's he crying for, Mama?' asked Elizabeth with interest.

'Hush, Elizabeth.'

But there was no quelling Elizabeth. She marched up to the heaving shoulders and thumped.

Indignant at this unfair approach, Arthur whirled

around. 'She hit me,' he wailed, more in surprise than hurt.

'Not very hard,' Elizabeth pointed out. 'It's silly to cry.'

Arthur's face puckered anew and grew even redder.

'Mama, he's just a crybaby,' pronounced Elizabeth and, losing interest, took Owen by the hand and disappeared towards the garden. Arthur, realising part of his audience had departed, decided to regain it, and after a moment trotted after them.

Beth expelled a sigh. 'I'm sorry, Rupert, I –'

'It's good for him,' said Rupert. 'Besides she's –' He broke off and an unguarded look passed between them, which William caught.

'Let's see the house,' was all he said.

The house was as unkempt as the grounds. Despite the best efforts of the staff, it was damp and unwelcoming. It seemed unlived in and unloved for many more years than was actually the case. Putting a brave face on it, Beth climbed the majestic marble staircase under the domed roof, the balustrade yielding slightly under her hand. The corridors were dusty, empty, silent; the rooms cavernous, badly in need of decorating; bathrooms non-existent. But Rupert saw none of this. 'This floor is for convalescent patients, with staff above. Windows opening onto the downs, light, fresh wallpaper – flowered. The west wing for the patients who are still ill, a few cottages in the grounds perhaps for extra patients, or staff – and a laboratory – we must have a laboratory for research eventually.'

'And what about the East Wing,' asked William, clearly impressed by his enthusiasm.

Rupert hesitated – then smiled awkwardly. 'The East Wing is for those who can't afford so much –'

'You're too generous, Rupert. You always were,' said Beth warmly.

'It's a board decision,' he said. 'I have a board of governors you see who will administer the funds and help our capitalisation. I could only afford the house, not to equip and run it too.'

'And they thought it a good idea?'

'Yes,' said Rupert stoutly. 'After a while,' he added honestly.

Beth laughed. 'But the world being as it is, won't your rich patients object to being side by side with people who are paying less for the same treatment? Won't it worry them – both sides – and when lack of worry is important in recovery, isn't that a bad thing?'

'Perhaps,' he said simply. 'But it would not be much of a memorial to Marie if I let people like her die without care that I could give them.'

William looked at Beth. Hitherto he had sat quiet in his chair. Now he said, 'Well, what do you think, Beth? I've no objection if you be of a mind.'

'No,' she said, more sharply than she meant. 'Rupert, I'm sorry, but I can't do it. My life is the Wheatsheaf and my children. If I work here, the Wheatsheaf will be neglected. I can't do it, Rupert, much as I'd like to. But,' she hesitated, glancing at William, 'I can do this. You've a lot of work to be done here, before this is going to be fit for patients. I'll help you get it ready, help you choose staff, decorations, furnishings, just until it's opened.'

'I thought that would be your answer,' he replied

sadly. 'But what have you decided about Arthur? Owen might like another boy to play with.'

'No,' she said violently, looking from one to the other. 'He needs to be with his own kind. You *must* see that, William? Rupert?'

But neither answered.

'Besides,' she went on recklessly, 'I believe you want me to do it for the wrong reasons. You want Arthur to be down here close to where Pippin used to live, to have a link –'

Rupert was the nearest to being angry that she had ever seen him. His lips compressed and he looked at her with bright challenging eyes, as he interrupted: 'And what of you, Beth? What of *your* reasons for refusing? Are you perhaps not scared to have my son?'

She cried out, flinching both from the truth and from the fact that William was witness to it. Mercilessly, Rupert had hit upon the source of her unease over Arthur: could she bear to see Elizabeth side by side with Rupert's son? She wanted no further link with that past life, nothing to remind her of Richard. She had managed to convince herself that Elizabeth was theirs, hers and William's. But with Arthur there how could she? William gazed stolidly at the floor, Beth hid her face in her hands, and Rupert stood watching her quietly.

It was Elizabeth who settled the matter.

'I've called him Mud,' she said happily, bursting through the library door and tugging after her a toddler scarcely recognisable under the thick coating of pond mud that adhered to every portion of him, and for the large smile which covered his small face under it. The name stuck as close as the filth.

And so it was that Mud Bonner came to Shepham.

'What do you think, then, William?' She had to break the silence that had fallen between them. William continued to brush his teeth – for longer than usual – his broad back turned to her.

'You're against it, then,' she went on relentlessly. No matter if this was the wrong moment, she had to have things straight before she went to bed – *their* bed.

'What do I think about what, Beth?' he replied, avoiding her eye as he turned at last.

'The hospital, me – oh, William, you know,' she went on impatiently.

'There'll be trouble,' he said matter of factly, drying his hands on the small towel, and climbing into bed. 'Folks won't like it.'

'Trouble?' she said, arrested in the act of pulling her nightdress over her head by this unexpected reply. 'What kind of trouble about opening a sanatorium?'

'A consumptives' sanatorium, Beth. You're not thinking straight. Folks'll think they can catch it.'

'But that's nonsense,' said Beth robustly. 'It's not a hospital, they won't have people with galloping consumption there. Anyway, you don't just *catch* consumption like measles. You have to live close to someone.'

'They won't like it, Beth,' said William obstinately. 'You mark my words.' And he blew out the candle and lay down.

Beth, still standing by the bed, stared at the back turned towards her feeling irrationally irritated with him. 'And what about me, William?' she demanded. He did not answer. 'Answer me, William. Do you mind my helping Rupert?'

He shot up in bed, his cheeks flushed. 'Now you listen to me, Beth. Yes, I mind, but 'tis your decision. You want to do it. You said you won't be up there once 'tis open because of me. Very good of you, but I reckon you'll be there all right. You'll see. You're restless, Beth. I seen it as soon as he arrived here, bringing the past with him. It won't do a bit of good whatever I say about it, or whatever I think about it. You'll be there.' He did not speak angrily. Merely resignedly.

Remorseful, she climbed into bed and put her arms round him. 'No, I won't, William. Am I really so contrary?'

'You can't help it, Beth,' he replied slowly, staring at the ceiling. 'You're like a caged bird. 'Tis all right when the hoppers are here. You're busy enough. Excitement, see. But other times when 'tis quiet and I like it best, you get bored. Dulled, like. Even the children don't keep you busy enough, I seen you, your eyes far away.'

She was alarmed. Had she even been aware of it? She had believed she was happy in the Wheatsheaf when there was little to do during the long winter evenings as hardly a soul came to the bar. Surely William must be wrong? Those odd restless thoughts, surely she had quelled them, not allowed them to show?

'Have I ever said I was bored?' she demanded, not gently now but urgently.

'No, Beth, you ain't. You don't have to. I known you too long. Now blow your candle out, girl, and let's get some sleep.'

But she was not satisfied. In the dark of the room she

spoke again in a low voice. 'You've made me happy, William. But you're right. Part of me *would* like to see what happens at Chartboys – it's exciting. To be in at the beginning. It might help the Wheatsheaf too –'

'Help the Wheatsheaf,' his voice was snorted in the dark. 'Having a lot of consumptives coming down here – that'll help trade a lot.'

'But they'll have friends, relations coming to see them,' her voice brightened. 'They'll need looking after –' Her old vision of the carriages with coronets outside the Wheatsheaf came to life once again. They would need food, beds – the Wheatsheaf Hotel. Perhaps now it was not such a dream. A wave of excitement surged over her; for an instant she was the Beth Ovenden of old. And suddenly the thought of Rupert's boy living there became possible, and at the remembrance of his small muddy face, a pleasure.

As if divining her thoughts, William reached out for her, to bridge the chasm that had briefly opened between them, and took her in his arms, fiercely and with a possessiveness she had rarely known from him before. It crossed her mind, briefly, afterwards, that he might be afraid of losing her. How little he knew her if so.

'There'll be trouble, Beth.'

The Squire paced round the library, echoing William's words. He often did pace, when Beth was around, as though he could not face her directly. By mutual, but unspoken agreement, they had kept their distance from each other at first after the tragedy, the problem of their future relationship too deep, too delicate for either to wish to face. It was made easier by the fact that Beth was busy at the Wheatsheaf in her early days of marriage and her pregnancy. When Elizabeth was born, the Squire – as she still thought of him – had sent bunches of grapes, gifts for the child. But he had not come to see her. So the chance was missed of their growing closer together, of their relationship becoming a reality. If ever Beth thought about it, she came back to one inescapable barrier: Pippin.

It was William who, when Elizabeth was two months old, had gently suggested to Beth she should take the baby to see him. She had refused at first. ''Tis our child, William.'

But meeting her eyes squarely, William had said, 'And his grandchild, Beth. You owe him the right to see her.'

'Owe him? I owe him nothing,' she said proudly.

'Then favour him, Beth, out of your generous heart.'

'Suppose he turns me away?' she said mutinously, not feeling in the least generous.

'Then you'll have done the right thing,' said William firmly. 'I'll come with you if you like.' And she had turned to him gratefully. They had taken Elizabeth, sleeping peacefully for once, one late spring day to Medlars.

'Thought you might like to see our first-born, Squire,' said William levelly.

The Squire had looked at them then at the baby, black curls already in evidence, a dimple hollowing her right cheek.

'She takes after Beth with her hair,' said William stolidly.

'Bonny,' said the Squire gruffly, turned away, then back again for a second look.

'And Beth and me was wondering, Squire, whether you'd stand for her at her baptism – be her godfather.'

Beth's eyes flew in astonishment to William. They had never discussed it, and she felt a moment's anger that she was being committed even to this insubstantial acknowledgement of their relationship.

At first the Squire had been speechless; then he took another look at Elizabeth and said slowly, 'I'm obliged to you, Parslow.' He hesitated, 'I'll do it.'

Since then they had taken Elizabeth, and then Owen as well, regularly to Medlars once a month, and the ritual of those visits replaced for Beth memories of that older, more established pattern of walking up Medlars' drive to see Pippin. All mention of Pippin was avoided. Then a month ago when the door of his study was open, Beth saw a photograph of Pippin standing with a sailor-suited toddler by her side, and a baby in her arms, clutching at her fashionable new look dress with its absurd 'S' shape. Don't suit her, thought Beth instantly, she never did have any taste. There was no husband in the photograph, and the lurch in Beth's stomach subsided. But her imagination peopled it with his figure, a tall handsome man, the wildness gone from his eyes, replaced with a proud soft look as he stood, proprietorially, with his family. All that night she lay awake, then disciplined herself and put it from her mind.

She had never managed to talk on easy terms with the Squire. It was a problem both avoided. A barrier existed which neither seemed willing to break. If Pippin came to visit Medlars Beth did not see or hear of her, and as Squire was away in London for long spells Beth presumed that he stayed with them in their London home.

So it was rare for Squire to summon her to Medlars and, curious, she had obeyed the call at once. After much humming and hawing he had come to the point. Chartboys. 'Can't you talk him out of it, Beth?'

'No, Squire, I can't. And I wouldn't want to. The village should be proud to have a sanatorium here.'

'Proud? The old traditions going, Chartboys being turned into a commercial establishment. And you think Shepham should be proud?'

'Rupert's doing something to help *everybody* – not just the rich, but East Wing's going to be for the poorer people.'

'*What*?' The Squire's eyes bulged. 'The fellow's a crazy idealist, Beth. I tell you, don't get mixed up in it. There's going to be trouble, and if you're involved it will be worse.'

'Why?' she asked, startled.

'Because Hamlin's out to stop Sir Rupert's plans.'

'Hamlin? But why? It's nothing to do with him or the brewery.'

'He wanted Chartboys for himself,' said the Squire grimly, 'Rupert Bonner outbid him. He'll not forget that in a hurry. He'd like Medlars too. But he knows he can't get rid of me. For one thing, I've shares in Teynham's. Not a big stake, but something at least.'

'But there's nothing he can *do*, Squire,' Beth pointed out robustly. 'He can rant and roar all he likes, but, 'tis all agreed now, it can go ahead.'

'He can stir up enough trouble in the village and Faversham way so that Sir Rupert can't make it a success,' said the Squire, 'I don't say he will, mind. But there are plenty of ways. Get the local shopkeepers stirred up, so that he can't get supplies, or people to work for him.'

'Then Rupert can get everything from Canterbury,' Beth said.

'He'll think of something, if he can. There's that right of way, for a start. Just be careful, Beth.'

The Squire was right. Whether Hamlin had anything to do with it or not, there were mutterings in the village, heated conversations in the shops that stopped as Beth entered, the subject being abruptly changed. Finally she took the bull by the horns. As she went in to the butcher's, she caught the words, 'Ain't right. Bringing death to village, that's what 'tis'.

Daniel Harbutt glanced up from his angry chopping that seemed to be emphasising his feelings, and stopped whatever his reply had been going to be.

'Do you agree, Mr Harbutt?' asked Beth firmly.

Harbutt lay down his chopper, rested his hands on the wooden bench and said slowly, 'Reckon I do, Mrs Parslow. I'm a good Christian. I want to see these folks well again, much as anyone. But I don't want my Jane catching it. Nor me, neither. That's the truth.'

'But it's not catching, Mr Harbutt.' From their blank response she knew they did not believe her.

'Then why did my sister's kiddies both die of it, then? Tell me that, Beth,' demanded one of the customers.

'It's in the family – that's what Sir Rupert says,' answered Beth. 'I'm no doctor, but I believe him.'

But it was clear they did not. The subdued protests went on: 'Don't hold with it, 'tis disease, ain't it. We got the Kent and Canterbury Hospital. What we want more for?' That was the general view. But gradually the mutterings grew less and, as the months went by, more local people were employed on the rebuilding at Chartboys. Beth was relieved, sure now that the plan was accepted. There was no sign of Hamlin.

'Rotten,' said Rupert in disgust, poking at an ornate cornice in one of the bedrooms, 'Nothing been done to it for decades.' He sighed. 'I thought this wing was sound enough. But no!'

'Are you sorry you started, Rupert?'

'No,' he said, 'I'll never be sorry. I'm just impatient for it all to be ready, and every time we start on a new room the workmen are reporting yet more problems. We'll never be ready by May at this rate.'

'It's only November yet, Rupert. There's another six months. Surely it doesn't matter if everything's not perfect right away?'

'Yes, it does,' he said simply.

'Even the East Wing?'

She'd meant it as a joke. The East Wing was in the worst repair of all, having not been lived in for forty years.

'Especially the East Wing,' replied Rupert firmly. 'You see, I haven't fully explained about that wing – I'm going to call it the Marie Bonner Wing.' Avoiding her eye, he went on, 'It's going to be entirely free, Beth. It's for people from the East End, hoppers in particular with consumption, the kind of people who were her family and neighbours.'

'But –'

'Have you ever been there, Beth?' he asked fiercely.

'Seen how they live. No, of course you haven't. I hadn't till she took me. Whole families in one room, no furniture, no heating, no water except the damp in the walls, sick people sleeping by healthy ones – the children dying before they're a year old, it's dreadful. And this is the twentieth century. They have no money for the doctor and the doctors that will come for a promise or for nothing are very few – there are few hospitals, and none for those already dying of the disease. Oh, the hopelessness in their eyes, Beth. This is the whole reason for this place. We'll care for the rich and their money will help those with none.'

She stared at him speechlessly.

'Do you think I'm crazy, Beth?'

'I think you're impractical, Rupert. It's a wonderful idea – but it won't work,' she said despairingly.

'Why?' he demanded. 'Why shouldn't it work?'

'Because the people the hospital will depend on, lords and ladies, and rich people and such like, won't like being next to East Enders –'

His mouth took on the obstinate twist that Beth was beginning to know. 'When they get used to the idea, they will. They're all sick. And they'll all get the best advice, the best treatment –'

'It won't work.'

'Beth, what's happened to you? I thought you'd be the first to champion me. It's not like you to be so pessimistic. What happened to the Beth that fought so hard for her own? Now you're condemning me for doing the same thing.'

He was right, she admitted to herself. The old Beth would not have hesitated for a moment. The odds were against it working, but she had never let the odds worry her in the past.

'Very well, Rupert. I'll do all I can to help make it work.'

The next six months were a whirl of ordering workmen about when Rupert was not there, since Rupert was absent much of the time at hospitals seeking patients and staff.

Slowly the place came right: the kitchens modernised with Barnard, Bishop and Barnard professional ranges and electric ovens; the laundry enlarged and equipped with Sellars' washing machines and electrical items; lavatories and bathrooms installed; furniture bought, comfortable beds, discreet commodes; the bedrooms were re-decorated; heavy-coloured Victorian hangings gave place to lighter florals as befitted the new century. The lighter the colours the lighter the heart, Beth had said, and with doubts about her sanity the builders had departed to obey her wishes. She had trips to London to Messrs Gamages and Whiteleys, wishing that the kitchens of the Wheatsheaf might be equally provided.

Finding staff proved an easier problem than the Squire had forecast. When it came to earning money, Shepham folk decided to put their principles aside. Kitchen staff, porters, odd-job men, housemaids, gardeners – there was little problem with any of these, despite the murmurings of discontent that still occasionally flared in the village. Jobs were welcomed wherever they were, and the dissenting voices were suddenly stilled with the lure of Rupert's fair wages. With the nursing staff, however, it was different.

'No, Beth, I won't take any local girls, unless they're

fully trained by the Nightingale method. If not all Queen's Nurses, then they should at least have been to one of the training schools. We'll give them their own uniform - you can decide that. Now, about the gardeners, Beth.' He swept on, not giving her a moment to intervene.

'You want *me* to engage gardeners?' Beth saw the funny side.

'No, it's serious, Beth. Don't laugh. When the patients start recovering they need exercise, gentle walking to the village and back maybe –'

Beth thought of the Squire's warning, 'Perhaps the other way, Rupert, might be better.' But he paid no heed.

'And gardening. I want you to arrange the gardening so that they can help just a little - the flower gardens, maybe.' He stared out over the bleak wilderness of Chartboys' gardens, deadened by the winter and by neglect.

'We need Bill the hedger,' said Beth decidedly.

'Hedger - but –'

'Bill's a gardener, too, 'Course he's over seventy now, but he could advise.'

Rupert was clearly doubtful, but Beth was adamant.

'The old orangery - that is for the patients who are well on the way to recovery to sit during the winter and spring.'

She looked at the broken glass and empty pots, the odd piece of statuary flaunted nakedly in its desolation. 'Yes, Rupert, I'll see to it,' she murmured resignedly.

And so it continued until under the trees at the back of the house, where they were sheltered, a few daffodils struggled to emerge from the grip of the winter. Otherwise the landscape appeared still dead, poised to emerge triumphant at a hint of warmth, but as yet silent.

Two more months, thought Beth gloomily. Would it ever be ready? The house smelled everywhere of paint; it was in her nostrils, in her throat all day long. She had developed an acutely sore throat which kept her away from Chartboys for several days while she fretted impatiently. At the Wheatsheaf William was busy with the spring brewing and had no time to listen to her problems. When she returned to Chartboys, it was to find that apparently nothing had progressed. The house still looked an empty shell.

'Don't worry, Beth,' Rupert had said cheerfully. 'It only needs people in it to bring it to life.'

What did he see, thought Beth? Warmth, colour, enthusiasm, where she saw merely emptiness? Was the old Beth so dead, that she had no vision any more, no strength to make dreams come true, even one as worthwhile and challenging as Chartboys? Yesterday had been a dispiriting day. The new chef had come down from London, a tall thin man with a lugubrious expression and a cockney accent. He appeared supercilious, offhand, but his eyes darted everywhere and his demands were exacting. By the time he had departed, orders issued, she felt like a dried-out sponge.

Within a few days, however, a certain excitement did take hold of her, a tension in the air she could not ignore. Chartboys Sanatorium. Things were beginning to happen. It was beginning to assume a reality. Like the spring, it was waking up. But it had been a long, hard winter, coping with her frequent visits to Chartboys in the cold damp weather, her duties at the Wheatsheaf – and the difficulties of a strange child in the house.

Nervous, shy, anxious to please, Mud crept around like a ghost. She had started by calling him Arthur. Then, a month ago, they had celebrated his fourth birthday. Arthur Bonner had greeted his coming of age in the children's stakes by falling in the stream and arriving at the Wheatsheaf door for his party covered in slime. As he waited anxiously for wrath to fall on his head, 'Oh, *Mud*,' was all she could say. At which his small face broke into smiles. He was accepted. She still heard him crying at nights and went often to comfort him, resolving that she would send him back to Rupert at the first opportunity for his own sake. But before that opportunity came, she arrived one night to find Elizabeth had beaten her to it and was deeply involved telling him the story of Gawaine and the dragon, presumably to calm him. She had not intruded, and thereafter the two children slept in the same room. Beth was relieved, it freed a room for the guests that might or might not stay at the Wheatsheaf. Not that this was likely at present, for the Wheatsheaf was passing through its bleakest time of year, when people ceased to need the cheer of winter in the bar, but were not yet bitten with the bug of spring. But the warmth in the Wheatsheaf did not diminish, and Mud became an inextricable part of their family.

'Gizzards and gallstones, woman, what do you call this?'

Beth dropped the bottle she was holding, the unexpected, unfamiliar voice startling her, and caught it again just before it reached the ground and whirled round unsteadily and angrily.

Two even angrier eyes met hers and she decided not to say what she had intended.

'This,' he repeated, sweeping his arm round the room. The clarion voice belonged to a short, dark wiry man with black beard, large nose, gimlet eyes, wearing a Homburg hat at least one size too big for him – which he did not bother to remove – adding to the sinister effect. In one hand he held an Oxford stick with which he was gesticulating wildly; too wildly, for the matchbox and matches it contained in its handle were distributing themselves over the floor, a factor he impatiently waved aside.

'Who be you looking for, sir?' said Beth, completely flustered, and relapsing into Kentish idiom.

'I be looking, as you put it, young woman, for whoever's responsible for this monstrosity.'

Beth looked round the room with its oak shelves, carboys and shoprounds and the two rows of drug runs.

''Tis the dispensary,' she said with a frown.

'It may be a dispensary to you, madam. To me, to *me*, it is a – pop-shop!'

Beth stared at him as though he and the world were mad. 'A pawnbroker's?' she asked blankly, believing herself locked up with some lunatic.

'A half witted peasant,' said the man, casting his eyes and stick heavenwards, 'Pop shop, woman. Pop. Pop goes the weasel. Ginger beer. Fizz, fizz, fizz.' He made his point clearer, if it needed it, by making the popping sound of a cork.

Seven months of hectic activity had not blunted Beth's

spirit enough to take this. 'If you be from old Hamlin's brewery – sales, are you? – *out*! Out, out, *out*! We got our own suppliers. I met you town swells before. You and your fancy weskits,' she said with scorn, looking at the ornately embroidered garment that sat uncomfortably under an ordinary lounge suit. Not that this man cared much for sartorial appearance. He had other matters on his mind.

His eyes bulged. 'A brewer? You think I look like a *brewer*? I would have you know, madam, that I am Samuel Goldstein, doctor in charge of this establishment and I demand you take me to your employer, someone responsible for this disaster.'

'And I'm Mrs Parslow, and I'm the only person *responsible*, as you put it,' retorted Beth coldly, her heart sinking. She'd never believe it. This little prancing madman the new doctor? She'd never seen anyone quite so ugly. When Rupert said he had engaged a specialist, a brilliant doctor, she had envisaged a tall grave, serious man of calm quiet dignity.

'*You*?' echoed the man in equal horror.

There was a silence while they weighed each other up. Beth was suddenly all too conscious of her white pinafore – no longer white – of the hair escaping down her back from its confines, of the dust that no doubt adorned her face.

Suddenly the man smiled. A huge smile that lit up his ugly face showing white teeth gleaming above the black beard. For a moment a radiant charm flashed out. Then it was gone. 'Well, Mrs Parslow,' he rasped. 'Explain this monstrosity.' He rested his hands on the top of his stick.

Beth flushed with anger. 'I don't have to explain anything, Dr Goldstein. You're the doctor. Sir Rupert has put in a dispensary for you. He took good advice, but it can be changed if you wants. But what you can't change is *us*. If you are coming to live in Shepham, you can't be treating folks like they was dirt. Perhaps you do in London, but here we're people, no matter how poor we look, how simple to your eye. We goes by what people does, not what they look like. And we don't hold with rudeness, either.'

Goldstein looked at her in amazement. Then his attention was sidetracked by a bronchitis kettle which he studied with interest. As if her words had just registered, he said, 'Rude, Mrs Parslow?' in complete amazement. 'You think I was rude? How strange. How very strange,' he muttered. 'Now tell me, what arrangements do you have for dispensing?'

Swallowing her frustration, Beth began to point out the new bench scales, the mortar and pestles and the cachet machine.

'Infusion pots?' he rasped. She pointed and he nodded, 'Satisfactory.' Then he examined the carboys and bottles so far filled. His brow darkened. 'Cod liver oil. Sputum mugs. Carbolic. My dear Mrs Parslow, this is a druggist of yesterday. Not for today. You may not be aware of it, young lady, but medicine is on the threshold. Trembling on the brink of destiny. Tell me, what momentous event took place last year?'

'The old queen died,' said Beth, blankly.

'The death of the monarch,' said Goldstein scathingly. 'Inconsequential! A nothing. No, what happened last year was that Almroth Wright pledged himself to fight against bacteria.'

'Who?'

'Who?' he screeched in disbelief. 'Not heard of Wright? You fool, woman. He's the Professor of Pathology at the Army Medical School in Southampton, of course. The world of medicine will be turned upside down by him.' He looked at her without seeing her. 'Hitherto the world of medicine, Mrs Parslow, has been trying to fight bacteria with outside agents. Lister, great man, great man, but wrong, wrong, *wrong*!' He thumped his hand so hard on the dispensing counter that the bottles shook. 'Away with this carbolic acid, I say. No use but to clean the floors with. *Your* job.' He glared at her.

She struggled for words, and it was only when he flashed that smile again that she realised that this passed for a joke. She compressed her lips. 'So you know the answers and Lister is wrong. Is that it, Dr Goldstein?' she asked ironically.

He answered her seriously. 'No, I do not have the answer. Even Almroth Wright does not have the answer. But he knows where it lies. We must fight like with like. Pasteur discovered *fifteen* years ago that we must use bacilli to fight bacilli. To immunise. And Koch discovered the tuberculosis bacillus *twenty* years ago. And Ehrlich showed *twenty-seven* years ago how to use the magic bullet.'

'Magic bullet. Sounds more like those conjuring tricks of Maskelyne and Devant than medicine.'

He frowned. 'Do not mock Ehrlich. The bullet will travel through the body to find the right spot and cure it, and not harm anything else. Dyes, chemical dyes. And now he is studying syphilis. You know what syphilis is, Mrs Parslow?'

Beth blinked. 'I –'

'The penalty of fornication, Mrs Parslow. No doubt you have heard of fornication down here?'

'Yes, indeed,' she replied forthrightly, 'But we don't go talking about it.'

'And that's why it's a disease,' he said, 'No one talks of it, yet it works insidiously like the tubercle bacillus itself.' His shoulders dropped. 'Yet with all this – Ehrlich, Pasteur, Koch, they each have one piece of the triangle, but we still don't know how to put it together. Wright will discover it though. Or if not Wright, then one of his pupils . . . Perhaps me. Perhaps not. But it will come. Then there'll be no need of Chartboys. No tuberculosis any more.' His eyes stared into a bright future.

'You'll be out of a job.' She was determined not to give an inch to this insulting man.

He turned to her impatiently. 'There will always be disease. As fast as man cures one, another will crop up for the times. Because we are a sinful race, Mrs Parslow. Are you sinful?'

'I'm too busy,' said Beth firmly.

He turned to her as if seeing her for the first time, studying her carefully. He noted the shabby clothes, the dusty apron, the untidy hair, then he saw the determined chin and the dark eyes that looked straight at him. What he saw evidently satisfied him, for he nodded to himself. 'Yes,' he said to himself. And to her: 'Mrs Parslow, I am a genius. Or will be. I have it in me. And now – this room.'

He proceeded to point out that the urinals were the wrong design, the syringes old-fashioned, the glass measures insufficient. Moreover the room faced in the wrong direction.

'Dr Goldstein,' said Beth with great restraint, 'there's nothing I can do about that.'

'We will choose a different room,' he replied calmly.

With sinking heart, Beth followed in his wake as he imperiously stalked round the house, hat still clamped to head. He cast wistful eyes on the kitchen, until she firmly closed the door. At last he drew a deep breath of satisfaction. '*Ah*,' he said, throwing the door wide open.

'It's Sir Rupert's study,' said Beth faintly.

'It is the dispensary, Mrs Parslow. I will explain to Sir Rupert, do not worry.'

And he did. By the next time Beth came to Chartboys Rupert's study had been transformed into a dispensary. The study was dismissed to a back room. It was better, certainly, but – suddenly she was glad that she had refused the job of manageress. The thought of working with this impossible man was too much. Her fighting days were over. When she thought of the struggles of the Wheatsheaf, she wondered how she had ever coped? Where was the passion that had lit her only those few brief years ago? Then she thanked heaven for the calm of her daily ordered existence filled with the things that really mattered – the children, William, the Wheatsheaf . . . She closed her eyes and hardly noticed the tear that trickled out beneath her lids.

Rupert had simply laughed when she told him of her stormy meeting with Goldstein, half expecting him to be angry over the loss of his study. He dismissed it as unimportant.

'Miss Wilton will be a match for him,' he said confidently. 'They'll be so busy battling with each other that Chartboys will run like a dream.'

'What's she like, Rupert?' she enquired curiously. What sort of a woman would be a match for Dr Goldstein? A real termagant, she supposed. It was, therefore, with some trepidation that she went to Faversham station to meet the new matron of the hospital on her arrival from London.

An imp of rebelliousness had made her bring the governess cart rather than Rupert's brougham which he now kept at Chartboys with a resident chauffeur. She would test the new woman's mettle. She would certainly need it at Chartboys, with the flamboyant Goldstein around.

She stood in the waiting hall, rather than at the railings where she had so often waited for the hoppers in times past, feeling herself the object of attention to others waiting thus from the Shepham district. News travelled quickly and Beth Parslow's association with the still suspect Chartboys was well known. Owen was with her, in clinging mood, tugging at her skirts impatiently. Belching smoke, the train chugged out, leaving a handful of passengers making their way towards the exit.

There could be no doubt which one was Mary Wilton, if only from the all-enveloping dark blue cloak. But was this tall, slim gentlewoman with the piled-up honey-coloured hair and the calm, dignified oval face the woman Rupert thought could hold her own against Goldstein?'

'Miss Wilton?' Beth began hesitantly.

The woman's head turned slightly, and two steady grey eyes regarded Beth. 'How do you do, Mrs Parslow. Sir Rupert said you'd be here to meet me. How kind.'

At this moment there was a yell from a child who had fallen over a hat box while his mother was inspecting the timetable. Beth ran to him, but Mary Wilton was quicker. A professional arm scooped him up, summed up grazed hand and the quality of the tears, murmured a few words and, perhaps out of shock, the wailing was suddenly cut short. The mother, casting a suspicious look at Beth and the stranger, tried to take him but the child would have none of it. Mary Wilton carried her burden outside, Beth and the mother leading the way with the porter, and placed him in the waiting cab. She turned and her eyes met Beth's and she smiled slightly as though she knew quite well what Beth was at. It was Beth who felt herself on trial. She and Chartboys.

'I hope you'll be happy here,' Beth said to her formally, as she showed her her quarters on the top floor of Chartboys. Mary Wilton crossed to the dormer window and looked out over the gardens that stretched away up the hillside at the rear of the house. 'You'll have the morning sun here – Have you everything you want?'

'Happy?' murmured Mary Wilton. 'Everything I want?' She smiled. 'Oh yes, thank you, everything.' But she did not seem to be thinking of linen and soap.

'Are you sure she's strong enough to handle Chartboys and Goldstein, Rupert?' asked Beth of him later, as they sat over a late supper, magnanimously prepared by the new chef, who envisaged greater culinary demands on his skills than the simple Kentish hot-pot requested by Rupert.

'She isn't very strong physically at the moment,' explained Rupert. 'She returned early from the war in South Africa, because she had been ill. She was in the siege at Kimberley, you know, and the privations she suffered have left their mark.'

'An army nurse?' said Beth in surprise. She could not imagine the swanlike Mary Wilton in the Army.

'No, a volunteer from the Queen Victoria Jubilee Institute. She's been a qualified Queen's Nurse for several years now, and when the South African war came and she heard of the appalling overwork of the army nurses, she felt she ought to go. The soldiers she nursed idolised her. A second Nightingale they said. She's not strong enough yet to take on full hospital nursing in the East End – which is what she feels she is called to do. So I persuaded her to take on this job meanwhile at least.'

'Nursing wealthy convalescent patients,' said Beth, frowning.

'All sick people, Beth. And don't forget the Marie Bonner Wing.'

It was to bring the first head-on clash between Goldstein and Mary Wilton.

'It will never work,' shouted Goldstein. 'You will see.'

'Do you not believe the poor have as much right to life as the rich, Dr Goldstein?' said Mary Wilton calmly.

'Of course,' impatiently. 'I am a doctor. But I am a man of the world – it will not work. Having poor patients from the East End side by side with paying patients, no, no, *no*.'

'If the world is to continue people must learn tolerance.'

'Perhaps, madam. But not in a hospital. It will not

work, you – you – disciple of Lister.' It was the worst insult he could hurl.

But for a Queen's Nurse who had nursed the sick in South Africa – 'I take that as a compliment, Dr Goldstein, to be a disciple of a man who has given so much to the world with the discovery of antiseptics, saved thousands of lives. He makes no difference between rich and poor.'

'And nor do I, woman,' he shouted, almost dancing in his rage. 'But I tell you there should be one hospital for the poor, another for the rich; they are uneasy in each other's company because that is the way of the world we live in.'

'So you will refuse to look after these patients whom Sir Rupert is sending from Bethnal Green.'

'You are insulting, madam.' Dark brown, almost black eyes glared fiercely at her. 'I will devote myself to them, I will pamper them, I will restore them to full health so that they may return to their flea-infested damp rooms and die. What achievement!'

'Our duty is only to try, not to judge, Dr Goldstein.'

At this moment Beth entered to give Mary Wilton a message from the chef. With a slight incline of the head, Mary Wilton departed.

'Duty, pah!' snorted Goldstein to Beth, but he was not looking at Beth. He was looking at Mary Wilton's slim figure in its neat grey dress walking down the corridor.

'Mud, you have to have lessons,' said Beth despairingly.

'Don't want to,' muttered the four-year-old.

'You want to go on living with Auntie Beth, don't you?' said Rupert, nonplussed at the sudden recalcitrance of his son.

'Yes.'

'Well, you must please her and learn very hard when Mr Tompkins comes to see you.'

'Don't want to.'

'Why not?' asked Rupert, appealing to reason.

Reason lost. 'Don't want to.'

'I know why,' said Elizabeth importantly, shouting down from the magnolia tree onto the lawn at Chartboys where they were taking a late afternoon tea just three weeks before the opening.

Rupert looked in the direction of the voice, guessed its hiding place, strode across and shouted up at her: 'Then suppose you come down and tell me, Miss Elizabeth.'

'It's because he wants to come to school with me. But he can't. Because I'm *big*.' The last word was shouted in a cry of triumph.

'Then that gives you responsibilities. Come down here, young lady.' An unusual note of firmness in Beth's voice, as she came out in support of Rupert, made Elizabeth for once decide to obey. Lithely she clambered down the tree, and stood nonchalantly before them.

'What's responsibilities?' she asked with interest.

'It means you've got to look after Mud, and help him, because he's younger than you. Like you do Owen.'

'Owen's my brother.'

'All the more reason for looking after Mud, because he hasn't got a sister.'

Elizabeth thought this over. 'Don't like responsibilities,' she pronounced finally and scampered off.

'Doesn't like responsibilities,' said Rupert ruefully. 'How like her father.'

Beth said nothing, and glancing at her face he said contritely, 'I'm sorry, Beth. It just slipped out.'

'It doesn't matter,' she replied. 'He *is* her father and no amount of pretence can change it. What's to become of her in Shepham, Rupert? I worry about it. It'll never hold her. Just look at her.'

'Does Richard know yet?'

A chill crossed the air. 'No,' she managed to say. 'How could he? I have not seen him since he married.' She tried to let them be just words, have no meaning.

'He'll have to know sometime,' said Rupert matter-of-factly.

'No,' she said sharply. 'I forbid it, Rupert. Elizabeth's our child now, mine and William's. And that's how it's got to stay. For all our sakes.'

'Even Elizabeth's? If not now, then tell him when she's older so that he can decide her future –'

'But William –' she cried in anguish.

'Elizabeth must come first.'

'No, Rupert,' she said obstinately, her heart pounding in fear. 'I won't let Richard back in my life. Ever. Not by letter, not by word, not by thought –'

'As bad as that still, Beth?'

'No,' she cried again. 'No, it's *not* bad. But it could be, don't you see, it could be!'

Later she tossed and turned, beside a peacefully slumbering William. Even the mention of his name could upset her, she was forced to acknowledge. Without mention of him she could live contentedly, but now the past rose up to haunt her, as she lay restlessly, half-sleeping, half-waking. She tried to banish him, but he would not be banished, and the highwayman haunted her dreams for the rest of that troubled night.

* * *

'No washerwomen in the sky today, Mary,' Beth said brightly, busy with a completely unnecessary rearrangement of flowers in one of the rooms. Unnecessary since all had been ready since the previous day for the grand opening of Chartboys this afternoon.

'Washerwomen, Beth?'

'Clouds coming over the sky suddenly when you're not expecting them. That's what we call 'em down here.' She shivered suddenly, wishing superstitiously she had made no mention of them. True, the village seemed to have withdrawn its opposition to Chartboys - she had heard little of the earlier discontent of late. But all the same, was it *too* quiet?

Mary glanced out of the window from the counterpane she was smoothing down. It was a clear late spring day, bright and fresh. She drew a deep breath of satisfaction. 'It's the kind of day I used to dream about when I was in South Africa. Oh to be in England now that April's there. You come to think that England is made of days like this, and of course it rarely is when you get here.' She inhaled the fresh downs' air. 'But it's a good omen for Chartboys, I agree.'

In mutual defence against Goldstein, Beth and Mary had become friendly, after an initial period of coolness. Beth had taken this as dislike at first on Mary's part, but had come to realise that it was the cloak of reserve the nurse had woven round herself to protect her in difficult, hostile situations. What experiences she must have had to endure in South Africa, what sights, what bestialities. No wonder she greeted the beauty and peace of the downs with an initial reserve, as though it were a shell that might crack to reveal a dung-hill beneath.

But upon this façade, Dr Goldstein had made no inroads, much, it seemed to Beth, as an observer, as he metaphorically danced round trying to lance it with mockery, with taunts, and sometimes direct onslaught. Each time her invisible armour flung him off, but back he would come all the keener for the contest, which more was a battle of wills than anything to do with the good of Chartboys, she sensed. Beth's concern was simply to stop matters from reaching Rupert's ears. He had enough to worry about.

By lunchtime everyone was tetchy. Even Mary was uncharacteristically snapping at her team of fifteen nurses, wearing their new uniforms of grey dress and white apron for the first time. The chef could be heard shouting at his underlings and, over all, the voice of Dr Goldstein rose shrilly to a crescendo of fury, tearing at all their nerves no matter who was the object of his ire. Even Rupert had a muscle twitching furiously in his face, and finally withdrew to his study and locked the door, not appearing even for luncheon.

Early in the afternoon the first carriages began to appear, some bearing crests, others station cabs. The afternoon disappeared quickly as people were shown their rooms, complained, were mollified and shown around. There was an unfortunate scene when the waggon arrived with the East Enders, pale and mistrustful of this thing called country, others welcoming their return to the land of the hops.

But the initial hostility disappeared as the East Enders were dispersed in to the East Wing and simultaneously tea and cakes appeared on the back lawns. It was a delightful scene. It might have been a scene from a country house weekend party, as patients sat with relatives, as the seven-strong board went round to each to introduce themselves. Rupert, Mary and Goldstein – impeccably behaved – did likewise, but Beth hung back feeling out of it, partly because she had no official function but more because she felt a fish out of water. She needed time to accustom herself to the fact that these lords and ladies, as she thought of them, were patients, human beings, her future daily companions perhaps, and not exotic creatures stepped from her vision of the Wheatsheaf's future.

She surveyed the scene, thankful that it was going so well, hardly knowing why she had been so ill at ease. Chartboys was open. But she had not heeded the sky. The washerwomen had approached unnoticed.

'What's that?' whispered Beth to Rupert. In the distance there was the rumble of noise, growing louder by the minute. Voices, shouting, drums surely?

'Gypsies?' asked Rupert, frowning.

'None around. Besides –'

All her life Beth was to remember that horror of realisation, that the dream they had worked for for a year was in jeopardy; that disaster trembled, awaiting its moment. Etched on her memory was Goldstein pausing in the middle of talking to an elderly dowager, Mary Wilton, teapot clutched in one hand, graceful head turned towards the source of the noise. Rupert standing by her on the steps transfixed in disbelief. And she, Beth, heart pounding, as the clouds gathered once more over her life.

Through the gate poured the source of the noise. Men, some women, all shouting, waving banners, a procession of hate bearing down upon them. No ill-disciplined mob, though. An orchestrated band with a leader striding at their head. George Hamlin. The Squire's words came back to her. 'Hamlin's out to stop Sir Rupert's plans.' And his throwaway – 'There's the right of way.' No wonder there'd been quiet in the village. They'd been building up for this.

'By God,' said Rupert, his face deathly pale, and started towards them.

Beth held him back. 'No, Rupert,' she said. 'Careful. It's the right of way.'

But there was no stopping him. They were surging along in front of the lawn shouting, banging tin sheets, gesticulating at the assembled crowd who sat frozen in disbelief. Rupert marched up to Hamlin who stopped his mob with a jeer as he saw him coming.

'Get this rabble off my land!'

'Right of way, Sir Rupert. No law says people can't sing and be joyful on a right of way.'

Be joyful? The swearing and the racket intensified. Higgins's supporters who had been so silent since his departure had found a new leader. And Tom the Higgler. Her heart sank. She went to move but felt a hand on her arm. It was Goldstein.

'Don't get involved, Mrs Parslow. Let Sir Rupert handle it.'

She turned to him fiercely. 'You don't understand, Doctor.'

How could he understand all her pent up anger at Hamlin for all he had done to her. She had had peace with him for five years – and now this. He would not hurt her or hers again. And the fire that was Beth

Ovenden came back to repossess Beth Parslow, that calm woman who had believed all passion dead disappeared briefly, and the old Beth was there again, heedless of anything save right and justice. The strength she thought had deserted her flooded back. And she ran across the lawns to push Rupert aside and face him herself – as he had wanted all along.

'You'll not succeed, Hamlin.'

'My dear Mrs Parslow, why the vehemence? A quiet Sabbath stroll. The village folk will be strolling along this right of way *every day*. Won't you, lads?' turning to the mob, who roared their approval. 'Right dangerous for them consumptives to be near a right of way as well. We've a right to complain about that.'

'Listen to me, all of you!' she shouted past him to the mob.

Hamlin went to push her aside, but big though he was she flung him off with a strength that surprised her. Whatever the motives that drove him on in his relentless quest for the Wheatsheaf, he would find Beth Parslow a match for him.

'Men of Kent you call yourselves?' she shouted. 'Or men of Hamlin? Don't you have minds of your own? Do you have to follow him like sheep? You, you, you, I don't know. But you, Jim Wilson, you Percy Twist, I've known you all my life. Isn't it you, Jim, that sits up with a sick animal all night? Wasn't it you, Percy, we all came to when we found a wounded bird? These are all sick *people* here. Do you care less for them? These doctors are trying to improve things, to find a cure for the disease, and you try to stop them? By God, you've followed this man long enough –'

Hamlin was shouting, trying to restrain her, but Rupert held him back.

'But we might catch it, missus,' said one braver than the rest.

'Nonsense,' she said. 'It's just not possible to catch it like a cold.'

'Mr Hamlin says so,' he said doubtfully.

'He's a brewer, not a doctor,' she shouted. 'Look at me. Do you think I'd put my children at risk by working here if there was a chance I'd catch it?'

This was a new idea and the opposition began to die down. Seeing she had their attention, she went on more quietly: 'There's men here followed Higgins, attacked me, burnt the Wheatsheaf – killed my father. Do you, Jim, do you, Percy, want to be with men like that? Do you now want to follow Hamlin and stop these people from getting better, kill them in fact? Jim, you spoke of justice once. Where is it now?'

Hamlin tried to rally them and those that worked for him marched stolidly on. But, standing irresolutely, Jim turned to the others. 'I don't say she's right, mind, but let's give the place a trial . . .'

From then on the opposition flickered, but finally died. If not welcomed with open arms, Chartboys was at least tolerated. Visits to the village were discouraged, and the right of way ceased to be disturbed. To quell the anxieties of those first patients had been a difficult task for several weeks. In the end, only two patients were lost to them, choosing to go to Switzerland, where the peasantry were kept at a distance. So Chartboys settled down to grind onto an even keel.

And with it, Beth. She had said she would stay until

the opening of Chartboys, but once Chartboys was open she realised with a pang that that was the end of her work. She resolutely stayed away, but was summoned to return by Rupert demanding to know with some surprise where she had been. 'No place for me, now,' she had said awkwardly.

Rupert had smiled. 'There'll always be a place for you at Chartboys.'

And so it had come about that Beth found herself responsible for the welcoming of new patients, organising the departure of the old, keeping the books for Chartboys and the patients' records – and increasingly keeping the peace between Dr Goldstein and Mary.

The opening of Chartboys and Beth's stand against Hamlin had brought about several almost imperceptible changes: Goldstein began to show an unexpected amiability towards her, born of respect; Mary Wilton became her friend; William grew more silent; and Beth's eyes began to sparkle again. But one thing could never change; Hamlin's relentless hostility.

CHAPTER TEN

'Where be you going?' William emerged from the cellar, wiping his hands on an old towel.

Beth turned in surprise. 'Only Chartboys, William.'

'Only Chartboys,' he repeated grimly. 'Maybe you best give Chartboys a miss for once, Beth. Look to your own.' His normally placid face was flushed red, and his eyes were bright with anger. As she stared at him in surprise, he continued more calmly, 'I don't mind you agoing there, Beth. But it seems to me you don't see what's agoing on *here*.'

'What's wrong?' she asked, puzzled, running her mind rapidly through the possible sources of problems; Mud was happy as a sandboy now, instead of the proposed year he had been with them well over two, no fatter but much happier; Elizabeth, Owen – nothing wrong there either.

'I've just been stocktaking, that's what's wrong. You ain't studied the accounts recently have you?'

She looked guilty. It was true that she was so occupied with the constant excitement of Chartboys that she no longer had the time to devote to poring over the Wheatsheaf orders, but left them to Ben, merely giving them a cursory glance before she signed them. William left the business side of things to her completely, handing the stocktaking records over to her to deal with. And she was immediately defensive that he had discovered her shortcomings.

'We're not in debt –'

'No, but it seems to me there's a powerful lot more beer being drunk but I don't see no extra profit flooding in. And there's less folk coming in nowadays, not more.'

'Costs have risen –'

'Not that much. Seems to me some of these monthly stock sheets want a bit of checking.'

'What are you suggesting – that Ben is dishonest?' she asked amazed, 'Or he and Hetty are drinking over their personal limits? Surely you don't mean they're making false returns. They wouldn't –'

'Wouldn't they? Why not?' said William. 'With no eye over 'em, 'tis all too easy. Now we've allus known there's a lot of long pulls when the hoppers around, but I think there's summat more, Beth, and you've to find out what it is.'

'But –'

'But nothing, Beth. 'Tis the Wheatsheaf we need to keep this family going, not Chartboys, even though 'ee do give you a good wage. But the future's here, not there.'

At this blunt statement from William, she was appalled. Her mind flicked back over the past two years since Chartboys had opened. Always something new: doing the books; helping Mary; acting as peacemaker between Mary and Goldstein; talking to the patients, meeting their guests; advising on the gardens; teaching the patients to care for the flowers; the excitement of being swept vicariously into other worlds as patients talked of castles, balls, servants. As Rupert's unofficial representative when he was not present she had a status that she could never otherwise have attained. Of course there was the other side – the constant problem of the Marie Bonner Ward, where Goldstein gave his professional, even devoted, care to the patients but still opposed any social mixing of the two groups of patients. Nor were the patients themselves easy to handle in the wing. Most were totally unused to the luxuries of modern living, and instead of benefiting from them, hankered after the ways that they knew. It was a constant challenge to keep both sets of patients contented. Yet she thought she had been carrying on her work at the Wheatsheaf with the same conscientiousness as before and never questioned that her heart lay there for ever. Now, panicking lest she was forced into a position where she had to give up Chartboys, she examined her conscience.

'I'll deal with it, William. Leave it to me. It's your afternoon for Canterbury, isn't it? You get off now.'

She took off her hat again. This afternoon she would remain here. Hetty had finished the lunchtime cashing up, there were no customers, and all was quiet in the bars. She got out the books and began to study them. An hour later she had got nowhere. The total sales at least were correct, the bought ledger tallied – yet consumption had increased with gross profit decreasing more than one per cent. A bad sign. Yet the books seemed right. It took another hour to pinpoint a grey area. The gauging of stock for the hogsheads of ale and porter. So easy to persistently gauge wrong and blame it on an error in calculating on the dip-rod method. There was no proof of course . . . But Beth was not one to let that stand in her way. She would confront Ben immediately.

She expected to find him in the cellars, but he was not there. He hadn't left for his coat and cap were still hanging in the hallway. She toured the Wheatsheaf unsuccessfully. Where was he? He must be in one of the outhouses used for storage. He wasn't.

She opened the door of the barn the smugglers used to use, more of a last gesture than anything else. She was aware of a sudden rustling as she stood, her eyes straining in the dark. One of the cats she thought, shut in? Then, as her eyes grew accustomed to the dark, she saw two intertwined shapes on the hay, motionless, guilty, staring up at her, white flesh all too evident. She had found Ben – and Hetty also.

Overcome with shock, she stood for a moment gaping, then, pulling herself together, slammed the door behind her and ran into the orchard. She needed to think, not to have to face William, while she wondered what she was to say to him. For this was her fault in a way. The cooling shade of the trees around her and the smell of the damp grass were comfortingly familiar, and she breathed more easily. So much for Hetty being a reformed character! So much for Ben the trusted lieutenant! This was what came of leaving the Wheatsheaf for Chartboys, she thought ruefully. Where was the fierce love for the Wheatsheaf that she had always proclaimed? Had she not clung to it in passionate possessiveness all these years; built it up again from the ashes? And now she had abandoned it. It was not too late. Ben and Hetty would go – they'd find more staff. But meanwhile – 'You were right, William,' she said to him later. 'I'll not be going to Chartboys from now on. The Wheatsheaf needs me more. I'll work up the preserves trade again. I've been letting it slip a bit, and your mother's always asking for more.'

William paused in the act of drying a glass and, almost as a trick of the light, she thought it was Andrew in his place.

'So you found out about Ben and Hetty at last, have you?'

'You knew?' she said in amazement. 'But why didn't you tell me? It's – it's horrible! Ben's poor wife –'

William shrugged. 'I suspected something was going on during my afternoons in Canterbury. But their private lives aren't our concern, Beth. So long as they does their job. 'Tis when they don't, I reckon we should take notice. And that's now, because they're cheating us. I don't like that.'

'But it *is* our concern, William. Ben's got a wife. They'll have to go.'

'Are you sure it's not just Hetty Didcot you want to go, Beth?'

She flushed a dull red. Why did William have to be so perceptive – seeing more quickly than Beth herself? Perhaps he was right. Perhaps she had always resented Hetty being in the Wheatsheaf.

'But they can't stay,' she said weakly. 'How would we ever trust them?'

'Not like you to be such a fierce moralist, Beth.'

The unfairness of it. How could William say such a thing? Her William. She looked at him, and saw an accusing stranger and her own guilt mirrored in his eyes.

The door opened, and Hetty came in.

'I wanted to thank you, Mrs Parslow, for keeping me on.'

Beth stiffened, ''Twas Mr Parslow's doing not mine,' she said coldly.

Hetty swallowed. Then she burst out, 'You're as proud and stubborn as ever, Beth Ovenden – I'm telling you woman to woman. Ben and I ain't doing any harm. You know it don't do no harm to Gladys. She's got her kids, Ben'll never leave her. What's the harm in him having some fun every once in a while? And me,' she added a little wistfully.

'He's another woman's husband, that's the harm.'

'And are you telling me that if Richard Lyle came down back to Shepham you wouldn't be out in the long grass with him?'

Beth shut down her heart, shut down her mind, fought to shut out the unforgivable . . .

Hetty took one look at her face and said, 'I'm sorry, Mrs Parslow. Forget I said that. It comes of –' she paused and went on awkwardly, 'I was allus jealous of you. Allus. You had it all; he enjoyed having me all right, but he *loved* you. Told me that he did even when I was carrying his bastard,' she added bitterly. 'So I used to look at you and wish – Well, allus so proud you were, never thinking of how others might feel. You were young, I suppose. We all were.' She sighed. 'It's a long time ago, Beth, and we got to get on with life. Make the best of what we has. And I can tell you, Beth, working at the Wheatsheaf is the *best* of what I has. But Ben ain't part of it. It don't mean nothing but a bit of fun. But the Wheatsheaf – it's come to mean something to me –'

Beth buried her face in her hands. 'Stop,' she said,

'please, *stop*. Just go. You can stay here. But please, please go.' Hetty slipped quietly away and Beth did not even notice. She would not, she could not, think of it. Her life was here, as it had always been, at the Wheatsheaf with William.

'No more Chartboys, William.'

'No, Beth. I won't be party to that. You go on, as you were, but maybe spare a little thought for those around you. I've had a word with Ben. You don't have to do that.' She looked at him gratefully. 'No more long pulls. No more underestimating the stocks. Now he knows we're watching, I reckon it'll make all the difference. Only thing is –' he paused '– he won't give Hetty up. All he'd say is that it won't happen at the Wheatsheaf again. Seems fair enough to me. We ain't the keeper of their souls.'

'No,' said Beth dully. 'You're right.' She felt as though Shepham was slipping away from her, she was not part of its world, nor part of Chartboys – William and the Wheatsheaf were her only anchor . . . she was coming near to losing it. She shivered. How could she have been so blind, so confident that William and the Wheatsheaf would always be there. Only a few years ago she had had the same confidence about her father, yet he had died, and the Wheatsheaf had been all but lost in the fire.

She would give up Chartboys. It took too much time from the Wheatsheaf. She would build up trade here, regain the ground William said they were losing, find new outlets for her energies, new paths to walk along that would benefit the Wheatsheaf, not Chartboys. For here was her world.

As if reading her thoughts, however, William said: 'I

want you to keep going to Chartboys, Beth. You need it. 'Tis all right when the hoppers are here, but rest of year I reckon, 'tis dull for you, with just me and the children.'

'No,' she said fiercely. 'Not dull. *Never* dull. It's just – I seem to want to do everything and can't bear to give anything up. Can you understand that?'

'Reckon so. You was allus the same. Look at all that time you spent at Medlars. Chartboys has taken Medlars' place, that's all. You go, Beth, but just you come back again, that's all I ask,' he said, in a matter-of-fact voice.

She put her arms round him and buried her face in his neck. 'Steady, Beth,' he said gruffly. 'Steady now,' his arms creeping around her as if they could never let go.

'Evening, Mrs Parslow.'

Beth stopped short on the threshold of the parlour, when she saw who was sitting there with William. She took off her hat and coat and drew off her gloves, taking an unnecessarily long time about it.

'Good evening, Mr Hamlin,' she said at last. 'What can we do for you? A drop of Ovenden Mild Ale perhaps? Or perhaps you've come to give me an order for pickles and ginger beer for all your tied houses?' True to her word she was busily involved in expanding the sales of her wines and preserves to other pubs in the area.

'Now, Beth,' he said easily. 'You got to learn that in business it pays to get along with folk, be diplomatic. That right, Mr Parslow?'

'We'll hear you out, Mr Hamlin,' said William stolidly, refusing to be drawn.

Hamlin had not improved with age. He must be in his

mid-fifties now, Beth calculated. Portlier, but slyer. Still wouldn't trust him further than a dog in Dover, she thought, for all his wealth and position.

'I expect you know why I've come –'

'Not to offer to buy us out?' she said sarcastically.

'Right, Mrs Parslow. I don't suppose you'd agree to it?'

'Quite right, Mr Hamlin.'

'So I've another suggestion. Part ownership. It would give you some capital to do things in this place. That's a reasonable offer.'

The vision of the Wheatsheaf Hotel flashed momentarily through her mind before she dismissed it. 'And whose might the major share be in this plan?'

'Mine, naturally. But that still don't give me too much to do. We'd have an arrangement whereby you went on running it. I don't mind that.'

'You're too kind,' murmured Beth, but warily. He had something up his sleeve.

'You'd switch over to Teynham Ales naturally –'

'Look,' said Beth exasperatedly. 'We don't need capital. We don't need you.'

Hamlin smiled, but the smile did not reach his eyes. 'You haven't heard then? Trade news takes a time to reach you snug in your village inn. Why bother to join the trade associations? Perhaps you ought to. Might be things you should know.'

'Such as?'

'The Compensation Act, for example.'

Beth looked blank.

'Ah, perhaps you've been too busy with your Chartboys work to notice. It's law now, you see, effective 1st January, 1905. Four months' time. There's too many public houses, you see. Now the magistrates have got the power to close 'em down.'

'That!' said Beth scornfully. 'That's been discussed for years, and nothing has ever happened.'

'Different now,' said Hamlin smugly. 'The act never went through before because, quite rightly, it was thought unfair that landlords and owners should be put out of business without compensation. But with the Compensation Act you can be closed down if the magistrates don't reckon there's enough trade to support it and compensation is paid. It'll come out of a fund all the inns and pubs contribute to.'

'I don't believe it,' said Beth angrily. 'Anyway, nobody'd close us down, the only pub in Shepham.'

'Small village,' pointed out Hamlin. 'And your trade's falling off. Noticed that? Must be because that pub at Westling's coming on nicely. And one at Charing has opened up. Had something to do with that myself,' he said casually. 'Trade coming on nicely. And the Temperance is strong round here. Of course I know all this because I've a friend still on the licensing board.'

'Friend!' said William violently. 'Old Ted Morrison's got shares in Teynham Breweries.'

'Friend,' said Hamlin, still smiling. 'And what if he has? So's the Squire come to that, and he's hardly what you might call a friend of mine. But if I were part owner – even minority owner perhaps – of the Wheatsheaf.'

'No,' said Beth violently.

'Perhaps you should discuss it with your husband,' Hamlin said smoothly.

'She don't need to,' said William evenly. 'I'm of a mind with her. There's no way we'll be closed down.'

'I'll do my best, Beth.' The Squire's face was tired and grey. He was ageing quickly, thought Beth, with a pang of remorse that she was not closer to him. 'But unless you and William can put up a good case, Hamlin will have too much support and he'll close you as soon as the new act comes into force next year.'

'Shepham *needs* us,' she said obstinately.

'No, Hamlin's supporters say that it can be served by Westling and Charing. Your revenue was down –'

'That was due –' she stopped. She would not betray Ben. That was over now. 'It's nonsense and you know it, Squire.'

'It's politics, Beth. I tell you, Shepham isn't the place it used to be. You used to be able to talk to these people, call at their homes, talk to them. They cared for the land, for their neighbours, for values. It's the twentieth century and things are changing. Now it's business interests all the time everywhere. Even Shepham. The word of the Squire isn't enough any more. You'll need some very good reason to make them change their minds.'

'It won't happen, will it, William?' she said to him when she returned to report the failure of her mission. In his silence she was alarmed. A hollow pit opened up in her stomach as she realised the possibility of closure had once more crept up in a clear blue sky and the storm overtaken them. What could they do? How could they suddenly produce some other reason for the Wheatsheaf's existence? After all, Hamlin *wanted* the

Wheatsheaf. Without a licence he could not run it. Suddenly she saw his plan. With the Wheatsheaf closed down, he could expand his Charing Inn, make a hotel even. Her alarm deepened – he wanted the Wheatsheaf but if he couldn't have it, he would see that she didn't. She saw it so clearly – and she saw no answer. Hamlin had won.

'You look like a twig with no sap,' was Bill's greeting to her as she went up to Chartboys that afternoon. He was busy pruning a fig tree, handling its leaves and emerging fruit with love in his gnarled fingers.

'The yew walk looks good, Bill,' she said, not commenting on his greeting.

'He wants me to cut 'em all shapes, but I says no, Mus Rupert, 'tis flying in the face of nature. If the Good Lord wanted His trees to look like dogs He'd have given 'em tails to start with. The natural way is good enough for me.'

The formal garden was in fact too ordered for Beth's taste; she preferred the wilder areas of the Chartboys' grounds, the vegetable gardens, the wilderness beyond the pond at the far end where the lilies grew. But most of all she loved the walled herb garden with its surrounding peach trees. There, sheltered from the winds, the sun could work its best, entrapping the scents and smells in the air, in a timelessness that could take her far away from her day to day problems.

'What be wrong, Miss Beth?' he asked bluntly.

'Another shot by Hamlin to close down the Wheatsheaf,' she said. 'And this time he'll win.'

He carefully clipped another branch, and then

descended the ladder. 'Now, look, Miss Beth,' he said. 'I don't be knowing about these business matters. Ain't had no call to, but there'll be an answer somewhere, if you only look. Can't Mus Rupert help?'

'He carries no weight down here, as far as licensing is concerned. Even Squire doesn't think he can help, and he's on the licensing board itself.'

'He be all there, Sir Rupert, for all he wants me to cut these bushes into the darndest shapes. 'Ave a word with him. And don't you worry, Miss Beth. You'll come through. You be like this fig tree.'

In spite of herself she laughed. 'A fig tree, Bill? I've been called quite a few things but never a fig.'

' 'Tain't no joking matter,' he said severely. 'I be serious. Nothing funny about a fig tree. If you trim the roots, like what Hamlin's adoing to you, it flourishes up top and starts bearing fruit, but if you let un be, the roots go all higgledy-piggledy, and start doing a power of damage. I reckon no one ain't pruned your roots for a while, Miss Beth, so you could say old Hamlin's adoing you a favour. Ah.' He spat on his hands and, turning his full attention to the tree, climbed up the ladder again.

Grateful to Hamlin! thought Beth wryly, as she walked up the steps, being whitened for the second time that day. Perhaps she would speak to Rupert, although it seemed unfair to burden him with her problems when he had all his work cut out running and supervising the hospital as well as his family estates, but she needed a friend. As she passed the dispensary, however, she could hear upraised voices. She immediately quickened her step. She was in no mood to cope with Goldstein and

Mary in yet another clash. She was too late, however, for as she passed the open door, Mary saw her. Her face was flushed with anger. 'Beth,' she called, 'can you spare a moment?'

Unwillingly Beth entered, to see Goldstein standing in front of the fire, legs arrogantly apart, beard jutting out fiercely, hands locked behind his back in classic male pose.

'Call in your cohorts,' he said, glaring at them both. 'Romantics, idealists, the monstrous regiment. You do not see things clearly.'

'There is nothing wrong with my eyesight, I believe, Dr Goldstein,' Mary replied spiritedly. 'In South Africa I saw people dying of leprosy, of disease, of wounds. I saw death make no distinction between officer and ranker.'

'But you had officers' and men's hospitals. And why do you think that is, you stupid woman? Because both want it that way. Officers aren't at ease with the men, the men aren't at ease with –'

'You've been in the front line, Dr Goldstein?'

'I've worked in the Southampton Army Hospital.'

'One hospital,' she snorted. 'Not in the field –'

'What *is* all this about?' pleaded Beth.

'Dr Goldstein has objected to the Marie Bonner Wing working in the same garden as the paying patients.'

'Yes, Mrs Parslow, because I wish to see *all* these patients get well. That is my concern. I do not wish them to be a social experiment, and people get on best with the people they have most to say to. My duty is to my patients, not to a nurse and not, Mrs Parslow, to you. Is that clear?'

'And my duty, Dr Goldstein, is to look after this hospital,' said Mary.

Beth desperately sought for a Solomon-like solution. 'Why not allow them both to work in the garden but arrange their free time so they are not there together?' It was a feeble solution, but they both stopped and looked at her.

'Very well,' said Goldstein slowly. 'I will accept that for the moment. But there will be trouble if we do not think of a permanent solution.'

'I don't accept it –'

'Mary,' said Beth, giving her a straight look.

Mary bit her lip. 'Very well,' she said, 'but for the moment only, Dr Goldstein.'

As she left to see Rupert, however, Beth had the strangest feeling that the quarrel between them, ostensibly about the patients, was actually about something quite different.

'You must go to Rupert,' said Beth, firmly.

'No, I won't. But, oh Beth, sometimes I'm near to walking out, much as I love it here. I feel I could be so much more use elsewhere.'

'You're needed here. You can't say that because people are convalescent they don't need you just as much as if they were dying of gangrene. Particularly in a sanatorium where the convalescence is so vital and the patients need educating for the future.'

'Yes, I suppose that's true, and particularly in the Marie Bonner Wing. If they take back what they've learned here to the East End and spread the lessons around, I would feel I was accomplishing something.

But even so, I get so weary of the constant fighting with that man. If it was not for –' she said unguardedly, then broke off with a quick look at Beth.

'Rupert?'

Mary went scarlet.

For some time now Beth had become aware that Mary Wilton was in love with Rupert. Perhaps it was something in those calm grey eyes when she talked of him, something in her very stance as Beth saw them walking round the hospital together, perhaps the unobtrusive way in which all irritations, all small obstacles, were cleared from his daily path. Beth was saddened, for she had seen no answering light in Rupert's eyes.

'Does he know?' Beth went on bluntly.

Mary grimaced. 'Is it so obvious?'

'Only perhaps to me,' said Beth.

'No, he doesn't know,' she said after a moment. 'I don't think he even notices me as a woman. Was he so devoted to his dead wife? It's as though he goes around on a saintly plane of his own.'

Beth was silent, wondering whether she should speak. Yet it was part of her own past as well; she had a right if she so chose. For Mary's sake she decided she would. 'The past is very strong, sometimes. I think, Mary, that Rupert is desolate and sick of an old passion. And not for his wife.'

'Then I am lost,' said Mary simply.

Rupert's room was tidy. A photograph of Mud in sailor suit stood on the mantelpiece, next to one of his parents, but they were the only personal effects in the room. It was as though indeed he had carefully packed away parts of his life that he did not wish to remember. Yet Chartboys stood in the heart of the very countryside that had brought his tragedy about. He was an odd mixture, decided Beth.

He listened quietly and attentively as usual.

'So that's what will happen unless a miracle occurs, Rupert. Now even if we lose the licence, there's no way that we'll sell the Wheatsheaf. We'll go on living there. Find something else to do. Would there be something at Chartboys perhaps?' she asked diffidently.

'Beth, what's happened to you?' he said at last. She flushed. 'How many times have you fought Hamlin off in the past? Aren't you even going to try to save the Wheatsheaf? Have you grown so tired of life?'

'That's unfair, Rupert,' she replied in a low voice.

'Is it? The Beth I used to know would have fought with every ounce in her body before the Wheatsheaf was sold.'

'I have tried,' she cried. 'But this time it's impossible. There's no answer if they take the licence.'

'You must go before the board yourself – give them the arguments.'

'We have to produce a good new argument to stay open if we're to win. But there is none. We're a small country pub. We have good business only six weeks of the year.'

'Then I can't help you, Beth. There's nothing I can do.'

Her face fell, and she realised how much she'd been counting on Rupert's support even if only moral. 'There's an answer, Beth,' he said, 'but not for someone in your state of mind. There is a way to save the

Wheatsheaf, something I've had in mind for some while, but not for a quitter. We need accommodation nearer than Faversham for people coming to visit their relatives.'

'But the Wheatsheaf's not big enough,' interrupted Beth dejectedly. 'I thought of that already. But it's no good, I've not the capital to build a hotel.'

He looked at her. 'Think, Beth,' he urged. 'Those cottages.'

'Cottages?' she said doubtfully. 'Those old tumble-down ones on the side of the green?'

'Yes. They're up for sale. Now I have no spare capital, but suppose I could raise some to buy them and fit them out into an annexe to the Wheatsheaf just for Chartboys' visitors? You could manage it, and share its profits. Wouldn't that give you your argument to put before the board? Not a hotel, perhaps, but bed and breakfast accommodation, right here in Shepham, with a steady trade.'

That had been six months ago. Filled with enthusiasm her arguments had swayed the licensing magistrates once Rupert had raised the capital - from where he did not say and she did not ask. Enough that he had outbid Hamlin, who, immediately Ted Morrison told him of the plan, had tried to buy them. In vain. The Wheatsheaf was Shepham, and the owner wanted it kept that way.

''Tis a big change,' said Mrs Parslow senior in tones of deep disapproval, looking at the clouds of dust gathered on the green as the old walls were renovated. 'Them's allus been dwellings.'

'They'll still be dwellings, Mother,' said Beth cheerfully, wiping a smut from her face. 'Only this'll be people's temporary dwellings, instead of permanent ones. They'll be spending lots of money in your shop,' she added cunningly.

'Huh,' snorted Mrs Parslow. 'Money is as money does,' she muttered darkly. 'Allus be at summat new, Beth, my girl. If you want summat new, have another baby now.'

'Oh Mother,' said Beth, for this was a well-worn theme. 'Don't you think I've enough to do . . .'

'Nature'll find a way,' uncompromisingly.

'Not if I have anything to do with it,' whispered Beth to herself, as Mrs Parslow stumped over to peer in the windows. 'Not yet awhile,' she added hastily, in case whatever gods might be were listening and thought but poorly of this impious utterance.

She picked up the copper paint-tin and eyed the door thoughtfully. Was blue the right colour?

'Aren't you going to cover them beams up?' asked Mrs Parslow.

'No, we're going to leave them like that,' said Beth. 'We like them better that way than plastered over.'

'Leaving the job half done,' said Mrs Parslow. 'You'll never learn, Beth. When I think of the trouble Mr Quested went to to put that plaster on and here are you tearing it off . . .' Shaking her head ruefully at the ways of the young, she retreated to the sanity of the post office.

Beth had flung herself with her old enthusiasm into the redecoration of the three cottages, determined to make the scheme work. Hamlin, in vengeance for her successful defence of the Wheatsheaf's licence, had forbidden any of his tied houses to stock her preserves, so that small source of income had dried up.

Now only the last cottage remained, nearly finished. She walked round to the rear to the neglected garden to paint the back door. It was a fine spring day. In the overgrown garden a few daffodils poked their heads through the dead mass of uncleared weeds and birds were beginning to sing with hope of spring in their voices. Her old pinafore was covered in paint, and she had to hitch her skirts up to avoid the mud that surrounded the cottage. Her hair was pulled back, tied loosely with a ribbon to keep it off her face. She was humming, listening to the chaffinches behind her as she painted.

'Hello, Beth.'

The world stopped. She stayed very still. Then she turned round slowly to face him.

And the wound she had so carefully plastered over for eight years burst wide open.

'Richard,' was all she whispered.

He was thinner. There were lines on his face that had not been there before. And a shadow over it that dimmed the light from those blue eyes. The face of a prosperous man. Richard, and not her Richard. She began to breathe more easily.

'Rupert said you'd changed,' he said abruptly, staring at her.

She was conscious of her unruly hair, of the paint, of the sight she must look to anyone else's eyes, but his. 'And have I?' she heard herself saying.

'I don't know,' he said simply. 'To me –' he hesitated, then a flash of that old crooked smile, 'you're my Beth.'

A lance caught her heart, and anger welled up that it should be so.

'Even with paint on your cheek.' He took an instinctive step towards her as if to touch it. She stepped back, in fear of something she didn't understand, and he stopped.

'Why didn't you tell me, Beth?' he said, in a low voice.

No pretending she did not know what he meant. 'Rupert told you then,' she said dully.

'No. Rupert never said a word.' His lips tightened grimly. 'It was Arthur.'

'Arthur? You mean Mud?'

'He told me about –' he stopped, as though it were an effort to speak, never taking his eyes from her face, 'about your daughter Elizabeth, nearly a whole year older than him. I became curious. Her birthday was in March. That means you were sleeping, loving, with William that June. I can't believe that, Beth, not that June –'

'She's mine,' cried Beth. 'Mine and William's. Think what you like.' There was panic in her eyes. The outside world had disappeared. They were alone, just her and Richard. To fight. Her will against his. 'She were early.'

'Then let me see her. I'll know.'

'No.'

'Why not, if she's William's? Beth, I want to see her. I must. I could have gone to see her with Arthur then, but I wouldn't, not without your knowing.'

'Still the honourable gentleman,' she said bitterly.

He flushed. 'Let me see her,' he repeated.

Beth hid her face in her hands. 'No,' she moaned. 'No, you can't do it, Richard. Leave me, please, I've my own life.'

He regarded her pitilessly. 'I have to see her. If not now, then I'll return and return again until I do.'

She threw back her head, defeated. 'She's in the orchard,' she said dully.

'And William?'

'He's in Canterbury. I'll tell him afterwards. There's no secrets between us.' She looked at him, but her glance fell. She would not tell William, and he knew it. Yet as she led him to the orchard, she felt a little easier. This was not her Richard, the ghost she had feared. This was some stranger to whom she had a duty. Her heart felt lighter. She felt curiously relaxed. This pain, this grief, she had been holding back with such an effort of will all these years, had been wasted – it was already evaporating, brought into the cold light of day.

'Elizabeth,' she called. But as usual it was Mud came running.

'Where's Elizabeth, Mud?' she said resignedly.

Mud smiled, recognising Richard. 'You show me, old chap,' said Richard, bending down to give Mud a piggy-back. With cries of glee, digging his heels into Richard's back, Mud pointed: upwards. Richard dumped him off, stood at the foot of the cherry tree and looked up. A heap of petticoats was all that could be seen of Elizabeth.

'Elizabeth, come down,' called Beth faintly.

Elizabeth looked down and decided the prospect did not seem inviting. She was an expert at the note in her mother's voice.

'Don't bother her, Beth, I'll go up.' Taking hold of the lower branches, Richard swung himself up into the cherry tree, regardless of his smart grey suit. And there, amid the cherry blossom, Richard met his daughter.

Beth walked quickly away, she could not bear to watch, opening the gate to the field. Then he was with her again, catching her up in the meadow, bright with celandines.

'Why didn't you tell me, Beth?' he said gently, his face a mask of sadness. 'You know nothing, *nothing* would have taken me away – even if I'd had to go to jail. Nothing,' he repeated vehemently. There was nothing withdrawn about his face now; the lines were set deep.

'I didn't want you staying acos of that,' she cried in anguish. 'You had to stay acos of me. And you didn't want me enough.'

They stared at each other separated by the chasm of the years.

'Your stupid pride,' he said bitterly. 'All because of your pride. You cheated me, Beth.'

'Cheated?' She was furiously angry. 'I cheated *you*?'

'You cheated me of happiness, Beth, and so cheated yourself. *You*. *Your* responsibility.'

'You made up your own mind what mattered to you. And it wasn't me.' The pent-up hurt came bursting forth after all the years.

'Beth, what's happened to us two? Look at me, a sober law-abiding barrister. Nothing before me but one predictable line of so-called success. And look at you. Where's the fire? The eagerness. You've no hope in your eyes any more, Beth.'

'I'm happy,' she cried in answer.

'Are you?' He twisted her round towards him viciously, took her face roughly between his hands. For a moment she felt faint as she thought he would kiss her and she would be lost, but he did not. Instead he tore the ribbon from her hair, releasing it over her shoulders as he had done all those years ago, and groaned.

'You've not changed,' he said almost bitterly, as though it presented some challenge. 'You're still the same. Buried, deep down there. You've got to come back. To life. You say you're happy? You're content, that's all. Not happy. Do you remember our haystack? Our dreams? Our great adventure?'

'Stop,' she cried in anguish. 'Stop, Richard, no more.'

'I want Elizabeth, Beth.'

'No,' she interrupted. 'She's mine and William's. William's legally and morally. We've brought her up, loved her, cared for her –'

'I want you Beth, and if I can't have you, by God I'll have Elizabeth.'

'*Me*?' she said faintly. 'You want *me*?'

'Come with me. William will get over it. He'll have the Wheatsheaf. And Pippin doesn't need me – nor do her children, for they are hers and not mine. We two will find the life we were meant to have. Still can have.'

Panic surrounded her in waves, till she thought she would faint of it.

'Elizabeth's *my* daughter, Beth, whatever you say about William. She's what came of our love. And I need that love back, more than anything. To say yes again to life, my love. With you in my arms. Beth, you must come, you *must*.'

She pushed him away with all her strength, as he took her in his arms again.

'We made our choice,' she said quickly, before she could regret it. 'There's no going back. Not now.' How she found the strength she did not know. So long as he did not touch her again.

His face tightened. 'Very well. I can't force you, Beth,' he said flatly. 'If you insist on ruining our lives again.'

'I love William,' she said vehemently. Empty words. But an anchor.

His face darkened. He seized her roughly. 'Does he kiss you like this?' he hissed, and his lips were on hers, and eight years fell away into the abyss of Lethe. Kissing, demanding, then tantalising, till every nerve in her body cried out for him, and her heart ceased to struggle. Enfolded in his arms, feeling his hands holding her close through the roughness of her dress, it seemed to her that she had come home; a gasp that might have been hers, an ache in her body that cried for relief, a joy that flooded her heart, and her lips hesitated, opened and flowered beneath his. For one moment. Then he released her as quickly as he had seized her, his face triumphant.

'You see?' he said quietly.

'Go back to your wife,' she said steadily. Then as he did not move, 'Richard,' she pleaded, 'please, *please*, I beg of you. Leave me alone.'

An intense loneliness filled his face, as he turned and left her alone in the meadow.

CHAPTER ELEVEN

It tore at her night and day; when she saw William's face, and when she walked in the orchard where he had so lately been; but most of all when she looked at Elizabeth. Now it would not be suppressed; he had told her their separation was her fault. But how, when he had betrayed her? Yet the memory of his bitter face, which she had known always to be laughing and carefree, haunted her dreams and smothered her as she went about the business of the pub.

At the same time there was a kind of relief. He had come, she had seen him, and she had had the strength to send him away. It was over. Yet she felt the roots of her existence had been torn out of the earth and left bruised, and exposed in the glare of the midday sun.

William had said nothing; she had said nothing. As she had feared, she did not have the courage to look upon the hurt she would see on his face. If William glanced at her questioningly, she pretended not to notice. If he reached for her at night, she stiffened and, seeming to understand, he let her be. One kiss, and she should feel like this, its memory still stinging on her lips. It tormented her until in desperation for relief from that memory she turned to William and found his patient arms still there.

Chartboys, even with Rupert there bringing memories

of the past, became a refuge, and so she found herself spending more and more time there, leaving the children to Hetty's care in the afternoons after school. Richard's visit had not gone unnoticed in the village, and Hetty's eyes rested on her as if in sympathy. Proudly Beth turned her head away, ignoring the unspoken overture.

Then a crisis occurred at Chartboys that absorbed all Beth's physical and mental energies, and left more personal anguish as a dull ache in her stomach that flared into life only during the few quiet moments that she had. Her responsibilities over the patients' welfare usually sat lightly upon her. She enjoyed them. But this problem was different.

It began over the barberry. Beth arrived one day to hear the sound of raised voices from the gardens. Hurrying partly in duty, partly in curiosity to find the cause, she found a group of patients gathered round two contenders. One, she saw with sinking heart, was Lady Tatsfield, a long-term patient who had already been there for nine months and whose gentle nature made her popular with staff and patients alike. So it must be serious. She was in tears. The other, Beth saw, heart sinking even further, was Ethel from the Marie Bonner Wing who had been here three months and whose initial timidity and bad health had improved so wonderfully in the downs air that she was back to full fighting cockney strength. She too was popular, but not for her lack of aggression.

''Tis mine, innit,' she was saying belligerently. 'I were supposed to be workin' this bit. Old Bill said to clear it up. Anyway, 'twas only a dull old bush.'

'It was,' wailed Lady Tatsfield, 'my barberry. Cultivated for its berries. And it looks so lovely in autumn.'

'What's the use of a bush don't look nice till autumn. I says we need summat bright to look at, not all this dull stuff.' Ethel looked scathingly round the square patch that Lady Tatsfield had been nurturing all the summer, in the hope of providing fresh herbs for use at Chartboys by reviving the long overgrown and defunct Elizabethan herb garden.

Lady Tatsfield would have retired vanquished at this point, despite rallying cries from her fellow patients, had it not been for the arrival of the Comtesse de Merville. The Comtesse had elected the downs as her chosen home for a particular reason. She had left her husband and thus scandalised French society. While having no regrets on the matter whatsoever she had decided, solely in the interests of her health, that it would be prudent to eschew the more usual and fashionable sanatoriums of Switzerland. The Comtesse had no doubts about Ethel's place in the order of things compared with herb gardens.

'You have no taste, woman. *C'est le jardin des herbes*. The important part of the garden. *Et vous, vous êtes folle*, you destroy it.'

'Who you callin' a fool?' And, undoubtedly provoked, Ethel retaliated by throwing a clump of weeds with unerring aim into the Comtesse's face.

Appalled, Beth rushed to the rescue, as the Comtesse began icily to remove the debris from her immaculate face with a dainty lace handkerchief.

'Comtesse, I'll handle this.'

'Handle it, Madame Parslow? Please do so. We are to pay for the privilege of being assaulted by the scum from the sewers of London?'

Attracted by the noise Mary and Dr Goldstein arrived simultaneously. Without knowing the cause of the disturbance, they both instinctively grasped the reason. An inimical glance at one another, and Mary went to the aid of Beth to calm down the Comtesse, Dr Goldstein to the irate Ethel, on whom he had a magical effect, Beth noticed. She was laughing by the time he led her away, one hand firmly underneath her bony arm. Half an hour later, when Beth had had a word with Old Bill and the gardeners and arranged a new, tactful division of responsibility for the gardens in order to keep possible conflicts at bay as far as possible, she went in to face the battle she guessed would be raging within. A battle within a war.

She had timed it well, for the battle appeared to be over, Mary was emerging from Goldstein's room with an angry expression.

'It's quite impossible, Beth,' she said vehemently. 'Impossible. I cannot work with this man. He will never even try to see my viewpoint. How on earth does he expect these people to get on with one another if he segregates them all the time? We need to encourage them to work side by side and then these conflicts will never arise, or if they arise they will be settled amicably.'

The door flew open. 'Ah, Mrs Parslow, the ladies' committee meeting, I see. Well, you see what your idealism has achieved, ladies. It will lose us our patients, all for the sake of your social revolution. To hell with their health. No doubt you will be impressing us all with public oratory shortly, Miss Wilton, like the estimable Pankhurst ladies. Or waving banners for Votes for Women. Ornamenting the House of Commons –'

'If progress was left to you, Dr Goldstein, we would be back in the dark ages.'

'And a good thing too,' he said, triumphantly. 'Back to your proper role of rearing sons and cooking in iron pots.'

'Rupert, I'm serious. You'll lose either Goldstein or Mary, and half your patients, if this goes on. Goldstein is impossible. He holds such strict views and seeks to impose them on Mary. He either orders her around as though she was a student nurse, or patronises her like a fluffy kitten.'

'He's a first-class doctor, Beth. We need him. He gives people hope. Both sides, as you describe it. He has all their interests at heart, you know.'

'Perhaps,' said Beth drily. 'But it's turning Chartboys into a bedlam, and the patients who pay are getting restless. It could so easily be smoothed over if only he'd be diplomatic with Mary. If they worked together, instead of fighting each other all the time.'

'I don't think he understands the meaning of that word, Beth.'

'Then,' said Beth firmly, 'you must take a hand yourself. I think Mary may be on the point of leaving.'

'She is,' said Rupert, slowly. 'I don't know why. I suppose this affair with Goldstein? She says she feels she's stifled here, that she can do a better job for sick people elsewhere now that she's regained her strength, and got Chartboys on its feet.'

'No,' Beth was appalled. 'You can't let her leave.'

'I can't let Goldstein go, either,' said Rupert. 'Quite apart from the fact that he's a first-class doctor and patients trust him, there's another reason.' He hesitated. 'He's got money in the business, Beth.'

'Goldstein has?' asked Beth incredulously.

'I didn't have the courage to tell you at the time, but when we bought those cottages Beth, I hadn't the capital. They belong to him.' He looked at her horror-stricken face. 'Do you mind very much?'

'Yes,' she said quietly. 'You should have told me, Rupert. I won't be beholden to him.'

'It's for Chartboys, Beth. And for the Wheatsheaf. It did help you save it. It will make no difference that he owns them. You'll see.'

Perhaps not, but it was unwelcome news. It put her under an obligation. 'Then what about Mary?' she asked.

His face saddened. 'I can't talk her out of it. See if you can change her mind. I doubt it now this business has cropped up.' He sighed. 'I don't find people easy, Beth. Ideas are much easier to control.'

There was a pause, then: 'I saw Richard, Rupert,' said Beth abruptly, surprising herself for she had not meant to tell him.

'My poor Beth.' He came across to her chair, knelt by her side and took her hands in his.

She saw the question in his eyes, and answered gently: 'No, she wasn't with him.' Relief flooded into his face. 'I sent him away.'

He held on to her hands the more tightly, then lightly kissed them, and stood up. 'And Elizabeth?'

'Stays with me.'

He nodded slowly. 'So it's you and I still, Beth. Alone.'

*　*　*

'I must go.' Mary stood before the window of her room, implacable and obstinate.

'But Rupert will have a word with Goldstein – we'll get this matter sorted out. It's only a matter of discussing things after all. You've always said every reasonable person can talk things out.'

'Goldstein is not a reasonable person. Besides, there are other reasons.'

'Rupert told me how you feel.' Beth deliberately misinterpreted what she meant. 'You think you can do more good elsewhere. But can you? Isn't that pride getting in the way? I know myself how that can happen,' she said bitterly. 'Look at all the good you do here –'

'It's a backwater.'

'You can't be in wars all the time,' Beth said practically.

'There's constant war against poverty, sickness, bad information, bad living conditions – I could be fighting those. But even that's not the real reason. You know that, don't you?'

'Yes,' Beth admitted. 'Of course I realise. And I'm sorry.'

'I can't stand it any longer. He stands apart, godlike, all the time, and I feel I can't reach him because he's so good. Almost as though he's forsworn women, taken a vow of chastity. Was he *so* devoted to that woman, whoever she was?' she asked pleadingly.

Beth wrestled with her conscience. 'Yes,' she unwillingly admitted. 'And still is. It's a combination of loving her and feeling guilty about his wife.' She felt a traitor to Rupert, yet on the other hand she owed something to Mary too. Mary would be a wonderful wife for him.

'Then there's no hope for me,' said Mary quietly, 'and I must go.'

'How like a woman.' On the threshold of Mary's sitting room stood Goldstein, who had come in unobserved. 'Quitters. All of them.'

'This was a private conversation, Dr Goldstein,' said Mary, confusion battling with outrage.

'Private? Nonsense, woman, you were talking about leaving Chartboys. Hardly a private matter, is it? It affects me, after all.'

'I can't feel you'll be sorry to see me gone.'

'Women drag personal feelings into things all the time. That's what's wrong with them in business. Give them the vote. Pah! They'll be saying the Speaker's in love with them. Or they can't stay to debate because they've got a headache. Fragile things, women. Physically and mentally. No stamina in either.'

'Stop,' said Beth, 'oh, please stop before you go too far.'

He glanced at her dispassionately. 'You mean well, Beth, but this is between Mary and me.' Humiliated by the rebuff, Beth got up. 'You needn't go, you damnfool woman. Just keep quiet. What happens affects you as much as anyone. I expect you want Mary to stay.'

Mary had turned her head slightly at his use of her name, and he spoke to her directly. 'You're a professional woman, you claim. You do a good job here. Stick to it. Isn't finished yet, is it?'

'I've done all I can,' she said obstinately.

'Bloody nonsense. We may fight a bit but we both

want the best we can for the patients, don't we?'

'Look at today,' interposed Beth.

'Ah, today was the beginning,' said Goldstein with satisfaction. 'Things will start happening now. They'll sort themselves out one way or the other, if we leave them to it. You do a good job, you know, when you forget all your Keir Hardie nonsense. Things'll change in their own time without you giving the world a spin.'

Beth saw the tears welling up for the first time ever in Mary's eyes and made a movement towards her, but Goldstein was quicker. He took her hands and spoke as though no one were listening at all. 'You stay, Mary. I need someone to fight with. And as for the other business, well, you can rise above that, can't you? He needs you, too. Like we all do. And that's your job as a professional, isn't it? To stay where you're really needed.'

Elizabeth hopped up and down and finally clung onto the railings in an ecstasy of excitement. 'I can see it, Mama.'

Beth stood at her side, trying hard not to think of how it had been. Thus had the train steamed down the track, thus had Pippin been at her side. Thus had Richard come into their lives.

At last the train drew in with a triumphant chug. Doors opened and disgorged luggage and people in a milling heap. The hop-picking season had begun. Shepham had battened down its hatches, and put up its barricades against the yearly invasion. Nothing would persuade the villagers other than that they were about to lose their livelihood to petty thievery and robbery. And, to do them justice, perhaps a few would. For the whole summer, Elizabeth had been awaiting the arrival of the hop-pickers, and had come to think of 'the Hoppers' as mysterious beings from a far off wonderful world rather than the unruly loud rabble who filled the Wheatsheaf to overflowing a few weeks a year. Potent, unfamiliar, not altogether pleasant smells filled the air, and her mother was busier and yet happier at hop-picking times than at any other. They became invested in a magical power of their own for Elizabeth when they descended from that mysterious place called London once a year to fill their lives with noise, bustle and song. This year she had demanded to be in at the beginning, as the hop-pickers arrived and Beth, with no logical reason save her own misgivings as to why she should not do so, had brought her down to the station. Nothing had changed from the nineties. She remembered the same atmosphere of excitement, the same solid family groups that swarmed off the platforms in the same garish hats and costumes, bringing the smells and sounds of London with them. Elizabeth leapt up and down unable to contain her glee, her dark eyes wide open in wonder. One of the hoppers, a man in his thirties, noticed her and came across: 'Here, luvvie,' he said, and handed her a paper windmill.

Entranced, Elizabeth puffed away at this sophisticated novelty.

All so much the same. Yet with one difference. No Richard now. Beth watched, holding firmly onto Elizabeth's hands, as the hoppers settled their luggage and clambered into whatever conveyance they had. She saw the Medlars' cart set off, the driver nodding to her. They had announced in church that the Medlars' picking was beginning a week earlier than most other farms this year.

'There,' said Elizabeth with satisfaction, as the last cart pulled away. 'It's all over now.'

'Yes, all over,' Beth echoed softly.

This season the hop-picking was to be troubled by a host of minor irritations, outbreaks of petty pilfering - and sometimes not so petty - quarrels and fights on the fields, a violent disagreement on the Home Farm about the tally money, the discovery of wilt in one field.

It affected the Wheatsheaf, since the hoppers split into groups, each group choosing its own pub from the villages around, preferring to travel to Westling or Charing than meet their opponents. On the rare occasions they did all gather at the Wheatsheaf there was much ill-will, sometimes erupting into fighting that had William rushing into the barn to contain the trouble. The disaffection spread through the village like contagion - the hoppers had never been less popular. It spread even to Chartboys where patients in the Marie Bonner Wing, forbidden to join relations and friends in the fields, were discontented and often openly defiant.

But more was brewing. From where it stemmed was never known, but there was a conflict between the gypsies, normally peaceable except amongst themselves, and the East Enders. Due initially to the manager of the garden siting them too close to one another instead of putting the gypsies to another field, the trouble flared into a continuous battle. The East Enders saw no difficulty in dealing with a pack of gypsies after the Lascars they were used to warring with. But they were mistaken.

The binman of the gypsies' battalion was accused by the East Enders of going too slow in order to avoid moving his forces on to a bad patch, with the result that the East Enders found themselves allotted to it. There was no proof it was deliberate, but the East Enders did not require it. The row was smoothed over, but the seeds festered. Small altercations broke out, were hushed down, each side retreating into uneasy co-existence. It all erupted on the day of the children's monthly visit to the Squire. As a special treat, Beth took them through the hopfields, since Elizabeth had displayed such interest in the mysterious hoppers and their doings.

As she approached the Home Farm hop gardens, she could hear the sounds of altercation but, assuming it to be no more than the usual fracas, she decided to press forward, especially since surging up behind her from the oast houses was a group of men, also bent on finding out what was going on.

The field was only half picked, but a fight was going on between half a dozen gypsies and a dozen or more East Enders. Reinforcements were arriving in ones and twos. Iron pots, contents tipped over; men punching; bines trampled underfoot. The gypsies once their anger was turned outside their own tribal disputes, were no mean fighters, with more order and precision in their attack than the East Enders. The women were screaming, whether from encouragement or fear Beth could not determine. Bystanders were egging them on. The cause this time had been a complaint from the oast house about the number of leaves left in the pockets with the hops: whose pockets were they? Who was the binman whose job it was to check? A rumour had gone round that no tally would be paid for the morning's work. Whether it was true or not scarcely mattered, as rival factions battled onwards.

Horrified at the sight of what was clearly beyond an easily settled dispute, Beth tugged at Owen's hand and called to Elizabeth. Her way back was blocked by the crowd of men behind, her way forward in the Medlars' park blocked by the Squire, with a hastily summoned retinue, who had come in person to find the cause of the uproar. The sight of good bines being trampled underfoot made him see red. Seizing the binman's horn, he put it to his lips and blew once, twice, then a third time. Recalled to reality and the threat of dismissal from the gardens, the men unwillingly and slowly broke off combat.

'That's enough. Do you want the police to you?' roared the Squire. 'I'll have no more fighting in these fields, or the lot of you will be banned from picking on this farm again or round these parts at all, if I have a say in the matter.' To families who had picked for generations on these fields this was a dire threat and they were still.

'I don't care who's in the right and who's in the wrong of it. It's to stop now, and the damage put right. You'll be stopped no money this time,' – the Squire was a shrewd man – 'but any of you so much as raises a fist against someone on my gardens again and you'll be dismissed immediately, no matter what the cause. That clear?' There was a series of disgruntled nods, animosity still flaring in their eyes, but tempers cooled.

Or so they would have done. But the minute the Squire had climbed down from the binman's chair, which he'd used as a vantage point, someone took his place.

Beth's heart sank. It was Hamlin, in Homburg hat and overcoat for all it was August. What on earth was he doing here? It boded no good for him to be concerning himself with the picking.

'What do you want, Hamlin?' demanded the Squire. 'This is no business of yours.'

'I'm here, Scoones, because I've got a business to run and a contract with Home Farm, that's my business. My sampler tells me your hops are undercured, but your drier tells me the quality's down because of the way they're being picked. Mishandled, they are.'

'Listen here, Hamlin,' the Squire roared and the workforce gathered to listen. The Squire never took kindly to criticism, and was suddenly on his pickers' side, much to their amazement. 'You've no place in these fields. You're a buyer, but we're in charge here. I won't have you interfering down at the oast. If you don't like our hops, then don't buy 'em. There's plenty as will.'

'That's true, and I'm one of them,' said Beth, unable to resist a thrust at her old adversary. She needed double the quantity for she was now supplying Chartboys with Ovenden Beers.

Hamlin slowly turned to look at her, and his inimical eyes went in glee from Beth to the Squire.

'Of course you'll buy his hops, Beth Parslow. That's how business is done in Shepham, isn't it? Quality don't count any more. You don't care what load of muck you produce and call it beer – not Squire Scoones and his bastard daughter!'

Would he never let her alone? Now this – the world swam around. She looked fearfully towards the Squire who, red in the face, was clutching hold of Hamlin and shaking him like a terrier, big man though he was.

Beth ran forward to pull him back, leaving Elizabeth

crying behind her. 'Father, don't –' she cried. The word came out naturally and it was not until later that she realised what she had said. 'Leave him be.'

'By God, Hamlin,' said Scoones, dropping his hold. 'I'll have you yet. You've been a scourge on this village too long. I'll not have it any longer. You thought you could bully my daughter here, and she was too much for you. Now you think you'll try me. Get off my land, and get out of our lives.'

'Look to yourself, Squire,' said Hamlin menacingly, his pale eyes full of hatred. 'I'm going, but you, your bastard and *her* bastard,' his eyes rested malevolently on Elizabeth who cowered fearfully behind Beth, 'take note. I'll have Medlars and I'll have the Wheatsheaf before I've done. By God, I took a vow once. And I'll not forget it. The Scoones and the Ovendens have had their day.'

It was an ugly interlude in a troubled summer. But it was to get worse. William came rushing into the bar the following day. 'Beth, my lovely. Thee's wanted.'

'Where? Chartboys?' she said absently, busily stocktaking at the bar.

'No, Medlars. 'Tis the Squire. He's had a heart attack. He's pulled through, but only just and they don't reckon he'll last long now.'

Her legs felt weak at this new blow.

'He's asking for you, Beth. You'd best go.'

'Will you come, William?' she faltered.

'No, 'tis you he wants,' he said gently, then seeing her pleading look: 'I'll come with 'ee to the house if you like. Ben can mind the bar.'

* * *

The Squire's eyes fluttered open as she sat stiffly by his side, unable to take in that this was the powerful, masterful Squire lying grey and helpless in the huge old bed.

'Beth, you called me Father out there –'

'Yes,' she said simply.

'There was talk at the time you were born. No one knew. But he must've heard the gossip. Beth – we've not been close. We should have been.'

'It came too late,' she said sadly. 'Too late for us both.' Then, anxious lest he thought this a reproach, she said gently, 'It was for the best. Would you have wanted me to grow up knowing I was a love-child, not Andrew's daughter?'

'No. But I've not done right by you.'

'You tried. No one could do more.'

'Pippin –'

She grew cold. This was what she had feared.

'Try, Beth. Try.'

Try? Try what? She shut the thought out, pretend he had said nothing about Pippin.

'I've looked after Elizabeth in my will, Beth. Owen too. But most for Elizabeth. She will need help. You're strong, Beth. You will cope. But the little one –' A tear escaped from under the lids as he closed his eyes from the effort of speaking.

She, Beth, strong? Why did everyone think that, when inside she was weak, curled up against the world. She felt a moment's bitterness at his care for Elizabeth – too late. Elizabeth should have been his legitimate grandchild. Then she quelled the bitterness as she looked at his worried eyes.

'Father,' she whispered, gently putting her lips to his forehead. Some of the trouble went out of his face and he fell asleep again once more. Tears pricked behind her eyes. What could she have made of the last years, had she devoted more time to him? She had thought him a kindly enough but dominating, assured man; now she saw only a tired, frightened one.

She tiptoed out and ran down the stairs to where Jervis was waiting to show her out. He looked more human than she'd ever seen him before. 'He's not well, is he, miss?' he asked gravely.

'No,' she said. 'Not well at all,' and passed out of the door lest Pippin should arrive and find her there.

She did not see her father again.

'I won't go.'

Beth stood mulishly in their bedroom. William sighed and patiently pleaded with her. 'Beth, you must. Thanks to old Hamlin, everyone knows you're his daughter and they'll be waiting to see whether you turn up at funeral.' The Squire had died in his sleep the day after Beth had seen him. Regrets that she had not grown closer to him had swept over her, saddening her ever since.

'Then I won't give them the satisfaction.'

'No, 'tis all the more reason to go. They'll think otherwise you're ashamed to face them. Ashamed of being his daughter. Are you, Beth?'

Her head was flung back proudly. 'No,' she said. 'Of course not.'

'Then you go.'

'But how can I, William? *She'll* be there,' she pleaded

piteously. She might have added, 'And *he'll* be there' but the thought lay unspoken between them.

'You ain't never been one not to face up to things, Beth,' William pointed out.

She regarded him strangely. How odd it was that even those closest to you could sometimes not understand. She was tired, so tired. The Squire's death and the village now knowing their relationship had been enough to cope with. To have to face Pippin was another thing altogether. Her half-sister – no, she could not, would not, think of it.

Beth sat rigidly in the pew, William staunchly by her side in his best black suit. Her mourning clothes were sadly out of date, stemming from the nineties, the same she had worn to Andrew's funeral and all the funerals since. Every nerve in her body awaited the arrival of the mourning party. Coming into church, seeing the villagers' heads turning, had been easy as she was swept along by a greater fear. When Daniel Harbutt as usher showed her to one of the front pews she had wondered why, then remembered that everyone knew now. A slight flush on her face, she had not demurred but taken her place quietly.

Rupert slid into the pew on the other side of her from William, his face pale. She looked at him gratefully and squeezed his hand companionably. The organist struck up with the funeral march.

Dear God, they were coming. She gripped Rupert's hand tightly as, unsteadily, she rose to her feet. The funeral party took their places on the other side of the aisle, as the funeral bier came to rest borne on the shoulders of six men. She glanced at the coffin, remembering for a moment with affection the Squire who had given her so much in her early years. But then a pit opened in her stomach. One of the bearers had been Richard, now making his way to stand by – she consciously turned to look at Pippin.

She knew Rupert was looking too, by the muscle working on his cheek. She summoned her courage and looked again, across William, who continued to look stolidly towards the front. A slight figure in black, gold hair under the very newest small hat, so different to every other woman there. Features chiselled, jaw set, as she stared straight forward, no emotion on her face, to where the rector was taking his place to begin the service.

Beth breathed easier. The worst was past. Was that cold, slender figure really Pippin? How could she have been afraid? Instead of the monstrous figures that had haunted her dreams, they were two perfectly ordinary people, husband and wife. She swallowed hard, and tried to concentrate on the service.

At the graveside she stood back, held between Rupert and William as she watched, with no emotion at all, Pippin sprinkle dust on the coffin and then the coffin disappear from sight. Later she would grieve, think of the early happy days at Medlars, but for now – she desperately wanted to be back in the safety and warmth of the Wheatsheaf kitchen. Pippin glanced up and saw her. Blue eyes stared coldly at Beth with no trace of recognition, then she gave a slight bow as she passed by on Richard's arm. A gleam of something lit her eyes as she passed Rupert. Then they were gone, Richard sweeping past Beth to greet Rupert. It was over. They could depart with dignity, and need never see each other again.

But she was wrong, it was not over and Rupert could not support her the second time. She had forgotten about the reading of the will. Having received a letter, she decided not to go, until the solicitor called in person at the Wheatsheaf to ensure her presence. Resigned, she went into the small parlour at Medlars to find a large gathering, perhaps forty people, present. Many she recognised as Medlars' servants, some she did not. She sat down in a corner, hoping to evade notice. She refused to let her eyes search for Richard. There was no need. He dominated the room.

He stood behind Pippin's chair as though patriach in a grouped family photograph. But there was no sign of their children, for which she was relieved. The will was much as she expected. Medlars and its whole estates went to Pippin in trust for her son. Bequests to servants and family. Then she heard, 'To my beloved daughter, now Elizabeth Parslow, my shares in Teynham Breweries and the sum of £200; to my grandson Owen Parslow £500; and to my granddaughter Elizabeth Parslow £1,000'.

She dared not look at Richard, but she sensed his sudden movement. So he hadn't known . . . How ironic. And how little it mattered. She sensed movement from Pippin too – staring across the room at Elizabeth, her face a mask.

'My beloved daughter'. Squire had called her his beloved daughter. Beth felt humbled, wondering again about her mother. He loved her for her mother's sake. But perhaps a little, too, for herself, thinking back to the days when he would greet her as she arrived at Medlars for lessons.

She knew she could not stay here; so hated. She rose to go as soon as the reading was over.

'Beth,' the well remembered ice-cold voice. Pippin came right up to her, so close Beth could smell her perfume. She was face to face with the woman who for so many years she had thought her best friend. She forced herself to stop, not to tremble. 'Elizabeth,' Pippin was saying now in inarticulate fury. 'Elizabeth.'

To Beth this meant only one thing at the time, 'You knew,' she found herself saying dazedly, 'you knew I was his daughter, didn't you?'

'Naturally,' came the hard voice.

'All the time?'

Pippin would not answer at first, but simply stared at Beth. 'It was the way he looked at you,' she said eventually. 'The way he looked at you –'

It was only much later that Beth realised what Pippin had meant by 'Elizabeth'. She had known already about Beth being her half-sister, but had now, after the bequest, guessed the truth about Elizabeth.

When her thoughts had calmed a little, Beth remembered what also had been said at the reading of the will: 'My shares in Teynham Breweries'. *Shares*! In Hamlin's firm! Even in her anguish, a small smile came to Beth's lips. A weapon at last. A small one perhaps. But at least a weapon.

Rupert greeted her as she entered his study on her next visit to Chartboys, looking at her almost apprehensively. She thought he would ask her about the funeral, the reading of the will, but he did not. Instead he said heavily, 'I've bad news, Beth.'

She drew in her breath sharply. 'What?'

'Pippin and Richard are returning to live at Medlars.'

Something seemed to hit her in the pit of her stomach. Why had she not ever thought of this? Of course, Medlars belonged to Pippin. Of course she'd come back.

'But Richard's career?' she asked faintly.

He shrugged. 'He fancies himself as the new manager of the estate, I gather.'

She laughed wildly. 'Richard? Manage the estate? He'll never do it. Where's the stage he needs in that?'

'Perhaps he's changed. Or perhaps he'll remain in London and continue his career during the week. I don't know.' There was a world of weariness in his voice, as he asked bleakly, 'What's to happen to us, Beth? What's to happen?'

CHAPTER TWELVE

The last of the autumn leaves had fallen. The lanes were piled high with soggy masses of brown and yellow leaves. The softness of the landscape spangled with spiders' webs had hardened in preparation for the winter. Hedgehogs and squirrels sought cover; golden hues gave place to grey and the east wind blew mournfully over the downs, a herald to the storms that would come.

In the Wheatsheaf, the logs burned brightly on the hearths; the polished red tiles glowed with the warmth no longer to be found outside. Here within its walls, the smell of baking from the range in her nostrils, the paraphernalia of pub life around her, Beth was safe. Her children were world enough - even though Mud was missing. Now eight and away at school during the week, he returned full of that mysterious other world to impress Elizabeth and Owen on Saturdays and those of the holidays he did not spend with Rupert in Buckinghamshire.

Beth shut her ears, and her heart, to all mention of Medlars. They had not yet arrived. She knew only that. She could not share her worries with anyone, certainly not with William, not even with Rupert who had not mentioned the matter after that first conversation.

Thereafter their conversation was confined to Chartboys, not to the prospective occupiers of Medlars. Yet she needed to talk, if only to help distance the problem.

At length, in desperation, having wrestled with her pride, she spoke to the one person who could, who might understand. Hetty was occupied in the never-ending chore of cleaning the copper.

'I'll give you a hand with that,' said Beth abruptly.

Hetty looked up in surprise and some suspicion. Beth did not often work alongside her, much less choose to when there was no need.

'How old's James now?' Beth asked.

'Ten,' replied Hetty warily.

'He's a fine-looking lad,' said Beth awkwardly, and conscious that she was sounding a false note. But it was the truth. He was the image of Richard, so resembling Elizabeth that she wondered the whole village did not remark on it. Perhaps they did, she thought. He was a bright-eyed lad, but sly, silent, looking at her with quick intelligent blue eyes that had all of Richard's cunning and none of his warmth.

'What's on your mind, Beth?' asked Hetty evenly, intimately. 'Not my son, I'll be bound.'

Beth flushed, but desperation drove her on. 'Hetty, he's coming back. To live.'

Hetty dropped the pan she was holding. Perhaps deliberately, for she turned her face away so that Beth could not see her expression. ''Tis no odds to me, Beth,' she said at last, straightening up again. 'But what are *you* going to do? I heard he come down in the spring. You saw him then didn't you?'

Beth nodded, feeling the relief of catharsis.

'I thought so; you was proper pother-headed for days. Look, my business it's not, but you brought it up. Richard Lyle will bring trouble, even if he don't mean to. He's just that sort. Can't help it. 'Tis all right for me. But not for you. You've more folks depending on you. Hold out, Beth. No matter how hard it be.'

'I've told him –' The colour drained from her face.

'Telling's no good,' said Hetty slowly. 'You got to feel it, mean it. He knows his power. And he'll use it. Oh, yes. Sure as there's a dog in Dover he'll use it,' she said bitterly.

Beth knew she must set her energies, both physical and mental, to other things – but what? The cottages were doing nicely, bringing in a small but steady income. Hetty was organising the housekeeping with the help of a local girl. The preserves trade and the wine trade were still blocked by Hamlin's actions in preventing local inns from purchasing them.

Yet how could he stop her, if she really wanted to carry on? She frowned. There were other outlets after all. Chartboys for one. Why hadn't she thought of it before? And why not take the goods to Faversham shops, as she had dreamed of long ago.

With an unexpected rise of excitement that for a moment quenched the ache in her heart, she went to see Rupert.

'I could give you a regular supply,' she said eagerly. 'Now I know Dr Goldstein thinks there's nothing to getting folks well but chasing those bacteria, but the old ways aren't done for yet. And my herb wines have been doing people good for a few centuries now. As well as the wines, I could give you preserved cucumbers and Indian soy and walnut catsup, mushroom too, preserved oranges perhaps, and of course –'

'Stop,' he said laughing. 'Bring all you want. And if it's used, I'll pay you. If it's left then you don't get any new orders.'

But it wasn't left. And once Chartboys had led the way, Faversham shopkeepers were quick to follow, until she was forced to organise regular daily deliveries by old Percy Brown's waggon and then to turn one of the unused barns into a workroom, whitewashing the walls, equipping it and hiring a girl from the village to help.

Yet, with all this, she had only to stay a moment in her restless drive for that familiar ache to begin once more.

Shortly before Christmas, Beth stood at the door of the Wheatsheaf and knew the time had come. At the far end of the green from the Faversham road appeared the familiar Medlars' carriage, then the governess carts, piled high with luggage, the carriage going by. She saw two children peering out of the carriage windows, and forced herself to face whatever came next. Now that it had come it did not seem so big an ordeal. But the sight of the Panhard motor car was a different matter. In stately, ostentatious fashion, it drove slowly past the green, Richard at the wheel, a hatted, veiled woman at his side, her fair hair visible even at this distance. A wave of sickness passed over Beth, but she forced herself to remain at the Wheatsheaf door, whether they saw her or not, watching the Panhard's progress, almost silhouetted against the bleak November sky; Richard's goggles and the monstrous veiled effusion at his side seeming to present a threat to the privacy of Shepham.

She re-entered the Wheatsheaf with heavy heart. It would not be easy. Tongues would soon be wagging. It was over nine years ago but, in villages, memories are long. Fortunately the spearhead of her enemies had gone; those that remained might be more sympathetic, she reasoned. But would they accept Richard as the new Squire? They remembered Richard Lyle as a hopper, a wild student, a man who, it was said, should be in prison if he had had his deserts. And what of Tom the Higgler and his mob? Tom was in prison and his followers no longer bothered Shepham, but news would travel. Although the Rawlinson brothers had 'retired' so it was said, from the 'trade', there again memories were long and old scores remained to be settled. There was no organised smuggling now, just small scale efforts. They would look to Richard, however, to turn a blind eye to their activities. Would he become a magistrate? *Would* he run the estate? Would he remain a practising barrister? She found these and a thousand other thoughts running constantly through her mind until, with a great effort of will, she turned her attention to the plum cake for Christmas and paid great attention to the chopping of the candied citron and raisins.

She saw him in church, she saw him walking with the children in the village. She saw him everywhere. Was it deliberate? Surely not. He never looked at her, never acknowledged her, she anguished alone. William had said nothing, for there was nothing to say, but his expression grew sadder. 'He's the sense to stay away from her,' she overheard him say one day to Ben, and was filled both with anger that he chose Ben as his confidant and with sorrow that he could not speak of it to her. But she did nothing.

'Now the winter's here, Jim, we'll have to reduce to two barrels. Do you mind?' It had been a shock to discover how overstocked they were when she went to the cellar to check the position. It was a constant niggle between herself and William as to whose job this was. It made sense for Beth with her business nose to do the actual ordering, but nowadays, more and more frequently, she found in effect she was controlling beer stocks as well. That should be William's job but it seemed the more energy she put into the running of the Wheatsheaf, the less he did, preferring to disappear for long periods to Canterbury, in theory to see the bank manager and discuss business with the malt suppliers but she suspected also it was to while away a few hours in its many hospitable public houses away from the cares of the Wheatsheaf.

'And, Jim,' she went on rapidly, 'can you give me longer credit this time?'

He pulled a face. ''Tis mounting up a bit, Beth. How long?'

'Three months?'

'As it's you, Beth, and I know you'll do as you say, I'll say yes. But not for ever, mind. Things not going well then? Hamlin still after you, is he? The Wheatsheaf that is,' he amended hastily.

'It'd be easier if it were me he'd an eye for,' she said ruefully. 'But he's keeping quieter now, now he knows I'm a shareholder even if a very minor one. He hasn't given up though,' she shivered.

'I heard he's buying up the old Bell at Westling Forstal,' said Jim, 'Another one gone. He's still up to his old tricks. Offered the Bell a loan, then made them buy his beer only as a condition of repayment. He didn't get far with your father though, nor with you and William.'

'Thanks to you,' said Beth. 'But it can't be easy for you either.'

'We do all right, because we serve a big area north of Maidstone. 'Tis more difficult for you.'

'We've got to beat him, Jim,' said Beth. 'Otherwise, in the future, quality will disappear, there'll be no room for the small brewer, no room for the small free house. It's important for us to stand firm now.'

But how? she wondered, as she left Jim's offices. She was still pondering the question as she entered the Star pub in the middle of the town. The landlord had set aside her usual private room, and she sank down thankfully on the small sofa, while he arranged for her lunch to be brought. She poked the small fire into flame, glad to be on her own for a short while away from Shepham, away from the Wheatsheaf, away from the children, away from anything that had claims on her.

'That was quick, Ernest,' she said idly, as she heard the door open behind her.

'It's not Ernest.'

She could not look round, she dared not. It couldn't be . . . dear God, please not.

'What are you doing here, Richard?' she asked wearily, facing the inevitable.

'Following you,' he said cheerfully, taking off his coat and tossing it over a chair. 'I've brought your luncheon.

Do get on with it. Don't take any notice of me. We can talk afterwards.'

'We have nothing to talk about,' she said desperately, looking wildly for a means of escape. There was none, for Richard was firmly planted in front of the door, arms crossed, eyes laughing.

'Ah yes, Beth. We do. Now eat your lunch like a good girl.'

She glared at him. 'I'm not –' she began, but gave up. There was no arguing with Richard in this mood. She ate her lunch as slowly as she could, conscious all the time of his eyes upon her. She was glad she was wearing her burgundy red bolero suit, conscious that it suited her, and the thought gave her a strength – a ridiculous one perhaps, but invaluable. When she had finished eating, she rose to her feet composedly and walked towards the door.

'Where do you think you're going?' he enquired pleasantly.

'Where do you think I'm going?' she replied with well-calculated irritability. 'I've just drunk a pint of Ernest's best mild and bitter!'

He eyed her suspiciously. 'I want your promise that you'll come back.' He seized her wrist, pulling her so close to him she shut her eyes. 'Either that, or I come with you and wait outside the door. Now,' he said teasingly, 'you're an honest broker. Which is it to be?'

She wrestled with her conscience. A broken promise – what was that where her sanity was concerned? But a lifetime's habit won. She returned to the sofa and plumped herself down. 'It was only half a pint,' she muttered, grinning despite herself.

'That's my Beth.' Swiftly, before she could move, he was at her side and his arm round her.

'No,' she said sharply, trying to pull away. 'Suppose somebody –'

'The door's locked.'

'That'll do my reputation a power of good,' she said tartly. 'I come here regular. They all know me.'

'Then hear me out quickly. I've got a proposition to make.' He did not release his hold. She could smell the soap he used, had always used. Imperceptibly, unconsciously, she began to relax. 'I want you back. I've got to have you back.' She gasped, and tried again to pull away. 'No, hear me out. It's no good. I can't live without you, not now I've seen you again, now I'm living here. I promise I won't make trouble over Elizabeth, if –'

'If what?' she asked angrily. 'Richard, I told you – I *can't*. William's good to me. I – I love him. I'm *married*. Doesn't that mean anything to you?'

'Yes,' he said in a clipped voice. 'It means I can't call you mine, can't love you and be proud of you as I want, have you at my side every day laughing and loving, or in my bed at night. It means I can't have any more children by you unless –'

'No,' she cried. 'Stop, Richard, oh, stop. It can't be. Can't you get that into your head? You left me. You chose Pippin. There's no going back. The whole of the village, as well as your wife and my husband, is watching us. There's no way –'

'There's always a way – if there's a will.'

'No will,' she said fiercely. 'Richard, I can't. You must see that. I can't ever, ever love you again.' The words rang hollowly in her ears. They had no meaning for her, they seemed to be spoken by some other person. 'I'll never be in your arms again.'

'You will, Beth, oh you will,' he murmured at once. He was confident, assured, smiling. Her words had produced no effect at all. Very well then, she must act. She got up and he did not hold her back. She walked unsteadily and turned the key to unlock it. But as she went out, she turned, impelled by a force stronger than her determination. He was smiling lazily, as though some lingering doubt had been quelled for ever.

She dreaded every moment that he might appear and bring her face to face again with her own heart. She trembled lest he appear at Chartboys, the church, the Wheatsheaf even, but when he did not, she began to relax, busying herself with her other concerns and especially those for Christmas. All the rooms were booked for the Christmas holiday, and right through to New Year's Day, for on New Year's Eve there was to be a dance at Chartboys for patients, guests and staff. Occupied as she was with preparations, Beth's worries over Richard's intentions were forgotten. He had been joking, she told herself. He knew as well as she that there was no future for them together.

But he had not been joking.

The children were Richard's first target. She sat with William and Rupert and the children in the Chartboys' pew, stiffly, barely acknowledging Richard and Pippin next door. She had schooled herself to incline her head politely towards them, by pretending they were completely different people whom she'd never met before. Indeed, as she glanced sideways at Pippin, she felt perhaps this was true. The chiselled features, the ice-cold eyes, bore little relation to the friend of her childhood.

'Mama, who is that lady?' whispered Elizabeth.

'Mrs Lyle, dear,' Beth hissed. To refuse an answer would create a passionate interest where now only idle curiosity existed. Elizabeth was determined – like Richard, the thought involuntarily came to her. And he was sitting there, not ten feet from her.

'She smells nice,' pronounced Elizabeth, 'but I like Uncle Richard best.' Beth froze, but nothing more was said, and William did not notice. And that would have been that, save for Mud.

'Uncle Richard,' shouted the small boy, after the service. Appalled and unable to stop him, Beth and William stood still on the pathway, William grasping her arm. Rupert was pale, as he grabbed Mud by the shoulder. But the boy tore free and ran to Richard, followed eagerly by Elizabeth.

'And you're Elizabeth,' said Richard softly.

'Yes,' said Elizabeth importantly. 'And you're the Cheshire Cat. I met you up a tree a long time ago.'

'Come along, darlings.' Pippin, her face a mask of hatred, came forward to claim her husband.

Beth gradually relaxed as she served the Christmas goose which Rupert was sharing with them at the Wheatsheaf to be with Mud. William had said nothing walking home from church, and she glanced at him once or twice anxiously. He had not joined the group in the churchyard but stood apart by the lychgate waiting for them to join him. Did he fear Richard's return as she did? If only they could talk about it. But she knew it was impossible.

Because of Elizabeth there could be no talk between them of Richard Lyle.

'Beth, I have to tell you something.' Rupert had followed her into the kitchen where she was unmoulding the plum pudding. She finished pouring the brandy over it and then gave him her attention.

'The New Year's dance at Chartboys,' he said awkwardly. 'I've asked Pippin and Richard.'

'Rupert, what are you doing?' she asked wearily. 'Oh, be careful. For yourself I mean. For I can't come.'

'Nonsense,' Rupert said firmly. 'I've thought all this out very carefully. We at Chartboys either have to mix socially with them – or create a noticeable feud. It isn't quite the same for you –'

'Because I'm not Society?' asked Beth, flushing.

'You know I didn't mean that, Beth. But you have a family around you, you have the Wheatsheaf. When I'm here, I'm a bachelor, I have to have some social life and –'

'These are excuses,' she cried. 'You want to meet them again, don't you? You say it's because you're a bachelor. Very well. Marry then. Marry Mary.'

Blank astonishment was written over his face, and she was furious with herself for having revealed Mary's secret.

'Beth, you and your romantic ideas. Mary doesn't care a fig for me.'

'Doesn't she?' said Beth drily. She'd gone too far now to pull back. 'Of course she does, Rupert. She's loved you ever since she first arrived. You accused me once of being blind. Now I say the same to you. *And* I'm warning you to take care, Rupert.'

* * *

Red. As red as the flames of jealousy that would lick her, burn her when she had to see them together once more in the same room. Dancing together. Man and wife. The dress was second-hand, given to her by Lady Tatsfield. It was out of fashion but on Beth this did not matter. It clung to her form perfectly, giving her skin a glow that even the months of working outside at Chartboys had not given it. Her black hair was only loosely caught up, so that it hung in curls to her shoulders. By Heaven, she'd go in fighting, she thought, looking at her reflection in the mirror critically.

William gave her a glance of approval. He had not wanted to go, especially when she told him who would be there, but he had not refused. It was almost a silent acknowledgement that this had to be faced. The dinner jacket looked even shabbier this year, but William wore it confidently, an unusual assurance in his step and look that surprised Beth.

The former huge Chartboys drawing room, used by the patients during the daytime, had been transformed, glistening with lights and decorations. For once, Goldstein had relaxed his rules of quietness for the patients. Those that were not well enough to attend were packed off to a distant ward – those that were were in full regalia, the tiaras and dress suits of the richer patients and guests intermingled with colourful – often gaudy – attire.

The dance was already in progress when Beth and William arrived. Her heart leapt and panic began to sweep over her as she saw Rupert already talking to Pippin, who was immaculate in a white low-cut Empire line satin dress. She shouldn't wear white, thought Beth instinctively, she hasn't the colouring for it. She began to feel better, especially as she saw the Comtesse de Merville join them. An ally, for although she knew nothing of Beth's personal story, she was a friend. As they hesitated, she saw Richard walk up to them, two glasses in his hands. It was the first time she had seen him in evening dress: and she had not realised till then quite how good-looking he was, the black formality complementing his dark curly hair and blue eyes. Yet he was so far removed from her gypsy highwayman lover of the past that it was oddly reassuring. She glanced at William questioningly.

'Aye, Beth,' he said simply, in silent accord. Together they walked up to the group. 'Pippin,' Beth said gravely, and bowed. 'Richard.' A slighter bow. 'Good evening, Rupert.'

A welcoming smile from the Comtesse. A cold bow from Pippin. Richard, as if divining her motive in her bold approach, took her hand and kissed it. A gauntlet had been thrown down. The Comtesse, sensing a stillness in the air, looked sharply at them. Sensitive as ever, Rupert asked Beth to dance and William took Pippin's arm, much to her disapproval. Richard turned to the Comtesse, mockingly aware of Beth's tenseness.

The evening wore on and Beth was an automaton. She did not know if she was enjoying herself; it was something to exist, to keep moving, keep drinking, keep talking, anything, but keep away from Richard. Midnight approached, and soon, soon she could go home, take this smile off her face and collapse. At least Richard was behaving himself. He was keeping away from her. He could hardly do otherwise with William and Rupert present, she thought. Then William chose that moment to replenish his and Beth's glasses to welcome the New Year. Thus it was, in ironic parody of that other New Year, that Richard, seeing Pippin dancing with Rupert, came upon her momentarily alone.

With a grin of triumph, Richard swept her off with not a chance to refuse short of causing a public incident, for William was nowhere to be seen. He returned to see Beth whirled like a red flame in Richard's arms.

'Happy New Year, darling,' Richard whispered. 'Do you remember –'

'No,' said Beth succinctly. 'I'm Beth Parslow now, and my husband is watching. It's New Year and I should be dancing with him.'

'He doesn't deserve you,' murmured Richard. 'Look at you. A flame reaching out for wilder worlds, to be freed, to soar into the skies, meant for –'

'Not meant for you,' said Beth, determined to quash this rhetoric before she began to listen to it with her heart as well as her ears.

'I'll not try to persuade you any more, Beth,' he said huskily as the clock began to strike the New Year. 'One day you'll come to me. I know that, more clearly than I've ever known anything before.'

'Let me go,' she said fearfully. 'You hold me too close.'

'No, Beth,' he said gravely. 'You only imagine that I do.'

She looked down and saw that he spoke the truth. The bonds that held them close were not physical.

* * *

The worst part of winter lay ahead, and the conspiracy – for so it seemed to Beth – thickened around her. Her preoccupation affected the Wheatsheaf, and trade, never good in the winter, slackened. When the snows came, first Mud, then Elizabeth, then Owen went to Medlars to play snowballs, to ride on their sledges down the Home Farm grazing slopes.

'I hit Uncle Richard with a snowball,' said Mud importantly. 'He laughed.'

'I don't have time to play snowballs, young Mud,' said William shortly, obviously feeling this as a reflection on his manhood.

'It doesn't matter,' said Mud generously. He was devoted to William. Then, as William sank into his armchair with a sigh of relief, 'You can build me a snowman instead.' Even William had to laugh at that, breaking the tension that Richard's name had created between Beth and himself ever since the New Year dance.

'Mama, I don't like Genevieve. She's mean.'

'She's not very used to the country yet, I expect, darling.' Privately she shared Elizabeth's reservations. 'But I like Jasper,' Elizabeth added thoughtfully. 'He kissed me,' then looked at them anxiously. She had not meant to part with this information.

'What did you do to deserve that?' William said evenly, but from the look he gave Beth he was sharing her thoughts. A danger they had not thought of. But Beth pushed the problem aside – Richard's children would soon be going away to boarding schools, thank Heaven. Then the thought crossed her mind. And what of Elizabeth? That was what the Squire's money was meant for, surely? She must talk to William.

The next round was unwittingly won on Richard's behalf by Pippin, who had carried open warfare into Beth's own territory. One day Beth went to Chartboys only to find Pippin arranging spring flowers in the drawing room.

'I just thought I'd bring a few up, Beth,' said Pippin with a quick artificial smile. 'They're from the Medlars' woods. You remember? I popped in to see Rupert, but couldn't resist arranging them myself. Pretty, aren't they?'

Pippin had lost none of her old power. Immediately Beth slipped into her old role. She could see it clearly now. Apparently submissive, Pippin was, had always been, the dominant one.

'It's good of you,' Beth managed to say coolly. But I should take the initiative, she thought desperately. 'But not that vase though. It's valuable –'

'Rupert said it was all right,' replied Pippin. 'Don't worry about it.' She gave Beth a sweet smile.

That was the start. Every so often after that Beth would arrive to find Pippin carrying out other small jobs. Always helpful, always meek. She made herself invaluable to Mary. It became clear to Beth then. Pippin had designs on Chartboys and on Beth's power there. With some alarm Beth saw a friendship blossoming between Mary and Pippin and coldness on Mary's part towards herself. In Dr Goldstein, however, she had an ally.

'Don't, Mrs Parslow,' he said through gritted teeth, 'allow little Miss Puss in Boots past my door. I hold you responsible.'

'She's Sir Rupert's friend,' pointed out Beth crossly, 'I can't stop her. I wish I could.'

He looked at her directly. 'Beth,' he said informally, 'where's your fighting spirit?' As she looked at him blankly, he said sadly, 'In the end, Beth, honesty may win through; but it will take a battering first. Can you take it?'

'Be careful, Rupert,' Beth pleaded. 'I know you're just trying to have a normal friendship with them, but be careful for Chartboys' sake.'

'You're jealous, Beth,' he replied quietly. 'I understand you don't like seeing her here, but she's doing no harm, she just wants to help us. And I find the more I see her, the easier it is to bear. It's good for me.'

'It's dangerous,' she said forthrightly, but he set his lips obstinately and changed the subject.

When the crisis came, it was unexpected. It seemed a normal evening – it was early August, the nights were warm and the evenings long – and Beth decided to slip up to Chartboys one evening to see Mary, leaving William in the bar.

The air was cooling only slightly after the long day, and the Chartboys' gardens were full of the scent of late roses and pinks. There was no sign of Rupert or of Mary in their rooms.

'On the terrace, miss,' one of the nurses volunteered, and Beth went through to the back of the house.

The sun was setting behind them. In stark silhouette, sitting at dinner on the terrace, candles flickering on the tables, she saw Mary, Dr Goldstein, Rupert – and Pippin and Richard. She stood in the doorway, aghast, unnoticed, a sick feeling creeping over her. She was transported back to that evening in the Savoy so long ago, of feeling excluded from the group she had the right to join.

She knew clearly then that there was no part for her in the social world of Chartboys, and perhaps no part at all. Pippin had succeeded. Succeeded in reconciling Richard and Rupert, thus drawing Rupert back into her toils, and by the same stroke excluding Beth.

Beth had been betrayed a second time, but this time by Rupert. The realisation forced an inarticulate cry from her lips, a cry of pain, and the diners looked up from their conversation, hands poised in tableau on wine glasses. A flush spread over Rupert's face. So she had not imagined it. It was a deliberate exclusion.

'I was good enough to help you create this place,' she burst out furiously to Rupert. 'But not good enough to dine with you, I see.' Mary cried out, Goldstein rose to his feet, napkin still tucked in under his chin. Richard sat still, not looking at her. And Pippin – one glance at Pippin's face and Beth knew she had not been imagining things. This was Pippin's revenge – to exclude her from Chartboys.

'Beth,' said Rupert, leaping up after a startled moment, real anger in his voice.

'What's the matter, Rupert? Am I breaking the rules of polite dinner society? Ruining your dinner party? I wasn't invited, so it don't matter.'

She caught Richard's eye for one moment, and her courage failed her. She turned and ran.

* * *

'Beth, let me in.' There was a pounding on the Wheatsheaf door.

'Go away, Mary.'

'Let me in,' said Mary firmly. 'I'll stay here till you come out otherwise.' Reluctantly Beth unlocked the door and let her in.

'Well?' said Beth mutinously. 'Are you going to tell me how dreadful I am, how petty, and how marvellously Pippin behaved?'

'No,' said Mary, shaking her head. 'I just wanted to say, I understand.'

'You're kind, Mary. But you don't mean it. And you can't understand. As I told you, it all began a long time ago.'

'It's him, isn't it?' said Mary. 'Richard Lyle.'

Beth was still. 'Rupert told you?'

'He didn't have to. I saw the way Mr Lyle looked at you at the dance, saw the way he tried not to look at you just now. There's an atmosphere between you when you're together – I can't describe it, but you're different. Not the Beth I know. You're wilder somehow.'

'I can't do anything about it,' said Beth pleadingly. 'It's there – but I'm not – I wouldn't –'

'I know,' said Mary quietly. 'After all, it's the same for both of us. Rupert knows now how I feel about him. I feel so ashamed because he's so gentle with me, so kind. But when he looks at *her* –'

'So you know that, too,' said Beth.

'Oh yes,' said Mary wrily. 'I've been blind. I didn't realise till tonight. Then I realised she'd deliberately been cultivating my friendship, partly against you and partly to see if she had any competition for Rupert's affection.'

'She's not all bad you know, Mary. I remember –'

'No,' said Mary, the peaceful reasonable Mary. 'But I'd like to strangle slowly the bit that is.'

Beth went no more to Chartboys. Rupert endeavoured to see her, but she refused all contact and he went away. Let Pippin have her victory. She wanted no more dealings with Medlars or with Rupert. He had gone over to *them*. Perhaps indeed he had never left them. He was no friend to her now, of that she was sure. What was to become of her now there was no Chartboys? Her days could be full but not her thoughts – save of one person. She must turn them away. Should she concentrate on the wine and preserves trade? It was fully established though, with a girl coming in from the village to help part-time and regular deliveries being made to outlying hamlets and to Faversham. The accommodation at the cottages? It ran efficiently enough but was no challenge, merely a series of bed linens constantly to be changed. Now if she had capital, the hotel, the dream, could be a reality.

But she didn't. She was finished. Doubtless Pippin, now established at Chartboys, would find ways of poisoning Rupert against the cottages. Sunk in gloom, she prowled around the house; she shouted at the children; she was moody in the bar; she left the hoppers' barn for Hetty to cope with; she skimped on the baking. Finally she shouted at William.

'Will you shut up, woman?' he roared in reply. 'You're nothing but a bear with a sore head. Grow up. 'Tis your stupid pride won't let you go to your beloved Chartboys. If you'd an ounce of cunning in you, you'd win over Pippin. Or learn to fight her. You have to turn things to your advantage that's all. But you're not interested in even trying. You're nothing but a tattery child.'

'I'm not,' she shouted. ''Tis always the same here. Work, work, work when the hoppers come. 'Tis you, you never have a moment to help me.' She paused, trying to think of some crime she could fling at William's head then, abandoning this line, said crossly, ''Tis more fun up the hop fields than it is here!'

'Then *go* ahopping. Earn some money that way, now that with your high and mighty tantrums you've given up Chartboys.'

'Money!' she hurled at him. 'That's all that's important, is it?'

She was unjust and knew it, but she didn't care. How dare William say she should grow up. Smarting under the injustice, after all she'd done, all she'd been through, all the troubles she'd shouldered. Everyone respected her except her own husband. Very well, she'd go to the hop fields, and earn some money. They could always do with extra hands. The weather didn't help her mood. It was hot and humid. Quickly she changed into old clothes, taking off her corsets and slipping with relief into an old pale-blue cotton dress and rolling up the sleeves so the air could get to her arms. Seizing her cotton sunbonnet belligerently, she marched indignantly out of The Wheatsheaf up to the hop fields. She found a set where they were short-handed and joined them. They were gypsies, but she didn't care. She'd show the strangers that the natives could pick as hard as them. The pole puller threw a bine across the basket she'd found, and she set to work.

She'd forgotten how rough picking was on the hands.

Fortunately her hands were tough enough with the work she did at the Wheatsheaf and with her gardening, but all the same she began to wish she'd brought gloves. She picked industriously, head down over the basket for two hours, the basket being emptied by the measurer, and she received her tokens. Then something made her glance up. There at the end of the set, with the golden glow of the sun behind him, was a figure. She could not see properly for the sun in her eyes but somehow there grew into her gaze a slim figure, dark-haired, dressed in old flannels and blazer, a bright kerchief at his neck, mobile, laughing, joking. There was a mist in her eyes, as the years fell away. Along the station platform, the sun behind him, strode Richard Lyle . . . Lying above her, in the meadow, the sun behind his head, was Richard Lyle . . . She was eighteen again, she was Beth Ovenden, proud as a queen, the belle of the village, with her life and Richard before her.

She must have made some slight cry, for the sound of his laughter stopped as he glanced around and saw a dark-haired girl in a pale blue summer dress staring at him. He made no move, but the light of the devil or Heaven was in his eyes, and she rose to her feet. Slowly he moved towards her. He was coming. She took one step towards him, then another and a last immense stride before she was in his arms. Only for an instant, before he drew away and took her hand.

Without a word being spoken, he led her out of the gardens, and through into the meadow.

''Twas the other gate we used,' she said at last. 'The one with half the slats missing.'

'So it was,' he said simply.

The grass was warm when he laid her on it. He knelt by her side, and said softly, 'You're sure, my Beth? It's not for any reason other than that you love me. Tell me that, Beth.'

With a great effort she thought of Pippin, of all that had happened, thought briefly of the life that might lie ahead, the deceit, the lies, of William who loved her, of the children who needed her. Then she looked into the face of the only man she'd ever loved. 'I love you, Richard.'

The bitterness and lines that the years had placed there fell from his face, and he lay down beside her and took her in his arms. 'It'll be quickly now,' he said, whispering to her passionately. 'I want you mine again. Later we can learn each other again. But now, oh Beth, tell me I have you for myself again.'

'With my heart, I'm yours.'

He slipped the dress from her shoulders, and half hiccuped with laughter. 'No corsets as usual, I see.'

'I do usually,' she said indignantly. 'It was only because –' Then she saw his tender laughter and fell back to his embrace.

And there in the sweet-smelling grass, with only the buttercups and a curious robin to see, Richard Lyle claimed her for himself for ever.

CHAPTER THIRTEEN

She kept her two worlds apart. It was her only means of survival. When she left the cottage at Westling that Richard had managed to rent again, she would walk home through the fields, and arriving at the Wheatsheaf, the children running to her and the routine of the pub claiming her attention, restored her to that other world, for that too she loved.

Afterwards she wondered how ever she could have faced William that first time when, aglow with love, with stars in her eyes, she had to return to the Wheatsheaf to prepare the supper. They had returned to the hop garden, swallowed up amongst the incurious East Enders, busy with their concerns and not regulars at the Wheatsheaf. There had been no need of words, no need of anything save the occasional touch of the hand, the intimate smile, the certainty that there would be a tomorrow.

In the event it had been easy returning to the Wheatsheaf. The familiar rush of affection swept over her as she saw William poring over the account books. He glanced up at her, greeted her and turned back to his studies. Owen clamoured for attention for his broken train, Elizabeth was nowhere to be found.

William grunted. 'Up at Chartboys, then?' his earlier irritation gone.

'No, I gave a hand with the hops like you suggested. They needed extra hands.'

'Fresh air suits you,' said William, glancing at her, looked for a moment and said no more.

And thus it had been for nine months now, till summer was on the point of coming again. She lived in the two worlds: one everyday, and none the less real and loved for that: the other, a world of dreams of excitement, a voyage into unknown territories, the land of adventure in his arms that he had promised her all those years ago. She was grateful that, when she had thought her chance past, it had come again and flowered beneath her. What matter if she were thirty-two? There was more than half of her life to go, a life suddenly full of colour and hope.

And the guilt? She had expected to feel remorse every moment, but she did not. She was to William her usual affectionate generous self, finding it easier, not harder now that Richard was back, as if she were so full of love herself it spilled over to those around her.

'Chartboys must have been awearing you out,' remarked William watching her playing with Elizabeth one day and tearing round the garden. 'You've more energy now than you used to.'

'Don't let's talk about Chartboys,' she said panting, as she stopped and came in for a glass of ale. 'That's over.'

'You allus were an all-or-nothing person, Beth,' he said. 'Daft I call it. You give all your time to building Chartboys up, and then just as you starts being able to enjoy the benefits, you have to get cruppish over who Rupert invites to dinner.'

'It's the principle,' said Beth scowling. 'Anyway, they don't need me. They'd have sent for me if they did.'

Against her will, she thought unwillingly of Pippin. Her name was never mentioned between Richard and herself. It had been only once when, unheedingly, she had asked if Pippin suspected anything. 'Be careful, Richard, won't you?'

He had been silent for a moment, then said, awkwardly, 'You saw the worst of her, Beth. She's selfish, very selfish. But aren't we all when it comes to someone we love?'

A chill struck her. So he still loved her. She had been nurturing an unfair hope that all was not well between them.

She dressed and left quietly. When they next met nothing was said, but he held her the more passionately, the more possessively, as if to reassure her and it was never referred to again. That he might be equally jealous of William never occurred to her. Her heart was wholly his; he must know that.

It was Hetty who first broke that barrier into Beth's other world, one morning when they were alone in the bar. 'Beth,' she said abruptly, awkwardly, 'you remembers what I said about there being trouble if –'

Beth stiffened. 'Yes,' she said coldly, and turned to go into the other bar.

But Hetty was not put off. 'I just thought I'd mention – I don't know of course, but Sylvie Thomas has been hanging round here a lot.'

'Well?' said Beth icily, not giving an inch.

Hetty flushed. 'You know as well as I do, she's got it in for you, marrying Mr Parslow. I thought you'd like to know, that's all. *And* she looks like the cat that got at the cream. Call it the gypsy's warning if you like, but I don't like it. So if you've anything to keep secret, Beth,' she said, carefully polishing a glass, 'remember what I says.'

Beth thought about this for a day or two, then dismissed the thought from her head. William was her husband, solid and dependent. He would not give Sylvie a second glance now. She had seen no sign of Sylvie lately, and it did not occur to her that she noticed very little of the atmosphere of the Wheatsheaf these days. She was spending more time there, that was the important thing, and trade was picking up, though not so quickly as she would wish. The baking was up to date. The pub had once again struggled through the winter, doing well with the letting of rooms in the cottages, and with the hopping season to come, all seemed set fair. Parslow Preserves, as the labels now declared them to be, were selling in greater numbers, and Alice Baker was now a full-time employee. Thanks to glowing reports carried home by Chartboys' patients, she had even had an enquiry from Messrs Jacksons in London, an enquiry that opened up awe-inspiring possibilities.

So, if William took a day or afternoon off every now and then, it was only his due, and it certainly wasn't to see Sylvie! So accustomed had she become to the ordered routine of the Wheatsheaf again that she was not only surprised but dismayed to receive a card from Mary, pleading with her to visit Chartboys. She telephoned to her from the post office.

'I can't come, Mary, you know that. 'Tis almost a year. Not unless Rupert comes and asks me to return, that is.'

'He doesn't know what – Beth, I'll come to tea, if I may. We can't talk over the telephone.'

Beth baked an almond orange cake and wondered what on earth had gone wrong. Despite her vow to forget Chartboys, she was intrigued.

Mary looked thinner, the air of calm was gone, her eyes were anxious.

'This time I must resign, Beth. You don't know what it's been like since you've been gone. I almost welcome the fights with Samuel –'

'Samuel?'

'Dr Goldstein,' said Mary, reddening, 'because at least he makes me feel human. If someone does you the honour of fighting with you, you know you exist,' she said bitterly. 'Rupert placidly listens to me, calms me down, and sends me on my way. No, the cause of the trouble is –'

'Pippin,' said Beth, wrily.

'Yes, it's not that she does anything to interfere. Nothing one could object to, that is. I wish there were something. It's just that she's always there, talking to the patients, acting the gracious lady of the manor, helping patients do this, do that, helping the nurses. She's so damned *good*, Beth, I want to hit her.'

Beth laughed, relieved that Mary should have such human reactions. 'I'm sorry to laugh, Mary, but that was always her way. Half of it is genuine. That's her charm –'

'And the other half?' enquired Mary.

'It's her way of ensuring Rupert doesn't marry you,' said Beth forthrightly.

'Oh Beth.' She hid her face in her hands. 'You know, before she came, there were times when I was sure he was fond enough of me to – he ought to marry again, oughtn't he?' she said in appeal.

'Oh yes,' said Beth, 'but Mary, I pity his wife while Pippin's around. You see, it's not as though he doesn't know the truth about her. He does. She led him on although it was Richard –' she said his name steadily '– she really wanted, and used any means to get,' she added. 'So there's no rude awakening likely for Rupert. He knows exactly what she is.'

'Then there's no hope for me,' said Mary sadly. 'I'll have to leave.'

'Would you like me to talk to Rupert?' asked Beth hesitantly. It was the last thing she wanted to do.

'Would it do any good?'

'It might,' said Beth consideringly. 'It would be difficult though.' Much as it suited Beth to have Pippin spend so much time at Chartboys, there was Chartboys to think of – and Rupert himself. Not to mention Mud. He saw little of his father now that Rupert had been swept into the social life of Kent, with Pippin and Richard.

'Beth?' Rupert's eyes lit up with pleasure. 'Come in and sit down.'

'You may not be so pleased to see me when I tell you what I come for,' warned Beth, taking off her gloves. 'It's Pippin, Rupert. She's playing havoc here.'

'Ah,' he said abruptly. 'The old story. Beth, the

patients love her. She's an asset. You haven't bothered to come near the place yourself –'

'No, I've seen enough,' said Beth angrily. 'And –'

'You've been talking to Mary, no doubt,' said Rupert dryly. 'Beth, it's difficult to say this, but don't you think Mary may be as prejudiced as you are? She was used to doing everything here, and naturally feels her nose out of joint. Besides which –'

'She's in love with you? You belittle her, Rupert. She's worked for you all these years and you insult her by saying she's done it just because she's in love with you? Besides, it isn't just Mary, it's Goldstein.'

'He's always difficult,' said Rupert. 'If he wasn't such a good doctor –'

'You're blind, Rupert. I warned you there'd be trouble.'

'And how about you?' he asked defensively. 'You left here because you didn't like seeing Pippin here. I understood of course, but I hardly think you can expect me to agree with you. I take a different approach.'

'Very well. But do please come to talk to Goldstein and Mary, otherwise you will have no senior staff left.'

'But what exactly do they object to?' he asked, bewildered.

'They'd better tell you.'

When they arrived at Mary's rooms, however, they heard the sounds of an altercation within. Familiar voices: Mary's, Goldstein's and a third – Pippin's.

'But I was helping her,' came her plaintive voice.

'You're not helping Lady Tatsfield by doing things for her, woman,' said Goldstein. 'Patients have to do things for themselves. You're taking away their confidence.'

'I don't see why.'

All their voices spoke together then.

Red with rage, Rupert strode into the room. 'What is all this about?' he demanded.

'Rupert,' said Pippin, turning to him quivering with hurt. 'I'm so sorry. I just didn't understand. I thought I was helping.' Her eyes flickered over to Beth, and a shutter seemed to come down over them.

'I'm sure this is a misunderstanding that can easily be ironed out,' said Rupert, his face softening.

'No misunderstanding,' shouted Goldstein, glaring. 'Direct question, Sir Rupert. Who does Mrs Lyle take orders from? Me, Miss Wilton, or you?'

There was dead silence. Rupert looked unhappily at Pippin. 'From you or Miss Wilton, naturally, Dr Goldstein. You are responsible for the health of the patients. In matters like this –'

'I understand that, Rupert,' said Pippin, her voice trembling, 'but I thought tea parties were more of a social event, and I might help.'

'Nonsense,' cut in Goldstein. 'I told you before, this damnfool mixing of the patients has to be done slowly. You come along and the first day out you put Lord Benfield with a hopper. And you expect them to chat away like old friends. Comfort. Reassurance for the patients. Bah!'

'It is good for them,' said Pippin passionately. 'They can learn from each other. There's no inequality in sickness.'

Mary, whose theme song this had been for so long, was silent.

'How often do you invite your labourers to tea?' said Goldstein.

Another dead silence. Pippin turned with dignity to Rupert. 'It seems to me I'd better not come again, Rupert. My services clearly aren't of use.'

That did it. Rupert burst forth in one of his rare rages. 'Goldstein, apologise for that.'

The doctor's eyes bulged. '*Apologise*? Mere question, that's all. Doesn't the woman practise what she preaches?'

'You don't understand what she's trying to do.'

'I understand too well,' said Goldstein. 'But she won't practise her Karl Marx theories on my patients. They'll mix when I think they're ready for it. Otherwise we'll have a bloody revolution *here*. When they get well, *then* is the time to get them all together. Not on their first day here, woman.'

Rupert, torn between the two, looked to his one salvation. 'Mary, you agree with me?'

'No,' she said shortly. 'I agree with Dr Goldstein.'

Goldstein's head slowly turned towards her. 'What the devil for? You never have before!'

'In principle, no,' she said, red in the face. 'In this instance, yes. Mrs Lyle ought to be answerable to one of us, and in this case, the tea parties were tried on patients who were too ill.'

Rupert stared slowly at his two senior staff, and then, 'Beth?'

Torn with all sorts of emotions, as Richard's wife looked at her coolly, waiting for her to use her power,

Beth said: 'Of course, Pip – Mrs Lyle must work under Dr Goldstein's and Miss Wilton's orders, as they're responsible for the hospital, but I'm sure she has the good of the patients at heart. There's a lot of valuable work she can do here under their direction and I think, when she reflects, she'll see the sense of it, and Dr Goldstein and Miss Wilton will be glad of her services.'

Sheer amazement filled Pippin's eyes, then they were clouded with an emotion Beth could not fathom. Rupert looked at her with real gratitude, took Pippin's arm, and led her away.

Left to themselves, the three of them drew a deep breath.

'Why so magnanimous in victory, Beth? I find that strange,' said Goldstein.

'I try to be objective when it comes to Chartboys,' said Beth weakly.

'Umph,' said Goldstein. 'I wonder,' to himself. Then to Mary: 'And you, Mary, you defended me. Why? Because of Mrs Lyle's presence?'

'No,' she shouted, suddenly irate. 'Can't you get it into your head, Samuel, that women are capable of rational thought and not motivated by personal emotions all the time?'

'No,' he said simply.

'Oh!' She was outraged; her emotions spilled over. She picked up the nearest object which happened to be a china toby jug and flung it at him with no strength spared. She was a bad shot. Hurled vaguely in the direction of his chest, it struck him a glancing blow on the temple sending him reeling backwards and collapsing into an armchair.

Beth rushed to him in horror, but Mary was quicker, pushing her aside.

A trickle of blood was running down the side of his face into his beard and Mary seized her handkerchief to mop it up, while he stared at her bemusedly.

'I didn't mean – it wasn't you – have I?' she muttered incoherently.

'Will you marry me, Mary?'

Beth thought she must have misheard the whispered words, but she did not miss Mary's answer. It came quite clearly:

'Yes, Samuel. Yes, please.'

Dr Goldstein and Mary. They would be an incongruous couple. But Mary loved Rupert – had she accepted Goldstein simply because of pique? Beth wondered, totally bemused. Yet somehow she knew it was not so simple as that. Mary was too strong a character. But what other reason? Giving up the puzzle as insoluble, she turned with dread to her own motivation in defending Pippin. Why had she left Pippin to continue at Chartboys when it had been in her power at that moment to stop her? Was it integrity, or was there indeed a knowledge that if Pippin were occupied at Chartboys she would not have so much time to spare for her husband? She dismissed this unwelcome thought too from her mind. She had acted as seemed right at the time. There was no point in judging. She turned her mind to happier subjects. Today was Thursday. Tomorrow she would see Richard when he returned from his London chambers.

* * *

She dressed carefully, sweeping up her dark hair, but not too tightly, so that it would swirl around her shoulders when he released it. Her heart began to beat faster. She put on a blue cotton skirt and matching blouse, and took up her sunbonnet. She would not think of Richard. Not till she had left the Wheatsheaf, and was hurrying along the footpath to the cottage. This was part of her ritual to keep the guilt away.

Richard was there at the cottage before her, sprawled on the shabby bed, reading, still half-dressed in his London clothes. He brightened as she came in and threw aside his book. But she resisted coming straight to his arms, and sat on the side of the bed, until he swung his legs over beside her and slipped an arm round her shoulders.

'What's wrong, Beth?'

'Nothing really,' she said, hesitating to voice a trouble so unspecific. 'I forgot to salute a magpie this morning, that's all. And – I saw Pippin yesterday.'

His grip tightened. 'And?'

She told him, finishing anxiously, 'She's staying on at Chartboys. You don't mind, do you?'

He frowned. 'That she's continuing to see Rupert? No. He's too much the knight errant to take advantage. Anyway, she'd never be unfaithful.'

She moved from his arms, indignant and hurt, 'But why does it matter? You are.'

He looked at her in surprise. 'I never thought of it that way. It doesn't, I suppose. And yet . . . what would you say if William were unfaithful?'

William? She shivered. 'Don't let's talk of it, Richard,' she pleaded. 'This is *our* world, isn't it? Ours, now and forever. No intrusions from the outside. Nothing can harm us here. Not now we're together again.'

'No,' he said. 'Nothing.' He lay down drawing her onto the bed with him, and they lay there quietly, the afternoon sunshine streaming through the window. She opened her eyes lazily, to see him staring out of the window, his eyes fixed on the tree outside, its leaves waving gently in the breeze.

'You're restless,' she said sadly.

He turned, and his hand went to her breast, 'No,' she said, gently removing it. 'I didn't mean that. I meant you feel confined, don't you? You're bored with Shepham. Bored in London. You want to be moving –'

He frowned. 'What?'

'Not with me, that I know well enough. But you're wanting to be travelling overseas and adventuring. Like,' her voice trembled, 'like we said we'd do, didn't we, once we was wed. I thought you'd settled down after you married Pippin, given up the smuggling and all that, but you haven't, have you? You haven't changed at all.'

His arm tightened round her. 'People *don't* change, Beth. They just get tied down with responsibilities, until gradually the spirit, the will dies, and they say it was all a dream of youth –'

'Am I a responsibility, a chain?' she asked.

'No, Beth, you're part of the dream. And dream enough for me if need be. If you won't leave here, then it has to be. I'll dream through you, and with you, and by you. I couldn't leave you again . . .'

'You'll throw your life away. You could travel, see the world. Take Pippin with you –' It cost her nothing to say this, for she knew that would never happen.

He turned his head back again from the beckoning sun, and put his hand on her so fiercely, so possessively, that she exclaimed in pain. He did not draw back and took off her clothes quickly, then his own. When she looked at him, his eyes were blazing, a wildness in them she had not seen for many years. 'There, my highwayman,' she murmured, and his face grew gentle again as he held her, murmuring sweet words of passion to her, until she called for him and he entered her, oblivious of the sun outside.

'I want another child by you, Beth.'

He said it calmly, matter of factly, as he pulled straight his tie. She, ready five minutes since, could not believe what she heard.

'No,' she said, flatly. 'That can't ever be.'

He shrugged, and smiled wickedly. 'Suppose I –'

'You wouldn't,' she answered in alarm.

'No,' he said. 'I'm not quite so selfish. But think about it.'

'Think about it!' She stared at him aghast. 'Richard, are you –' Her voice rose.

'Oh, Richard,' came Pippin's clear high voice as she thrust open the door. 'How nice to have you come down early for the weekend.' The ice, the triumph, the victory dropped into the void. Behind her stood Sylvie, eyes vindictive, glorying in her achievement. No sign of shock from Pippin, of horror or – Beth registered even then – loss, of love for Richard.

Richard groaned, and sat down on the bed again, folding his arms and gazing out of the window. Ostrich! accused Beth to herself. It was left to her to face Pippin.

'I understand now why,' said Pippin coolly, 'you were so co-operative about my staying at Chartboys. I did wonder at it, Beth.'

'I have no apologies to make to you, Pippin,' said Beth, more evenly than she felt. 'I've done to you what you did to me with far less cause all those years ago.'

Pippin's eyes showed some emotion. 'Yes,' she agreed, as if they were discussing the plans for a dinner party. 'Yes, but it's different now, isn't it?' She gave a bright artificial smile. 'Because I'm his wife. I think, on the whole, don't you, that Shepham will see my side of it?'

There was an exclamation from Richard at the window. 'No, Richard,' said Beth without turning. 'Don't you say anything. I'm sure Pippin will see 'twill make her look ridiculous for Shepham to know she took my lover once, only for him to come rushing back to me as soon as he could. Doesn't say a lot for you, does it?'

It was cruel, it was underhand, it was all that Beth wasn't, but in fighting Pippin she had to use the weapons that she, and Sylvie, would understand. She was fighting for Richard, and for her own survival.

Pippin regarded her sardonically. Then she turned to Sylvie. 'I think,' she said carefully, 'we'll keep it between the four of us. Six of us, I should say. We four, and William naturally, and perhaps I'd better mention it to Rupert –'

There was a sharp intake of breath from Richard. He stared across at his wife, then his face went blank, quite blank. I should have expected it, thought Beth. What else? No hope of keeping it from William with Sylvie there. Hetty had tried to warn her. But as usual she hadn't listened.

Beth's head went up proudly. 'You've had what you wanted, Pippin. Now out.' There was force, venom in her tone. 'You can leave Richard and me together quite safely – to say goodbye.'

'I thought you'd see it that way, Beth,' said Pippin, and departed victorious. She glanced amusedly at Richard. 'Don't be long, darling.'

'She has you and Rupert now,' observed Beth flatly, sitting down on the bed.

He disregarded this. 'Goodbye?'

'Of course,' she said wearily. 'What else?'

'Goodbye,' he muttered. 'God, where did today come from? What happened?'

'Where it allus comes from – ourselves,' she said wrily. 'We created this situation, not God. Only ourselves to blame if it comes to an end.'

'Not yet, my queen, not quite yet.' He threw back his head and laughed. 'Though we cannot make our sun stand still, yet we will make him run . . .' He strode to the door, and belatedly locking it, he came towards her purposefully, his face a mask, his eyes slits of wildness and passion.

Later, tired, exhausted emotionally and physically, she went slowly towards the Wheatsheaf, to face what awaited her there. Time enough for Sylvie to have told him now. Would it have made a difference, if she had told William herself? No, it might have been worse. Or was that cowardly? She pushed open the back door, and Owen's bellow of rage over some small problem rang out from upstairs. But she had no time for his troubles now. She had to find William. She found him in the bar with Hetty. One glance at her and he looked away. So he knew. They were busy that evening, and it was not until half way through the evening that she managed to force a meeting. Better now than bedtime.

'So you heard then. Sylvie told you?'

He looked at her. 'Hardly come as a surprise, Beth,' he said bleakly.

'You *knew*?'

'No, I never. But I knew summat was up this past year. I thought 'twas just having him near. I never thought you –' He broke off and she went to him but he pushed her away angrily. 'Whatever I thought of you, Beth, and you was silly enough, Lord knows, I never thought you were a cheat.'

She shook her head dumbly. 'I didn't want to –'

'Didn't want –' he said in disgust. 'It were my fault, I suppose. He comes here and beckons and you give yourself to him with no thought of Pippin, me, the children. And you so high and mighty about other folks. I tell you, Beth, if I'd anywhere to go I'd go – no matter about money. But I won't leave Owen and he needs you.'

'*Owen*?'

'Other one's his bastard, ain't she? I know we pretend different but it's a fact. What d'yer expect me to do, thank him for it?'

She gave a low moan, ran past him up to a bedroom – not their bedroom – and lay on the bed. So it was over. Everything. Richard, her life of content, and she'd broken William's heart. Even Elizabeth must share in her own rejection now. Too low even for tears, she lay face down, head buried in the pillow, until an arm came round her shoulders.

'Drink this, Beth,' said Hetty. 'It'll do you good.'

'I –'

'Drink it,' she commanded, and shuddering, Beth forced a few drops of brandy down her. ''Tis paid for, don't worry,' said Hetty anxiously.

In spite of herself, Beth began to laugh weakly. If fiddling the accounts was all she had to worry about now!

'I don't see anything to laugh at meself,' said Hetty worriedly. 'Mr Parslow's in a real state. I can see that. I know what's happened, see.'

'Sylvie,' said Beth, bitterly. So much for keeping it quiet.

'I saw her around, and guessed summat was up. So I forced her to tell me. Don't worry, Beth, she won't be telling anyone, I seen to that.' Yes, she'd seen to that, underhand maybe. Threatened to spread it round the village that William Parslow was spending quite a few afternoons at her cottage. Not that Sylvie would mind it getting back to Beth, but she did mind her children hearing about it at school, their mother being laughed at. Her children were going to get on in the world, Sylvie had determined. It had been bluff on Hetty's part, but it had worked.

'Oh.' A sigh of relief. 'But why –'

'Silly, ain't it, after the rollicking you gave me over Ben, and now here you are – beg your pardon, Beth, don't mean to, but we might as well have it out. There was allus something about that Richard Lyle,' Hetty went on wistfully. 'I know what a way he's got. I don't say you should have done it, mind, but I understand why, and . . . oh Beth.' There was a light in her eyes, a sadness, that made Beth remember what she had said once about being jealous.

Beth saw the look, saw the pity in it, and hugged Hetty to her, their tears intermingling.

She could not bear to go on living in Shepham, but there seemed no alternative. Perhaps Richard would work in London all the time. She hoped they'd move from Medlars, but she knew Pippin would not abandon Chartboys and Rupert now. Beth walked out into the garden and saw the mulberry tree in its new leaf. How many years it had seen, how many seasons' fruit it had borne. How many troubles at the Wheatsheaf it had seen come and go. There was always the garden as a refuge. And there was Elizabeth – every time she had looked at her, she had seen Richard. And now so would William. The desolation hit her anew.

It was Mary who brought her the news. A happy Mary awaiting her wedding the following week; but now her eyes were full of concern.

'What a lovely garden,' she said inconsequentially, finding Beth struggling with the ground elder under the lilac trees.

'You didn't come here to admire my garden, Mary,' said Beth quietly. 'What is it? More trouble at Chartboys?'

'No,' Mary shook her head, then took Beth's hands. 'I've some news,' she said awkwardly. 'I don't know if it's good or bad. It's Richard Lyle.'

Something must have shown in Beth's face, for Mary clutched her hands tighter.

'Not dead,' Beth whispered faintly.

'No,' said Mary. 'Left.'

'Left?' repeated Beth dully. 'Left where?'

'Left Medlars, and, I gather, left Pippin.'

'You mean he's gone back to live in London?' said Beth impatiently.

'No, gone abroad, left his chambers, too, and left no address. Only his solicitors know where he is, and their instructions are not to reveal it to anyone. Pippin's screaming the place down. He's never coming back.'

Never to see Richard again. Beth had thought her pain could not grow greater, but she had been wrong. He had gone, to his life of adventure, and despite all his fine words, left her, Beth, to battle alone. How like him, oh how *like* him, and a wave of love so fierce welled up in her that she moaned.

He should have taken her, was her first thought. No, he had spared her that. She would have refused. Wouldn't she? He had left her to the life with which she had claimed content. Left without a word. She looked slowly round the Wheatsheaf garden. ''Tis good news, Mary, good news.' In time she would believe it to be true.

Later that night she gazed out towards the Channel in the starlit night and whispered, 'God speed you well, my highwayman.'

William did not speak to her save for essential matters. To everyone else, however, and to the children – both equally – he was placid and affectionate. But from Beth he withdrew physically and emotionally.

A week later, when they were getting ready for bed, for he had not moved to another room, he said abruptly, 'Beth, we got a long time to live together yet. I've been thinking. I reckon what happened between us happened a long time before he came back on the scene. Some of the blame rests on me. I thought I could make you happy. I couldn't. Simple as that. You had Chartboys then, when you didn't, you had him. Well, you've neither now, so we must make do as best we can.'

'Bless you, William,' was all she said, and kissed his cheek. He did not return the kiss but, in the middle of the night, he turned to her gently, slowly, so slowly she was only awoken by the moisture of his tears on her face.

CHAPTER FOURTEEN

'She's old enough, William. It's time.'

'Too young, Beth. She's never been away from us.'

'She's eleven, William. You just won't face it.' But that wasn't so, she thought to herself. He was doggedly determined to give reasons why Elizabeth should not go away to the boarding school her quicksilver intelligence needed – and her grandfather's money was there to pay for.

It was not that William did not want her to go. Beth guessed he would welcome it and, in his usual fairness, felt he should dissuade Beth from sending her. For in the last year the old bond between William and Elizabeth had been broken. She had seen William conscientiously straining to recapture it, but it did not come. She saw Elizabeth become more serious as a result, more withdrawn, less impulsive. She had drawn immeasurably closer to Beth, she guessed to William's relief. She knew he had to force himself now to see Elizabeth as his daughter, and for that she, Beth, was entirely to blame. The guilt she could not feel while Richard was present, was heaped upon her now he was gone.

Gone. Without one word in a year. No word to her and, according to Rupert, no word to Pippin. No word to the children, no money – not that Pippin needed it. It was as if Richard Lyle had never swept into their lives, and Shepham seemed metaphorically to shake itself down with a sigh after his departure, the ranks closing behind him. The Wheatsheaf, too, had healed its wounds, though the scars were still there. She and William resumed their former life, but the past lay between them, and now had come between William and Elizabeth.

Owen was a different matter. He, conversely, had grown closer to William, a happy-go-lucky child now nearly nine years old who skated through life skimming on its surface and never letting anything trouble him. He cheerfully sailed through his school work. Reports of 'could try harder', 'could do better', never bothered him. Not for Owen the prizes that Elizabeth carried off, the row of leather-bound books that filled her shelf in her bedroom. Yes, Beth acknowledged, she was ready to learn to face a challenge. But would she adapt to a public school after these years in a village? She was not eager to go away to school yet fretted continually at the limitations of the village school. So much quicker than the others, she studied at home with the help of the rector's library and permission to wander at will at Chartboys' library, though Beth tried to discourage her visiting there. Wistfully, Beth thought back to her own lessons at Medlars and the vast library there – denied forever to Elizabeth.

Eventually William conceded the battle. Elizabeth would go to school for the summer term to see how she liked it. 'Sevenoaks,' grunted William. 'Where's that then? And how's she to get home?'

'The railway,' said Beth firmly. 'No matter if she is the only child not delivered in a horseless carriage.'

The year that had followed Richard's departure had not been easy, not only for her and William personally, but also in the trade. The importation of foreign hops was dealing a serious blow to the Kentish hop industry and more and more farmers were giving up hops. Their lack of prosperity meant a lack of prosperity for Shepham, and less trade for the Wheatsheaf. The preserves and wine trade was temporarily hampered by the difficulties of regular deliveries during the winter, and the cost of buying in supplies to cover a hoped-for expansion of trade.

To escape her problems, Beth found herself taking refuge in fantasy, planning what it would be like to have a *real* hotel, not just rooms available. She'd buy that land by the side of the cottages and build, or to the side of the old barn. In her vision she saw its roof soaring up, a long sloping peg-tiled roof. The old barn should be a restaurant – no, she couldn't do that for where would the hoppers go? No, the restaurant must be part of the new building – at the back, overlooking the gardens. There was plenty of space that side of the green. Only that cottage of Mr Tucker's stood in the way and now he'd gone to live with his daughter he'd sell. The hotel would not be large: perhaps fifteen bedrooms, and three bathrooms. She'd need a lot of staff. And the catering – a chef. How to work out how much food? How many would a sirloin feed? She'd talk to the Chartboys' chef.

Pippin had, Mary told Beth compassionately, naturally fled to Rupert with her tale of woe after Richard's desertion; the wronged wife. When, shortly afterwards, Beth saw Rupert pass by in his motor car, he did not look her way. Six months later, however, urged on by Mary, she had taken the bull by the horns and gone to Chartboys to see Rupert on business. Half fearing to be shown the door on her arrival, she found the contrary to be the case. Rupert, a little pink in the face, came to meet her, both hands outstretched. When a month later there was a dispute to be sorted out in the apportioning of tasks in the garden, he sent for Beth to ask her help. Which was gladly given. She had, it seemed, been forgiven – by Rupert at least. Thereafter she visited Chartboys once or twice a week – on days when Pippin was not present.

But the name of Richard Lyle was never mentioned between them.

Chartboys provided another source of escape as well. Samuel Goldstein and Mary were living in a cottage on the Chartboys' estate. Marriage suited Mary and they appeared blissfully happy. In marriage they had miraculously achieved the harmony they had missed in their working lives. There was a gentleness in Goldstein's voice when Mary's name was mentioned, and a laughing happiness in Mary's eyes that Beth envied.

So their home became a refuge for Beth, provided, of course, she avoided the days when Pippin visited. Pippin . . . how had she really taken Richard's disappearance? Beth wondered. Her children were away at school and Pippin, having brought in a manager for the estate, spent much of her time in London. Only twice had Beth ever seen her since that fateful day. She was not interested in Shepham, and Shepham who had seen little of her as a girl, cared little about the woman. The fiction commonly held in Shepham was that Richard was abroad in the army, but that the gossip continued, Beth knew through Hetty. They still speculated as to whether his disappearance had to do with Mrs Parslow or with trouble with the law. Beth paid no heed, lest she were hurt once more, and her attitude stilled the wagging tongues. They needed the Wheatsheaf too much to let the gossip go too far, and the sight of William and Beth still firmly in partnership helped greatly.

Gradually things improved, and Parslow's Preserves became almost an industry. Beth took on a second helper, and converted another outhouse for the wine-making and storage. They became almost an obsession with her, taking the place of that other dream which she had no hope of realising. She expanded the range into hop liquor – 'It's been curing Shepham folk for years, and will do as well in London,' she declared – and her bergamot pomatum. Unable to pick all the produce she needed for the preserves and wines herself, she was buying from local farmers; and many villagers earned the odd pence for scouring the hedgerows for nettles and dandelions. Scenting prosperity in the air, Percy bought himself a motor van, the first seen in Shepham, for his daily deliveries to Faversham railway station for the London train. 'Never thought I'd learn new tricks at my time of life, Miss Beth,' he chuckled, setting his driving cap at a jaunty angle. 'But change comes to us all, don't it?'

But change was once again on the way for Chartboys.

Beth was busily labelling the latest batch of preserves when Mary arrived, pink-cheeked and excited.

'Beth, such news. I'm going to have a baby.'

'I'm so glad,' said Beth wholeheartedly, holding out her arms. They hugged.

'It's been two years, I hardly hoped. After all, I'm thirty-seven but there's no doubt. If I'm careful, Dr Hipson says.'

Beth had an irresponsibly wild picture of what a baby born of the ugly Goldstein and the beautiful Mary might possibly look like, and tried to suppress it.

'Of course,' Mary added hesitantly, 'it means I shall not be able to continue at Chartboys as manageress. But Samuel says he can find another head nurse from St. Mary's. It won't be difficult. It's a lovely job – now,' she added honestly. 'The storms are over.'

'What about Mary's replacement, Rupert? Have you found one?' she asked casually a few days later.

Rupert stared out of the window. 'Let's go for a walk, Beth,' he said abruptly.

'Walk?' she repeated blankly. 'But it's raining.'

He turned round almost violently. 'I need fresh air.'

Taken aback, she picked up her coat and umbrella, and obediently accompanied him. Rupert turned out of the Chartboys' park, towards the lane that led over the downs to Westling. Children were playing in the cottage gardens, a cat strolled by the beech tree that had been struck by lightning – these and a hundred other details etched themselves on her mind as Rupert talked, fast, angrily, a bright red spot on his cheeks, contrasting with his pale face.

'Dr Goldstein has found a replacement nurse for Mary. We debated whether to promote Miss Hargreaves but decided it would be better to start afresh. Her name is Ruth Barton, a widow, wants to move to the country. A good nurse.'

'Why do you emphasise "good nurse", Rupert?' asked Beth quietly.

Rupert picked his way carefully along the bridle path, swiping at the hedgerows with his walking stick.

'Because I've decided – the board's decided – to divide the job in two in future. A head nurse and another lady to be manageress.'

'And you want me to be manageress, is that it?' asked Beth, puzzled. What else could he mean? And yet –

'No, Beth,' he said quickly. 'No, Beth, I didn't mean –'

'Then who?' Beth broke in feeling foolish in the extreme, her face red with embarrassment.

'I've asked Pippin to be manageress and she's accepted,' he said matter-of-factly.

A cold hand seemed to clamp down on Beth's stomach – why did she never see these shocks coming? she asked herself. Of course, he would ask Pippin. How stupid she had been. 'Well,' she said bitterly at last, 'you allus said I was blind, Rupert. And now I feel an idiot too. I suppose you want me to stay away completely again.' It was a statement, not a question. Chartboys had never seemed so dear to her, her work more precious, as the prospect of leaving them once more swam before her.

'Of course I don't, but –'

'But how can I work with Pippin, that it? Rupert,' she burst out, unable to control her impetuosity, '*no one* can work with Pippin, don't you see? Dr Goldstein, does he know?'

'No,' replied Rupert coldly. 'Not yet, but it makes no difference. He sees Pippin's virtues –'

Does he? Beth thought sarcastically, but wisely did not say it. Although earlier differences had been smoothed over, Pippin the occasional volunteer was not the same as Pippin as manageress.

'Why this continued hostility towards Pippin?' burst out Rupert. 'Can't you *ever* forget? She's sweet and loving. She's the easiest person in the world to get on with.'

'Rupert,' cried Beth, her restraint gone. 'You're thinking of the girl you thought you fell in love with fourteen years ago, not the woman she is today.'

'Don't you think you're prejudiced, Beth?' They stood facing each other, as bitter antagonists for the first time in their lives. This was a subject they could not discuss, could never agree on.

'I may be prejudiced, and with reason,' said Beth. 'But you think Goldstein is? That Mary is?'

'They all have their reasons –'

'Rupert,' exploded Beth. 'Use your eyes. *You're* the one who's prejudiced. You're still hopelessly, blindly, in love with her. Pippin is Pippin, solely devoted to her own interests, sweet and loving only when nothing threatens them. That's not what you need in a manageress.'

'My board,' Rupert threw at her, almost inarticulate with fury, 'believes that Pippin is exactly the person we need to attract and impress new patients. You're –'

'I'm just a village girl. Is that it?' she asked bitterly. 'Like I always was. You, Pippin, Richard – and me, the publican's daughter.'

'Not Richard. He's gone, and gone for ever.'

'He's still her husband, Rupert,' said Beth quietly, trying to ignore the sick hurt in her stomach. Time enough to tend that later. Now her own affection for Rupert *must* make him see he was facing disaster for himself and for Chartboys.

'There's divorce,' muttered Rupert.

'Rupert, you're crazy. Pippin would never divorce. The disgrace.'

'If she loved me.'

'Rupert –' She put her arms round him. 'Don't think that way. Remember how you used to warn me about Pippin? Now *you* take heed.'

But he unwound her arms from him, and stood apart. 'I know you mean well, Beth. But you're too devoted still to Richard for me to listen any more to your blackening of Pippin.'

Then she knew without a doubt that his friendship was lost to her.

The disaster she foresaw so clearly was not long in coming. The first blow was the discontinuation of the Chartboys' order for wines and preserves.

'New manageress says they're not being used. Whole caseful of the elderflower I've got returned here. She's ordering some fancy foreign muck instead. Miss Pippin that is,' Percy said, face cocked inquisitively.

Of course Pippin would stop any contact between Beth and Chartboys, even if it did mean cutting off a large part of Beth's livelihood. Beth knew she should have expected it. But how was she to manage? The conversion of the barn still had to be paid for, supplies ordered in good faith on the strength of the Chartboys' business . . .

Then Mary came to see her one afternoon in the Wheatsheaf parlour, Goldstein accompanying her.

'Beth, darling, I've come to say goodbye.'

'*Goodbye*?' Beth stopped in the middle of her huffkin. 'Oh Mary, just because I can't go to Chartboys any longer, you don't mean –'

'Beth, it's nothing to do with you. You know nothing could stop me seeing you if I were here. But Samuel and I are leaving Shepham. Leaving Chartboys, in fact.'

'Leaving?' Beth said blankly.

'I'm afraid so,' Goldstein said gravely.

She looked slowly from one to the other. 'Because of Pippin?' She said at last.

'Yes,' said Goldstein. 'You may find it ironic, Beth, that I'm leaving because I cannot work with a woman, but there it is. It is more than dislike, I hope you will appreciate. It's the Marie Bonner Wing. Madam Lyle has all but persuaded Sir Rupert to charge people for it. She points out unfairly, but accurately, that it has been a bone of contention all these years because it's free. And that would mean that those for whom it was intended would no longer be able to come there. It would end up being the same as the other wards. So I find myself hoist with my own petard. Sir Rupert uses my own words against me.'

'Charge for the Marie Bonner Wing?' repeated Beth uncomprehendingly. She could not explain even to these friends what that signified – the betrayal of his dead wife, and the betrayal of the very principle that had led him to open Chartboys in the first place.

'Mrs Lyle is no doubt an invaluable ornament for Chartboys, but that is no qualification for managing.' Goldstein glared at Beth as though she were about to take issue with this. He took off his thick spectacles and polished them vigorously with his red silk handkerchief. 'I want to return to St Mary's. Fresh fields and pastures new, Beth. Dr Wright and his pupils are on the verge of opening up whole new worlds in medicine. They are almost there, I am sure –' He was lost for a moment, then recollected the purpose of his visit. 'However, I regret this for your sake, Beth.'

'Why?' asked Beth, puzzled.

'Because it affects you as much as Sir Rupert,' Mary said sadly.

'But why?' Then the answer hit her like a sledgehammer. The cottages belonged to Goldstein. Her rent money went to Chartboys, but he was the owner.

'You're going to sell,' she said flatly.

'Have to sell,' said Goldstein. 'I need the money to support us in London. Can you raise the money?' he asked bluntly.

'No,' said Beth wearily. How could she? She needed every penny she made from the bed and breakfast, and her preserves, to keep the Wheatsheaf going.

'The money you told me the Squire had left you, perhaps?' asked Mary. 'Those shares in Teynham Breweries?'

Beth thought of the Squire's words: 'You're strong, Beth'.

'I won't sell them,' said Beth obstinately. 'They wouldn't be near enough to cover it, anyway.' She couldn't explain it, but even knowing that they were up there in her desk drawer gave her a sense of power, power that she clung to as a refuge.

'There must be some way you can use them,' worried Mary. Then when Beth gave a hopeless shrug: 'Have you told Rupert, Samuel?'

'Not yet,' said Goldstein. 'But I have no great hope there.'

'Don't sell to Hamlin,' Beth said abruptly. The spectre of his owning the cottages suddenly rose in front of her.

'I can wait three months. Only that.'

Stifling her pride, she wrote a stiff little note to Rupert asking what his plans might be for the future of the cottages.

William came into the parlour to find her holding a letter slackly between her fingers. He took it from her and read: 'Dear Beth, I very much regret that Dr Goldstein's departure has left Chartboys with a large financial problem and that we will be unable to . . .' He read no more but tore it up, throwing the fragments in the fire.

'Good morning, Jim.' She sounded brighter than she felt. The three month deadline hung over her like a sentence. If they lost the cottage trade, they would only have the Wheatsheaf and her preserves' revenue to fall back on, and that she knew would be insufficient in these turbulent times.

The hop farmers were protesting, marching through the streets of Kentish towns, demanding the imposition of tariffs on imported hops. Banners were held high, their slogans protesting the plight of the hop trade: 'Over five thousand acres grubbed since October in Kent alone'; 'One hundred and fifty thousand pounds lost in labour alone'. May 16th was decreed as Hop Saturday for a huge rally in Trafalgar Square for grievances to be aired and demands of duty of £2 a hundredweight to be imposed on foreign goods. But it couldn't achieve anything quickly enough to help the Wheatsheaf. The price of home hops was high. The free houses endeavoured to increase their home brewing, to avoid being dependent on the large breweries, but the customers were drinking less. It was a vicious circle. No one had the money to drink, nor often the will to. Young folk, their best customers, were leaving the village for the towns, and who could blame them? Life on the factory floor offered a more lucrative return than an uncertain, inclement life in the fields, with an uncertain livelihood from year to year. With yearly contracts only who knew if they'd have a job next year?

'No, it isn't a good morning, Beth. Not by a long chalk.'

She stopped on the threshold, horrified to see Jim's normally happy face so downcast. 'What be wrong?' she asked sharply.

'Bad news, Beth. I'm going to have to sell out.'

She should have expected it. Bad news never comes singly. And of course the small breweries, more dependent on the home firms than the big combines, were suffering. Jim had premises to run, staff to pay, a family to feed.

'Is it –' she could not frame the word.

'He offered the best price, Beth,' he said apologetically, avoiding her reproachful look. 'Moreover, the only one. No one else was interested. Times are hard, even for the big breweries.' He hesitated. 'You know what this will mean, Beth?'

She was puzzled for a moment, then it hit her: She flushed. 'Our bill! I've let the credit run up.'

'I didn't say anything, knowing you've a struggle. But now that Hamlin's taking over, you realise he'll call in the credit.' It had gradually been creeping up and up; it was still not a great deal of money – but it was money she didn't have. And where now could she find it, with the bank manager urging William and herself to sell out, cash in on the business they had built up?

'I'm sorry, Beth. He'll not be so bad maybe. After all, you'll be a customer.'

'I'll be no customer of Hamlin's, Jim. No matter if we have to brew every pint of beer ourselves.'

'Could you do that?'

'Of course –' she said without thinking, then stopped. You needed capital for brewing. Capital she didn't have. She needed to work on credit. 'No,' she said bleakly, 'I don't have the money.'

'Well, then,' said Jim, 'there's no way out.'

'There's my shares in Teynham's,' said Beth suddenly. He looked interested. 'Too small to count, though. And they wouldn't fetch enough,' she went on.

'How many?' asked Jim abruptly.

'Two per cent, I think.'

'Have you talked to Ted Morrison?' he asked thoughtfully.

'No. Why should I?'

'Reckon you'd have something to talk about, the pair of you.'

She left without much hope, her thoughts still on

Hamlin. To give in to him now was unthinkable. Goldstein said he would not sell to Hamlin, if he could avoid it, but was it fair to expect this? He needed the money for his new home and his child. Hamlin could offer a good price – if he wanted the cottages, of course, she thought suddenly, a ray of hope shining. Why should he, after all? He could do nothing with them. Then she realised he would be her landlord. He would guess how much she depended on the income and he would use it as a lever for the Wheatsheaf. She stabled the cart and mare and went into the bar to face William with the news.

'You're back early, Mrs Parslow,' said Ben, taken by surprise and returning hastily to his glass washing.

'Where's William?' she asked.

'Slipped into Canterbury,' said Hetty, glancing at Ben. 'Don't you worry. We can manage.'

Finding that she was indeed not wanted, she decided to go for a walk to think things out. No cottage trade, no suppliers. They'd find another maybe? But where? Small breweries were being swallowed like minnows all over the county. No one would want to take on the uncertain credit of a free house at this time. They needed the security of tied houses. Anyway, Jim's beer was the best, and she didn't want to lose more trade.

Deep in thought she turned into the lane that ran past the Medlars' estate, and was astounded to see William cross the lane in front of her, climbing a stile onto the footpath back to the Wheatsheaf. She shrank back against the bank lest he see her. What on earth was William doing here? He was supposed to be in Canterbury. Then she whispered, 'William – and Sylvie.' There could be no other explanation. She lived in one of the cottages on the Medlars' estate. Hetty would lie for no other reason. She remembered the slight tension in the bar when she came back early. The silence that meant nothing at the time, but she understood now. He had made a fool of her. Everybody knew but her! She wanted to run after him, cry after him, you're not the William I know. I'm *Beth*. I'm your wife. But then she remembered Richard Lyle and knew that she had no right. Her life was crumbling around her. She took hold of herself. It should not do so, if she could help it.

She hammered on Sylvie's door. The woman opened it, and her face changed, first to fear, then to mean triumph.

'Mrs Parslow, what an honour, I'm sure.'

'Keep away from me and mine, Sylvie. You've done me enough harm, but you'll not harm William –'

'Harm William?' Sylvie snorted. 'You can say that? After what you done to him? He only stayed with you 'cos of the Wheatsheaf and the kid. Not the bastard. I mean Owen . . .'

Beth slapped her face so hard she staggered back. Then, recovering herself, she said more calmly, 'You can hit me all you like, Beth Ovenden, but it don't alter facts. The Wheatsheaf be going through a hard time, bain't it? Better take care lest the birds be aflying. I've no man here now. Reckon I'd like one.'

Ashamed of her outburst she said nothing to William on her return, and suffered alone. She pleaded tiredness when he reached for her, and he did not persist. He rarely did now, and she knew why. Sylvie. She had failed William. Failed at everything that mattered. Failed at

Chartboys, failed at running the Wheatsheaf, failed at being a wife. How could she in justice blame William, even though everything in her screamed in protest?

She forced herself to wait several days before telling William of Jim's news – perhaps because she lacked the strength to face this new problem herself.

He cursed softly.

'Not good, is it, William?'

'You know 'tis only the cottages and Jim's credit keeping us going, Beth. Without them we're done for, seems to me,' he stated baldly. 'First thing old Hamlin will do is call in the credit. How much is it, Beth?'

'Four hundred and fifty.'

'*What*? Saints alive, Beth, how did you let it get so big?' And when she didn't answer, went on grimly, 'You was at Chartboys, eh? Never really noticed. Thought it would be all right.'

Again she was silent.

'Well,' he said at last, 'that's it then. We're finished at the Wheatsheaf. We'll have to put it on the market, I reckon.'

'Sell?' she said blankly. '*Sell*?'

'Dammit, Beth, don't act so daft. There's no alternative. Sir Rupert told me this afternoon that Goldstein is putting the cottages on the market, and you know as well as I do who'll be buying them.'

His chilling acceptance of the situation galvanised her into desperate action.

'There *is* a chance, William,' she cried. 'The shares. Jim said I should talk to Ted Morrison.'

William laughed scornfully: 'Ted Morrison? What

interest is he going to take in your handful of shares? He's a friend of Hamlin's.'

'I don't know,' said Beth. 'But there's no harm in asking. I'll not see Hamlin in the Wheatsheaf. I'd leave Shepham sooner than see that.'

'Leave Shepham?' William was startled. 'Come Beth, don't go that far. We can find summat else to do. We'll find a small cottage. You've got your preserves trade. 'Tain't that bad –'

Her chin went up. 'We leave Shepham,' she said. 'I'll not wait here and see Hamlin in the Wheatsheaf. Besides,' she could not resist adding, 'I know why you don't want to leave Shepham.'

'Why's that then?' he asked steadily, meeting her gaze.

'It's Sylvie, isn't it? I saw you and then she admitted it.'

'Yes, she told me.' There was no emotion in his voice. 'Well, now you know, Beth.'

She stared at him blankly. 'Is that all you've got to say, William. Are things that bad?'

'No,' he said, 'they're not. But they're not good, are they? You've still got Richard Lyle with you the whole time. 'Tis worse now he's gone than when he's here. Can't blame me, can you?'

She stared at him in horror. 'Sylvie claimed,' she made herself say, 'that it was only the Wheatsheaf kept you with me. That and Owen. And if the Wheatsheaf went, then you would go to her, now her husband's walked out on her. Is that true?'

'She'd no call to say that to you, Beth,' he said levelly.

'But is it true?'

He was silent for an agonising moment. 'I don't know, Beth,' he said at last. 'And that's the truth. I just don't know.'

She could not believe it. She had waited, assured he would say no. She buried her face in her hands, then ashamed of her weakness she got up. Then sat down again. She must face this. 'Do I deserve this, William?' she asked. 'Tell me. When I tried so hard after it had happened.'

'No, Beth, you don't. But a lot of things happen that folks don't deserve. It just hasn't worked out, that's all. We weren't right for each other, as I said before. I need a bit of peace. You need – well, you need forever something new. I can't keep up – and, to tell the truth, I don't want to no more.'

'But I love you. And you loved me,' she cried in agony. This was a stranger, not her faithful, loyal William.

'Yes,' he said heavily. 'But we can't talk in terms of love no more. It's more habit. And I suppose I've got into the habit of being here with you. Don't seem likely I could change that easy. Maybe we'll get back into the habit of loving too, eh, Beth?'

But his eyes lacked hope.

William was right. Ted Morrison merely laughed at her. Sitting in his stuffy parlour, smoking away like a chimney till the smoke got into her eyes and made them sting, he dismissed her businesslike proposal shortly.

'I'll buy your shares, Mrs Parslow. Market price, no more. Four hundred.'

She bit back the anger she felt at his sneering,

patronising tone. For a moment she was tempted. It wouldn't pay off the whole bill to Hamlin. But it would help. Should she . . . She wavered, noticing his watchful eyes on her, at odds with his relaxed, don't care attitude. She took a gamble.

'No, thank you, Mr Morrison. That's not enough, I'm afraid.'

She lost the gamble. He shrugged, said nothing, but his eyes followed her thoughtfully as she left.

William was desultorily adding the finings to one of Jim's casks when she went to the cellar to tell him, dreading his reaction.

'Well, you threw away our last chance then, Beth,' he said, concentrating on his task, and not even bothering to look at her.

She bit her lip, staring at his broad shoulders obstinately turned to her. 'I couldn't sell when it came to it, William.'

'We'll put the Wheatsheaf on the market then, like I said. The cottages are sold now. Letter this morning, from solicitors.'

'But there's no need,' she cried. 'The Wheatsheaf is self-sufficient especially with the preserves' trade. We'll raise a loan to pay Hamlin –'

'Raise a loan?' he repeated scathingly. 'With the bank manager hand in glove with Hamlin?'

'The preserves' trade . . .' Her voice faltered. Without the Chartboys' trade, it was going to be a long uphill struggle to get back to where they were, with no money free to subsidise the Wheatsheaf. It had its own crippling bills to pay, since they had ordered supplies to cope with the Chartboys' demand. And with the money spent on converting the second outhouse the trade was at this moment a heavy liability. She had staked everything on improving the London trade. As yet, it had not happened.

The posters of the auction went up. Beth went around in a dream unable to believe that the nightmare she had dreaded for so long was actually happening, and happening so quickly. The Wheatsheaf up for sale. How had it come about? How could she have let it? She threw off all murmurs of sympathy, and went dry-eyed about the plans to dispose of the furniture, and what would fit into the small cottage that she and William had found to rent, temporarily at any rate.

'On 10th June 1908. At the Wheatsheaf Inn . . .' She could read no further. Hamlin would buy. Of course he would. To spite her, if for nothing else. Endless visitors tramped round the pub, measuring, appraising, peering everywhere, into every outhouse, every bedroom, every closet, testing the humidity of the cellars, checking stock; a few private buyers, but mostly breweries. And Hamlin's was one. Finally she made up her mind.

'I'll not sell it, William. We'll live in it, work elsewhere, take in lodgers here.'

He shook his head. 'Talk sense, Beth. We ain't got the money to fit it out. Everything changes, Beth. You'll have to accept this. 'Sides, is it fair to Shepham to take away their pub?'

'Has Shepham been fair to me?' she asked fiercely.

'They're but folk, Beth, and maybe you deserved it.'

His offhand remark took the last of her fighting spirit.

She could not battle alone. She needed William, and William was no longer there.

For a moment time slipped. As she went into the bar she saw Hamlin, arms resting on the bar possessively, somewhat fatter now which only served to increase his repulsiveness. She remembered when as a girl of eighteen she had seen him standing just so; he had not got the better of her then, and would not now.

'I'll thank you to leave, Mr Hamlin. You're not welcome here,' she said with a flash of her old spirit.

He did not take offence, picked up his hat and clapped it on his head. 'Have your moment of glory, Beth Parslow. I'll be owner here next week.'

'You seem very sure of it. There may be other bidders you know,' she said tartly.

'Even if there are, rest assured I'll win.' He paused. 'Now, about those paltry shares of yours, Beth. Ted Morrison tells me you've been to see him. I can afford to be generous, now. Once I'm in the Wheatsheaf I'll take them from you, say no more about your bill, and give you and William jobs here as long as you want and two hundred pounds more on the shares for capital. What do you say?'

'What I say is no, Mr Hamlin,' she flashed. 'Not for sale.'

'Come m'dear, the money would help you fit out the cottages better. Improve them.'

'I'm not improving any of your property.'

He looked blank. 'My property?' His eyes narrowed. A smile came to his lips. 'As you like, my dear. As you like.' He moved past her to the door.

'Why?' she called after him. 'Why does the Wheatsheaf mean so much to you?'

He paused for a moment, then continued on his way without answering her.

She dressed as carefully for the occasion as if it were a visit to London. She took one brief glance round the room before composedly taking a seat next to William at the back of the room.

The auctioneer from Faversham, fussily important, a little nervous. One or two local brewers, a few men whose faces she did not know, and of course Hamlin in person. Ready for his victory, he was not acting ostentatiously. He had no need to be. He had his solicitor with him, she noticed – the one who had been hers. Hamlin raised his hat politely. There was no need to sneer now, for victory was within his grasp.

'Six hundred.'

'Eight hundred.'

'One thousand.'

The droning, unreal voices went on. Hamlin was contentedly puffing a cigar, his solicitor intent on the bidding.

'Fifteen hundred.'

'Sixteen.'

She longed for it to be over. There were only two bidders now. Hamlin and an unknown man. Whoever he was, he would not hold out against Hamlin, much as she approved of the price being forced up – and up.

'Two thousand.'

She blinked, and even William looked excited. They had hoped for fifteen hundred pounds.

Hamlin muttered something to his solicitor, who promptly put in two thousand two hundred.

'He'll give up now,' thought Beth, heart sinking, looking at the unknown man.

'Two thousand three hundred.'

Hamlin's face was suddenly angry. There were stirs of excitement in the audience. 'Two thousand three hundred pounds for a country pub.' Something was afoot.

'Two thousand four hundred.'

'Five.'

Hamlin, red in the face, talked furiously to his solicitor who was expostulating vehemently. Then grim-lipped: 'Two thousand six hundred.'

'Three thousand.'

Beth shared in the gasp that went round the room.

Hamlin leapt up. His solicitor grabbed his arm and pulled him down, murmuring in his ear. Then: 'Has he the money to pay?' Hamlin's irate voice boomed out again.

The auctioneer stiffened in fury, then remembered Hamlin was still Hamlin. 'We're satisfied that – er – our client –'

'I'm not,' Hamlin swept out in a fury, leaving his solicitor to go into a huddle with the auctioneer and the victorious party. Beth stood to one side, with William, dumbfounded by what had taken place.

The successful bidder tried to escape, but Beth seized his arm.

'Who be you then?' she asked bluntly.

'Pendlebury and Pendlebury of Canterbury, Mrs Parslow, and now if you'll excuse me –'

'But who are you – a brewery? Please, you must tell us.'

'Solicitors, Mrs Parslow.' He looked unhappy.

'Then who are you acting for?' And when he was silent. 'I've a right to know who I'm selling to,' she said.

'Ah. Strictly speaking, no, Mrs Parslow. Provided the money is forthcoming.'

'But I must know –' she looked defenceless.

The man softened and said nervously. 'We're acting on behalf of London solicitors – that's all I can tell you. That's all *I* know.'

'Who?'

'Jacobs and Trumpington,' he replied with dignity. 'Now if you'll excuse me, I must leave. You will be hearing from me.'

Two weeks later, on tenterhooks, everything packed and ready, they had heard nothing. They continued to serve drinks, every barrel she opened she thought would be the last. Eventually, she went into Canterbury and demanded to see them. Mr Pendlebury still looked nervous.

'I'm instructed to tell you, Mrs Parslow, that my client wishes the property left in your name. And that, ah, includes the cottages to the left of your inn, at present being –'

'My name,' she repeated blankly, 'but, if it's in my name –'

'Precisely Mrs Parslow. The Wheatsheaf is still your property, and now the cottages too.'

'You mean, your client bought it *and* the cottages for me?' she said stupidly.

'Yes.' The look on his face was one of disapproval at this irregular proceeding.

'But who is it?' she asked blankly. 'Sir Rupert? Dr Goldstein?'

'I cannot reveal our client's identity. Indeed, I don't know it –'

'You must know,' she said angrily. 'You tell me someone's made me a present of three thousand pounds and yet I can't know who it is?'

'Those are our instructions . . .'

'I'll find out –'

'There's nothing you can do.' But he spoke to thin air. Beth had left, flying on winged feet to find William.

'It's still ours.' The truth was beginning to sink in. 'We're safe. And with the money, we can pay off the creditors and fit out the cottages properly. But I've got to know who it is, no matter what they say.'

'Sure we want to find out, Beth?' said William slowly.

'Why ever not? I shan't feel the place is really mine till we do. Ours, that is,' glancing at him. 'William,' she went on quietly. 'What'll you do now the Wheatsheaf's safe again?'

He looked at her. 'Nothing, Beth. We'll go on running it, same as we always have.'

'But what if we'd lost it?'

He stared out at the mulberry tree. 'Reckon I'd have stayed with you, Beth, like I said before. You make your choices in life. To stick to them is all one can do.'

'I don't want you if you don't love me –'

He smiled sadly. 'We're too old for all that now, Beth. You know as well as I do there's more ways than one of loving.'

'But Sylvie. I'll not share, William, 'tis time for choices again.'

He got up. 'Reckon it's time I opened up.'

'Sylvie, William.'

''Tis up to you, Beth. There'd be no need of Sylvie if –'

'If?'

'You'd open your heart to me again.'

The mulberry tree was in full leaf, the roses in bloom, and a linnet gazed inquisitively at a daisy on the lawn. Slowly she embraced him in her arms: 'I will, William, I will.'

She had a dream that night. She had a dream long ago. And both were the same. Of a hotel, warm and welcoming, herself at the door to receive her guests; of carriages stopping, and coroneted heads emerging, of travellers passing through bringing tales of lands far away, of people far from home finding a haven within her walls. Then midnight struck. Cinderella should have fled, her ballgown in rags, her carriage changed to a pumpkin. But this time the dream went on, then became confused with Hamlin. Something he had said, something he had not said. A question unanswered.

She woke calm, and accepted that some mystery yet to be resolved was going to give her a second chance in life, not only to devote herself to the Wheatsheaf, but something else. There was more ahead. But the more she groped after the intangible, the further it sped away from her grasp. Giving it up, she turned to William and smiled.

'It's going to be a lovely day, William.'

It was while she was washing at the huge old willow patterned bowl in their room that it came to her. Why had Hamlin come that day to see her – and why had he offered her, in effect, over the market price? There had to be a reason. He wasn't the sort to be magnanimous in victory, unless it suited his pocket. Suddenly she knew she was right. She whirled round soap in hand splashing water over William who sat up spluttering in protest.

'Now don't make a fuss, William, about nothing. Just *listen*.'

It was a week before Goldstein, the only person she could approach, reported back to her. Even he seemed excited.

'You were right, Beth. Hamlin's in trouble over his shares. His brother who held forty-five per cent, like Hamlin himself, died suddenly three months ago, and his shares went to his widow, who Hamlin thought he held in the palm of his hand. Unfortunately the widow upped and married again, shocking the neighbours and shocking Hamlin even more. Now her shares belong to High Rock Breweries at Tunbridge Wells. They've managed to get another four per cent, two percent are in Ted Morrison's hands, two per cent in yours, and a further two percent are floating around in various hands. The quickest way to gain control of Teynham Breweries lies in buying your two per cent. In effect you control the whole lot.'

'Explain it to me again, Samuel. More slowly,' she commanded, her head reeling with disbelief. He did so, and she sighed with pure happiness.

'I'll see Hamlin for you, Beth?'

'No,' she said, already glorying in her triumph. 'I'll do it myself.'

* * *

She dressed as carefully for victory as for defeat. Even Hamlin flicked an eye over her trim figure as she sat down in his office, no longer the suppliant.

'I'll need three thousand pounds, Mr Hamlin.'

His eyes bulged. 'Three thousand? For those paltry shares?'

She laughed. 'Come now, Mr Hamlin. Not paltry for you, are they?'

'Six hundred I said, and that was a generous offer.'

'Not for control of Teynham Breweries.'

His face changed, as though a mask had been ripped off, colour came and went. But Hamlin was a realist. He could adapt quickly. He swallowed hard. 'Fifteen hundred,' he said. 'Take it or leave it.'

'Leave it,' she said. 'I'll keep the shares and control of Teynham Breweries.'

'Bluff!' But he said it uneasily. 'I can't raise three thousand pounds from the bank just to buy two per cent of the shares.' There was a silence, then, 'Two thousand maybe.'

'Two and a half,' she said sweetly, as she had intended all along. 'I'm a generous person.'

'I've no choice. Two and a half.' His face was drained now, white and blank of expression. He raised his head slowly. 'You may think you've won, Beth Parslow. Don't be too sure though. You've the Wheatsheaf, and two and a half thousand pounds into the bargain. You're a rich woman now, but things change.'

'Mr Hamlin,' she was laughing openly, triumphantly, 'I owe so much to you.'

'Owe?'

'You've given me –' she stopped. 'My dream,' she finished at last.

The women passed directly in front of her. Women clad in white, carrying banners, calm, dignified, well-dressed. Not the shrieking harridans she read of in the press. Despite the urgency of her mission, she stood back from the roadside to watch further, a frown crossing her brow as she heard the ribald comments of the men around her.

Already it had been clear when she emerged from the railway station that something was astir in London. Huge posters adorned the hoardings. Posters of the women who would be speaking at the huge rally in two days' time, on Sunday June 21st in Hyde Park. Emily Pankhurst, her daughters Christabel and Sylvia, her henchwomen Annie Kenney, Mrs Pethick-Lawrence, Mrs Despard – and the 'General'. Only yesterday she'd read in the newspaper that the intrepid Mrs Drummond, the 'General', had hired a motorboat and with a megaphone addressed the terrace of the House of Commons at tea-time inviting them to the demonstration. Last Sunday thirteen thousand women had marched the streets of London to the Albert Hall, an impressive demonstration which the newspapers forecast would be eclipsed by the Hyde Park pageantry this coming Sunday.

From the newspapers, she had gathered the Suffragettes were ill-disciplined, mere caricatures of women, law-breakers. Now she could see differently. These were women with the light of justice in their eyes, enthusiasm, dedication. Just as she, Beth Ovenden, had once been, when fighting for the Wheatsheaf. And now as she would be again – pursuing her dream. The Shepham Hotel was a practical possibility at last. This time nothing would stand in her way. A miracle had – apparently – restored the Wheatsheaf and she vowed that never again would she let her heritage slip from her grasp.

'I must know, Mr Trumpington.'

'I understand, Mrs Parslow,' said the solicitor blandly. 'I'm afraid, however, that we humble solicitors have to take instructions from our superiors, as you ladies from your husbands.'

She gasped at his patronising condescension, something she was not used to in Kent. It crossed her mind, even in the turmoil of the moment, that newspapers were run by men. It was hardly surprising the Suffragettes were depicted so unfavourably.

'*My* husband sees sense,' she said bluntly. 'Maybe if you try talking to your client, he will too.'

'I'm not prepared to question his instructions, Mrs Parslow.'

'But this is ridiculous,' she said, beginning to lose her temper. 'I need to know whether the Wheatsheaf and the cottages are mine, to make all decisions, or whether I'm holding them in some way in trust for him.'

'They are yours, Mrs Parslow. I can assure you of that. My client does not want to be involved.'

She found herself gently ushered out of the well-appointed Mayfair offices, frustrated and angry. She would not return home yet. She needed time to think. Perhaps she would write to the owner. The solicitor must surely be obliged to forward a letter. A horrible suspicion was beginning to form in her mind, a ridiculous notion that she dismissed immediately, then had a lingering doubt. She walked briskly along by the Serpentine past children with their nannies feeding the ducks, walked over the bridge and into Kensington Gardens, still deep in thought. By this time her boots were beginning to hurt, and she sat down in one of the deck chairs and closed her eyes.

The day was swelteringly hot and humid, and she began to doze and then to dream. A dream of Richard and a meadow long ago, of the love in his eyes, of a time when responsibility and care were far away, and they were free to love.

'Beth.'

She was instantly wide awake. The voice that called out of her dream was no dream. It was Richard. He plumped down in the deck chair next to her, sprawling out lazily, laughing at her, blue eyes twinkling, as though fifteen years had never passed.

' "Bess, the landlord's daughter",' he quoted. ' "The landlord's black-eyed daughter". Your highwayman has returned.

"Look for me by moonlight;
Watch for me by moonlight;
I'll come to thee by moonlight, though hell
should bar the way!" ' he declaimed softly.

'It was you, wasn't it?' she said softly.

'Of course.'

'Why did you say I wasn't to know? And how did you know?' she added suspiciously.

He hesitated, then said ruefully, 'Through Mary.' And seeing her look blank added, 'I couldn't go away and not know what was happening to you. I swore her to secrecy except to Samuel, of course. That's how I knew about the cottages. Don't blame her. And I really didn't want you to know about my buying the Wheatsheaf. When I saw you again, I couldn't resist it. I was in the adjoining office while you were with old Trumpington, and well, I – you're getting plump, Beth.' He grinned.

'I am *not*,' she said indignantly.

'More rounded then. I don't mind. I like you that way.'

'It's no concern of yours whether I'm fat or thin *or* whether you like me this way,' she said firmly, struggling to get up from the low chair.

'Don't get up. I can afford to pay for your deck chair,' he said grandly, glancing at the deck-chair man who was approaching for their payment.

'How come you're so flush with your money then?' she flashed. 'And you running away and leaving everything behind you.'

'Unlucky in love, lucky in cards.'

'You won it gambling?'

'No.'

'How then?'

'This and that,' he said carelessly.

'Where? And how? And what have you been doing all this time?'

'Now is that any question to ask of a highwayman?'

'*I* can ask it,' she said in a low voice, 'I have the right,'

'Yes,' he said, 'you do. Let's just say I'm in business abroad.'

'Good business,' she said sharply, 'to buy the Wheatsheaf. Oh, Richard, surely you can't afford it?'

'Yes, I can, Beth,' he said seriously. 'Easily. It's small recompense for what I did to you.'

She was silent for she could think of no words to thank him for the Wheatsheaf, especially since there was a desolation there, a feeling that it cleared the scorecard. She would never see him again. He had paid his dues, and would depart into the unknown for ever.

He broke the silence first. 'How's Elizabeth?'

'At school doing well. But shouldn't it be Pippin and your children you're enquiring after?' she said bleakly.

'Don't be cruel, Beth. Very well, how are my dear wife and children?'

'Don't you care?' she asked, scandalised.

'Not very much, if truth be told.'

'But they're your children.'

'Her children,' he corrected her.

'You don't mean –'

'No, I sired them, but they don't seem like mine, Beth. She brought them up to be little Pippins. I feel I have to apologise for being their father. They're better off without me.'

His indifference stunned her. 'Don't you care about anything, Richard?'

'Yes, Beth. I care about you, always you, and Elizabeth. Nothing else.'

She said nothing, but the air around them was suddenly sweet with the air of lovers. She turned to him with a low cry and he took her hand gently, 'Beth, I'm asking you now for the last time. I can't live without you. Leave William and the Wheatsheaf, now Elizabeth's at school, and come with me. We'll live abroad . . . Just disappear. Don't go back. Come *now*.'

'Oh Richard.'

He read the temptation in her eyes and a joy came into his face that made her task even harder.

'I can't, Richard,' she faltered. 'Oh, I can't. I gave William my word we'd try again. And Owen still needs me –'

The bleakness shuttered his face. 'You don't want me any more. You haven't the courage.'

'Richard, I love you, I'll always love you. If it were just my love, I'd up and come with you now. But it isn't. I've my pride in myself and I promised. I've failed people time and again, and I can't do so again and live with myself. Can you understand?'

'No, Beth. To me it's simple. You love me or you don't.'

'Four pence please.'

The ticket collector stood between them like Nemesis. Dumbly, forestalling Richard, she counted out four pennies and handed them over.

'There,' she said when the man had gone. 'Don't say I never pay my creditors,' she laughed, but the tears were streaming down her face. 'A deck chair for the Wheatsheaf.'

'The Wheatsheaf for a death sentence,' he replied.

'Don't dramatise, Richard,' she tried to say lightly. 'You'll survive.'

He watched the tears running down her face, then said noncommittally, 'Perhaps.' He stood up and stared at some invisible horizon. Then, without a word, he strode away, and did not look behind him.

CHAPTER FIFTEEN

Plans for the Shepham Hotel were started and then became bogged down in detail and frustration. It wasn't possible, said the builders, and maintained their opposition till she could have cried with frustration. She didn't. She seized the pencil from the architect's hand and made bold determined strokes on the paper.

'This is what I want. And *this* –'

'But –'

'And *this* –'

The men studied it glumly. 'I suppose it might, I say just might, be possible.'

And so the dream had at last been given tangible shape.

'You lay the first stone, William.'

No, Beth, 'tis your doing, this place, not mine.' She glanced at him anxiously but saw only a gentleness there, not bitterness, so she picked up the stone and laid it in position. Kentish ragstone laid on Kentish soil to build a hotel that Beth was determined should be the best in the country. The old idea of building onto the barn or incorporating the barn in the design had been abandoned; the tithe barn remained as proudly independent as it always had.

The Shepham Hotel was to have its own identity, though merging in appearance with the cottages it abutted. She resisted all demands by the architect for high gables, crenellations, wings. Low and rambling, set back off the road, tiled roof and built of warm ragstone, the hotel looked as though it had been there nearly as long as the cottages themselves, yet inside all was modern comfort. At the back overlooking the fields was the restaurant. A cook and two helpers were employed. The first cook came and departed within three weeks, his 'French' cooking failing to please customers, and his temper failing to endear him to his colleagues. After yet another, even swifter, débâcle with French cuisine Beth came to a decision. She gave the current gentleman a month's wages and hired in his place the recently widowed butcher's wife from Shepham. Daniel Harbutt had been a happy contented man and part of that was undoubtedly due to the good home cooking of Mrs Harbutt. So chicken pudding replaced *la poule au pot à la crème Normande* and primrose pie *crème aux fraises*. And trade increased.

The villagers were half fearful and half proud to have a hotel of their own, but as soon as it was clear that the Wheatsheaf remained as it was and that Beth had not abandoned the bar for the hotel completely they accepted the situation cheerfully, peering at each carriage that arrived with friendly inquisitiveness.

It had not taken Beth long to realise that even she could not be at the Wheatsheaf, run Parslow's Preserves and run the hotel, much as she would like to have done. So she came to a decision.

'Me, manageress?' repeated Hetty in wonder,

smoothing back her hair and tidying her apron subconsciously in preparation for her greater status. Some emotion rushed over her face, but she merely said simply, 'You won't be sorry, Beth.' She nodded gruffly. 'I can do it. Since Jamie's gone to sea, it's quiet back home, so I reckon I'll welcome it.'

She had been nervous at first, flustered at so much direct contact with the 'lords and ladies' as she referred to them, and Beth had to come to her rescue when she became overwhelmed by the Christmas and New Year rush. But with the slowing down of trade in January and February Hetty had first come to terms with it, and then enjoyed her new position. Ben, left in command of the bar, was equally content now that he had an underling barman who jumped to his very word.

That had been over eighteen months ago, and the hotel had done well. Even Pippin had not been able to prevent the hotel being the centre for visitors to Chartboys, though other contact with Chartboys had been virtually non-existent. Some gossip Beth heard through hotel customers, little snippets that was all. But now there was something worrying which brought Chartboys back into her life again.

Beth lifted out the heavy ledger with the previous year's returns, and went through them carefully. There was no doubt. Even with the increase in the prices, revenue from the hotel was well down for the first nine months of 1910. She had been aware that the rooms were less occupied than usual, but was unaware how much the deficiency had mounted up during the year. Less rooms. Less guests to Chartboys. And this was the end of the summer season when they should have been full all the time.

She frowned. She had no positive information, but it was clear to her that things were not well there. The new doctor, Alan Proctor, was not the character that Goldstein had been. But this failed to account for the falling off in the number of visitors. Did this mean there was a similar falling off in the number of patients, or merely that times were harder and people did not stay so long to visit? The conclusion was inescapable, however. She had to find out.

Outside the window, falling leaves drifted past, and Beth's spirits were low. Face Rupert, face Pippin perhaps, and without her ally, Mary? But she summoned up her courage – it was, after all, she told herself, purely a business call.

She hurried through the old dining room; logs were burning on the hearth, the smell of the beeswaxed beams was in her nostrils and the clink of glasses and murmur of voices came from the bar. Elizabeth, Owen and Mud had left for the autumn term, and the old inn seemed empty with just her and William.

'I'll have to go to Chartboys,' she told William. 'To see Rupert.'

He looked at her questioningly. 'Wise, Beth?'

'We don't have any choice,' she said. 'We must know what's happening.'

'Want me to come?'

She thought about this, then shook her head. 'It's good of you, but no. It might make it worse.'

He grunted acquiescence, but she could see that he was hurt, once more feeling shut out of her life. She had denied that she had found out anything at all about the mysterious benefactor who had preserved the Wheatsheaf for them, but she sensed that he did not believe her and a silence fell between them whenever the sale was mentioned.

She took the back way to Chartboys, the way they had walked all those years ago, when Rupert first brought her here to explain his grandiose scheme. She had thought him idealistic, a philanthropist, almost a saint; and now he had given it up for Pippin. That's what it amounted to. Was there still a Marie Bonner Wing, she wondered?'

'The pity,' she whispered. 'Oh, the pity.' A dream forgotten in the harsh light of day.

Before she went to Chartboys she had a visit to make however. Bill was in retirement now, but she knew he had contacts with all the Chartboys' gardeners, who regularly called in to see him and ask his advice. Moreover his daughter, with whom he lived, was in service there.

'What's this then, Miss Beth?' he asked warily. 'Staking out your ground before you starts planting?'

She grimaced. 'I wish you couldn't see through me quite so clearly, Bill.'

'Ah!' He spat some baccy out into a spittoon. Some of it missed. ''Course it's all talk perhaps, but my Rose do say that things have dropped off proper badly there. That Miss Pippin,' he said casually, 'she don't know how to run a cabbage patch, let alone an hospital. She stakes 'em up when they should be free-standing, and let's 'em straggle all over the place when they should be pruned regular. That's what Rose do say.'

'I don't think that could account for the fall-off in trade though.'

'It's a part of it, ain't it? Then Sir Rupert, he started charging for the Bonner Wing. Not a lot mind, but folks do say 'tis the principle of the thing. Either 'tis free or you pays the same as everyone else. Neither flesh nor fowl, now. Pocketful of dead hopes, that's what 'e got there.'

'Beth.' Rupert came out to greet her after she had given her name to the formal, offputting receptionist, new since her time. It was after all two years since she had been to Chartboys and now that Mud was at school, her and Rupert's paths did not cross there either. She stood awkwardly, waiting for him to approach her. But she had underestimated Rupert, for he simply took her in his arms and kissed her, to the obvious disapproval of the chilly lady in black. 'Come up to my study.'

It was the same room, the same view, but he, Rupert, had changed. He was thinner, older than two years should have explained, his hair already streaked with silver in places, although he was only, she calculated, thirty-seven. She sat in the old leather armchair, glad that this at any rate had not changed. There were no traces of Pippin's influence in this room – and she was grateful.

'Mud tells me all about you, but it's not the same as seeing you, Beth.' He paused and tiredly rubbed his eyes. 'You shouldn't have stayed away –' He broke off as he saw her reproachful look. 'Are you coming back? No,' he said immediately, 'of course not. Foolish of me.'

'I've come to find out why business is falling off, Rupert,' she said bluntly.

He looked harassed. 'What concern is it of yours?' he asked almost belligerently. 'You made it clear that Chartboys was not your concern.'

'No, but *my* hotel is,' she reminded him. 'I own it, and the income is going down. I need it. Why aren't there so many visitors any more, Rupert? Do you, or the new doctor, discourage visiting?'

He got up swiftly and stood by the window. 'No,' he said at last. 'There's a very easy explanation, I'm afraid. Your business is going down, because ours is.'

'Why?' she asked, horrified now her suspicions were confirmed. 'You aren't telling me people do not suffer from consumption any more?'

'I don't know,' he said dispiritedly. 'I simply don't know.' He sounded querulous, almost apathetic. 'The board keep asking me . . . He's a good enough doctor.'

'And what's all this I hear about charging for the Marie Bonner Wing?' she cut in.

He turned on her angrily. 'It makes sense. One can't afford idealism in today's world.'

'You, Rupert?' she cried. 'Do you remember why you started this whole venture? It was in memory of your wife. The Marie Bonner Wing was the focal point for the whole scheme.'

'It doesn't make sense for it to be free. The board agreed that we should charge for it.'

'You, Rupert, you of all people,' she said bitterly. 'You've sold out to –'

'To whom, Beth?'

Pippin, elegant, coiffured, cool, clad in a fashionable tunic style dress, stood on the threshold; she walked in, and closed the door behind her. 'We don't want the whole hospital to hear, do we? This is supposed to be a sanatorium for peace and quiet. I ask you again, Beth, to whom?'

'To the devil,' said Beth bitterly.

Arched eyebrows. 'And no doubt you equate the devil with me?'

'If you've had anything to do with this decision to charge for the Marie Bonner Wing, yes,' replied Beth bluntly.

'I make my own decisions,' interposed Rupert angrily.

'Do you, Rupert?' Beth flashed. 'Then why have you not this time? She has you under her thumb - like she always did. There's only one difference. In the old days you could see her for what she was. Now you can't.'

'Do I have to listen to this, Rupert?' came a thin voice.

He looked at Pippin with devoted eyes. 'No, Pippin, you don't. Beth –'

'I'm sorry for you, Rupert,' Beth would not let him finish. 'You started with a grand ideal, a dream. And you're deliberately destroying it, driving patients away. Does your wife mean nothing to you any more? Do you want to be set down as a failure? As you will. You started with a dream and you'll end with a bankruptcy.'

'What eloquent words. You always were an idealist, Beth. Perhaps that's why you've landed up as an adulteress with a bastard child.'

Beth sprang from her chair to fly at her, but one word from Rupert stopped both of the women in their tracks. Just one word: 'Marie.'

Pippin, her invective forgotten, stared at him and, alight with sudden hope, Beth moved towards him. He turned to her: 'What must I do, Beth?'

The answer was simple. She had thought it out long since. 'Bring back Goldstein.'

Pippin's outraged 'No' was disregarded. So was her, 'If you do, Rupert, I leave.'

'Proctor's a good doctor,' he said slowly.

'But a bad diplomat. Get rid of him, Rupert –'

'I can't –'

'If you don't act now, you never will.'

Rupert turned pleadingly to Pippin, but found no help in her stony face. Yet somehow this made him the more resolute. 'We must do something, Pippin. We shall have to close down, if this goes on. I'm sorry you don't like him, but it's worth trying. It needn't affect you at all.'

'You listen to *her*, not me . . .' She was inarticulate with fury.

'This is business,' he said absently. 'It doesn't matter who says it if it's right. I'll write to him – no, go to see him, and Beth, I want you to come also . . .'

'I haven't ridden first class since that time Pippin and I came up to London to see you and Richard,' Beth said reflectively. She edged away from the window lest soot blow in and smear her best grey costume.

'A long time ago,' said Rupert, sighing. 'And now look at us. The most you can say is that we've tried, Beth. I suppose we just weren't meant to be winners.'

'There are no winners, no losers till the game's run its course,' said Beth stoutly. More stoutly than she felt. She was tired, run down, from being caught in a never-ending whirl of trying to make ends meet. She was dogged by a series of colds and small complaints that she could never shake off. The last thing she wanted was to be travelling to London on a rainy October day to try to be persuasive to Samuel Goldstein, much as she would enjoy seeing Mary again.

Goldstein and Mary lived in a small house in Dulwich. Rupert and Beth had taken the chance of their being at home and had chosen to arrive unannounced. Rupert sent in his card by the maid who retreated into a drawing room, leaving them standing in the hall. After a moment, the door opened and Mary almost flew out.

'Rupert – oh, Beth,' she cried. Beth ran to her, kissing her warmly. Then Mary looked from one to the other, and smiled slightly. 'Is this an official mission? If so, you'll need some tea, because Samuel isn't here yet.' Ushering them into the drawing room, she pulled the bell rope.

The preliminaries of tea ordering over, Mary said laughingly, 'I can't believe you've come here just to see our first born.' His presence was indicated by a yell from above.

'And another on the way,' said Beth forthrightly. 'I'm so pleased.'

Mary blushed. 'We were very lucky,' she said. 'Samuel makes a good father.' She looked from one to the other. 'Now, is it trouble?' she asked gently.

'Yes Mary, we need your help at Chartboys.'

'To persuade me to come back, eh?' Goldstein had silently entered the room, casually flinging his overcoat and Homburg on a chair. He had aged not a bit, nor had his looks improved. He was uglier than ever, thought Beth, but from the adoring look Mary gave him it was obvious her views were not shared.

'Yes, Dr G – Samuel,' said Beth simply.

He grinned. 'That's what I like about you, Beth. No beating about the bush. Things going down the drain, eh?

Knew they would. Said so, didn't I?'

'Dear,' murmured Mary in embarrassment. 'Rupert –'

'Sir Rupert can face facts. He has faced them or he wouldn't be here. Well, he can face another one. I'm not coming.' He settled himself in a chair and took up a cucumber sandwich with great enthusiasm.

'And as usual you won't even listen to the arguments,' said Beth.

He looked up. 'I know them Beth. You don't know mine, that's the trouble. Needed here, you see, at St Mary's. Things are moving now. Research is getting somewhere. They are good fellows I'm working with, London is where it happens.'

'And is that the only thing that's important?' asked Mary.

He turned to her in surprise. 'You used to think so.'

She glanced down at her stomach. 'That was before we had Jacob. Now I think of clean air, and the downs . . .'

'No,' he said warningly. 'No, woman. You can think you can do what you like with me. But I'll show you –' He stopped. 'Means a lot to you, does it Mary?'

'I've never liked London . . .'

He considered, then spoke crisply: 'Three conditions, Sir Rupert. One: house on the estate. My children are not going to live in the hospital. Two: I spend one day a week at St Mary's. Three –'

'Three?' echoed Beth, delighted.

'Three: that woman goes.'

Rupert blenched.

'Mrs Lyle,' Goldstein added, to make the point quite clear.

* * *

She was in the garden when she heard the Seven Whistlers again. She could not believe this time they portended ill. All was set fair at Chartboys: Rupert had conceded to Goldstein's demands; Dr Proctor had elected to stay on under Goldstein. If all worked well, Chartboys should recover its revenues. At the Wheatsheaf, the autumn revenues were up, the beer safely brewed for winter stock. All was well with William and the children.

But still the curlews called. She coughed. It must be a chill she caught when going to London. And when you were feeling ill then everything seemed to portend bad times ahead. She shivered and went indoors.

She sat alone in the parlour during the afternoon, cold despite the fire. They had feared the Licensing Bill in 1908 would stop their opening in the afternoons, but the bill had not become law and all was well. Not that there was much afternoon trade now. She used to do well with Chartboys' visitors taking afternoon tea; now perhaps that trade would pick up again, if Goldstein succeeded in turning the fortunes of Chartboys round.

The door flew open with a crash. Pippin stood in the doorway, her cheeks red with anger. Beth stared at her, completely taken aback by the sight of her. Pippin had *never* come to the Wheatsheaf, even when they were friends.

'Whore,' said Pippin viciously.

Suddenly Beth felt quite calm. 'If you've come for tea,' she said slowly, 'you'd best sit down. If you've come to insult me, you can go.'

Pippin sat down.

'In that case,' said Beth, 'I'd best lock the door. We

don't want half of Shepham hearing your ladylike conversation.'

Pippin's eyes were blazing. 'Well done, Beth,' she hissed. 'Are you gloating over your triumph?'

'What are you talking about?' asked Beth in bewilderment.

'You persuaded Rupert to give me the sack,' she said. Her eyes were slits of fury.

'I was there, but 'twasn't me. Mind you, I agreed with –'

'Goldstein,' supplied Pippin. 'Yes, and *you* persuaded Rupert to bring him back. Is there anything else you can do for your petty revenge?'

'Not revenge, Pippin. It's Rupert's and my livelihood. It isn't your fault. It's a difficult task running a place like Chartboys. You weren't trained for it.'

'Thank you very much. I'm relieved to hear that you don't blame me,' she spat out. 'To think that I, from Medlars, should have the course of my life dictated by a barmaid. My father's bastard. All my life you've prevented me from having what I wanted. No more, Beth Ovenden. You've gone too far.'

'How have I?' cried Beth.

'You wanted what I had, you took what I had. Then you took Richard away from me. You thought he was yours. Well, he wasn't. He was mine. All along. From the beginning. And now it's over. Richard's *dead*, Beth!' She was shouting in her triumph, eyes blazing, her final overwhelming victory.

'What?' Beth whispered, unable to take the words in.

'Dead,' Pippin jeered. 'I thought you should be the first to know. After his legal wife, that is.'

Dead? The word made no sense. She tried to comprehend it.

Pippin stopped as she saw Beth's face, wavering between the need to have her revenge and her old love for her friend. Then she went on more quietly: 'The Foreign Office told me ten days ago. He's been killed mixed up in some fighting out in the Balkans somewhere. Turkey perhaps, I don't remember. Typical of Richard, anyway. Never could carry through anything successfully. Always found out in the end.' She began to laugh, crazily. Hysterically.

'You're laughing, and he's dead.' Beth's senses were reeling, unable to make sense of this maniacal woman, who was laughing yet seemed to be telling her that her husband was dead. Richard. Her lover. Her highwayman.

'Yes, laughing. Because that's what comes of grand passions. Where's your great love now, if it ever existed? He just lusted after you, Beth. But he married me. And nothing you can do can change that now. Nothing. Not now he's dead.' Pippin burst into hysterical tears, and caught at Beth's arm.

Beth brushed past her blindly, unheeding, unlocked the door and staggered into the other bar. Hetty saw her pass and cried out.

'Beth,' Hetty rushed up to her in alarm, but Beth pushed her aside, oblivious of this impediment in her way. She reached the kitchen door and saw William stirring a pot on the range. He saw her, dropped the ladle and ran to her.

'My lord, Beth, what –'

'Richard's dead,' she managed to croak and collapsed into his arms.

* * *

The rain made splodges, hazy patterns of light on the windows, sometimes light, sometimes dark, sometimes a rainbow, if she stared long and hard enough. The wall-paper danced in patterns around her, the roses came out and swallowed her in their perfume; assuming monstrous faces they peered at her, strangling her, wrapping their stems round her throat, choking her, till she lacked the strength to throw them off, and the stench filled her nostrils, the perfume nauseating. Her lips were forced open, she was drowning, drowning in beef tea, cough it up, no, it hurt too much. Easier to lie, unresisting, watching the rain come and go, or was it snow? Jack Frost her mother used to call him, knocking on the window with his patterns. Black faces loomed threatening, shouting at her to drink, to fight. Fight? Fight what? Were the Balkans here? It was more peaceful just to drift. Richard was in the Balkans. He fought. And he was – a cry of agony escaped her lips.

If they turned her the other way, she saw the flames of the fire. Flickering, jumping all the time. She wanted to move but could not. It was Hell. It was certain Hell, and she was damned. And here was the devil himself! She screamed, and the devil laid a soothing hand over her forehead, and the devil was saying: 'You must fight, Beth. Fight. Come on now. Don't give up.' A long tube, a Jacob's ladder from Heaven to Hell was forced into her. She tried, she tried to climb it. But she was back in Hell. But it wasn't the devil. It was Goldstein. What was he doing here in Hell? Her eyes clouded in bewilderment, then she relapsed again into semi-consciousness – somewhere she could hear Goldstein, or was it the devil, murmuring, 'She doesn't want to try. It's useless. She's slipping.'

Slipping? Where was she slipping? On the ladder? No, the snow perhaps. Out in the snow. She was so cold, so hot. Then two hands were grasping hers firmly, hurting her.

'Beth, girl, come back, you've got to come back. We need you.'

Who needed her? Was that William? He looked thinner, sad. Why? Was it the Wheatsheaf . . . the Wheatsheaf . . . She was walking up the side of the green to the front door of the Wheatsheaf, bathed in morning sunlight. If she could get through to the back garden she'd see the mulberry tree and the wistaria. But the Wheatsheaf receded as she reached out for the door. She must make another step. The Wheatsheaf seemed to need her. This time she tried harder. She reached out, pushing hard against some immovable, invisible object and grasped the old lion door knocker, holding on to it with all her strength; she pulled herself towards it slowly inch by inch, never letting it out of her sight.

And the door opened and she fell into the Wheatsheaf's welcoming arms.

'Is it opening time yet?' The painful whisper only just reached his ears. Slowly William turned, an unbelieving joy in his eyes, a happiness she had not seen for many years.

'No, lass, you lie quiet,' he choked. 'I'll see to opening time.'

He went to the door and shouted, then returned to the bed and gripped her hand.

'How long have I been here, William? It's afternoon again.' She frowned. The sun was setting. 'All day?'

'Six weeks, Beth.'

'*Six weeks*?'

'Aye, 'tis New Year, that's the bells starting to ring.'

'Have I been ill?'

'You've had pneumonia, Beth. 'Twas that chill, turned to pneumonia after you had a shock.'

Shock? No, she could not think about that. 'Am I all right now?'

'Aye, you're all right now.'

But it was another few weeks before she was able to sit in the basket chair by the window, staring out into the garden, where the first spring daffodils were coming into flower. Golden harbingers of a new spring.

'They wouldn't let me see you before, Beth. I wanted to.'

Slowly she turned at the unexpected voice, as if some great obstacle prevented her. Pippin, not the grand lady now, but simply dressed in an old blue blouse and skirt, stood hesitantly inside the door.

Beth turned her head back and looked out at the daffodils again.

'Don't turn away, Beth, please. I've come to say how sorry I am.'

It began to sweep over her again in a rush; the pain, the anguish. Richard . . . She refused to think of it.

'William says I mustn't tire you, but I wanted to tell you.' Her voice broke. 'Oh Beth, I –' Pippin came quickly to her and knelt by her side. 'Oh Beth, I thought I hated you, but I didn't. I never did. I was just so jealous.'

Beth turned her head once more with enormous effort,

and looked down puzzledly at Pippin. What was she apologising for? It was just Pippin, wasn't it? Her friend. No, her enemy. Which was it? She made an effort to remember.

'Do you remember all the good times we had as children Beth? We loved each other so much. Don't you think – we might again? If we tried. I need a friend, Beth. I need *you*. I know that now. When I heard you were going to die, I realised how much you meant to me, and now you're well again, nearly well, it seems as though God is giving me a second chance. Please, Beth.'

She had been so wet, so bedraggled, when Beth pulled her out of the stream. So very wet. She looked like a puppy dog, dripping with water and weeds. Beth grinned. 'Towser, that's what I called you,' she whispered.

'I haven't changed, Beth, I've only got a better hairdresser,' Pippin laughed shakily.

Yet there was something bothering her, thought Beth, some enormous stone that stood between them. She must make the effort to rescue Pippin. Save her life. Save her friendship. Which? 'Richard?' she said through cracked and painful lips, and it came back, the pain, the bitterness. The years between.

'Oh, Beth. William said I wasn't to talk of him. But I must quickly, then never again. First, you see, there was Father. There was something in his face when he looked at you, and I found out we were sisters, half-sisters. I was so jealous. And when Richard came, it was worse. I thought I loved him, Beth. I really did, or I would never have taken him from you. I convinced myself he loved me, that he would love me, that you had dominated him, and when he was free of you, he'd love me. But he didn't. He liked me, wanted to look after me, but it's not the same thing, is it? I – I irritated him, I think. Then one day I realised I didn't love him . . . didn't love anyone in that way. But when he came back to you, oh, it was unbearable. My pride, I suppose.' She stopped, the tears blurring her eyes, then went on. 'Oh, Beth, you know, I think if you said you'd be my friend again, I'd give him back to you if I could.'

She buried her head in Beth's lap and slowly, slowly Beth's hand came to rest lightly upon it.

CHAPTER SIXTEEN

Beth drew a deep breath and sniffed. Consciously, deliberately. The ground, still damp from the light rain an hour before, released to her all its earthy, fresh smells, surrounding her with its fragrance. She had come up here to this hillside to snatch a few precious moments away from the Wheatsheaf, away from the hotel, away from Chartboys, away from everything that laid claim to her. It was September now, and the leaves were already beginning to show signs of yellow, the light was growing softer and the sweet fruitful smells of autumn beginning almost imperceptibly to fill the countryside.

To her right she could see Chartboys, on the crest of the downs, which swept down majestically towards the Weald. The fruitful county of Kent, its lanes, its paths, its red roofs, its harvest. Where else could compare? She hugged her knees to her, oblivious of the damp beginning to rise through her skirts, happy in the midst of her homeland. There was the damson orchard that used to belong to Miss Monk, and now was sold to Medlars. A ladder was left carelessly against one tree, promising imminent harvest. Filbert nuts ready to be picked, long, milky pale coffee-coloured amongst their nest of leaves.

Time soon for her walnut catsup. And the blackberry

wine. And the new brewing season. With a sense of excitement, she began to run through her mind how she would organise her autumn. Which to do first, the cider or the beer? Or the hop liquor? Everything was ripe together, that was the excitement of autumn, of Kent. How could anyone bear to live anywhere but in Kent? she sometimes thought, pitying poor folk condemned to live in Sussex – or even further away, even London.

'Mine be a home on some sweet Kentish hill,
'Screened by ancestral oaks from winter's chill.'

She remembered the poem her father used to recite to her when she was a child. It meant nothing to her then, but now – 'Here would I live and die where I was born – in lovely Kent.' For her the Wheatsheaf, its daily life, the seasons of the year unfolding with their different duties. And now autumn was coming. A sudden shiver went down her spine which she could not account for. The trees around her for a moment seemed to hold menace in them, till she laughed at herself for being fanciful, drew her shawl round herself once more, and thought again of the walnut catsup.

Walnut catsup was important, for dreams had now departed for ever, she had learned, and everyday life must supply what compensations it could. The part of her that had been the wild Beth Ovenden had been quelled for ever. And she was busy enough, goodness knows. The children were still at home, in this late summer of 1911, for the autumn term had not yet begun. Mud too was with them while Rupert was at Chartboys.

To them, he was still just Mud, though at school he was Bonner, Arthur, a thirteen-year-old who took himself and the world seriously. Only Elizabeth could conjure laughs and smiles at will from that anxious face.

Elizabeth . . . willy nilly, Beth began to think of her rebellious daughter, always in trouble at school and at home. Several times she had had to plead with the school to keep her there; she was thought an unsettling influence on other pupils. There was no harm in her; she was just . . . Richard's daughter. What lay ahead for her, once school was over? Condemned to a life in Shepham? Go to London and with her rebellious spirit become a suffragette? Become a governess? There were only two more years to solve that problem. And meanwhile Elizabeth unconsciously made a constant barrier between herself and William. Beth watched with pain as William tried to love Elizabeth as before, yet there was a distance between them. In his outward behaviour he was as affectionate as ever. But deep down was something different . . . something that Elizabeth must have been aware of, for she was quieter now towards him, less spontaneous.

It had taken a long time for Beth to get back to full strength after her illness. When she did so, a shadow once again lay between them, a shadow that centred on Elizabeth, as though Richard's death had made William the more aware of his legacy to them. Was it simply her imagination, that deep within her lay something she dared not examine, that she had overlaid with so many layers that she discounted its presence?

She could hear someone calling. She shaded her eyes against the late afternoon sun.

'Wherever have you been, Beth?' Pippin panted. 'You're late. I've been waiting and waiting.'

'You look like you did when you used to rush out to meet me at Medlars,' said Beth laughing. 'You look no more than eighteen, either, not in the least like thirty-five.'

Pippin made a moué and pulled her to her feet. 'Now don't be horrid, not when I've something so wonderful to tell you.'

'Wonderful?' asked Beth. 'Old Mrs Fitzmaurice has pulled through then?'

'Yes, no, I mean yes she has, but no it isn't,' answered Pippin laughing, muddled.

'It's Jasper – passed his examinations?'

'No,' pouted Pippin. 'Oh Beth, *can't* you guess? It's me, *me*. I'm going to be – Rupert and I are going to be married.'

'Married?' said Beth blankly. Then she put her arms round Pippin. 'That's wonderful, Pippin. You were right. I'm so pleased for you.'

'Are you, Beth?' asked Pippin anxiously, glancing at her sideways. 'I wondered –'

Beth had thought of it as a possibility in the years to come, but somehow never as an immediate reality. Yet why hadn't she? After all, there was no point in waiting. Pippin had been – something caught at her heart – a widow for a year now, and Rupert deserved to wait no longer. If for an instant, she felt once again the odd one out, the third of the trio, she stifled it. Why should she be jealous? She had a happy enough marriage. And one thought lay at the back of her mind, not consciously expressed even to herself: when Pippin married Rupert, she, Beth, would no longer think of her as Richard's wife. She could claim him as her own again. The last shadow that lay between her and Pippin would be removed.

After Beth had recovered from her illness they had tentatively met once or twice, then more often, both surprised to find how easy it was to slip back into the ways of girlhood. Yet there was one difference. Beth was always aware that now beneath the genuine affection was a determination as inflexible as her own. Once she had come to terms with this, the rest had been easy. Beth had resumed her work at a now thriving Chartboys and gradually Pippin had joined her there, both working amicably enough with the new matron. It had not been easy for Pippin to yield to Goldstein, but determined to make the effort, she had at last succeeded. Perhaps, seeing which way the wind might undoubtedly blow, Goldstein, too, had made the effort.

'Yes,' said Beth warmly in answer to Pippin's query. 'Oh yes, I'm delighted. Rupert deserves happiness. But, Pippin, do you . . .' she hesitated.

'Do I love him?' asked Pippin, forthrightly for her. 'Yes, I think I do. And before you say anything,' seeing Beth's mouth open –'I want to say it's not like before, but that's *good*. Because it was all wrong last time. This time it's something different I feel. Rupert's kind and good and we've always got on – and I think I love him, just like you do William.'

The irony. Beth said nothing. What was between William and her must remain there.

As they entered Rupert's study in Chartboys, he leapt up, eyes shining with devotion. 'You've told

Beth, I see,' he said smiling, taking Pippin's hands in his.

'Yes, I know you wanted to tell her, Rupert, but I've known her longer than you, darling.'

He looked at Beth anxiously as though her approval were all-important.

Beth kissed him. 'I'm so happy for you both, Rupert.'

Pippin linked arms with Rupert on one side and Beth on the other. 'The three of us, together. And it will stay like that, always.'

'So they're going to marry, William, as soon as possible.'

William continued to stoke the boiler unmoved.

'Aren't you interested?' she asked indignantly.

'Yes, I'm interested. 'Tis hardly unexpected though. Sir Rupert always loved her and Pippin needs a man.'

'Don't you think all women do?'

He shrugged. 'You don't, Beth.'

She was set back by this sudden flat statement. '*Me*? William, I do *need* you,' she cried.

'To light fires, haul coal, roll up the barrels, maybe.'

'No, more than that.' She was outraged at the bitterness in his voice.

'To copulate with once in a while.'

She said nothing. She could not. The chasm had revealed itself with awful suddenness between them. Her William to be speaking thus? He was instantly contrite as he saw her disbelieving, ashen face, came to her, taking her stiff body into his arms.

'I'm sorry, Beth. Shouldn't use words like that to you. You don't deserve that. Still, we can't call it love, can we?'

'Can't we?' Her voice trembled. 'I thought we could,

William. Oh, I thought we could.'

He sat down heavily, avoiding looking at her. She went to sit by him. 'You must answer me, William,' she said gently. 'It's gone too far to drop.'

'Reckon we make do,' he said at last, a kind of hopelessness in his eyes. 'That's more than a lot of folks have.'

'But I thought after – after I was ill, that you loved me, that things would be all right again. I tried, didn't I? It wasn't my fault?'

'Yes, you tried,' he said. 'Wasn't your fault. Wasn't mine.'

'But there was –' she swallowed, then braced herself. 'Richard. That was my fault. I started it.'

He sat, not looking at her. 'I'd be less than honest if I said yes, Beth. That started it, maybe, brought it to a head. But fact is, deep down, I just need a quiet life, a quiet woman. I can't be doing with all this Chartboys stuff, running hotels –'

'I'll give them up,' she said eagerly.

He put out his hand and covered hers, smiling despite himself. ''Tis more than that, Beth. It's you yourself. There's a streak of wildness in you, won't ever let you be. Nothing I can do about that. Can't live with it, can't live without it. Found that out when you were ill.'

'Then you do still love me?' she said.

He hesitated. 'You're my whole life, Beth. Can't say anything else.'

'Sylvie?'

He shrugged. 'Over long since. No one but you. But I can't seem to make the effort somehow. To reach you. Understand, do you?' He looked at her hopefully.

'Yes,' she said, her voice breaking. 'I feel the same. Yet

so guilty, whatever you say. And you, so good to me always.'

'There you go again, Beth. Seeing yourself as all bad, and me all good. It ain't like that. We're none of us all good, Beth, none all bad. We're just folk, I reckon. To get along as best we may.'

As best we may . . . that might be good enough for them, but not for the Wheatsheaf. Their own dissension seemed to run through the pub. Perhaps it was her imagination but the talk in the bar was less lively, people melted away earlier to their homes. There was not quite so much chat between bar and customers. Fears that her suspicions were correct were confirmed when she looked at the monthly takings: down by twelve per cent. Anxiously she compared the figures with previous months. There was no doubt about it; they were running less and less profitably. The feeling she had that the place was less cared for, less sparkling clean, and less welcoming was not just in her imagination then. Carefully she examined the stock sheets. There was undoubtedly something wrong and her anger rose. This was what came, William would say, of her going back to Chartboys to work. Ben was up to his old tricks. Perhaps even Hetty was in on it. They were betraying them, feeding on their good will.

Arms akimbo, she faced Ben. 'It's the long pull again isn't it, Ben? Trying to keep in with your old pals now the hop-pickers are back.'

Flushed, Ben stood up from his task of adding the finings to the beer. 'What's that you say, Beth?' he said slowly.

'You heard, Ben. And I'm Mrs Parslow, not Beth,' she replied shortly.

His mouth opened slowly. 'Mrs Parslow.' For a moment he looked like the old Ben, the man she had so detested, with his sly expression and roving hands. Then he slipped back to the Ben she knew. 'Takings down, are they, Beth?' he said soberly.

'As you well know.'

'I give Mr Parslow my word, an' I ain't gone back on it. Now leave it be, Beth. An' Beth you'll allus be to me, so don't come the old pearly queen with me.'

She gasped with outrage. 'Do you think I'll just leave it there? Did you hear what I said? The takings are down *twelve per cent*!'

'Yes, I heard. We got less custom, that's all.'

'Too busy with Hetty, are you?'

'By God, you've got a tongue on you when you choose, Beth,' he said violently. 'Look to your own, that's what I say.'

And he went off, leaving her standing alone in the cellar. Fuming, she set to to finish adding the finings herself, muttering with frustration. She was still there, hot and flustered, finishing work in the cellar when Hetty came in.

'Mrs Parslow,' she said, eyes glittering, a dangerous sign. 'What's this I hear about you attacking Ben?'

'I have a right to question my own staff, I suppose?' said Beth stiffly, by no means sure of her ground.

'Yes, but not when you accuse them of summat serious without cause.'

'Without cause indeed,' exploded Beth. 'Up to his old tricks again is Ben.'

'No,' said Hetty defiantly.

'You would defend him.'

Hetty flushed. 'If you had eyes for anything, Beth, you'd have noticed that me and Ben left off all that years ago. But I'm not going to see him attacked without cause.'

'Hetty,' said Beth wearily, 'what other answer can there be? Falling returns, falling stock. Ben's been putting his hand in the till again –'

'No,' said Hetty angrily. 'Not Ben. William. Mr Parslow.'

'*William*?' said Beth blankly. 'But I don't see –'

'You never do see, Beth. That's your trouble and allus will be,' said Hetty quietly. 'Even when it's your living. Mr Parslow's not himself, hasn't been these past couple of years. Now he's letting things slide. So folks stopped coming. Then to attract them back, he does it the easy way, the long pull. But it don't work in the long run. And it's no use you looking like that. I can prove it, Beth Ovenden.'

Ignoring Beth's protests, Hetty led her round the bars and outhouses, and to Beth's horrified eyes she saw the things she had passed a hundred times without taking in their significance, the pile of unclaimed credit tallies behind the clock, the stock of Ovenden beer diminished with insufficient return, the half-empty wine racks which should be full, the space where the new malt should already be stored ready for the new brewery, the letter from the manager of the Farmers' Union cancelling the private room once a month – all small things in themselves. But, together, ominous.

* * *

Elizabeth worked speedily, her nimble fingers stripping the hops from the bine with her thumb and middle finger, regardless of the way they tore at her hands. She should wear gloves she knew, like the other women, but she welcomed the contact with the hops themselves, the roughness on her hands, the smell more pungent it seemed. She was singing. Hopping always made her sing. It made some people sleepy but she wanted to sing. Right from that first time when Beth had taken her to the railway station to see the arrival of the hop-pickers they had cast a magic spell over her life. For her as for the growers, the driers and most of the village, the year was dominated by the hops. The arrival of the hop string, the wearisome winding into balls, mysterious men high on their stilts, like Jack in the Beanstalks, up in the air stringing the poles. Huge friendly giants who'd wave at her, and shout out to her, and on one glorious occasion had whipped her up with them, swung the little girl high, high into the air, so she was flying like a bird. Then there was the endless hoeing and dressing; nibbling of the young hop shoots, watching them for signs of wilt, all leading up to one glorious culmination: the arrival of the hop-pickers, that mysterious band from faraway. It was no use Mama telling her it was just London. These strange folk were not of the London she had seen when she went to the pantomime. After her first introduction to hop-picking, she had never missed a year, and as soon as she was old enough to steal away on her own she would sneak up to the fields to be near these wondrous people. She could hear them in the Wheatsheaf barn after she was meant to be asleep, listen to their songs, their shouts of laughter, mingling into her dream world.

They breathed a vibrancy and life that was not to be found in Shepham, bringing with them strange odours, strange talk and songs, strange goods, brought by their tradesmen who followed them from London. It was a world pulsating with life, a life she craved.

As she grew older, she began to notice other not so pleasant things; the brawling, the ugliness, the lack of hygiene. Once straying into the meadow she had seen two heaving figures in the grass, then a couple in the hop garden itself, and added a knowledge of the raw side of humanity as well as of animals. But she noticed it all with a detached curiosity that did little to break the spell the hoppers cast. It seemed all part of one whole, far removed from the Wheatsheaf and its loving security, or the grim outside world of school. She marked her remaining months there off on a calendar. There were far too many to go. Years, and endless years. But she would not think about school. For now was hopping timc.

'William, I must talk to you.' Beth burst in to the parlour where William was sitting, with a pint of beer, staring into space. 'William, I've been doing the accounts. They're down again and Ben says –'

'Oh yes,' he said, straightening up belligerently. 'What does Ben say? And how come you discuss the accounts with him, not with me then?'

'Because – oh William, don't be difficult. I thought he'd been fiddling them again. I was afraid you'd say I'd been neglecting things. So I thought I'd straighten it out myself.'

'And Ben tells you what?' he grunted.

Miserably she told him. 'Ben just denied it, but Hetty showed me how bad things are getting. Is it true, William?'

He flared at her. 'I've a right to do as I wish in my own pub, ain't I? No cause to be told what to do by my own barman. By God, I'll give him the sack right now –'

'William, you can't if he's not done anything. It's not fair.'

'Fair,' he shouted, then quietened down. 'It's only temporary, Beth,' he pleaded, trying to soothe her. 'See us through a bad patch. Get the customers back. Free pint now and then –'

'But this isn't a bad patch, William,' she said bewildered. 'We're in the middle of the hopping season and full every night in the barn.'

'What the hell's it matter?' he said. 'We've enough to live on, ain't we? Thanks to your lover, that is,' he flung at her with unexpected and savage vehemence.

She gasped at the suddenness of his attack. 'But –'

'It were him, weren't it? Bought the Wheatsheaf back for you? Think I didn't guess, did you? Take me for a fool? Bought it for his fancy piece and his bastard –'

'William,' she moaned, 'please –'

But he swept on. 'She behaves like she owns the place too. No mucking out the bar for her. Where is she now?'

'I don't know.'

'You *should* know where she is. She's your daughter. You let her go running all over the place. She's wild, Beth, like –' He did not finish the sentence, but strode angrily out into the garden where Owen was reading. 'Where's Elizabeth?' he shouted.

Owen looked up. 'I don't know,' and went back to his book.

William fumed. 'Seems to me no one knows anything round here.'

'William, be reasonable,' pleaded Beth. 'Let's discuss one thing at a time. The Wheatsheaf –'

'Yes, more important than the kids, isn't it?' William was conscious of being in the wrong. 'Where is she, Beth?' he demanded implacably. It was at this moment that Mud came through the garden door.

'Mud, where is Elizabeth?' Beth asked despairingly to get the matter settled.

He glanced at her quickly. 'I don't know, Auntie Beth.' She looked at him, slightly puzzled. Mud *always* knew where Elizabeth was. He remained as devoted to her now as he was at four years old. For some reason he did not want to tell. Unfortunately William also divined this. 'Mud, tell me,' he roared. 'Or I'll beat the living daylights out of you.'

Mud went white. It was a threat which still carried weight, though never carried out at the Wheatsheaf. 'I don't know,' he stated uncharacteristically, shifting from one foot to the other.

'On your honour,' said William through tight lips.

Mud went scarlet this time. 'On my honour,' he muttered.

'Mud, tell me,' said Beth resigned. Better to get it over.

He looked at her. 'She went hopping,' he mumbled, and seeing that retribution was not about to fall on his head escaped thankfully.

'William, don't look like that,' said Beth alarmed. 'She's a child.'

'She's nearly a woman, and I'll not have her disobeying my orders – whoever her father is. Maybe you don't need me wrapped up in your business successes, but *I* look after Elizabeth. So make your mind up, Beth. Is she a village slut or Squire's granddaughter?'

Elizabeth twitched irritably at the sleeves of her blouse under her liberty dress. It was far too hot for long sleeves. She longed for the freedom of her new gym slip, the only thing she did long for at school. The sunbonnet which Mama insisted she wore lay discarded on one side, her dark hair with its scarlet ribbon cascading in the sun. Her basket was filling up nicely, and the measurer would be round soon. It was still near the beginning of the season, but far enough into it for people to be settling down, and the laughter and chatter were loud, and she had been adopted by one East End family and allowed to share their midday meal.

She could have wished for a different companion than James, however. He was always trying to get her to come into the fields with him. Still, he was amusing, and he had a look in his eyes that told her he was as hungry for adventure as she was. It was that which attracted her to him. He intrigued her, too, because she sensed that Mama did not approve of her seeing him. Just because he was Hetty's son. It was ridiculous. Everyone should be friends with *everyone*, Elizabeth thought. She did wish James would stop following her about so much though, even if he did have more life in him than the rest of Shepham put together.

'I'll come round and help you with your bine, Lizzie,' he declared, bright-eyed. 'We'll work quicker that way.'

He stood behind her, so close she could feel his warm breath down the low neck of her dress. She pushed him away indignantly.

'That you won't, Jamie Grayston. You pick your own bine.'

He grinned and went back to his own seat. Peace reigned for five minutes.

'Look, you have this bine,' he said, tossing it across.

'Why?' asked Elizabeth suspiciously, picking it up with care.

'It's got a hop with a teat on it.'

'So what?' said Elizabeth carelessly, slightly embarrassed.

'That means it's a lucky one,' retorted James. 'Aren't you going to thank me?'

'Thank you very much,' she said gravely.

'That's not a thank you. This is.' And before she could demur, he had run round to her, seizing her in a bear hug and planting his lips on hers.

Several sensations went through her, chiefly of indignation that he should take advantage of her, surprise was another, and a certain curiosity was another. He drew back to see how she was taking it and, seeing she did not instantly slap his face, kissed her again, this time more gently. Now she was sure of her reaction. Pure outrage, but she was not able to express it before William caught up with her.

Beth caught at William's hand before he struck Elizabeth. He flung her off, but made no attempt to repeat his attempt to hit Elizabeth. James took one look and disappeared through the bines to the next set and safety.

White to the lips, William seized Elizabeth by the hand, dragging her away, leaving Beth to pick up the discarded sunbonnet, a minor symbol of rebellion. She looked round the hop gardens in despair. Always the scene of trouble. Always the magnet. How could she blame Elizabeth when she had done the same herself? But Jamie Grayston. The full horror of it struck her as she hurried after them. Why had she not thought of the dangers of letting Elizabeth near James? Jasper she could not stand, but James had Richard's temperament, so like her own. She flinched as she heard William hurling abuse at Elizabeth.

'William, please,' Beth pleaded. 'Stop.' They were round the oast houses on the way home, and she had to struggle to keep up. Elizabeth was crying, William still had his vice-like grip on her arm.

He glared at Beth. 'Just like her mother. Keep out of this, Beth. You've spoiled her. See what comes of it. Just because you roved all over the hop fields, and look where it got you.' She quailed beneath his frightening anger, his frustration, his bitterness against a dead man, now being taken out on his daughter.

'It's not Mama's fault,' cried Elizabeth spiritedly. 'She didn't know where I was going. And –'

'Kissing at your age,' William roared.

'But –'

'And don't you answer me back. I seen you with my own eyes. You've got the devil in you just like your father –'

'William!' Beth's cry rang out, as Elizabeth taking in only the anger of his words, not the meaning, tore her wrist free and ran, ran to escape from this frightening stranger. Running, running blindly . . .

'Elizabeth!' Beth's scream rang out just as William, marginally in front of her and unhampered as she was by long skirts, threw himself towards Elizabeth. They could see what she could not, that the waggon fully loaded with pockets of hops ready for market was running uncoupled, out of control, down the slope towards the point where Elizabeth any second would rush across behind it. With a last desperate effort William hurled himself on her, pushing her collapsing, sprawling forwards on the rough gravel, but free of the wheels that ground William relentlessly into the ground.

Beth had been here before. The still, racked body on the ground. The people that tried to shield her, to prevent her reaching it. The obstacles she must battle through before she could kneel at his side, hear his last whispered, 'It were for our daughter, Beth,' before he died. Mist blurred everything, and Beth Ovenden stood once more by her father's body while William Parslow sheltered her from the storms of life. Then, and ever. Till now. The oak had fallen.

She took her daughter in her arms, cradling her with her tears, and together they shared their grief.

The funeral passed in a blur. After all, it had nothing to do with William. William, like Andrew, was still in the Wheatsheaf, tending the bar. Later Beth remembered only one scene from the funeral: Elizabeth, quiet, tight-faced, hand-in-hand with Owen, supporting him, and Mud behind them, gravely watching over both. A strange threesome, three different fathers, yet united, complete. A family.

Now Hetty and Ben were running the Wheatsheaf and the cottages, Pippin and Rupert attending to the business matters. And she Beth was doing nothing, not thinking, not blaming, just nothing. Once before she had run to Bill the hedger, but he was dead now, a year since. She wandered out into the garden wondering what he might have said. Not that it mattered. Nothing mattered any more. She was numb. She had lost her father, William and – Richard. All through her own folly. It would be comforting to take all the blame, to be able to sink into an abyss of guilt, a welcome catharsis. Yet every time she did so, William's words came back to her: 'We're just folk, I reckon'. Guilt there must be, but how much? She could talk to no one. Slowly she went into the orchard to find the empty hives that had lain there decaying since her father had died. William had always been going to start the beehives again, but somehow he had never got round to it. She smiled sadly to herself. And that brought the agony to the fore.

'Our daughter,' he'd said. At the last he'd broken through that barrier, reached her, united them again. But what use was that now that he was gone?

The hives were lying unused and rotting in the corner, but buzzing round them, in search of clover on the grass beneath, was a solitary bee. And so she began once more to whisper to the bees the news that the master of the Wheatsheaf had once again died. As her lips moved quietly, she found some strange absolution in the rite, as though by framing the words, she was the more able to accept their message.

'Mama,' came a whisper. Startled, Beth looked up, shamefaced at being caught, but Elizabeth seemed to notice nothing odd. 'Mama, you never talk to me now. Do you blame me for Papa's death?'

'Blame you? Darling, no. No blame. Papa was angry with me if anyone, not you. He loved you.'

'I thought he did, but he was so angry. I don't know why. I suppose he must have loved me though,' she said hopefully, 'or he wouldn't have . . .' her voice trembled '. . . saved me, would he?'

'No,' said Beth simply. Not for a fourteen-year-old the turmoil of emotions; how resentment, love and coldness could conspire together.

'But why should I be alive when he's dead?' she whispered.

'Because he chose it that way,' Beth said firmly. 'He loved you, like he loved Owen and me – and the Wheatsheaf – and protected us all.'

'The Wheatsheaf's only a building, Mama,' said Elizabeth, a cloud passing over her face.

'Never say that,' Beth said forcefully. 'What one works for, loves for, lives in, becomes your spirit, part of you. And Father's spirit is in the Wheatsheaf, and that's why we must work together to carry it onwards. We have no choice.'

'We'll help you all we can, Beth,' said Pippin anxiously.

'I'm sorry, Pippin, what did you say?' asked Beth, bewildered. What was this talk of justices?

'The licence, Beth,' said Rupert patiently. 'You need a new licensee now.'

'The justices,' repeated Beth. Then the sense of his words came home to her. Why on earth had she not thought of it before? In the Wheatsheaf she had gone on from day to day, living somehow, anyhow. She had not thought about the licence.

'Whom will you ask?' said Pippin anxiously. 'Ben?'

'Yes, I suppose I could make Ben manager,' said Beth without enthusiasm. She did not see Ben as a manager. He wasn't the type. He needed an eye kept on him, and more than Hetty's. She pondered it for some hours, and it was only when she was harvesting the rest of the tomatoes left still green on the plants when she knew what she must do.

This time she would herself be licensee. She knew this quite categorically. The Wheatsheaf was hers, and she would guard it jealously. Through the numbness of her grief came a spurt of excitement. So there were no women licensees. Why should there not be? Hetty could run the hotel. She could get in a new barman, and have extra help at hopping time in case things got out of hand. William's broad figure – something caught at her throat – was enough to quell any disturbance. Ben, being an ex-hopper himself, did not carry so much authority. But they would make do.

'I heard you put in an application that your good self should be licensee now that poor William's dead, Mrs Parslow.' Hamlin sat podgily in one of the saloon bar armchairs.

'You never give up, do you, Mr Hamlin?' Beth said without animosity. Nothing had the power to hurt any more. 'Time you retired.' He must be over seventy by now, she reckoned.

His eyes narrowed, and he laughed artificially. 'Not quite, Mrs Parslow. Not quite time yet. There's still a need to see things run properly. Give advice on what to take over, that sort of thing. Keep my eye open when there's an opportunity.' His eyes roamed acquisitively round the old oak bar. 'I'd like to see this place mine before I call it a day,' he continued conversationally. 'Call it a challenge, if you like. This time I'll succeed, or I'll be a Dutchman. We don't take kindly to militant ladies here in Kent. None of your Suffragettes. I think the justices will see it my way.'

'Don't be too sure, Mr Hamlin,' said Beth, more confidently than she felt.

'Got another husband up your sleeve have you? Going to ask Ben to divorce Gladys, or bump her off?'

'No need of rudeness, Mr Hamlin,' she replied evenly.

'You're right, my dear.' He laughed. 'No need at all. This time, this time,' he choked at his own wit, 'I think the licensing justices will see it my way. Mrs Pankhurst . . .'

She dressed decorously in her dark blue costume, and set off calmly and fatalistically. If she lost she would face the problem when it came. She was not thinking of losing, however. She was thinking of winning.

She had accepted Rupert's offer of a carriage to take her to Canterbury. Pippin had been eager to accompany her, but she had refused. She needed time to collect her thoughts. The arrival of the Chartboys' brougham at the town hall was noticed, she was pleased to see. It drew up next to the carriage of Sir Thomas Poulter, whom she knew would be her biggest obstacle on the board. He had the reputation of being interested solely in large businesses and to favour big brewery amalgamations. He and Hamlin's man, Ted Morrison, together would be formidable opposition. Together they would sway the board. Unless she could achieve something spectacular.

Her lawyer, Mr Parkes, met her, looking as though he wished he were anywhere but there. He clearly expected nothing spectacular from her. Word had already gone round about the woman who was presuming to be a licensee, and the crowds were gathering.

Beth was temporarily thrown by the large formal room and the grouped semi-circle of chairs behind the table facing her. The justices' courtesy was overwhelming: chairs were fetched, her coat taken, every effort was made to make her feel at home. But it meant nothing.

She finished her speech of explanation to silence. It was impossible to tell whether or not the justices had been impressed by the arguments she had so carefully marshalled together.

'Our inspection was satisfactory,' remarked Tom Morrison, 'though the beer itself was below par.'

Hypocrite, thought Beth instantly. Pretending a lack of bias.

'A death doesn't leave much time . . .' she said. It was a mistake. Instantly she had classified herself as an emotional bereaved widow, not as an independent businesswoman. She had to work hard to overcome the impression, talking in hard facts and figures about the proposed improvements to the hotel trade, to the barn.

'I understand that you work at Chartboys also,' put in Sir Thomas quietly.

'I should give that up, naturally,' said Beth quickly. 'And I already have someone to run the hotel side of the business. My assistant Mrs Grayston.' It seemed to go down well. She tried to subdue the tension in her stomach.

'You understand, Mrs Parslow, that we have to be careful - um - as to character. Especially in view of - um - your sex. Now Sir Rupert has spoken highly of you.'

Beth was instantly wary. Something was coming.

'But there are no woman licensees. We can't get round that. It's just not a job for a woman.'

'I explained why I don't agree with that. Women are taking all sorts of jobs nowadays.'

'Even aspiring to Parliament,' murmured Morrison, shooting a look of glee. His moment had come. 'And breaking windows to show how qualified they are.'

'What are your views on the Suffragettes, Mrs Parslow?' said Sir Thomas casually.

Beth caught her breath, and Morrison stirred eagerly. Why had she not foreseen the trap?

'I see no reason why eventually women shouldn't do every job that men do,' she said firmly and irrevocably.

'And do you approve of the means by which they are trying to achieve this goal?' asked Sir Thomas.

She was caught. The Suffragettes were the talk of the day. Their militancy, stone throwing, chaining themselves to railings, even setting fire to property, their prison sentences. If she said she agreed with them, she was siding with violence, with the very thing that licensees must avoid at all costs. She would be labelled as a reckless, dangerous person. If she said she disagreed with it, she would be lying.

She seemed to have no choice. Looking straight at

them, she began slowly, picking her words with care.

'When I was a girl, I saw more violence in Shepham than ever the streets of London saw. I saw a mob using violence against people in the name of Temperance, of religion, a man who called himself their leader using force against me personally. A means to an end, so those men defended themselves afterwards. Well, against burning people to death, against rape, against mob savagery, violence against postboxes doesn't seem so bad, breaking a few windows, as a means to an end. The end being to attract attention to the cause. I've seen the Suffragettes myself, not just read about them. For years they marched peacefully and got nowhere. Calm dedicated women, just marching, stating their case, but putting fear into weak men that their position would be threatened in some way. So they attacked them, just as the mob attacked me that time. Attacked them with ridicule, with words in the press, then when that did not deter them, with prison sentences, and when that still didn't stop them, because they believed their cause was just, with physical violence. They attacked them in the street, attacked them in prison with forced feeding, turned hoses on them, divided mothers from infants, anything they could think of if vindictive enough. You ask me if I approve of violence. No. But it's violence against *people* that I disapprove of.'

Morrison started to say something, but she swept on: 'Women just want a chance to have a say in the process of law that decides their fate. That's all. Just as I need a chance to run the Wheatsheaf myself, the job I've done for twenty years in all but name.'

Morrison snorted with a gale of laughter, after a brief

silence. 'Suffragettes. A good spanking, that's what they need.'

'Indeed, Mr Morrison,' came a glacial voice. 'And would you administer this spanking to my wife?'

All eyes turned to Sir Thomas. 'Perhaps you are not aware, Mr Morrison, that my wife has recently been released from prison after forcible feeding for her beliefs. How would you like a tube pushed into you, Mr Morrison, with Teynham Ale poured through it? That's what forcible feeding is. It takes six warders to hold one woman down, apparently. A tube is then forced up her nostrils and Valentine's meat juice poured down it. My wife is likely to suffer for it for the rest of her life. Yet she is ready to go back as soon as she is on her feet again.' His calm deliberate voice was at odds with his impassioned words. He turned to Beth.

'I find your arguments impressive, Mrs Parslow. You will be notified in due course of our decision.'

His tone was impassive, but as she left she could have sworn she saw the suspicion of a wink in one eye.

Huddled in the carriage, her nerve gave way. Pippin had been there to meet her in the carriage.

'I came because I thought you might like company on the way home,' she said anxiously in case she might not be welcome. Beth was so proud sometimes.

'Oh Pippin.' She burst into tears. 'I think it's going to be all right.'

And all right it was. She was the new licensee of the Wheatsheaf, at least for the next year. She read the letter twice to make sure and sank thankfully into a chair by the inglenook. There was no fire yet, and the morning was chilly. She must open soon. Suddenly her victory seemed hollow. The children were at school. Hetty and Ben were not yet arrived, and there was no William.

William. She missed him more than she thought possible. Her grief was overwhelming, now she no longer had to keep her strength for Owen and Elizabeth. Should she have married him? Or he her? What if Richard had not come back? Impossible to say. Now it was possible only to mourn, to cherish his memory, and to love what he too had loved - the Wheatsheaf. She walked to the front door and looked out upon the green, running her hands down the smooth wood of the oak lintel. The Wheatsheaf. Her inheritance, now in her trust completely at last. But an empty victory now. Slowly she turned and went back inside, closing the door behind her.

CHAPTER SEVENTEEN

'We're calling her Annabel,' Pippin said, peering down fondly at the fair-haired scrap in her arms.

It had been ten days since the baby had been born, and only now had Beth been allowed to make the journey to Buckinghamshire to see her. It had not been an easy birth, with Pippin now thirty-seven and so slightly built, but she was lying looking pale but happy back on the pillows.

'That's a pretty name,' said Beth, stifling the unexpected pang of jealousy that overcame her at the sight of the tiny baby. A sudden craving to hold a baby of her own in her arms once more swept over her. An impossibility now, and she laughed at herself for such a ridiculous thought.

'It seems a happy name,' murmured Pippin contentedly. 'Oh Beth, how fortunate I am. I've all I want now. Rupert, Jasper and Genevieve and now Annabel. And, Beth, I'm so lucky. I have you as my friend – whenever you can be bothered to come to see me,' she pouted.

'Oh Pippin!' Beth was outraged.

Pippin laughed. 'I was teasing. I know how difficult it is. But much as I like it here, I do miss you – and Medlars,' she added wistfully.

This had proved the one problem in their marriage on which they had differed. When Pippin had become pregnant, Rupert had decided they should live in Buckinghamshire, at least until such time as Mud was of age, in order that Mud should become acquainted with his future inheritance now that he was older and stronger. Pippin had pleaded to retain Medlars, and Rupert had agreed, somewhat reluctantly, that at least for the moment it should only be let. Now that Jasper and Genevieve were away at their boarding schools, Pippin found it lonely when Rupert went to Chartboys. 'There's no one here I can talk to,' she complained, 'I don't know anyone.'

'That's only because you're used to Chartboys, and London society. I could never imagine that, somehow. It didn't seem like you.'

Pippin answered her quietly. 'That's a life that has gone, Beth. I needed it then. So did,' she hesitated, 'Richard. It was a way, I suppose, of avoiding being too much together. It was like,' her brow furrowed, trying to recall, 'opium I suppose.' She laughed. 'That sounds ridiculous. But in a way it's true. The more we drugged ourselves with being with other people, the more we could ignore the fact that –' she looked straight at Beth '– we didn't love each other.'

Beth reached out and squeezed her hand. She knew how difficult it was for Pippin to have spoken so.

'Now,' said Pippin more firmly, 'I just want to try to make up to Rupert for what I did to him. And Annabel,' she planted a kiss on top of the tiny head, 'is the seal.'

It was the first time Beth had left the Wheatsheaf for more than a day since William had died eighteen months ago. At first driven by continued shock and grief into apathy, it had been as much as she could do to get through the daily routine, establishing the standards to which she expected the inn and hotel to be run. Hard work, but not emotionally demanding, had been her salvation. There had come a day when quite calmly and rationally she knew that the worst time had passed, that the agonising tearing at her conscience, the bitter grief for the death of a good man, was over. Now she had to go forward, plan a new life at the Wheatsheaf. Now loss and grief could merge into the other strands of life, be set side by side with memories of his strength, his kindness, his love, and used to build a future. So dry-eyed and determined she had set about devoting herself solely to making the Wheatsheaf and the hotel into something William would have been proud of, that the children would have after her, and cherish as she had cherished it.

She was determined, however, not to let the village feel the Wheatsheaf was no longer their pub. It should remain so: muddy boots would always be tolerated in the Wheatsheaf. There was no reason however that the Wheatsheaf and the hotel could not prosper together. But dreams are one thing and realisation another, thought Beth despondently, as she looked at the latest accounts. Reluctantly she was forced to face the fact that improvements were out of the question at the moment.

'Where's your vision, woman?' Samuel had roared at her one evening when she was explaining this.

'Where's the money?' Beth replied wrily, then instantly regretted it when he responded.

'No worry about that, Beth.'

'I don't want –'

'Great leaping ladybugs, woman, of course you do.

Did it once before. Only difference is this time you know it's me. But,' he paused, white teeth gleaming amid his dark beard, 'this time we're friends. Aren't we? Eh?'

'Yes, Samuel,' said Beth meekly. Mary winked at her, then blushed as Samuel caught her doing it.

'So tell me what you've got in mind, Beth.'

She hesitated, fearing lest her plans were too far-fetched, and he laughed at her. Then she gathered her courage. Of course they weren't. They were *possible*.

'I want to expand the wine business,' she said, darting a look at his face and seeing only encouragement there. 'Into France.'

Then he did laugh. 'Into France, Beth - oh come now.'

'I knew you'd laugh,' she said, 'but look at this.' She waved a letter in the air. 'It's a letter from Fauchons, in Paris, the famous food store. They've heard from Jackson's how well my fruit wines sell in London. They want to try them - and my preserves - as part of a special English corner. Not just for all the English people in Paris but French people too.'

He stopped laughing and looked at her, shaking his head good-humouredly. 'Oh Beth, you and your dreams. Follow your rainbow, then. I'll support you with the capital, provided . . .' and he went into a stream of financial ifs and buts which passed over Beth's head.

She was so busy with her new obsession that former concerns passed into insignificance. One of them was Hamlin. He had opposed the renewal of a licence for the hotel through Ted Morrison, as he had every year, but it had almost been perfunctory, with no real effort behind it, and it brought him no dividends.

Perhaps it was age. Whatever he said about not retiring, he must be over seventy now. Perhaps at long last he had lost interest in his vendetta against the Wheatsheaf. It was all the more surprising therefore when he appeared in the Wheatsheaf bar one day and invited her to lunch with him. Taken aback, she demurred, pleading pressure of work. Whatever he had to say, she was not interested, and would certainly not accept his hospitality.

'Ashamed of your cook, that it?'

'No!' She flashed back.

'Then why not?' Since there seemed to be no answer to this, she assented warily.

'Why?'

'Old times' sake, Beth. Feel I can call you that again now.'

'Do you indeed?' she replied tartly.

'You've made a nice place here.' His eyes roved round the restaurant, decorated with Cecil Aldin prints, the comfortable chairs upholstered in red plush. His small sharp eyes returned to her face. 'I didn't think you had it in you,' he said abruptly. 'All fire and flame you were. Thought you'd give up. Not been easy, has it?'

'Thanks to you, no.'

His eyes narrowed. 'Not me, Beth. We make our own difficulties for ourselves, by and large. All I did was in the way of business.'

'No,' she said vehemently. 'No, you had some real need to get this place. More than just business. It's just one small inn, that's all. Nothing special about it. So why?'

He toyed with the chicken pie and pushed it to one

side. 'No disrespect to your cook, Beth. Not too hungry. I came to tell you I was retiring.'

'Retiring?' She could not keep the glee out of her voice.

'I thought you'd be pleased. Don't blame you. But you're too clever a woman to know that one man retiring can automatically help you. If Teynham's want you, they'll get you. Even with your fancy friends backing you.'

'Teynham's haven't done too well up to now. Nearly a quarter of a century and they haven't succeeded yet.' There was triumph in her voice. 'So I'll drink to your retirement, Mr Hamlin. I'm no hypocrite.'

'No, and so I'll answer your question, Beth. What do I want the Wheatsheaf for?' He hesitated, then drained off his glass. 'It was all because of . . . *her*, you see. Elizabeth. Just a slip of a thing, with her black hair and dark eyes, and the light of the devil in them. Always laughing she was, always. I was at school with her in Charing, but she never noticed me. Never. I was always on the plump side, you see. Then at the village dances it was the same. One dance with me for politeness, but her eyes were allus elsewhere. Not rude, no. It would have been better if she had been. Oh no, she was always kind. She just never noticed me, that was it. Then she fell for that lad.'

'My father?' asked Beth, muddled, then remembered. 'Andrew Ovenden.' But Hamlin was too engrossed in his story to sneer.

'No, not him. She were in love with the rector's son. No following in his father's footsteps for him. He were the roving kind. We all of us thought she'd up and off with him. But she never. Nothing came of it, and that made some of the heart go out of her, I reckon. She were very quiet for a while. I thought that was my chance. I was going to be making money, you see. I was sure of that. Some things you just know. But she wouldn't look at me. I'm going to marry Andrew Ovenden, she said, just like that. Afore he asked her, too. Why? says I, astounded. I've got more to offer than a struggling inn-keeper. She gave me a funny kind of smile and said, it's the Wheatsheaf, I suppose. There's just something about it, and I like Andrew well enough. She never spoke to me again, regretted saying as much I guess. She got back her pretty ways and her laugh, and married Andrew Ovenden. But something was never quite the same. There was that business with Squire –' he glanced at her and broke off.

Beth stiffened.

'No, Beth, don't take on. Time we got things sorted out. I'm retiring, but I'm still going to be around. You asked why I wanted the Wheatsheaf, and I'm going to tell you. It's simple, Beth. Because I couldn't have her.' There was no emotion on his face at all, as he cut himself a slice of cheese.

She gasped. 'Just revenge from a thwarted childhood romance?'

'No, more than that. There was the Squire at Medlars, Andrew Ovenden at the Wheatsheaf. Just sitting there smugly, secure in what had been handed down to them; all that –' He paused, then said explosively, 'Heritage. Born into it: Kentish bricks and mortar. They calmly accepted it as their right. Well, I was determined I'd show 'em anyone could take it from 'em if they worked at it. And then came Elizabeth. Marrying one and carrying on with the other.' He wiped his brow and looked at her apologetically. 'I'm sorry, but I wanted her, you see, really wanted Elizabeth. And you know I don't give up easy. I'd have made her happy, you know. I suppose Wheatsheaf came to mean her to me in a way. It meant something special to her, and so it did to me too.' He paused. 'She died and then there was you. Spitting image of her, only not so gentle as her. And you too took one look at me and decided you didn't like me either.'

'You didn't go out of your way to be pleasant.'

'You expect me to? You've got her eyes . . . So I thought, by God I'll get the Wheatsheaf now if it's the last thing I do.'

'But you haven't,' Beth pointed out, not cruelly.

'No,' he said slowly. 'Not it, nor you. I never wanted you in my bed; I wanted to see you just once at my mercy, coming to me for help for the Wheatsheaf, instead of running to everyone else.'

She looked at him and tried to feel pity, but she could not.

'So there it is, Beth. I'm retiring, but I'm still on the board. We won't give up. It won't be so personal now of course, but any chance of adding this nice little business to Teynham Breweries and we would take it.'

'And what happened to Mr Shurland when you took him over?'

He shrugged. 'Just business, Beth. No bad will. That's what there'll be between you and Teynham's from now on, eh?' He held out his hand.

She looked at it, heart pounding, and managed to

answer coolly: 'I won't take your hand, Mr Hamlin, but don't take it amiss. I don't look back and I don't hold any bitterness for all you've tried to do to me. But I won't take your hand as a businesswoman, either, because I don't believe in big companies. I believe in –' She searched for the right words '– things staying local. Personal. So I'll go on fighting Teynham's. But I'll fight fair and square.'

He hesitated, then nodded abruptly. 'Very well. It's war still, but the Queensberry rules, eh, Beth?'

'Exactly, Mr Hamlin.'

The full impact of his words was not fully brought home o Beth for some time; she was too shaken by the whole ncounter. She was blacking the old grate in the kitchen nd glanced wistfully at the oven. How long since she'd ad the time to bake her own bread. How her mother vould have disapproved. Her mother . . . the mother vhose face she could scarcely remember, except as the eatures in the one photograph Beth possessed, whose tiffly posed formality could not hide the gleam in her ye, the feeling of impatience waiting to be set free from he constriction of the studio. So Andrew had not been er first love. There had been another, an adventurer ho went off to other lands leaving her behind. Some ther Richard, who left his love to mourn alone. She sat own heavily in a chair, overwhelmed by a sadness and rief for lost opportunities that had not touched her for any a long day. It had sprung from her own mother, er streak of wildness, her desire for freedom, for adven-re. And she had passed on to Beth her deep feelings bout the Wheatsheaf. Poor Elizabeth Ovenden, caught in the beloved web she chose herself. The Wheatsheaf. And now Beth's own life was ruled by the same love.

'Mother, can I borrow your new hat, the one with the red feather?' Elizabeth erupted into the kitchen, a whirl of skirts.

'Where are you going, Elizabeth?'

'Only to Aunt Mary's, Mama.'

The answer was too meek. 'You're going to Chartboys, aren't you?' Beth asked sternly.

Elizabeth wriggled the toe of her boot on the ground.

'You know I don't like you going there so much. You're too young. It's unhealthy for you.'

'I don't go often,' Elizabeth said mutinously.

Beth eyed her sharply. She too had visited Chartboys recently. 'Are you sure these are all errands given you by Aunt Mary? Are you sure it isn't that rather attractive convalescent young gentleman, Patrick – Patrick something?'

'Fitzmaurice,' supplied Elizabeth helpfully. 'And yes Mother, it is. Why not? He needs visitors and – oh Mother, he's *fun*.' The eyes were pleading.

'Darling, he's consumptive. And you're not yet sixteen.'

'I shall be in two weeks' time,' Elizabeth replied mutinously. 'Mother, there's nothing to *do* here. The village boys are so *dull*. I just don't feel part of Shepham. Owen does, but I don't. But it's so exciting up at Chartboys. All the people are so interesting. Patrick – um, they all tell me about France and Switzerland and Italy – where his parents were in the diplomatic service and he's been everywhere. It sounds wonderful. I wish I could go there.'

But Beth did not hear her. Italy . . . Her heart gave a wrench. She looked at her daughter as she chattered on, black hair, swept up casually, dark, excited eyes. Richard's daughter. What would be her future? Surely she wouldn't really want to leave Shepham. She would want to stay at the Wheatsheaf – help run it perhaps. But marriage? Whom would there be for her to meet in Shepham, save at Chartboys?

'Elizabeth, isn't the Wheatsheaf enough for you? All the people you meet here. If you worked here with me –'

'Mother,' Elizabeth knelt by her side. 'I love it here, but I don't feel the same about the Wheatsheaf as you do.'

Beth heard the words but did not understand them.

'It's my home, and I'll always love it. But it's bricks and mortar and wood. I want people, I want adventure. I want mountains, lakes, gondolas. I don't want to stay here like you've done all your life. I want to be free to go anywhere I like.'

Beth felt as though her heart were being torn out of her. She must speak for the Wheatsheaf. 'It's more than that, Elizabeth. It's people's hopes and fears, dreams and security, for centuries it's sheltered and cheered people, they've poured their whole lives into it. How can you say it's bricks and wood? Your grandmother, grandfather and theirs before them lived here, and their spirit is still here. We can't just give it up.'

'Then Owen can carry it on,' said Elizabeth passionately. 'Not me. You don't understand.'

'Don't understand,' repeated Beth brokenly to herself. How could she not understand. 'Oh darling, I do. ut think how your father –'

'That's something else, Mother,' said Elizabeth tensely. 'When Father died, I didn't think about anything much. But afterwards I had those nightmares you remember . . .'

Yes, Beth remembered. Running to her in the night, holding her, comforting her in her distress, sending her on visits, anywhere, anything, to make her forget.

'And I thought about what he'd said that day.' Her face was white. 'He said something odd. He talked about my father as though *he* wasn't my father at all. What did he mean, Mother?'

She should tell her, but she could not. The wound was still too deep. 'William loved you, Elizabeth.'

'I know that now, but –'

'But no, he wasn't your real father,' Beth went or quietly.

A slight sigh. 'Then who is?' she demanded implacably

Who is? Just two words to demand so much. Treac lightly for the quicksand approaches. 'He's dead darling.'

'But who –'

'Elizabeth,' Beth broke in desperately. 'I'll make pact with you. Please, please listen. I'll tell you who you father was – but not now. Other people would be hurt.

The stormy look descended again across Elizabeth' face. 'But –'

'And in return,' Beth said quickly. 'I promise you somehow, in some way, I'll do for you what was nc possible for me. You'll be free of the Wheatsheaf, free c Shepham, free to do what you want, and I'll keep th Wheatsheaf going, for you to return to as your home.'

Elizabeth was held by indecision and for one momer

Beth thought she would protest. But the immediate carrot thankfully proved the stronger.

Just how she was to carry out her promise, Beth hadn't the slightest idea but do so she would. She looked at advertisements for governesses. Elizabeth a governess? In spite of herself Beth laughed. In service? She couldn't sew a button on straight. A lady on a typewriting machine? Work for the Suffragettes? But she was only sixteen. She talked it over with Rupert, with Samuel and Mary, for ideas. Train for a nurse was Goldstein's suggestion. Get her into St Mary's teaching school, said Samuel. But Elizabeth did not want to be a nurse. A doctor perhaps. Like Dr Garrett Anderson. Samuel was not receptive to the idea and quarrelling broke out until Beth begged for peace. It was stalemate.

'Do you know why I asked you to come, Beth?'

'To admire Annabel,' said Beth warmly, playing with the baby's tiny fingers. Only a week or two since she'd seen her but already she was beginning to take on a look of Rupert.

'No, silly,' said Pippin. 'I want to talk to you. As I'm still not strong you'll have to be nice to me, and pander to me. I can't be crossed the doctor says.'

'You never could,' murmured Beth affectionately. 'You always got your way in the end,' she said unthinkingly and a slight shadow fell between them.

'Yes,' said Pippin quietly, dispelling the shadow perceptively, 'and that's what I want to talk about. Richard.'

Beth swallowed. 'Pippin, no –'

'Yes. He left a lot of money, you know. He made a lot

when he was on the Continent – and it's all come to me. I've invested most of it.' Pippin covered Beth's hands with her own: 'Rupert and I want you to have some of it for Elizabeth. We think she ought to go to finishing school on the continent and Richard's money will pay for it.'

'Finishing school?' Beth burst out laughing. 'Oh Pippin, she's not one for finishing school. She isn't going to be a lady.'

'She's Richard's daughter,' said Pippin firmly. A look passed between them. 'Yes, I know I hated the idea at first, hated you, but that's all past. We've agreed that. I've had a lot of time to think about it. I disliked Elizabeth because she reminded me of what I'd done to you. But now it's different.' She glanced quickly at Annabel. 'You owe it to Richard's memory to agree, Beth. You're her mother. But he was her father. Had he been alive –'

'Stop,' said Beth, trembling.

'Is it still so bad? Oh, poor Beth . . .'

Beth got up abruptly and stared unseeingly out of the window. It was a peaceful scene: the ornamental lake, the stone lions guarding the flight of steps, a timeless symbol of a heritage that Pippin and Rupert took for granted. As had Richard too. Did she have any right to deprive Elizabeth of a chance to enter a larger world even though it might be a world into which she, Beth, could not follow? Elizabeth could have all the things that Beth had longed for. Her small battle was quickly won.

'Very well.' Beth turned round, and the smile on her face was whole-hearted and tranquil. 'If Elizabeth agrees.'

* * *

'Mother, don't look back that way. This way . . . over there!'

Standing on the deck of the steamer, trying to quell the rising nausea, Beth was watching the Shakespeare cliff recede into the distance, and Dover castle standing sentinel over the harbour, as though she were leaving home for ever. If this was travelling, she'd had enough already. Most passengers on this choppy late April day had taken to the cabins below decks; but Elizabeth, seemingly unaffected by the steamer's motion, had demanded to see *everything*. Bright-eyed she had dragged Beth on deck with her, just as the hooter boomed out their departure, shattering Beth's nerves.

'There,' said Elizabeth, 'you can see France. Look. Don't look back – over there.'

Slowly, with an immense effort, Beth turned her head away from England and towards that new horizon. A new life. For Elizabeth. In the distance there could be seen a purplish grey indistinct mass that was undoubtedly not England. They were making a fast passage and in an hour they were gliding past the lighthouse and pier of Calais. Clutching her new fur-lined travelling coat around her and tying down her hat even more firmly with another hat pin, Beth wondered however she would have the strength to face this strange life. Suddenly, her desire for adventure seemed to have vanished. Years ago, she might have enjoyed it. With Richard, she could have danced and sped as lightly as a butterfly to these fresh fields, as Elizabeth was about to. Now in this spring of 1913 she was nearly thirty-seven. How had she grown so old, so dull? In the passing years as the businesswoman flourished, what had happened to the old Beth Ovenden? Was she still buried down there somewhere, or had she passed the flame to her daughter?

Suddenly this strange thing France was upon them. Strange foreign voices shouted, blue-overalled porters with berets, yelling words she did not understand, harbour workers fastening ropes as the steamer inched its way alongside. Gangplanks were inexorably positioned, and the porters rushed up. Thank heavens, their baggage was registered through to Paris. To have to fumble with customs and this foreign money together would be too much.

'*Facteur*? *Facteur*?' A bright-eyed face was pushed underneath hers, trying to grab her hand case, speaking to her but his eyes on Elizabeth.

'*Non*,' said Beth firmly, shaking her head with a shrug. Her first small triumph. She had spoken a word of French in this new world. She gave a tentative smile at Elizabeth. Then it faded as she worried about the luggage. Where would they find it? It would be examined in Calais, she had been told. For a moment she looked enviously at all those women sailing through on their husbands' arms, protected from the trials of travelling. Then she rebuked herself. Was she not Beth Parslow of the Wheatsheaf, of the Shepham Hotel? She swallowed hard to remove the last traces of nausea, now vanishing miraculously with their arrival.

'*Madame n'a rien à déclarer*?'

'*Oui*,' she said firmly, her second hurdle faced, and produced the packets of tea demanded by the Comtesse de Merville, their hostess in Paris. Forbiddingly the cus toms officer consulted his list, then caught Elizabeth's eye. '*Mademoiselle*,' he murmured and waved them through, together with their tea.

'But it's dutiable,' Beth said, slightly scandalised to Elizabeth, who looked smug. Other places, other ways. They emerged into the cold grey of the April day onto the railway platform, the train already belching smoke as if eager to depart.

Despite their first-class compartment, the train seemed uncomfortable compared with English ones, and Beth sat uneasily for a while till she succumbed to Elizabeth's enthusiasm for the countryside they were passing. Quaint country stations, flat platforms, a countryside that was green, and yet not green as Kent, grey villages. How sombre compared with Kent's mellow red warmth, thought Beth. A huge meandering river, the Somme their map said. Flat, desolate land, hardly a horse or person to be seen.

'Mother, look!' Elizabeth's excited shout brought Beth out to the corridor where Elizabeth was standing. She pointed in the direction they were going. There shining in the pale sunshine was an enormous white church. Cathedral? Castle? Set on a hill dominating the buildings beneath, white round domes giving it an Eastern appearance.

'What is it?' breathed Beth. 'Do you know?'

'I think it's Sacré Coeur.' Elizabeth had her Baedeker clutched in her hand.

Beth stared at it as if hypnotised, as the train belched its way towards Paris. Excitement mounted in her. So this was Paris. This was France. What lay ahead? Perhaps, after all, life held promise of the unknown, of adventure, still for her. She began to look forward to her visit to Fauchons to discuss the wine sales.

Outside the railway station indecision struck again in the noise and confusion. Should they take the railway omnibus or a *fiacre*? Or a tram perhaps? Their porter had no hesitation and took their luggage straight to his company's omnibus, hand held out for his *pourboire*. Beth hesitated between a two franc silver piece or a fifty centime piece, opted for the two franc piece and was rewarded by his look of amazed gratitude.

'Mama, you gave him over two shillings. Did you realise that?' commented Elizabeth indignantly, with the scorn of the young for the dilemmas of their elders.

'Yes, no. Oh do be quiet, Elizabeth.'

It was not a long drive to the Grand Hotel, but a kaleidoscope of new impressions kept them both open-mouthed. So different to London with its comfortable grandeur. Here all was grey elegance in the buildings contrasting with the brightness and bustle of the little shops and cafés that dotted every street.

As the omnibus drew up outside the Grand Hotel, Beth wished once again that she had taken the *fiacre*. It was so *very* grand. Baggage porters took down their luggage with as much deference as if from a Rolls-Royce motor car.

'Look,' breathed Elizabeth, pointing not to the hotel or to the Café de la Paix by its side humming with life but to the end of the boulevard where a huge ornate building dominated the scene. '*That's* the Opera, where we'll be going.' She was almost jumping up and down in excitement in a most un-sixteen-like manner.

The Paris Opera with its columns, its domes and cupolas, the ornate carvings and statues, was the loveliest building Beth had ever seen. She stood and stared, a strange excitement welling up inside her that tomorrow she would be walking inside that palace.

Inside the grand lobby of the hotel, they found the Comtesse de Merville waiting. Always a friend since her first visit to Chartboys, now she was a friend indeed. As soon as Beth had given her assent, Pippin and Rupert had moved quickly. So had the Comtesse, and a school in St Germain speedily arranged. The Comtesse, travelling from her home in Fontainebleau, had insisted on their being her guests in the Grand Hotel *pour comprendre Paris un peu*, as she put it.

Now, muffled in furs, although it was nearly the end of April, she rose to greet them in the foyer of the hotel. 'Ah, Beth, *ma chérie*. I trust you do not object to my not coming to the railway station. So vulgar, railway stations.' She accorded Beth the honour of three kisses, while Elizabeth, overawed by the Comtesse as she had not been by Paris itself, received the statutory two. Then her critical gaze swept over them both. '*Évidemment*,' she said eventually, nodding, 'you are ready for Paris.' It should have been Elizabeth to whom she referred, but her words were spoken to Beth.

'Mother, I have something to ask you,' said Elizabeth, sweeping her hair towards the back of her head in the new style and admiring the effect in the mirror. 'How do I look?'

'That's all you want to ask me?' asked Beth, laughing.

'No, I just got distracted!' She twirled in front of the

long mirror in the drawing room of their suite. The highwaisted low-necked evening gown in pale pink georgette highlighted her dark beauty.

'How do I look, Mama?'

'You look – eager for life, darling.'

'You don't think I look too, well, *English*?' Elizabeth frowned. Both of them had been somewhat cowed by the elegantly dressed Parisiennes that surrounded them everywhere in their day and a half in Paris.

'You *are* English,' declared Beth robustly. 'And you look beautiful.'

'And so do you, Mama,' said Elizabeth generously, in a rare moment of perceptiveness.

'Do I?' Beth was pleased. 'Grand enough for the Opera?' In the spirit of adventure she had bought one of the new *brassières* and was very conscious of the different shape it gave her bosom. Self-conscious, but rather pleased. Her dress, also low cut, but with a more generous covering of lace over her neck and arms, was red. She had not worn red since that ball at Chartboys. She felt almost a girl again, instead of a staid businesswoman. Then she remembered. 'Not so much flattery, Elizabeth,' she said sternly. 'What did you want to ask me?'

Elizabeth hesitated, then burst out. 'When I go to the school at St Germain-en-Laye tomorrow, can I just go with the Comtesse? Please?' In just twenty-four hours she and the Comtesse had become firm friends.

Beth felt as though she had been struck.

'I don't want you to be hurt. It's just that it's special. I'm beginning a new life, and I need to do it alone. Not with your help. If the Comtesse comes, I will really feel different, almost French. I think I'd feel braver.' Her voice wobbled slightly.

In a flash Beth caught her in her arms. 'There, darling, yes of course. I don't mind at all. There's plenty to see in Paris . . .'

'The Dance by the Carpeaux, *chère* Elizabeth.' The Comtesse watched with some amusement Elizabeth and Beth outside the opera, Beth averting her eyes, Elizabeth staring unashamedly. At school they were hurried past such naked statuary, and the Louvre had been a spectacular success with her. The Comtesse's lips twitched. '*Alors*, *mon enfant*, for our older eyes, the glories are within.'

And such glories. Beth held her breath as they entered the grand foyer from the chill of the evening outside, straight into a Ruritanian world she had only seen on the stage before. No London theatre was like this. She had never been to Covent Garden, but she could not imagine its rivalling this in its magnificence. The grand staircase flanked with ornate balustrades overlooked by small balconies, divided into two halfway up, lit by a myriad of lamps supported by ornate statues. But the staircase itself was hardly visible; gliding up it was Paris itself *en fête*. Men in elegant evening dress escorted birds of paradise, bedecked with feathers, jewels and swansdown. No hobble skirts to be seen here now, but the very newest fashions, the best of Poiret and Worth. Amongst this glorious parade Beth felt as English and conspicuous as a maypole.

'*Alors*, Elizabeth, she resembles your mama, does she not?' The Comtesse watched Elizabeth marvelling at the arresting *statue de la Pythie* at the bottom of the grand staircase.

'Mother? You see *Mother* like that?' asked Elizabeth in amazement, looking at the statue of the tousle-haired rampant wild spirit warding off danger unafraid.

'Ah yes, my child. See the chain round the feet of *La Pythie*. A chained spirit, your mama, that should be wild and free. You should have seen her, as I have seen her.'

'I don't feel like a wild spirit,' said Beth ruefully.

The Comtesse glanced at her. 'Ah yes, it is there still,' she said. 'And one day the chains will break, and *voilà*, like St Peter you will be free.'

The curtain swept up to reveal Japan. Beth had seen the *Mikado*, but this was not the Japan of Gilbert and Sullivan, but a delicate, doll-like, poignant world a million miles away. Beth sat entranced by Puccini's music, new to her as indeed was opera itself. She could not understand the words, but the Comtesse had explained the plot to them, and such was the beauty of the music that even that seemed unnecessary. It was evident from the shufflings in the audience beneath them, that the opera came second to its social requirements, but Beth was oblivious to all save the enchantment of the siren-like voice of Madame Butterfly and the lilting tenor of the black-haired handsome Lieutenant Pinkerton. The Comtesse's box was close to the stage, but even so Beth felt impelled to raise her opera glasses to see him closer. That voice, that face. How silly, he was nothing like – Her attention was lost for a few minutes, and when she concentrated again the newly married couple were alone, awaiting the joys of their marriage bed.

'*Ora sei tutta mia.*' 'Now you are mine alone.' '*Vieni, vieni,*' Pinkerton sang. Oh come . . . The melodies of the music coupled with that face, that voice, distanced her from all around her. She was part of that scene, that newly married joy. Pinkerton had Butterfly by the hand, but in Beth's imagination they were embracing; he was leading her towards the quaint little Japanese house, towards a gate in a meadow, long ago, the sun shining warm around them.

'*Vieni, vieni.*'

They lay in the meadow, she and Richard. Yesterday, today, tomorrow. The witchcraft of the music beguiled her, these lovers in their happiness. 'Beth, let's make it real.' 'Forever my Beth.' She could look no longer, she must tear her eyes away from the lovers on the stage; she turned her head, drawn by the feeling of someone's eyes upon her from the box opposite to theirs on the other side of the auditorium.

Richard's eyes.

'*Ah, vieni, vieni . . .*' The curtain fell, the applause deafening, and stifling Beth's one small, choked cry. With trembling fingers that did not seem to be her own she picked up the opera glasses, focussed them: a muffled impression of a dark bearded face, and then it was gone. The energy drained out of her. There was just an empty space opposite.

'Beth, are you ill?' The Comtesse was concerned.

'Comtesse.' She stopped. She could not explain. 'Air. I just need air.' She could say no more but ran swiftly out of the box. Somehow, she must find her way round to that side of the auditorium to seek him. Just to put her mind at rest, that it had been a dream, an illusion. As it must, *must* have been. But everywhere people were flocking out of boxes, out of the stalls, to promenade in the foyers and vast wide corridors. She had forgotten that the Comtesse had explained it was the custom at the opera to meet all one's friends during the long intervals, to see and to be seen. At every turn her path was blocked. Twisting, apologising, desperate to get through, oblivious of upturned eyebrows at this strange unaccompanied woman, she hurried towards her goal. Why hurry, said Society. There was tomorrow, and tomorrow, and tomorrow.

The audience was milling down the grand staircase, and she stood helplessly in one of the little balconies overlooking the cage of the staircase, looking down at the tops of the heads of the people below. When a face looked upwards, she scanned it eagerly. But it was not *the* face. Eventually, quietly, ashamed of herself now the tumult had subsided, she made her way back to the box and apologised to the Comtesse.

'Mama, what's wrong?' demanded Elizabeth.

'I just felt a little faint,' said Beth mechanically.

'I have taken the liberty of ordering champagne here,' said the Comtesse, eyeing her thoughtfully. 'Perhaps the promenade is too much, *hein*?'

'Perhaps,' acknowledged Beth, emotion drained out of her. What was wrong with her? She was living in a fantasy world, seeing phantoms of the past, long dead. Had the music been that powerful?

The music began again, for the second act. No Pinkerton in this act, no dark hair and lilting voice to set feelings astir that had been buried long since.

But they had lain beneath the surface, waiting for some chance happening to stir again, and imagine the impossible. Beth fearfully raised her opera glasses to her eyes once more, focussed them first on the mandolin-like carving beneath the box, then slowly raised them to where that face had been. Again other men, a woman, but not *that* man. He could never have been there. She had imagined it. She was tired, so tired.

Elizabeth was sitting by her side and Beth reached out her hand as if to ensure she were still there, an anchor in a world that seemed suddenly at risk. The grip of her hand reassured her, and at last the curtain fell over the dead body of Madame Butterfly.

Slowly Beth donned her opera cloak, unable to take part in the social ceremonies that followed as the Comtesse met her friends, shaking hands, kissing, effusing. The grand staircase was packed as they slowly walked down: ahead of them was a sea of opera-hatted men and women en fête, a hubbub of twittering voices, a seething dovecote. Save for one still calm centre. Half-way down Beth looked over the balustrade. Standing in the bay at the bottom was a man in a cloak and opera hat half in shadow gazing up. He quickly turned away, but it was too late. She had seen the eyes in the unfamiliarly bearded face.

'Richard,' she whispered.

As her lips formed the word he moved swiftly, gliding through the crowds and vanished out of the main entrance. Coming out of her daze, Beth gave one cry and started to pursue him, then slipped on the steps. She was closed in, imprisoned by a sea of concerned faces. The Comtesse was nearest and helped her up, and to the bottom of the steps.

'Please, Comtesse, I'll be all right. I need air –' She pushed her way through the crowd in pursuit of that fleeing figure. The linkman looked at her curiously, noting her distraught expression. '*Un fiacre*, madame?' he enquired. She shook her head. 'That gentleman,' she stammered.

'Madame?' Polite incomprehension.

'The gentleman with the opera hat. With a beard.'

He shrugged and turned away. There were hundreds of gentlemen, with opera hats, with beards.

'Beth, what is wrong with you?' the Comtesse demanded, arriving by her side.

Gasping with thankfulness for an ally, Beth pleaded: 'Comtesse, I need to know. A man passed out just now, swiftly, alone, with a beard, he came out alone. Do they remember? Do they know him?'

Frowning, the Comtesse fired off some rapid phrases. There were long consultations but finally she turned to Beth explaining, 'They think they remember the gentleman, but no, they do not know who he is. They have seen him before but not often. No, they do not know where his *fiacre* went.'

. . . 'And now Beth, that we are alone, I wish you to explain,' said the Comtesse a trifle grimly.

Beth did so, wearily, leaving little out now. She could trust the Comtesse. But she made no mention of Elizabeth.

At the conclusion, the Comtesse said simply, 'If he is known in Paris we will discover him. Meanwhile, you rest.' It was a command. 'I will escort Elizabeth to her school and when I return, we set out to find this man, *hein*?'

She looked at Beth's distraught face. 'Do not worry, my Beth, *le bon Seigneur* disposes. If it is His will, he will find you or you will find him.'

But Beth could not sit and do nothing. Richard was in

Paris. Richard was alive. Reason told her this could not be so; her heart told her differently. Bearded the man might have been, but it was Richard. Not dead, though still wishing to be thought so. She could not rest till the Comtesse returned. At this very moment Richard might be leaving the city. He did not wish to meet her, that was obvious. He no longer loved her . . . No, he would not have returned for a second look if so. Unless he had come to see Elizabeth. The thought struck her with a pang. He might have come to see his daughter. No, she could not, would not believe that was all.

'Lyle. Mr Richard Lyle.'

She spelled out the name carefully to the bored official who condescended to see her in the British Embassy in the Rue du Faubourg St Honoré. Already her visit to Fauchons had passed into the back of her mind. She had been in a daze. The business completed quickly, pleasantly and satisfactorily - but she could not remember how.

'Of course, madam, we would not necessarily know of all British subjects resident here, but we have no one of that name listed.'

Heavy-hearted, she walked across to the Tuileries Gardens and sat down on one of the chairs, watching the Parisians promenading, the children playing with a marionette theatre, and felt bereft. She was alone in Paris and Richard was here. It must be possible to find him, but how, where? She thought again of the Comtesse's words: either he will find you or you will find him. But only if God so disposes, she thought wrily. Well, God helped those who helped themselves, she reflected, desperation making her brain work the harder. Richard was a barrister. Perhaps he would be at the Palais de Justice.

Excitement quickened in her as she hurried along the road by the Seine past the Louvre, scarcely now giving a thought to the museum she had marvelled at so recently, over to the Île de la Cité. She pushed her way through the milling tourists and found her way to the civil courts. Here, totally bewildered, she found a concierge. Who spoke no English. She enlisted the aid of an elderly Frenchman, to whom, pride smarting in her, she was obliged to confess she was seeking a former lover. His eyes gleamed. He understood *parfaitement*. But the concierge shook his head. She was directed to an avocat, still with her interpreter, sympathetically agog. He too shook his head. 'It is unlikely he practises here, Madame. He would need to be an *avocat français*. I regret, Madame . . .'

Dispensing with great difficulty with the services of her new admirer, she returned to the Café de la Paix for luncheon. She remembered the Comtesse telling her that if one sat here long enough all the world would pass one by. Perhaps she did not linger long enough over her *omelette aux fines herbes*, for Richard did not. Frustrated and near to tears, she wondered where to go next. April was a time for lovers in Paris, and yet they were apart. Perhaps she'd been mistaken after all, was chasing a will-o'-the-wisp. How could he be alive? Pippin would have known and told her –

The terrible thought struck her at once. Why had it not occurred to her before? Pippin! If Richard was alive, Pippin's marriage to Rupert would be invalid. The new baby a bastard. Illegitimate, she hastily corrected herself. If Richard came back, he would still be married to Pippin. She could not face the agonising questions that brought to her mind. No, she must find Richard first.

The linkmen at the opera had said they had seen him before but not often. Very well, so either he was a visitor to Paris – or he didn't like opera. No, that didn't make sense. If he lived in Paris, with Richard's love of society, he would be a regular attender at the opera. So he must be a visitor. She would first try the hotels. The *best* hotels. Even the Grand would not be grand enough for Richard. Should she take a *fiacre*? She looked at her small store of money. Her feet were hurting now, as much from the failure of her mission as from exhaustion. But she needed to husband her resources now. It might be a long search. She set out on foot down the Rue de la Paix to the Place Vendôme to the Ritz. Start with the best.

She found the uniform façades of the Place Vendôme off-putting, but intent on her quest found it no effort to walk into the portals of No 17 past the grandly uniformed doorman. She was surprised to find the lobby so small for such a luxurious hotel, and no place to sit as in most hotels.

Once again she had no luck. But the concierge, taking pity on her, became almost human. Madame, he suggested, needed tea to revive her. Madame looked weary. She was about to refuse, then for some reason changed her mind and the concierge pointed out the Salon de Thé. She consulted her list of hotels while she sipped her tea, inured now to fashionable Parisiennes around her. The Majestic, the Meurice, the Vendôme. Well, at least that one was near. But a feeling of hopelessness was already beginning to creep over her.

It was not until, footsore and weary, she returned to the Grand Hotel late that afternoon that the obvious explanation occurred to her. He had changed his name, of course. He had chosen to disappear again. Richard Lyle was dead indeed.

She put off returning to her suite for a moment, reluctant to face its emptiness now that Elizabeth had gone. She walked through the magnificent ballroom, but the cherubs staring down from the ceiling seemed to mock her. She felt tired, dirty, and ready to burst into tears. If she did not find him now, he was gone for ever. That she was sure of. One thing was clear. He no longer wanted - loved - her. She returned to the suite despondently and was glad to find the bath she had ordered ready. She blessed the Comtesse for giving her this luxury of a suite with a rare private bathroom. Perhaps it would enable her to see things more clearly.

She climbed into the magnificent porcelain painted tub standing proudly in the middle of the bathroom, so different from the old tin bath of the Wheatsheaf, or even the new small bathrooms she had installed in her hotel. By the side of this her hotel looked like a rabbit hutch!

Refreshed, she put on her underclothes and dressing gown and returned to the bedroom. Something was different, strange. What was it? Everything was as she had left it, yet - her shoulder purse was not here. Odd. She must have left it in the salon. She opened the white painted door - and stopped still.

He was there, lounging one leg across the arm of the chair, his old familiar pose. But his familiar smile had gone. There were lines on his face, more than were put there by the years.

'I talked my way in,' he said abruptly, his gaze travelling slowly up and down the blue dressing gown to the boudoir cap over her long black hair.

'Nice for my reputation,' she said, rallying slightly. The sight of him actually there in the room sent first waves of panic through her, then an odd calm. 'Richard –' She moved towards him, but he stopped her with a gesture.

'Don't come closer, Beth. Please.'

She began to tremble. 'You're supposed to be dead,' she said. 'Did you know that? Did they make a mistake?'

'No,' he said. 'No mistake. I did it purposely. It was very easy out there in the Balkans with so much unrest. I simply changed identities. A ship got sunk. Some were saved. Some not. It seemed better that Richard Lyle was not. I'm John Hargreaves now, officially. Soldier of fortune, as they say.'

'Why, Richard, why?' she burst out.

He looked at her almost dispassionately. 'It seemed better, Beth. That last time, when you refused me, I was going to shoot myself. Yes, I know it sounds melodramatic. But it really seemed that everyone would be better off. You, Pippin, the children. Even my father would be glad to see the back of me. Nothing but trouble, you see. I'd drifted over to Bucharest and the night I decided . . . something turned up. I was outside the casino, which seemed the right place to kill myself.

Gambled with life and lost. That was me. But before I did, I put the last money in my pockets on the tables – and won. And won and won again. I started chatting, won some more, met a few people – and, well, I always was a coward. I didn't shoot myself after all. I told myself when I'd lost all the money again, then I'd kill myself. But somehow I couldn't lose. Then I tried my hand at a few business deals. They all worked. However hard I tried, I couldn't lose that blessed money. Ironic, isn't it? I decided in the end life or God was trying to tell me something. Even when –' he hesitated, 'I met this woman, I found she had even more money than I had. Funny life. So it's been going on. Till I saw you. I tried to escape. But I couldn't resist another look to see if it really was you.'

'And why have you come now?' she said, stiltedly, hope dying in her heart at the flatness in his voice. A woman, he'd said.

'I knew you'd never give up trying to find me. I saw you taking tea at the Ritz. I *was* staying there. I knew you'd go on looking for me and might even tell Rupert. I couldn't risk that. So now I've explained. I'll just disappear and no one will be any the wiser.'

'But me?' she whispered, unbelievingly. 'What about me? Don't you care any more?'

His eyes were cold, disillusioned. This wasn't her Richard surely. Her highwayman. Back before the morning light with his prize of gold. Back only to vanish once more?

'Don't torment me, Beth. You'll never leave William I realise that.'

The room spun round her. Leave William? 'William'

You've heard nothing then from Shepham?' she blurted out.

'For Heaven's sake, Beth, I'm dead, aren't I?' he said irritably. 'Do you think I get a news bulletin from the Post Office?'

'William's dead,' she said flatly, 'eighteen months ago. And Pippin,' she swallowed, 'Pippin's married to Rupert. They've got a baby.'

A moment of shock, of silence. 'Dead?' he repeated blankly, looking at her suspiciously. 'Pippin married? Beth, I – oh, my poor Beth.' He swung his legs off the armchair and stood up. She thought he was coming to her, but he simply stood, staring at her unseeing, assimilating what she had told him, his face quite blank. Something that might have been a smile crept round his lips, but his eyes did not leave hers. 'A baby? Pippin's got a bastard?'

The smile became a laugh, and reached his eyes, lighting them for her alone. They were so intense, so blue, that she instinctively backed away towards the door behind her. Now he strode towards her, and she fled through the door into the bedroom, pushing it shut. But he threw his weight against it, and he was taking her into his arms, not fiercely, but gently as though she were not yet quite real to him.

'Mine, Beth,' he whispered in her ear. 'We're free –'

'No,' she cried. 'Richard, we must talk,' and she tore herself away, dodging round to the far side of the bed, poised to run again.

'Afterwards,' he hissed across at her.

'No!'

'Yes!'

'Madness!'

'Love.' And with a triumphant cry, he threw himself across the bed, catapulting off the other side and catching her as she fled round the end of it. In a trice she found herself upended on the bed, he holding her legs high in the air, her dark hair, free of the cap, spilling over the counterpane. She was pinioned as securely as she had been in the hop-pickers' basket nineteen years before.

'Let me go.'

She wriggled her body around frantically, but he gripped her the more firmly.

'Why should I?'

'I'm a respectable businesswoman, not a village girl any more. I'm a hotelier –' As she struggled, the skirts of her dressing gown fell about her.

'Respectable businesswomen don't lie upside down on beds waving their French knickers in the air for all to see.'

'Put me down.'

But his grip precluded all movement.

'Say you'll be my sweetheart again, Beth.'

She was dizzy with love for him, as his bearded face grinned down at her.

'Go away, Richard Lyle. I don't know you with that ugly black beard.'

'Ah yes, you do. You've known me since the world began. Remember?'

She could not answer, lost in a reverie of love, and knowing she would not move now, he let her go at last and joined her on the bed.

'Are you going to let me love you, Beth?' he asked softly.

'You daft rollocks,' she said without any conviction in her voice. 'No.' Then she recollected all that had happened. 'No,' she said indignantly, sitting up and straightening her skirts. 'You can't just come back into my life yet again. Not this time Richard. There's too much happened. Too much pain. And anyway, who's this other woman you've got?' She got off the bed and stood a distance away, fearful that close she could not resist her heart and would take him in her arms and abandon herself to him now, as she had done all those years before.

'No part of my life now,' he said. 'I go back to see her once in a while. But she married an art collector a while back.'

'Oh,' said Beth, partly mollified. But only partly. 'But you still can't just come in here and love me, as though nothing's happened these past seven years.'

'Very well,' he said offhandedly, and lay back on the bed, hands resting peacefully behind his head.

'That all you're going to say?' she said suspiciously. 'Don't care much, do you?'

'No,' he said casually. 'No. After all, if you won't come back to me, Beth, I can always come back to Shepham.'

She whirled on him. 'You'll *what*?'

'You heard me. Come back to Shepham. Reclaim my long lost wife.'

'But she's married. With a new baby. Richard, we must think what we're going to do about Pippin.'

'You must think what *you're* going to do, Beth,' he said blandly. 'Are you going home to tell Pippin all about me?'

'You know I couldn't do that to her.'

'After what she did to you?'

'It's different. We're friends again now, but even if we weren't I couldn't tell her.'

'Not even with the legal position to think of?'

'No,' she shook her head. 'Pippin would never stand the shock, the disgrace. Even if you obtained a quiet divorce –'

'Oh, it wouldn't be quiet,' he said dangerously. 'I want you, Beth. I need you now and for ever. I won't let you go again. And if I fail to persuade you to come to me this time, if I lose you, then it doesn't much matter to me what happens.'

He was smiling lazily, his blue eyes as watchful as a cat's, as he went on softly: 'I think I might like to see my wife again. It's a pity of course about Rupert and the new baby. Pippin will be upset. But it will be outweighed by her pleasure in seeing me again.'

There was a tense silence. He swung himself off the bed, and watched her conflicting emotions.

'Bluff!' she threw at him.

'Sure?' There was a dangerous light in his eyes.

'Yes,' she said defiantly. She was almost sure. But last time he said he'd wanted to kill himself. If she refused him again, might he not indeed carry out his threat to come to England. Was it not better for Pippin and Rupert that Richard Lyle remained dead, fallen in the Balkans years ago, dead . . . and forgotten. Better for them, better for his children. And for her, Beth? She began to open her heart to herself. If he remained legally dead, she could see him somehow. She would be making regular visits to France to see Fauchons. A new life would open up, not just for Elizabeth, but for her, Beth. The life she had dreamed of, had been promised years ago. New hope . . .

Seeing her face gradually change, the tenseness die to softness, he came to her and took her in his arms. He kissed the last of the doubt from her eyes, kissed her throat, then found her lips.

'My Beth, forever, my Beth,' he whispered, and taking her hand in his, he led her towards the bed.

More Compulsive Fiction from Headline:

Agnes Short

THE FIRST FAIR WIND

A delightful family saga of Scottish fisherfolk

The warm-hearted Christie family take in orphan Rachel and raise her as one of their own. Like other fisherwomen, Rachel gathers bait, coils the lines, wades into the icy sea at dawn to launch the boat, carries full creels to the market – and dreams that one day she might have a house and family of her own.

James, the handsome eldest Christie son, longs for a different way of life, more prosperous and more secure than fishing – he dreams of building a fine stout ship that will carry him to the trading ports around the world. But his ambitions bring him into a near disastrous conflict with a local merchant.

Set in the bustling fishing community of Footdee, *The First Fair Wind* is the first in a trilogy of novels that follows the fortunes of the Christie family.

"Agnes Short has created a memorable picture of daily life in a Scottish fishing community nearly two hundred years ago . . . She has a feeling for the period, and a nice sense of humour." *Irish Times*